# Never Cry Again

# Never Cry Again

To Ron

*Jim Cole*

| Library of Congress Control Number: | | 2016908553 |
| ISBN: | Hardcover | 978-1-5245-0469-4 |
| | Softcover | 978-1-5245-0468-7 |
| | eBook | 978-1-5245-0467-0 |

Printed in the United States of America.

Rev. date: 06/11/2018

**To order additional copies of this book, contact:**
Xlibris
1-888-795-4274
www.Xlibris.com
Orders@Xlibris.com
739257

# Contents

# Preface

WRITING *NEVER CRY Again* has been a chore, a delight, and a labor of love, and, finally, satisfying. While the story is not autobiographical, I, nonetheless, as a white boy growing up in South Texas in the 1930s through 1940s, observed the racial discrimination of those times. Unlike most white children, I had a number of friends who were Negroes. So elements of this book are things that I personally experienced, the racial discrimination of the times I saw through their eyes.

We in America have a long way to go as this nation struggles to reach equality in the way we treat and think about other races.

I am not political, and neither is this book. Rather, it is a story of the times that I wanted to tell. Though set in Arkansas, Louisiana, and Texas, it could have happened almost anywhere in the South. It is fiction, and I am compelled to say that any similarity to real places and any person or people, living or dead, is coincidental.

I have included a few historical personalities of the times and have put words in their mouths. They are my words, not theirs. In particular, I want to say that the references I have available to me say that Eleanor Roosevelt was in Dallas only once, and that trip was by train in 1940, not by airplane in 1942. Her meeting with Drew Neilan is, of course, entirely fictitious.

Dallas, Oklahoma City, Little Rock, and other locales are real places, but I have been loose and often deliberately confusing in describing specific locations in these cities. In fact, I have taken pains at times to deliberately confuse what are today real locations. Union City does not exist. There is a small community in Southern Arkansas called Newell, but the Newell as described in the narrative is entirely fictitious. The story is set against the backdrop of real events of the 1930s through 1940s.

Having said the foregoing, I want to note that many of the fictitious characters are composites of real people I have known. I have tried to capture the true character of these composites and hope that I have succeeded.

This book would not have been written without the wholehearted support of my family and, in particular, my wife of over sixty years, Marian, and my loving retired librarian sister, Linda.

I am especially grateful to my editor, Mark Cameron, and thank my lucky stars for that chance meeting we had one fall day in Houston. I sweated blood over rewrites based on his recommendations but knew deep within me that he was always right on target. He helped me polish and expand the narrative, and I shall always be proud of our association.

Jim Cole
Victoria, Texas
2016

# Chapter 1

# *The Cap*
## *1933*

T HEY HAD STOLEN his favorite cap. It was also his only cap, but Drew called it his favorite. He had run after them for a short distance, but they were older and he could not keep up. He didn't even know their names. They simply snatched away his cap and ran off laughing into the woods behind the oil refinery. He knew they did it just to tease him; the cap meant nothing. He also knew that they would throw it away somewhere in the woods where they went almost every day after school to smoke cigarettes made from Bull Durham caged from Wilkinson's Drugstore.

These same boys always shouted at him during recess and called him names. Drew often gritted his teeth at the insults and bullying and sometimes swore he would get even but admitted truthfully to himself that he did not know how he would do this. He was nearly seven but skinny with short legs and thin arms. He remembered that Reverend Thomas had once said, "'Vengeance is mine,' sayeth the Lord." But he did not think either the Lord or Reverend Thomas was going to get his cap back or help him get even.

Drew ran his hand across his sandy hair and was suddenly unsure if the heat he felt was from the sun or the anger in his head. It only served to remind him of the missing cap, like rubbing salt on a wound, as he opened the wire gate in front of the small house he shared with his mother. Several of the older kids at school had teased him about it being a shotgun house. Once it had been painted a bright barn red but now looked like a faded rusty train car, covered in peeling paint and splotches of dirt.

The yard was a collection of weeds, piles of junk, and dirt paths. One of his uncles had brought the junk of various types to the house in order to have a place to store it. Drew was never told the purpose of this and, as time passed, simply ignored the various bits and pieces of wrecked automobiles, old tires, an icebox with a missing door, and a dilapidated chifforobe, the veneer peeling off in strips. The dirt path to the porch wound through the weeds and rusting geography in the front of the house.

As he crossed the yard, he wondered if his uncle Henry had come by today. He always left more money than his other uncles. The obvious signs of this uncle were usually a restocked supply of liquor and, on rare occasion, a whole carton of cigarettes. Sometimes, after Henry's visit, his mother would go out and buy food.

He crossed the porch quietly. If his mother was sleeping, it probably would not make a difference, but there was no sense in making extra noise. The inside consisted of three rooms in a row; he slept in the front room, the kitchen was in the center, and his mother's room was at the rear. A lean-to that had gotten added to the kitchen served as their washroom. He put his school things down in his room and crossed into the kitchen. He saw the new bottle of Four Roses right away, already only three quarters full. A green-and-red carton of Lucky Strike cigarettes sat on the table. It too had been opened.

He looked into the icebox and saw that today must have been a banner day because his mother had bought milk, bread, and bacon. There was even a small brown sack with six eggs inside. She must have gone all the way to Mr. Martinez's store up the hill from their house. A fresh block of ice told him that she even had enough money for the iceman, who he sometimes thought might be an uncle even if his mother kept denying it.

Much of the time he thought the iceman was not an uncle. He was a colored man and his mother always said she hated colored people, although she used a word he thought of as a bad word. Still, he had seen the iceman coming from her room several times with that look that other men had after spending some time with her; heads sort of ducked down and hurrying away without trying to make conversation.

She had left her purse on the table, and he carefully removed a $1 bill and a handful of coins. She would notice the missing dollar long before she ever noticed the coins, but he thought if the day had been as good as it seemed, perhaps she would forget about it quickly. When he got into his room, he counted it and then pulled a once-gaily colored tin box labeled Mrs. Goldstone's Excellent Bath Crystals from under his bed. He added the dollar and 87¢ to the other coins and few dollar bills in the box and slid it back under his bed. The money would be useful next week in case Uncle Henry did not return.

He sneaked a look into his mother's bedroom. She was asleep, snoring softly, her table radio playing quietly. He went back into the kitchen and moved aside some of the dirty dishes and knives and forks on the kitchen table, then got his school things from the front room, and sat down with his arithmetic book for his lessons. An insolent cockroach crawled across the table, and he swatted at it. The cockroach moved away, stopping just under a dirty plate; but he could still see its legs as it waited, expectant, for him to leave.

His lessons needed to be finished by Monday, three days away, but he thought he might as well get started. A girl who sat next to him at school had given him some paper, and his books belonged to the school. They were free as long as they were returned in good condition. He had used old paper sacks to carefully make book covers.

This lesson was about adding compound numbers, which to him seemed unnecessary to know. Still, he carefully wrote his answers to the arithmetic problems from the end of the chapter. He wrote as small as he could to conserve paper. When he finished, he had used only half of the sheet, which he folded back and forth, and then carefully tore in a straight line. Miss Ryan would let him turn his work in on less than whole sheets, even though when he did, some of the other kids would laugh in that nasty way they had.

It was nearly dark when he finished; and he was beginning to think of frying some of the bacon, slicing bread off the loaf, and frying it in the bacon grease for supper. He wasn't good at slicing. Sometimes bacon he sliced was thick in the middle; other times the ends were thick and the middle too thin. It was the same way with bread, but he thought that if he kept trying, he would eventually get better.

He suddenly looked up, feeling another presence in the room. Eugene, one of his many uncles, was leaning against the doorjamb, an opened bottle of beer in his hand. He had not heard him come in or heard Eugene's old truck as he usually did when it labored and clattered along the sandy rutted road. He felt a little irritated at not noticing Eugene's entrance, especially since he seemed to be coming by more often than most of the others. Usually, when Eugene came, Drew made sure to go to his blanket out in the shed under the old chinaberry tree.

"Hey, Drew," Eugene said in his nasally whine of a voice. The way he drawled out his name sent shivers under his skin.

"Hello," Drew answered quietly, looking at Eugene. He was dressed in dirty overalls that were too large. Eugene rarely wore a shirt, and the hair sticking out from under his arms, Drew knew from experience, smelled bad. Eugene's teeth were yellow stained, and one in front was missing.

"Your ma's passed out again," Eugene said with a hint of an accusation. Drew wished Eugene would not call her *ma*. He called her *mother* and expected others to call her that too or at least call her by her name, Edith.

Eugene continued, "I come all the way over here, ready to party with your ma and everything. I got paid today too. Now, she's out like a light."

Drew couldn't think of a safe response. He knew Eugene had hit his mother some weeks ago, and with a little start of fear, he wondered if the man now wanted to hit him. He wished he would just leave. He got up and took his school things back into his room.

As he left, he heard Eugene walk over to the kitchen table and he heard the scrape of glass on wood. He did not turn around but knew that Eugene had picked up the whiskey bottle. The sound of the cork as it protested being pulled out proved him right, followed by the sound of a belch. Eugene must have gulped whiskey directly from the bottle and then followed with a large swallow of beer. The scrape of the chair as Eugene sat down at the table made Drew turn around.

He walked back to the kitchen and stood in his doorway, looking at Eugene.

"I don't know when Mother will wake up," he said, emphasizing his title for her. "She was probably pretty tired. I think she walked all the way to Mr. Martinez's store today."

Eugene looked at him for a while and then got those funny crinkly lines around his mouth, like he was trying to smile and frown at the same time. He had looked this way the time when he had hit his mother. There had been other times when Eugene had looked this way.

"Come over here," Eugene said with his funny crinkly lines somehow making his voice funny and crinkly. "I want you to sit on my lap. You're such a big boy now. You 'member you used to sit on my lap when you was just a little feller?"

Drew started to move away, but Eugene had long skinny arms that easily reached out and grabbed him and pulled him onto his lap. He brought Drew close to his face, and the smell of his breath, laden with the odor of rotten teeth along with cigarette smoke and whiskey, almost overwhelmed Drew. He squirmed and tried to move away.

Eugene laughed and held him tighter. And his hands! Unlike his arms, they were big and seemed to be everywhere! He struggled some more to get off Eugene, and then those big hands moved again, and he felt that he could not get his breath.

He knew without looking when his mother entered the room. Her scent of cigarette smoke, whiskey, and the latest free sample of the Avon lady's perfume always came into the room before she did.

Edith pulled her son off Eugene's lap, hugged him, and said, "How's my big boy today." This wasn't a question, and she didn't look at Drew. She was looking at Eugene. He saw that his mother was wearing only her green rayon robe, which she had not tied well, and he saw that Eugene was now staring at his mother's open robe. Drew was embarrassed to look at her.

Edith let him go and leaned over and kissed Eugene on the mouth. Eugene's hands moved again, this time to her open robe. She giggled a little, picked up the whiskey bottle, and took Eugene by the hand. Drew watched as she pulled him across the kitchen and into her bedroom, where she closed the door. Drew felt that he had not breathed for several minutes and took deep breaths.

His mother's bedroom door burst open, and she came back into the kitchen. Drew looked at the floor as he realized she had not retied the sash. She turned away from him, opened the top of the icebox, chipped ice into two glasses with a pick, smiled at Drew, winked when she caught his eye, and returned to her room. She shut the door again.

He heard the music on the radio get louder and knew it was time for him to go out into the shed where he was to stay when his mother had a party. Soon there would be noises that he did not want to hear coming from his mother's bedroom.

The uncle who had stored junk in the front yard had taken an old tire and made it into a swing and hung it from the old chinaberry tree next to the shed that held Drew's blanket. He sat in the swing as the afternoon deepened into a still, quiet evening twilight. Drew could faintly hear the sounds of singing from the colored church up the hill from his house, past Mr. Martinez's store. It was choir practice time at the Paradise Valley Missionary Baptist Church. The music from the hymns, indistinct but somehow soothing, washed softly over him.

He watched the early summer lightning bugs as they bobbed about. Sometimes, while waiting like this, he had caught one or two and squeezed off the glowing part of their body and made a fairy ring for his third finger. But it would not feel right tonight. His chest still felt tight, and he was shaking.

He cried a little. He was hungry and wondered how long Eugene and his mother would have their party. He hoped it would not be too long.

He found a wad of chewing gum in his pocket, wrapped in waxed paper. The girl who had given him paper for his homework had also handed him the gum. Her name was Kowanda. She had chewed it, and most had stuck to the waxed paper, but what little of the gum he got still had a little flavor. He chewed it while tears ran down his cheeks, and he waited for Eugene to leave so he and his mother could have a late supper together.

Maybe tonight she would stay awake and listen to him talk about school and what Miss Ryan had said. She sometimes did that, so he sat and wished and hoped and maybe believed just a little that tonight his mother would sit and talk with him. He continued crying and did not know why as the twilight turned into a clear, starry night. The soft and indistinct sounds of Negro voices singing their Christian hymns drifted about him.

# Chapter 2

⋇ • ⌒ • ⋇

## Lubbock County, Texas
## 1920—1925

EDITH PULLED THE covers tight about her. *Maybe,* she said to herself as she did every night, *maybe tonight he will not come. Maybe, maybe, maybe, oh, not tonight, please, please, please.* And some nights he did not come.

But most nights he did, and tonight would be such a night. Swaying, shuffling, and believing in his drunkenness that he was being quiet and that the child never heard, felt, or knew. But of course she knew. Of course she heard as he fumbled into the room and knew that the pain would come again. She felt him climbing into bed, felt him touching her, and when he spread her legs and entered her, she felt that too.

"Edith Ann, Edith Ann, oh, sweet little Edith," he sang softly to himself as he began to move back and forth, and the pain increased. She closed her eyes tighter.

Their small house had not been painted in many years, and it seemed to Edith that their house was as gray as the prairie it sat on, windswept and bleak. The grayness stretched unbroken to the horizon, with no trees or hills to disrupt the monotony. Edith thought that her life was gray—as gray as the land and the house.

Her father sharecropped and was permitted to keep one-third of whatever the land produced. But the land was poor, and the incessant North Texas winds were so severe that usually the land produced nothing except massive storms of swirling dust.

But each year Edith's mother produced a new baby, and each year her father went deeper into debt at the country store that was owned by the landlord of the property he farmed.

There was always work to do. Besides the babies and the younger children, there were clothes to wash, lamps to fill and trim, and the kerosene stove in the kitchen had to be kept clean of soot and greasy grime. Edith, as the oldest, had been permitted to attend only four years of school and then had to help at home. There was never enough for everyone to eat. It seemed to Edith that either her mother or one of the children was always sick.

It was a cold, gray winter day when her mother died giving birth. Edith heard her mother's dying screams for months afterward and blamed her father, believing the death was her father's fault. The baby was stillborn. Edith's primary emotion upon seeing the dead infant was a feeling of relief that there would not be another infant to feed, diaper, and care for.

It was about six months after her mother's death that her father took her to his bed. At first, it had been a simple sharing; his presence was a comfort to the grieving girl, and she began to forgive him for her mother's death.

Soon, though, the blame would return, along with resentment, eventually anger, and then hatred.

She never knew where he got his liquor, but each night he drank after supper. Her thirteenth birthday was the first time. She pretended to sleep through the pain, through the grunts and thrusting, through the soft under-his-breath singing until he shuddered and moved off her and began snoring.

Occasionally, he drank himself into a stupor, falling to sleep at the kitchen table. On those nights she was blissfully alone. She began to look forward to those nights, and she began bringing him his liquor earlier each evening after supper. She even started trying to choke down a little of the fiery liquid herself to encourage him to drink more. In time, it became easier to drink, and she learned that it could help her get to sleep. If she drank enough, she could even get through her father's fumbling with minimal discomfort, physically at least. So while still in her early teens, Edith learned to tolerate and enjoy alcohol.

There was shock and shame when she found that she was pregnant with her father's child, but the friendly alcohol helped her bear this too. When the pregnancy was three months along Edith wept and screamed at the hideous pain of miscarriage. The oldest of her younger sisters tried to help and indeed was of some assistance, but mostly the help hurt more than eased her pain. All the sisters wept at the sight of the poor bloody lump of stillborn tissue that had issued from Edith's body.

Spring came early to the North Texas plains the year Edith turned fifteen. One day, when the air was soft and balmy and puffs of cloud dotted the light blue of the Texas sky, it seemed to Edith that her housework was finished for a little while. She sat on the front steps of the house in a rare moment of rest while the other children played in the backyard. There was washing on a line in the side yard that flapped in the breeze. It would be hours before her father returned from the fields, and she already had fresh cornbread in two cast-iron skillets on the warming board, covered with cup towels.

She decided that it would be a good time to wash her hair. Afterward, it felt refreshing to let her hair dry in the light breeze. Her sisters always talked about how her hair was a shiny golden blonde. Today, its curls billowed about her shoulders, and the sensation gave her a new sense of freedom.

She noticed the wildflowers that sprang up in profusion beside the ditch at the side of the dirt road. Edith felt as if she'd never seen them before. She moved toward them, at first intending merely to look at them more closely.

As she stood, admiring the flowers, a strange feeling came over her. In some way she could not analyze the road seemed to be calling. Edith turned and went back into the house to the bureau where her things were kept. She pulled out a faded sepia photograph mounted on heavy paper. It had once shown two young people, standing stiffly for the camera. Edith had long ago cut the picture in half so that now it only showed a heartbreakingly young woman with a strong resemblance to Edith. She put the photograph of her mother in her pocket, went back to the road and simply walked away.

She walked away from the other children, from her father, and from the gray house that had been her life. She took nothing with her other than the photograph and clothes that she wore. She hadn't completely realized that she was actually going to leave. It was just that the day was so pretty and the road called so strongly that at first all she wanted to do was just walk. After a while, she wanted to see how far her feet could take her.

She slept on the ground by the side of the road when night came, her only thought being that on this night she was free from her father's approach. She did not think about the younger children who would be anxious and wanting their supper or about the wildflowers that she had so admired earlier and which now made a bed for her. She thought she would return home the next morning.

But she did not. As the sun crept over the horizon, Edith shook off the morning chill and kept on walking. She stopped at the first house in town that she came to and knocked at the back door.

A woman with a dirty head cloth and greasy apron opened the door.

"What do you want?" she asked in a whiny voice.

"Something to eat," Edith begged. "I'll work."

"I got nothing for you. You're some damn gypsy or something. Get out of here before I call the law!" The door slammed. Edith walked down the back steps and turned, looking up at the closed door. Then a window curtain parted. Edith could see the woman watching.

The door opened again, and the woman came out with a broom. She shook it at Edith.

"Go on, git! There's nothing for you here! Go home to your folks. I got all I can handle with my own kids."

So Edith walked on. Women at two other houses chased her away too.

She eventually found several large garbage cans in an alley behind the restaurant in the middle of town. Edith thought the largest might have some scraps she could get. A man came from inside the restaurant and into the alley and chased her away before she was able to scavenge anything. She decided to keep on walking.

On the other side of town, an oil derrick by the side of the new concrete highway was ringing with sounds of men and machinery. The smells of dirt, steam, grease, and sweat were heavy in the air. One of the men saw her watching and recognized the look of hunger. Something about the skinny blonde girl called him. He climbed down from the drilling floor and crossed the muddy machinery-strewn area between the rig and the road. The girl warily watched the approach of this man in his greasy trousers and aluminum roughneck's hat. The way she tensed up, and her eyes widened as he got closer, made him think of a frightened rabbit.

He called out, "Hey, don't run away. You hungry? I got a sandwich here."

So Edith Simmons met George Andrew Watson, a minor partner in the wildcat well. It was highly unusual for an investor to also work on the drilling floor, but George had worked for the principal partners on other wildcat rigs. When his wife inherited several thousand dollars, George took the money and invested in this well.

He asked Edith to sit down on an overturned barrel and handed her his sandwich. As she ate, George told her his name and asked for hers. He chatted easily with her; and she became calm and began to feel safe with this friendly, kind, handsome man. He was tall and slender, his straight white teeth flashed when he smiled, his dark wavy hair shone in the sunlight, and his intense dark eyes fascinated her.

"Would you wait for me to get off work?" George asked. "I could take you back into town, maybe give you a ride home. Are you from around here?"

Edith shook her head, wondering how much she should tell him. "I lived on a farm," she blurted. "I don't want to live there anymore."

George shook his head. What was he getting himself into? "Do you have someplace to stay tonight?"

Edith again shook her head. "No."

"Well," George said kindly, "maybe I can help."

Edith agreed to wait until his work was over. He left her his coffee thermos and returned to the rig. She remained, sitting on the barrel and whiling away the afternoon, not really thinking of anything, simply watching the men work.

As the afternoon shadows lengthened, George climbed down off the rig and led her to the largest newest automobile she had ever seen. He opened the door for her and invited her to ride with him. No man had ever opened a door for her. He took her to the Stetson Hotel in downtown Lubbock where he had a large room with a connecting bath. Edith's head swam at the luxuries this man enjoyed.

Edith, without really making the decision to do so, stayed with George for a number of weeks. He was ten years her senior and at first was solicitous and helpful. He told the hotel staff that Edith was his niece and had them bring a cot into his room for her to sleep on. He borrowed fresh clothes for her that first night when he took her to supper. Later, he bought her clothes and paid for her first trip to a beauty parlor. Afterward, they sat in a small park and talked while he ran his hand softly through her newly shining blonde curls. The beauty parlor operator had shown Edith a few cosmetic products and instructed her how to apply them.

When she tried the cosmetics at the hotel, George supervising, she began to realize that she might be more than simply a plain country girl. The cosmetics, along with her new hairstyle and new clothes, made her very attractive and appear older than fifteen.

George took her to restaurants. The luxury of eating food someone else had prepared shocked Edith into fits of giggles and blushes.

Edith had never known a man as kind, as handsome, and as rich as George Andrew Watson. He cared for her, he said, adding that she was so pretty she deserved to be treated like royalty. Edith wondered why her father had never treated her this way, cared for her like this. She deserved to be treated as George treated her. George said so. She was pretty. George said this too over and again. Pretty people deserved to be treated the way George was treating her.

As the days passed, it was inevitable that she would begin to fantasize about George, and it was inevitable that he would seduce her. At first, Edith was afraid to let him touch her, but George was not too selfish; and he took his time, teaching her that sex could be a more pleasant activity than she had known. Gradually, Edith relaxed.

George learned early that Edith had an acquaintance with alcohol, and he began giving her little drinks to help the process along. It was easier to learn how to enjoy George's attentions that way. In time, sex with George became tolerable; and she discovered that if she made moaning sounds and thrusting motions in response to his, he would become even more excited. She began to imagine that this was love and that eventually he would marry her. After all, George kept saying, she deserved to be treated well; and after all her hard work on the farm, it seemed only natural to have a man love her and take care of her.

However, as time went by, the thrill of it all began to fade for George.

Edith often spent her days in his hotel room, sitting before a mirror, trying new applications of cosmetics, admiring herself. Sometimes she wandered about the hotel, chatting with maids and other hotel employees. Other times she ventured about the town, stopping at restaurants or department stores, talking with clerks or waitresses. George always arose early and left for the well site. He often returned to the hotel late, was ravenous for food, and fell asleep shortly after eating.

But there were rare nights that he took her to the movies, reading the silent-film dialogue cards to her, and later they stopped at a speakeasy where George taught her to dance. When other men asked to dance with her, Edith found their attentions enjoyable as well.

On many nights during those later weeks, even if they didn't go out, Edith found herself having several drinks after dinner to help her sleep soundly beside the snoring George.

It was on one of Edith's walks about town that her fantasy of life was shattered. She had gone alone to a movie matinee and was walking along, eating the last of her popcorn. An arm reached out from the corner of a building, grabbed her, and pulled her into the alley. She was stunned to see that it was her father.

"I caught you, you little bitch!" He had been quick to hit her across the mouth. "Now you're gonna come home and help me with the kids!"

Edith twisted and turned with the hit, a cry wrenched from her throat at the impact. The remaining popcorn scattered. The bag blew down the deserted alleyway.

"I asked around, bitch!" her father spat at her. His breath stank of liquor. "I know you been shackin' up with that wildcatter." He hit her again. She tasted blood. This time she fell to her knees against the wall of the alley, ruining her stockings. He still held her arm tightly. She knew bruises would later show on both her face and arm.

"I'm gonna get the law on that feller! You're underage!" He hit her again.

"Don't!" Edith sobbed.

"Don't what? Don't get the law? I'll goddamn sure enough get the law. They'll put that bastard in jail!" He raised his arm again.

"Oh!" Edith shrank away from the impending blow. "Don't hit me again, please!" As she begged, her mind screamed at the injustice of this beast, taking away a life she'd only just discovered, a life that she deserved. Now her silk stockings were ruined! Anger stirred within her.

How dare her father hit her like this? How dare he demand that she return to the farm? She was done with that life. Let him find someone else to be his slave!

She remembered the few dollars she had in her purse. She strained in his grip to get away from his hand and, sobbing, pulled money from her purse. Among the few bills and silver coins was a $5 gold piece George had given her after the first night they'd had sex. She held all of it out to her father.

"Gold!" her father breathed. His eyes narrowed. "That bastard's got gold?" He grabbed the money out of her hand and let go of her.

Edith snuffled and rubbed the back of her hand across the blood and mucus on her face. "He's got lots of money. He's in love with me." An idea came into her head. "He'll pay you lots to let me go with him."

Her father's eyes gleamed. Edith could see the wheels spinning in his head and could guess what sort of plans might be forming there. He was thinking that he could get money from this wildcatter. He could still call the law afterward.

Her father grabbed her hand again and dragged her farther into the alleyway behind some trash barrels. He sat her against a building wall, took a dirty handkerchief from his overall pocket, leaned over, and roughly wiped her face.

"We need to clean you up a little," he said as he wiped her. "You've been staying at that hotel, right? Let's go there. We'll wait for that prick. He'll be sorry. Get up!" He pulled at her.

A loose brick lay in the alley next to the trash barrel. Edith picked it up as she was lifted from her position against the wall, her father pulling at her while still wiping her face. She hadn't known what she was going to do, but the anger had continued to build. She gritted her teeth. Suddenly, with all her strength, she swung the brick. It hit her father in the temple. He squalled something, fell backward, and sprawled into the middle of the alley.

She stood over him as he writhed. Something deep within her had snapped open, and the hatred that had been building for several years flowed through her veins. Hatred of this pathetic man that sought to ruin all she had earned. Even her new silk stockings were ruined! She was still holding the brick. She raised it with both hands; and as her hatred soared to a peak, gagging her, she crashed the brick down as hard as possible into her father's face.

She stood over him, still sobbing, breathing heavily. It occurred to her that he might be dead. She wondered if this could be murder. Then she felt a surge of victory. She had won! He would never hurt her again!

As she calmed a little, still standing over the man at her feet, she wondered if someone might have seen it happen. She looked about, back where the alley turned, then where it opened to the street. There were no cars passing and no one walking by that she could see. She bent over, grabbed her father's hand, and pulled him behind the trash barrels.

She knelt next to him and looked for signs of life. He wasn't breathing. His eyes were open. The expression on his face was one of astonishment. She nodded to herself; yes, he was dead.

She continued kneeling next to her father's body, now wondering how she felt. She stopped her almost-reflexive sobbing and knelt there for a few more minutes.

A grim but pleased expression crossed her face. *I won't have to go back to the farm now,* she told herself. *George will take care of me. He'll buy me another pair of silk stockings!*

The dirty handkerchief her father had used lay nearby. She picked it up. If only she had a little water, she could clean herself up. She left her father's body, crumpled against the trash barrel, and walked deeper into the alley, where it turned. She saw a Texas Company gasoline station across the street at the far end of the alley.

She quickly crossed to the station and around to the back to the restroom. She washed her face and rinsed out the handkerchief, wiping her face and arms. The bruises would show, but she thought she could cover most of them with cosmetics. She pulled her ruined stockings off and thrust them into a trash container. That was when she remembered her purse. It was in the alley next to her father's body. Had someone found it already? If they had, the police would surely be heading this way. There would be questions. She quickly left the station and went back across the street into the alley. She hoped no one had noticed her.

Her father's body lay where she left it, with the purse nearby. She picked up the purse and looked at her father's body one last time. She felt no remorse and was somehow detached from the corpse at her feet. This was no longer her father. It was simply a disgusting thing. A fly crawled across her father's opened eye.

Later, having done what she could to clean up her appearance, Edith walked back to the hotel. She needed to get her things and find George.

Walking down the hotel hallway, she felt in her purse before realizing the key was not necessary. The door was open. George was inside, filling suitcases with his clothes.

"Ah," he said, looking up, "the well's finished. I'm leaving town."

"I'll go with you."

"No, honey, we talked about this," he said in the calm tone of an elder talking to a child. "I'm married. I got two kids. I gotta go back to my wife and kids in Oklahoma City."

"My pa's in town," she said hurriedly. "He's looking for me. I barely got away. He said he's looking for you." A thought occurred to her. George needed to understand he might be in trouble. "He said he'd been to the police," she added, barely able to breathe. "He said he told them about you and that I'm underage. I gotta get away from him. Please!"

"Is that where you got those bruises?" His eye had caught the detail while she rushed to explain.

"Yeah. He hit me. But I got away," she repeated. She sobbed a little.

A frown crossed George's face. He began to worry.

His wallet was bulging with more than $5,000. Tool pushers didn't normally merit a bonus for completing a successful well, but as a minor partner, George had been given an advance share in the profits. There would be more—much more—where that had come from. Now, however, the likelihood existed that all the money in his wallet, and money yet to come, might now be taken by courts and lawyers. He suddenly realized there was a strong probability that he could go to jail. He realized that he had to leave Lubbock quickly, and there was no doubt in his mind that he had to get this underage girl out of town to cover his bases.

"Look," he said, resigned, "I can take you as far as Wichita Falls. I can give you some money. You can buy a bus or train ticket. You can go anywhere, get away from your pa."

"But, George, I want to be with you."

"Can't happen, babe. I told you about my wife and kids. Look, get your stuff together. We gotta get out of here."

Edith began moving quickly about the room, gathering her things and stuffing them into a suitcase George had bought her earlier. George picked up the bags and nodded to Edith. The two of them went into the hall and down the back stairway of the hotel where he had parked his car.

They drove through the night, stopping at dawn at White's Hotel near the railroad depot in Wichita Falls. They ate breakfast at the café down the block from the hotel and then slept until noon.

George woke Edith with a large cup of coffee.

"Honey," he began without preamble, "I gotta leave and go home to Oklahoma City."

"No, no," Edith replied groggily, "I told you I wanna be with you."

"I've told you that you can't go with me. I'm married. I gotta go back to my wife and my kids, and I gotta leave now." His voice had a harsh tone she had never heard before, and his face had a stern look. "See here, baby, I got you away from your old man. Here's $200. You need to find your own way. There'll be a train coming through later today," he offered. "You can go anywhere you want. I gotta go now. It's a long drive to OK city."

"George!" she said in a half whimper, half cry. Edith was still trying to rub sleep from her eyes. He was already backing away toward the door.

"No, I gotta go, baby. Look, it's been fun. Like I said, you're swell."

"George!"

He paused and looked at her. George was not insensitive, but he had responsibilities; he had to leave. He pulled another $50 from his wallet, tossed it onto the bed, and said, "Good-bye, babe!" He turned and went out of the room, closing the door behind him.

Edith turned into the pillow and wept.

George had paid the hotel for a week's rent, so Edith stayed, daydreaming that he would return for her. But he did not, and seven days later, she was told to either pay for another week or leave.

Edith used $37 of the money George had given her to buy a train ticket to Oklahoma City. She had no idea how she was going to find him, but she was sure he loved her and that true love would guide the way. She would show up and convince George to marry her. She knew she could take care of his kids. That other woman would just have to go and find herself another man.

It turned out that George was not hard to find at all.

As she exited the train, her eye caught headlines on the *Daily Oklahoman* lying on a seat in the waiting room. George's photograph was on the front page.

There had been an oilfield explosion. Seven men had been killed. One of them was her George.

In the back pages of the paper were photographs of several of the funerals. The paper identified George's grieving widow and two young daughters.

Edith's reading skills were severely limited. It took her several hours to fully decipher the story. She had to stop to weep and then go into the restroom to wash her face several times. She was trying to understand that George would never again be in her world. She did not notice the man who had watched her intently throughout the afternoon.

She thought that he was being kind when he approached her and inquired solicitously after her obvious sorrow. After she related the story, somewhat edited, he offered to buy her a meal. As the two of them ate in the station café, Edith looked more closely at this friendly stranger. He had a pencil-thin mustache, his hair was slicked straight back with pomade, and he smelled of the Bay Rum aftershave George had used. His suit was shabby and somewhat out of style, and his tie had grease spots. To her unpracticed eyes, though, he appeared prosperous.

She thought he had a strong resemblance to a movie hero she had seen recently. She began to like this kindly soul, and she thought about a possible future. Here was someone who could take care of her, treat her like royalty as she deserved. It would be what George would have wanted.

But later, in the backseat of his car, there was forcible, brutal, and painful sex. She was unconscious and bleeding between her legs when he pushed her out onto the pavement of the alleyway where they'd parked.

He kept her purse and the suitcase George had given her.

At the hospital where she was taken, Edith learned she was three months pregnant.

## Chapter 3

❖ ❖

# *Oklahoma City*
# *1926*

**O**NLY EDITH WAS seeking business on a night like this. She was clearly in an advanced stage of pregnancy. Her clothing, designed for neither the weather nor her current condition, was a pathetic compilation of skimpy skirt, tattered sweater, cloche hat, and lightweight scarf. She held the scarf about her face with one hand while the other was placed on an outthrust hip in a posture of intended sexuality but which, in fact, added to the pathos of the scene.

An elderly Negro woman—thin, frail, toothless, and wrinkled like a well-aged prune—was the sole passenger on the city bus that passed the corner of Fourteenth and Lincoln that night. She gazed at the girl standing in the cold from her seat in the rear of the bus. At first, she looked without interest, but then something about the girl caused Maude to look again. It was in that second glance that she saw the wisp of blonde hair, the too-young face, and the defiant yet gamine looks about her.

This girl, Maude considered, might have what it takes—once the pregnancy is done, of course. She'd have to be properly shown how to get cleaned up and work for a better clientele.

Maude Millar worked at Mrs. Lytle's Gentlemen's Club in Little Rock. She had never married, and now her only living relative, her sister, was dreadfully sick with advanced lung cancer. Maude had both high cheekbones and a broad flat nose that attested to her heritage: Native American blended with genes from the continent of Africa. Her skin, while black, had a touch of red. Her hair was gray and grizzled, held tightly under her woolen scarf by numerous pins.

Maude earned $12 a week at Mrs. Lytle's, carrying out slops, laundry, general cleaning, and kitchen duty for the establishment.

Mrs. Lytle allowed her to stay in the ramshackle cabin behind the main house, provided she paid $10 a month rent. Few of Mrs. Lytle's customers sought out Maude except for the occasional drunk who asked for special treatment. The performance of oral sex by a toothless woman sometimes became too good to pass up. She liked to joke to herself that since this was done underneath a sheet it was as if she were a phantom providing the service. Mrs. Lytle charged her customer $20 extra and gave Maude $5 of this, provided that the client didn't complain later. Few did.

She nodded silently again as she thought about the girl standing in the light freezing rain. There were possibilities. Maude knew that Mrs. Lytle needed to replace Louise, who'd come down with tuberculosis and was to be sent away to a sanitarium. This little young thing might earn her employer substantial additional revenue. Only coincidentally, her acceptance at Mrs. Lytle's might earn Maude a small bonus, which she desperately needed if she was to help pay for a proper doctor for her sick sister.

The unborn child would be a problem, but perhaps an orphanage could be arranged. Maude knew Mrs. Lytle had a relationship of some sort—a platonic relationship to be sure—with Monsignor Father Richards of St. Michael's Cathedral in Little Rock. Perhaps the good Father could be of help in placing the child.

The bus was six blocks past the blonde pregnant girl when Maude made her decision. If her initial impression was correct, and the girl indeed looked as if she could be fitted in at Mrs. Lytle's, she would go from there.

Maude rang the bell. As she exited, there was immediate regret upon leaving the lighted warmth. The street was dark, the cold wind seemed stronger, and the bus to Little Rock would leave in three hours. There would hardly be enough time to evaluate the girl, convince her to come along, wait for another city bus that Maude knew would be the last of the night, and then make it to the bus station on time. Nevertheless, she was on the sidewalk and committed. She pulled her headscarf more tightly about and walked hurriedly up Fourteenth Street toward the corner where she'd seen the girl.

The windswept dark corner by the shuttered grocery store was empty. The girl was not where Maude had seen her only minutes earlier.

Maude turned and walked to the alley at the rear of the store. There was nothing to be seen. The soft rain turned to sleet.

She walked back to the front of the store and saw, for the first time, the large closed saloon car parked across Fourteenth Street. The engine was running, and steam issued from the tailpipe. Maude stepped into the shadows away from the streetlights, out of the wind. She waited. It took less than five minutes.

The rear door of the saloon car opened, and the pregnant girl climbed out. She put her head back in; there was conversation, shouting could be heard, and then two loud pops. The girl closed the car door, turned, and walked across the street toward Maude. The engine in the car continued running.

"Prick!" the girl was mumbling to herself as she approached the lee of the store that was Maude's hiding place. "I told him five, he agreed to five, then said no money for me! The bastard! I showed him." Maude stepped into the light and used the instant of fright on the girl's face to study her. Yes, Maude thought, she will do just fine.

"Who the shits are you?" Edith shrieked in surprise as she backed away, stuffing something bulky in her purse. She was only seconds away from turning and running.

"Honey, Ah means no harm," Maude said quickly. "Please listen t'me. Ah is he'ar to offer y'food an' a place to have that young'un." She could see that Edith was starting to back away. "Don't run away!"

Edith did not seem convinced and kept sliding away from Maude, looking about in all directions as she did, seemingly worried about something other than the presence of the elderly Negro. She had begun to turn but hadn't yet started to run. She looked back, moving sideways, backing toward the street curb. "Who are you? I don't do women. Especially I don't do old nigger women! Stay away from me!" She reached the curb and stood there as if she could take flight from that vantage point, that height.

Just then, another car came down Fourteenth Street and slowed as it passed the idling saloon car. Edith was near panic. She turned toward the Negro woman, suddenly thoughtful and replaying her words in her head.

"Listen t'me!" Maude insisted again. "Ah kin hep. Lemme tell y'how!"

Edith Simmons listened. Partly she listened because she was tired, cold, and hungry. Mostly she listened because there was a dead man in the parked saloon car with his bulging wallet and small pistol now in her purse, and she needed to leave this part of town quickly. Edith wondered if she was feverish. She wondered if, in her hunger, cold, tiredness, and now fright over her recent actions, perhaps Maude was not real but some ghost or maybe an angel. Then she wondered if Negroes could be angels. She decided that they could not.

Edith accepted Maude's proposal. She saw it as a means of escape. Moreover, she saw it as a means of avoiding the nuisance of having to dispose of a baby somewhere. Five minutes later, when the last bus to run down Fourteenth Street loomed through the dark and sleety night, Edith boarded it and sat two seats behind the driver. Maude entered afterward and moved to the rear of the bus past the sign that read White Only on one side and Colored on the other. Edith relaxed. If the bus driver were ever to be questioned, he likely would remember the black woman, not the white; Edith would be quickly forgotten.

Just as they boarded the bus, a pedestrian hurrying along on the opposite side of Lincoln in the sleety night paused at the saloon car, noticing the engine still running. Edith saw the pedestrian look around and then bend down to look into the car. She slumped farther down in her seat, turning her face so it would not appear in the driver's rearview mirror.

She was sure that soon police cars and ambulances would be racing to the intersection of Fourteenth and Lincoln.

Maude heard sirens as the bus rumbled toward the Greyhound station but paid no attention, focused as she was on the argument she would have to make to Margaret Lytle.

Maude could not eat in the bus station restaurant or wait in the same waiting room as white people, so she gave Edith enough money for hot food and a bus ticket to Little Rock. Maude wondered if the girl would wait or simply take the money and return to the streets. But when Maude and the other Negroes were allowed to board the bus, she saw the girl sitting next to a window as she made her way to the rear section. Many of the traveling Negroes, including Maude, had to stand behind the sign separating the races since all seats in that section were filled. The bus lurched its way through the night on poorly paved, and some not paved at all, highways to Little Rock.

The bus arrived in Little Rock shortly after noon the next day. At one of the infrequent rest stops during the night, Maude had used some of her dwindling cash supply to send a brief telegram to Mrs. Lytle saying she'd be late.

Margaret Lytle was completely dismissive of the pregnant girl, telling Maude to remove her from the house at once. But Maude argued, pointing out how the young girl could be an interesting business prospect. Ultimately, Margaret relented and visited with the Monsignor. Tentative arrangements were made.

Six weeks after Edith arrived at Margaret Lytle's Gentlemen's Club, a squalling red-faced blond baby boy arrived. When he did, Maude did something she had never before in her life done: she fell in love. She begged Margaret Lytle. Maude would keep the baby in her little cabin. Later, she would see if someone from her church, perhaps Reverend Thomas, could raise the child. It all sounded like foolishness to the hard-bitten madam of the house, but then Margaret Lytle held the child. Uncharacteristically, she relented to Maude's pleas.

As Edith healed from a birth that had not been easy, two of Mrs. Lytle's ladies were assigned the task of instructing her. Maxine, the sillier of the two, concocted a scheme where Edith would pose as a newly arrived immigrant from Holland who was a virgin. That way, Maxine explained, Edith could wince from penetration so soon after giving birth without covering up her discomfort. The more practical Violet instructed Edith on the finer points of technique and came up with the idea of a vial of red fluid, which Edith would adroitly spill as a way to convince the client of her "virginity."

Maude reported all this to Mrs. Lytle who quickly saw the profit potential in the fantasy. She also realized that her liquor sales were going to have to increase if she was going to be able to convince several of her clients that a virgin could be deflowered more than once.

Four weeks following childbirth, a newly coifed, dressed, and instructed Edith began servicing Mrs. Lytle's clients. Margaret told them her new girl, a virgin, had just arrived in the United States from Holland; her name was Gretchen, and she could not speak English. It was a testament to the strength of Mrs. Lytle's liquor, as well as her skills of salesmanship, that several men each night believed that the blonde, pigtailed, and pinafore-dressed Gretchen was, in fact, a virgin who had been reserved especially for them.

It required little acting on Edith's part to wince in pain and sometimes cry as she spilled the tiny vial of red liquid. It was the rare client indeed who did not succumb to this act and urge the weeping Gretchen to stop crying. Most of the time, they gave her additional money. Sometimes it was $10 or more. Once, a man named Henry gave Edith a $5 gold piece. He returned again and again to see her and deflower her once more.

After several months, Edith's hairstyle was redone, and she was instructed to drop the phony Dutch, which she wasn't very good at anyway. Her clients were now told that she was an heiress, hiding from an evil stepfather. Henry was among the first to accept this story as strongly as he had accepted the Gretchen fabrication.

# Chapter 4

# Mrs. Lytle's
## 1926–1931

THE FIRST MONTHS of the baby boy's life were spent with Sister Beth Bailey, who attended Maude's church and had just weaned her own child. Sister Beth was happy for the $2 a week Maude paid her but would have nursed and cared for the boy as one of her own, regardless.

Each Sunday, Maude made the trip to the rural Ebenezer Church of God in Jesus Christ and held the baby boy throughout Reverend Thomas's endless sermons. She was always reluctant to leave for the coming week's work at Mrs. Lytle's and was jealous of the time she could not be with the baby.

Edith could not help but be reminded of George when she looked into the boy's eyes even though his were blue while George's had been dark. There was a look about him, nevertheless, so it seemed appropriate to use George's name. However, Edith reversed the order of the names. He was given his mother's last name and so became Andrew George Simmons. In time, no one remembered his full name, and most never knew why he had been so named. To almost everyone, he was called Drew.

Maude and Eddie Mackenzie, the piano player at Mrs. Lytle's, along with the entire congregation of the Ebenezer Church of God in Jesus Christ, raised him.

Maude truly did not remember a time in her life when she had been in love. She was in love now, though, with a blue-eyed pink little baby that was her joy and her life. The tall slender George Andrew Watson had dark-brown eyes and black hair. When his genes mixed with those of Edith Ann Simmons, they produced a boy with reddish-blond hair and eyes of a deep and dark blue. As a child, the boy's hair would be a sunny blond; but as he grew, it would become darker, turning into a rich auburn as he matured. One of Mrs. Lytle's clients, upon seeing the startling blue of the boy's eyes, said they were the blue of the deepest ocean.

Drew's earliest memory was of Maude. Her gnarled hands, worn by work and racked by arthritis, had the power to soothe him. They often did as she held him through the night while a fever ransacked the little body or his stomach rebelled against some unknown viral invader. As he grew and became more aware of life, it never seemed strange to him that her skin was black while his was white. It was just the way things were supposed to be.

When he began to form words, he tried to call her *mama*, but Maude shook her head. "Call me Maudie, little love. I am your Maudie."

But the little baby mind converted this into Mardie, and Mardie she became.

The other ladies at Mrs. Lytle's Gentlemen's Club began taking peeks at the pink little boy when Maude first brought him back to Little Rock from Sister Bailey's. He quickly won the hearts of those who lived and worked at the brothel. Even the hard-bitten Mrs. Lytle herself had been seen holding the baby while she cooed baby talk. When discovered, she had quickly put the boy back into Maude's hands, for Margaret Lytle believed that any evidence of softness on her part would diminish her control. She vowed after that first time that she would stay away from the boy.

But as the boy grew, she was not able to hold on to her vow. The child was winsome. Margaret Lytle, like everyone at the Gentlemen's Club except the boy's mother, came under his spell.

The club was a Little Rock institution. The physical structure had originally been a single-family residence with five rooms and a washroom/bathroom built as a lean-to to the original structure. The lot on Quincy Street behind the railroad switchyard near the cotton mill, was quite large, and Margaret Lytle had overseen the construction of additions to her little house as her business grew. In time, twelve tiny bedrooms and two more bathrooms, along with an enlarged parlor and a bar with a piano, had been added to the original structure. It sprawled over the lot in an array that from the inside was confusing enough to a sober person and incomprehensible to most of Margaret's clients who, by the time they were led into its recesses, were often in an advanced stage of inebriation.

The existence of the house of prostitution was well-known throughout Arkansas. Police had been lulled into complacency by generous contributions to the Policeman's Benevolent Association, as well as by the caliber of the clientele, which comprised most of the legislators and many of the officials of the Arkansas state government. Lobbyists gave elaborate parties at Mrs. Lytle's that sometimes lasted for several days. After these exhausting events, Margaret Lytle would always close for a day of rest for her ladies.

Prohibition was the law of the land, but it had no impact on the flow of liquor at Mrs. Lytle's. She proclaimed that, as a private club devoted to the relaxation and comfort of gentlemen, she was exempt from the Volstead Act of 1920. The lobbyists, legislators, and officials of the Arkansas state government agreed with her. The police could hardly have done anything different. In any case, both the chief of police and the sheriff, while not among Mrs. Lytle's regulars, had been known to visit, on occasion, so that they might personally check that no rowdiness was being promulgated. It was rumored that both worthy gentlemen had also visited with one or another of Mrs. Lytle's ladies, though if confronted both would have issued hot denials.

It was also common knowledge throughout Little Rock that a baby boy with startling dark-blue eyes lived at the brothel. When the information had first surfaced, initially as rumors, some of the preachers in the town had railed about the boy's presence, given as it was a new focus on their rantings. They had long since lost the interest of their male parishioners who, if not actual clients of Mrs. Lytle's, were for the most part tolerant of their fellow sinners and were tired of hearing further assaults on the house from the pulpit. Margaret Lytle had visited each of the town's churches following these tirades, arriving ostentatiously in her large town car driven by her light-skinned Negro chauffeur. She always arrived just after the Sunday service but while the ladies of the altar guild were still cleaning the communion ware.

No one ever knew what was said in her brief private meetings with the pastors in their church offices. However, following these meetings, there were fewer mentions from that pulpit about Mrs. Lytle's establishment. The church's general fund seemed to suddenly have a surplus.

Drew was the darling of Mrs. Lytle's Gentlemen's Club. The ladies of the house vied for his attention and approval, and as he grew and learned to walk, the labyrinthine hallways became as familiar to him as the fixtures and furniture in Maude's little shack. During their rest periods, in the late mornings and afternoons, the ladies would coo over the baby, hold and pet him. Hands that were more experienced in other ministrations to the male body changed his diapers, powdered his bottom, and dabbed drool from his lips.

On some level, Drew became aware as he grew that the woman they told him was his mother did not care for him. Where everyone else he met became an instant friend, his mother seemed to always want to sleep, or she would tell him she was too busy, to go away. When he cried and was somewhere she could hear, she would shout for Maude to take the "squalling brat" away.

Drew turned for love and nurture to Maude, and he got it. Time after time, Maude would say to him, "Honey, whun you popped outta dat blonde woman, so red and squallin', yore Mardie knowed you wuz to be mine. An' yore Mardie is raisin' you, best Ah can."

So black, skinny, wrinkled, toothless old Maude was the boy's mother during these formative stages of his life. As he learned to talk, Maude determined that his speech was not to mimic hers. She enlisted the aid of the ladies of the club, and they quickly moved to correct his pronunciation and accent when he began aping Maude's dialect.

Drew trailed around with her in the mornings as she cleaned and emptied the slops, and on Sundays, she took him to church when she'd finished cleaning from the Saturday night parties.

In the same way that Maude was Drew's mother and the ladies of the brothel his friends, his family was the congregation of the Ebenezer Church of God in Jesus Christ.

The rural Negro church, located five miles from the city limits of Little Rock on the banks of the White River, was precious to Maude. After her early Sunday morning duties at Mrs. Lytle's, she and Drew rode the city bus to the end of its route and simply walked the remainder of the way. Many members of the congregation walked to church along that stretch of gravelly country road, for few had the means to acquire an automobile. Reverend Aloysius P. Thomas had long ago begun driving along the road in his open Essex Phaeton, whose aged top had deteriorated into nothingness, picking up not only Maude and Drew but other parishioners as they walked to his service. Drew always shouted a welcome to his friends as they climbed into the overcrowded car.

Services at the Ebenezer Church of God in Jesus Christ often began late on Sunday mornings. Even when they started on time, they always lasted until late afternoon and included a lunch, which was called dinner, prepared by the parishioners. Choir practice usually was held early while the good reverend made trip after trip gathering his flock.

When services finally started, they lasted. Reverend Thomas could and did preach for hours.

The one-room clapboard building, set in a bend in the road, had once been white; but now paint was peeling, and the overall impression was of a gray building. The ceiling was low, and there was no electricity. In winter the place was heated by an ancient cast-iron wood stove, which overheated those nearest while parishioners farther away shivered from the cold winds that slithered through cracks in the exterior siding. The church had only a few wooden pews. Most worshipers stood or sat on the floor or on the few folding chairs kept stacked by the door.

In summer, and indeed on most fall or spring days, the interior of the old church became a sweltering oven. Sunday services were therefore held outdoors whenever possible. The outdoor services, under the huge old cypress trees that shaded the church grounds, were unquestionably preferable to services inside.

Every Sunday there was a huge meal of simple but nourishing food following the service. The food—fried chicken; ham; catfish when they were biting; watermelon in season; vegetables of all sorts, home canned or fresh; along with heaps of fresh cornbread—was laid out on several old rough-hewn picnic tables placed down the slope to the White River from the church. People simply filled their plates and sat on the ground, enjoying fellowship and the soothing sounds of the river. In summer, besides watermelon, there were often fresh peach or berry cobblers for dessert or pecan pies, buttermilk custards, and sweet potato pies. Once, for a particularly festive occasion, ice cream was hand cranked from a coterie of ancient freezers.

On Sundays when there was a baptism, the noon meal became an even larger event, with games, singing, and worship on the riverbank. Reverend Thomas would preach again, sometimes the same sermon he'd preached that morning. No one cared. His voice rolled and thundered: soft when he described God's love, rattling the rooftops and scattering startled birds from the cypress when he spoke of the misdeeds of the devil or those of his parishioners. When he thundered so, babies sleeping in their mother's laps would startle awake, only to be lulled back to sleep to the chorus of "Yes, brother," "Amen," and "Thank you, Lord Jesus" that came from the congregation and were sprinkled throughout the sermon. These were among the first words that Drew learned, and the two-year old boy loved to shout "Thank you, Lord Jesus" when the responses came during Reverend Thomas's sermons.

The people of the congregation accepted Drew, loved him, cared for him, and he grew up caring deeply for them in return. His extended family encouraged, without really realizing they were doing so, the natural open friendliness of the young boy; and his personality expanded in their wealth of love and caring.

The baptism Sundays were his favorite. He shivered as Reverend Thomas shouted for the angels to come and oversee the baptisms, and he wept at the often-emotional singing, songs that he later learned were called spirituals.

The baptism itself often seemed a game to Drew when grown-ups and sometimes older children would wade into the river with clothing or white robes to be dunked under the water by one of the deacons. Then, afterward, there would be more singing and clapping. Drew would race along the riverbank during the singing, shouting, "Thank you, Lord Jesus!"

The church services always continued late, whether or not there was a baptism. Often Drew and Maude would spend the night at one house or another since Mrs. Lytle did not open on Sunday nights. Sometimes they got a ride back to the bus stop early Monday mornings. They walked when they did not.

When Drew was three, Mrs. Lytle's piano player Eddie Mackenzie acquired an old closed Studebaker sedan. The top leaked badly when it rained. Two of the windows were broken, replaced by old isinglass taken from a wrecked touring car and taped into place. Eddie kept the engine running smoothly.

On those Sundays, when he didn't visit his sweetheart in Dardanelle, he was pleased to ferry Drew and Maude to church. Eddie joined the church after several months and was one of those adults whom Drew watched in fascination as they played that strange game with Reverend Thomas and one of the deacons, and all waded into the river.

It would have been appropriate for Eddie to be fat in counterpoint to Maude's lean, skinny frame, but he was not. Eddie Mackenzie was barely more than seventeen when he joined the cast at Mrs. Lytle's. He was tall, slender, and light skinned; and his eyes held a dreamy half-lidded look that belied his quick intelligence and sharp mind. He could play any musical instrument that was placed in front of him and could play any tune that he'd ever heard despite not being able to read a note of music. When he sang, his voice was mellow and soft. Love ballads sung by Eddie were the favorite of the ladies at Mrs. Lytle's.

Margaret Lytle had been concerned about Eddie's youth when he first asked for a job at her establishment. He was young, and she wondered, frankly, if he would be tempted by any of the ladies in her house. Then he played a popular love ballad for her, and she found herself plunged into memories of an earlier life that she'd once told herself to forget. She was almost won over as she listened to him play. She gave him the job when he told her, "Miz Lytle, ah unnerstans when you says you is concerned about mah depot'm't, so to speak, 'cuz you got some awful pretty young ladies here, and ah is a young buck. But you needn't concern yourself. Ah knows ah is black, ah knows the Ku Kluxers will be watchin' and Ah don't have no wishes to stretch mah neck in a rope. Besides, ah is Christian and ah got a good lil' nigger gal waitin' for me over in Dardanelle."

So Margaret Lytle hired him. He had Sunday nights off, of course, since she was closed; but she also gave him every other Monday night off so he could visit the girl she learned was named Maybelle.

Drew had been born with perfect pitch and an excellent sense of rhythm. At church gatherings, he sang with the rest of the congregation and the loud clear voice of the toddler, always on key, often could be heard over others. Frequently, he was invited to sing with the choir and many times as he grew older was a solo singer during some special point of the sermon. Eddie Mackenzie, whom Drew called Uncle Max, had bought Drew shoes with taps and taught him some elementary tap-dancing steps. In the evenings at Mrs. Lytle's, while Eddie played the old piano in the parlor, four-year-old Drew, dressed in a sailor suit, tapped his feet to the music and sang. The drunken patrons threw money at the blond child they called that poor little bastard. Eddie had thoughtfully placed his bowler hat on the floor next to the piano.

Mrs. Lytle kept quite a bit of the money thrown into Max's hat as Drew danced, and Max kept most of the rest, but Maude got an extra dollar a week, and an extra dollar went to Edith.

Sometimes Maude would leave Drew with Reverend Thomas after the Sunday services, and he would stay for a week or longer. He grew to love these times with the good preacher and his wife. There were often long walks in the woods or maybe excursions into town in the reverend's old car. Drew loved riding in the open car, especially when the bald reverend would declare that the wind had made both his and Drew's hair into a fright and then roll his eyes comically. Drew felt carefree and would laugh as though it was the first time he'd heard the joke and seen the face Reverend Thomas made.

Between Maude, Eddie, Reverend Thomas, and the people of the congregation, Drew learned many things. He learned Bible stories and how they applied to everyday life. He learned to sing, and he learned to love the hymns and spirituals. Eddie had taught him to tap dance, and the choir members used this talent in their Sunday performances. Drew also learned by watching the behavior of those in the church; and they taught him by example to be quiet, listen, and speak when spoken to. He learned to keep his own thoughts to himself and to wait until another time to take any action that would better his cause, whatever the cause might be. With the exception of Reverend Thomas, Drew learned, Maude, Eddie, and all the other Negroes that he knew, when they were around white people had an air about them that was subservient. They cast their eyes down and spoke in a drawl, mouthing words like *yassah*, and *ah knows*, and *ah will, suh*. It was as though they were waiting for something, and in the meanwhile, they would watch and learn.

But when the guides in his early life were not in the presence of white people, their true personalities came to the fore. Many could and did speak clear and direct English though often grammatically incorrect. They retained the blur and twang of other native Arkansans.

Many of Drew's Negro friends could not read, but they prized education that others had acquired and wanted to learn from them. Reverend Thomas's Sunday afternoon services often included educational topics, and all were eager to listen. The people who were Drew's initial life influencers lived for the most part in grinding poverty.

Yet they were wealthy in the currency of family, faith, and friends. Drew adopted many of the mannerisms of these wealthy personalities.

Reverend Aloysius P. Thomas had acquired knowledge beyond the Holy Bible. While he could and did quote not only verses but whole chapters from the King James Bible, he could also quote at length poems by Keats, Shakespeare, Shelly, and Whitman, as well as poems and essays by Thoreau. He sometimes confused his parishioners with his quotes, and some came to believe that William Shakespeare was also a biblical character.

Reverend Thomas also knew and could quote almost every recorded word that Abraham Lincoln had ever uttered. And he had an unshakable belief that the time would someday come when black people would have better schools than those currently available and that these schools would lead his people to a better life.

As he taught others of his congregation to read and write, he also taught the little white boy. By the time he was five, Drew could read almost anything that Reverend Thomas held out for him. Drew didn't know many of the words and their meanings, but he developed the ability to sound the words out and would later puzzle about their meanings.

Drew's life at both Mrs. Lytle's and at the Ebenezer Church of God in Jesus Christ was rich and full of meaning. It was far from being the life of deprivation that the bawdyhouse patrons, in their drunkenness, assumed. He was gaining a solid education in basic evangelical Christianity, some of the classics, a reverence for Mr. Lincoln, for reading, music appreciation, and how one handles himself around adults.

Drew, early in his life, had found the softness in Margaret Lytle that she worked so hard to hide. As the years passed, she found herself spending hours with the child, telling stories, teaching him games. Once long ago she had worked onstage as a magician's helper and from him she had learned various card tricks, which she often put to use in her weekly poker games. She taught the young boy several of these card maneuvers, and while his hands were too small to effectively hide cards, she felt he had ability and instructed him to practice. A number of times, she had him demonstrate his skills during her weekly poker games, and she complimented him on his progress.

But Drew's life was soon to change. In May of 1931 he turned five; and in the summer of that year, his mother and his new Uncle Henry took him away to Union City, in southern Arkansas, far from Little Rock, and far from his family and the life he had always known.

# Chapter 5

## *Leaving Little Rock*

HENRY DESCHAES WAS a wealthy businessman from a small southern Arkansas town near the Louisiana border. He had been a regular visitor to Mrs. Lytle's whenever business took him to the state capitol and had been one of Edith's first clients when she was still called Gretchen.

He had become enamored with Edith, then in her late teens, and had continued to visit her at every opportunity even after Mrs. Lytle changed her story and name.

Henry was no fool, and while he'd enjoyed the fantasies, he had never fallen under the spell of either of the stories Mrs. Lytle had put forth. Edith's speech alone would have dispelled the illusion that she was any sort of heiress, for she never lost the flat accents of west Texas or mastered more than the minimum of polite language skills. But Henry was blind to Edith's coarseness. He was also blind to her intake of alcohol.

Margaret Lytle was nothing if not a businesswoman, and when Henry's feelings for Edith became more apparent, she saw a way out of a growing problem that her business was facing.

Drew would need to start school by the following year. Margaret worried that women across Little Rock might become concerned that a boy who had been raised in a house of prostitution—and, therefore, was undoubtedly corrupted—would soon enter public school along with more innocent children. Politicians and lobbyists who frequented Margaret's establishment had begun to mention that maintaining the privacy and anonymity of their visits was becoming more difficult largely due to the issue of the boy and his perceived future unhealthy influence on the city's children.

Margaret had foreseen the problem for some time but had ignored its ramifications because of her strong feelings for the boy. There was now a degree of urgency to resolve the issue.

Thus, Margaret Lytle had begun, some months prior to Drew's fifth birthday, a not-quite-subtle campaign to influence Henry Deschaes to relocate Edith—and her son—to another town, perhaps one closer to the town in which he lived with his wife. It would avoid his frequent trips to Little Rock. Margaret admitted that relocating Drew away from his friends with a man who hardly knew him and a mother who couldn't care less about his well-being was certainly not in the boy's best interests. She could see no other alternative.

As a separate, but no less significant, factor, Arkansas's so-called Jim Crow laws not only forbade whites and Negroes from attending school together but also forbade the races to worship together. There were rumblings in and around Little Rock about the "uppity" Negro preacher, who so obviously cared for a white boy. He was that boy's teacher and mentor, and both allowed and encouraged the white boy to attend church with his Negro congregation. Comments around town were heard that Reverend Thomas was so uppity that he was even trying to talk like a white man, though everyone knew 'niggers' couldn't talk that way because "their lips were too thick."

Margaret cut the best deal she could with Henry, insisting that he provide a house for Edith and Drew and that he promise to pay all bills and put the house in Edith's name. Henry paid Margaret $500 for Edith, who was more than dismayed to learn that the deal included Drew and that he was to accompany her to the new home in Union City, near Newell, where Henry lived with his wife.

Edith considered that the reddish-blond blue-eyed boy was a great nuisance. When she learned that the house Henry had provided was not the grand palace she had imagined, she blamed Drew for what she considered her misfortune and wrung her hands at the injustice of having a crying brat on her hands. Her complaints fell on deaf ears as she wailed about her misfortunes. Her coworkers upbraided her and pointed out how grateful she should be for her good fortune. Even the silly Maxine angrily pointed out that Drew deserved better than he was getting, and she went so far as to say if she ever heard that Edith was mistreating the boy that she, Maxine, would personally travel to Union City and set her straight.

Edith retreated to her room, sobbing over the lack of sympathy she knew she deserved.

To Drew, it seemed that life was to start all over again. He was sad to be leaving Maude, Eddie, Reverend Thomas, and all his friends at the Ebenezer Church. He liked Henry, and even though he had never heard of Union City and had no idea where it was, he looked forward to his new life with some enthusiasm and a little twinge of fear.

Maude was devastated but was more a realist than Margaret Lytle and fully understood the impact of prejudice against the innocent. She, Eddie, and Reverend Thomas did their best to point out positive aspects of the move to Drew; and the youngster accepted that they also believed the move was for the best.

There was a going-away party of sorts late one sunny Sunday afternoon, with Mrs. Lytle and all her ladies dressed in their finest gowns. Edith was clothed in a new flowery frock. Henry had on his best suit, and the ladies had taken up a collection and had bought Drew a new white-and-blue sailor suit. Drew thought the sailor suit was a little scratchy and uncomfortable, but everyone bragged about how sweet he looked, so he didn't complain.

Maxine announced loudly that the leave-taking was "almost a wedding," and all the participants were in a gay mood. Maude had made lemonade, and Mrs. Lytle had broken out a bottle of her cheapest sparkling wine as a going away gift. The bottle was grandly and inaccurately labeled "Chapaign".

They all gathered at the front gate of the gentlemen's club at the end of the afternoon, where Henry had his car parked at the curb, engine idling.

Good-byes and hugs and kisses on the cheek that missed were passed around among the small crowd gathered at the idling car. Maude and Eddie took Drew aside and led him around the corner of the house.

They both knelt and hugged him. Drew realized they were on the verge of tears. He looked at them with his serious dark-blue eyes. "Don't cry, Mardie. Don't cry, Uncle Max. I'll come back, and we can visit!" Maude and Eddie exchanged glances as their tears started. They gave Drew the only thing they had to give.

"Drew, baby," Maude said as Eddie looked on, "y'gots t'kno you is betta than y'mama, betta than Henry, and betta than me an' Uncle

Max." Tears streamed down her sunken cheeks. "They gonna be good things in sto' for you. You're gonna have a good life."

Eddie nodded and said in his best interpretation to date of Reverend Thomas's diction lessons, "We won't forget you, not ever. You don' forget us. You grow up strong an' true and honest. Now, in school, y'study hard. Y' gonna be a good man." Tears were streaming down his cheeks, and he wiped them away with the back of his hand. Drew did not cry but wondered fearfully at the tears of these two that he loved.

"We'll see each other again," Drew said plaintively. Eddie nodded as more tears came down his cheeks.

"Mebbe so," Maude said. "But even so, you just 'member. Me and Uncle Max here, we love you and we wil' always love you. And Reverend Thomas, he do too. And eva' one at church, they all love you. All of us have done the mos' for you we could. You go now, and you go with your head high, and you don' eva foget: you're a good boy, and you're gonna rise above all this, and you're gonna make a good man. And tha's what life is all about, honey. You be the best man you can be, and Uncle Max and me, we'll go to our graves proud we got to be with you and love you as long as we did."

Eddie added, "Drew, Reverend Thomas has been teaching me to read and write." He continued, his diction somewhat better than Maude's, "I knows he has taught you too. You write us letters, and you tell us how you're doing."

"I don't know how to write a letter," Drew said, now blinking back incipient tears of his own.

"We fixed up envelopes for you," Eddie said, still wiping away tears, "w'stamps and everything. Here, in this box." He handed Drew a small metal box with a tightly fitting lid. The writing on the brightly colored box read Mrs. Goldstone's Excellent Bath Crystals. "We put in paper," Max continued. "Also, we put in pencils and stamped envelopes. You take a piece of the paper, write what you are doing, and put it in an envelope and give it to the mailman."

Drew looked at the envelopes. They were all addressed to the Ebenezer Church of God in Jesus Christ.

"Write to us, Drew," Max repeated. "When those run out, we'll send more. We love you. We want to hear from you."

And then, Uncle Henry had blown the horn on his Chevrolet coupe; and Edith was laughing and calling, "Drew baby, come on honey. Your new Uncle Henry is gonna take us to our new home." Maude hugged Drew one last time and then turned him in the direction of the car. "Go" was all she said as she gently pushed him from behind. Drew ran around the corner of the house, was hugged briefly by Margaret Lytle, and then Henry lifted him into the rumble seat of the little brown car with yellow wheels, placing him next to his mother's new large suitcase.

There was a chorus of good-byes and handkerchief waving from all the ladies as Henry tipped his hat, climbed in behind the wheel, put the car in gear, and let in the clutch. The tires slipped on the graveled road, sprayed gravel, and the car clattered away, leaving boiling red dust behind.

Drew turned in the open seat and looked back as the crowd grew smaller in the distance. He kept looking back as Henry turned the corner by the cotton mill, and he could see the side of Mrs. Lytle's Gentlemen's Club. Two figures raced down the hill from the side of the house, one in a flowing maid's dress and the other in a tight-fitting suit, losing his bowler hat as he raced to the fence line. Drew waved again, and the two figures also waved in the gathering dusk. Drew's eyes remained focused on the two figures; and he continued to clutch the small metal box with its paper, pencils, and packet of envelopes.

His sailor cap blew off and tumbled out of the car. It soon became a small white dot in the graveled roadway and then vanished from view as the car sped down the road.

# Chapter 6

# Union City, Arkansas
# 1931

"YASSIM, MA'AM, AH is Sistah Alma," the Negro woman said as she stood at the screened door at the little house near the oil refinery. Edith stared through bleary eyes at the huge woman, who was wearing a stained print dress, her frizzy gray hair pulled back into an untidy bun. "Ah has been sent by Mist Henry. Is you Miz Edith?"

Edith was dressed only in a light-green rayon robe at nearly two o'clock in the afternoon. She had been sitting at her unkempt kitchen table, smoking. She and Henry had had a party the previous night; and afterward, she'd stayed up, working on the remainder of the whiskey, drifting off to a boozy sleep while listening to late-night dance music on her secondhand Philco radio and then awakening to a pounding headache. She'd staggered to the kitchen, searching for her cigarettes, and had remained, staring in disappointment at the empty whiskey bottle. Where, she'd wondered fuzzily, was Drew? Usually, the boy was up early, whining and crying about wanting breakfast.

And now this fat old nigger had appeared at her back door. She did not understand how she had gotten to this point.

During the first years of Drew's life, there had been any number of hands to care for him. Edith often thought wistfully how for so long there'd been that old nigger Maude, who'd kept the boy all the time. And then the girls at Mrs. Lytle's had petted and cooed over him for what had seemed like hours on end, although for the life of her, Edith couldn't understand why. She'd had enough of crying babies and whining brats on her father's farm.

For just a moment, she frowned as she remembered with distaste the endless work that her younger brothers and sisters had been as they were born year after year on that barren windswept Texas plain. Her father's dead face leapt into her mind, and while her body reacted almost instinctively against the remembered pain, her mind continued to feel triumph that he was no longer alive. She muttered under her breath, *Nothing but pain—that's all I remember about that old man and all his squalling babies. Nothing but work.* She grimaced, not even wondering what may have happened to her younger siblings after her father died, and she abandoned them. She was thinking of Drew, still in her hair and creating unending work.

Sister Alma stood quietly on the stoop, saying nothing.

When Henry had proposed that she leave Mrs. Lytle's, Edith was hard-pressed to hide her dismay when she learned the offer included Drew. Now, in Union City, she had rediscovered that a young child was a lot of work. She resented the work and the boy. This was not how she should be treated.

Edith soon found that other than Henry's once-a-week visits, and sometimes not even that often, there was little to do in Union City other than an occasional matinee at the Rialto. In Little Rock, several times, Margaret Lytle had granted Edith and two of her coworkers a "vacation" of sorts: they could only be gone two days because the legislature, whatever that was, wasn't in session or some such foolishness, and they'd ridden the train to Memphis and stayed in a hotel. They had danced, flirted, and none of them had turned any tricks at all, although they hadn't considered it a "trick" when Edith slept with a handsome young black-haired Tennessean. He had been about Edith's own age, was especially attentive to her, and the next morning had proclaimed he was hopelessly in love with her. He had even followed all three women to the train station, begging for an address so he could at least write to her. It had been deliciously exciting. Each of the little vacations to Memphis had been similarly pleasant.

Edith sighed, walked to the kitchen door, and leaned against the doorjamb. She was bored with her life in Union City. She never got the rest that she deserved. She never got the attention she deserved either. And here was this nigger woman. At least it was something new, but that didn't mean she liked it. She tried to remember what the woman had said.

"Henry sent you?" she voiced the thought.

"Yassim, he sont me. He said you mout need a body to kar for your young'un, frum time to time," said the woman, patiently explaining again. "Ah ain't got no reg'lar job, so Ah got the time, and Ah does need the money. He done say he'd pay me when Ah teks kar of yr' boy, an' he done sont me down he'ar to meet you'uns. Kin Ah come in fo' a minute?"

"Ah, yes," Edith answered. She remembered saying something to Henry last night. She had cried a little over how much work it was to have a little boy around the house. "You come on in," she continued. "The door is open."

As Sister Alma stood calmly by the icebox in the kitchen, Edith sat at the table. She pushed aside some of the dirty dishes, knives, and forks before she ran her hand through her hair and pulled the robe tighter around her. "When can you start?" she asked. She sat up a little straighter and lit another cigarette. Her headache was beginning to ease. She wondered if there was any coffee in the house.

"Ah reckon Ah already has," Sister Alma answered. "Ah come by this mawin'. Ah seen the boy in the back ya'ard.

"Ah axed him iffen he wuz little An-Drew," she went on, "an' he say yassim tha's his name, 'sept folks call him Drew. Ah say whar's yore Ma, and he say you wuz in th' house. He say you wuz tared from las' night an' wuz still sleepin', an' he's not to bother you. So Ah axed him iffen he wuz hongry, and he say yassim he's hongry. So Ah tuk him home and fed him. Ah didn't have nuthin' but cole cornbread and some buttermilk, but he say tha's mighty good, an' he eat a lot. He's at mah house now, playin' with mah nephews. Is that OK?"

"Yes, yes," Edith answered dismissively. Her mind quickly grasped that here was an answer to the unending work of caring for a five-year-old. This old nigger was like a fat version of that other old nigger—Maude, that was her name—back in Little Rock.

"Do you do housework too?" she asked, wondering about the limits of Henry's generosity.

"Mist Henry, he says Ah is to come over he'ar once a week, tek the laundry to mah house an' do th' washin' and th' ironing, an' bring it back. He say, Ah is to clean the kitchen, too, but only do that once a week. He say you kin do the rest."

"Oh," Edith said, disappointed. She had hoped for a full-time maid. That would have been wonderful.

She stubbed out her cigarette in a dirty dish. "Well, can you do any of that now?"

"Noam," Sister Alma clarified, "Ah gots to git home. Ah lives mout a half mile from here, and Ah done walk it three times today, fust when Ah picks up An-Drew, Ah means Drew, an' teks him home, an' then to come back this enin to talk to you," Sister Alma continued with a genial smile.

"Ah gots to walk it once more, to bring Drew home. Tha's three miles jess' today, an' Ah is ole, an' mah knees hurt sompin fierce. An' mah nephews an' yo' boy is there rat now, an' they is alone. Ah gots to git home." She nodded to herself, hoping that Edith would understand her reasoning.

"Ah will come bak day after tomorrow, iffen tha's all rat with you," Sister Alma concluded. She nodded to Edith and said, "Good-bye, Miz Edith. Ah'm guine home." She turned and let herself out the door.

*Thank God Almighty,* Edith's heart sang. *I'll finally have some help with that little . . . little*—she couldn't think of an appropriate word. She hadn't wanted him. George had done this to her and then gotten himself killed. She did not understand why the kid couldn't have been left behind with Maude or the congregation at that country nigger church. They wanted him, she thought, but God knows why he was so much work!

She brightened again. *But at least now, I'll have a little help. I think I'll celebrate. A little drink should be just about right.* She stared again at the empty whiskey bottle, knowing that there were no other bottles in the house.

There was a knock at the back door. "Iceman," sang a voice she knew well.

Edith turned. "Come on in, Ezell. I need about twenty-five pounds today," she said with a lilt in her voice. She had not even heard the ice truck drive up.

A tall black man dressed in khakis, with the ice company emblem on his shirt, entered with a large block of ice on his back, held with enormous tongs. He removed the top of the icebox with one hand, shifted his body, and lifted the block of ice into the upper compartment. He turned and smiled, showing a mouthful of almost blindingly white even teeth, and reached into his rear pant pocket. He withdrew a pint whiskey bottle filled with a clear liquid that Edith's practiced eyes knew was illegal alcohol and no doubt extraordinarily potent.

"Ezell," Edith said, "that is a sight for sore eyes."

Ezell grinned again, turned away, took an ice pick out of its scabbard on his belt, and chipped ice into two glasses. He handed both glasses and the whiskey bottle to Edith.

"Ah had t' wait 'til Sister Alma left," Ezell said. "Ah don' think she saw me. Ah wuz around the corner." Icy water had dripped on the back of his shirt as he'd carried ice into other homes, and it was soaked. He took it off as he talked, displaying a magnificent physique, and draped the wet shirt across the back of a chair. His skin was the color of rich milk chocolate; his chest was hairless. He was broad shouldered and narrow hipped, lean and muscular from years of carrying ice into homes throughout Union City. Quite a few of Union City's housewives had sampled other of Ezell's attributes, though Edith was the only one that got free ice.

Edith had begun turning tricks soon after her arrival in Union City. At first, it was simply out of boredom, but it did not take long for her to appreciate the extra spending money and attention. Henry had sternly rebuked her drinking and smoking and had cut her allowance in a vain attempt to encourage her to reduce her intake of both vices.

But Ezell was different from her normal tricks. His aggressive sexuality excited her. It was enough for her to forgive his skin color.

As he kicked his shoes off and removed his trousers, Edith moved toward him, still carrying the glasses and whiskey. She put both arms around him, the ice-filled glasses rubbing his back; and as they kissed, his tongue opened her mouth and probed. His arms went to her shoulders and pushed against the robe. The sash slipped as the robe dropped away. She quickly put the glasses and liquor on the table and shrugged the robe all the way off. As it fell to the floor, she grabbed the glasses and whiskey again; and Ezell picked her up, kicked his pants into a corner of the kitchen, and carried her into the bedroom. *Today,* she thought with pleasurable excitement, *is surely one of my better days!*

Ezell had been wrong. Sister Alma had indeed witnessed his arrival at Edith's. She watched with disgust as he had turned into the yard of the little house and pulled his truck to the rear and carried the ice into the house. When he didn't reappear, her suspicions were confirmed. She thought, *Fool! Did he think no one knew or saw?*

She turned away, resuming her slow and painful way along the sandy road. *I'll need to keep Andrew—no, the boy said he wanted to be called Drew—a little longer,* she thought, *to be sure those two are finished. What a life that little tyke has! He's going to need a lot of care. His mother is no mother at all. No better than a stray alley cat,* her mind went on. *No,* she added in her silent soliloquy, *an alley cat is a better mother than that selfish woman. What on earth did Henry Deschaes see in her, bringing her down from Little Rock like that?*

She turned tiredly into her own yard. "An-Drew!" she called. "Drew!" she repeated the name again. "Whir is you, boy?"

A tousled head covered with reddish sandy hair popped around the corner of the house. "Yes, ma'am?" Sister Alma couldn't quite get over those startling blue eyes.

"Ah has talked to Miz Edith. She say you mout need to stay here a while' longer. Ah will git yawl sum supper aft a while." Sister Alma shuffled up the steps across the back porch and into her kitchen.

"Did one of my uncles come over?" Drew asked with unfeigned innocence.

"I've got lots of uncles," the boy added nonchalantly at Sister Alma's reaction. "When they come over, I have to go out in the backyard."

Sister Alma stared at the boy. "What iffen it's raining?" she asked.

"Oh, I have a place to play in the shed, out back. There's a blanket I can sit on, and I have some toys I keep in the shed. Not many. I don't have many toys." This last was a simple statement of fact.

"I can go to my room when Uncle Henry comes over. I don't have to go to the shed," Drew went on. "But most of the other uncles, when they come, I have to go to the shed. Sometimes Mother wants me to sleep out there. It's like camping out, she says. She lets me keep a coal oil lamp out there."

Sister Alma couldn't help herself. "Is th' ice man an uncle?"

"Sometimes I think he may be, but Mother keeps saying he isn't. I don't know." Drew shrugged.

"Does Mist. Henry know about your other uncles?"

"I don't think so. Maybe he does, but Mother always tells me not to tell him about my other uncles."

Sister Alma was beyond words. She could only shake her head. *Merciful Jesus,* she thought, *the boy's mother is turning tricks right in front of her own little boy.* She turned to her kitchen and said, "Ah will fix yawl sum supper in a little while, Drew, and then Ah will walk you home."

Drew followed her into the kitchen. "Was Mother all right?" he asked.

"Honey, she wuz jest fine. She's a little tired, that's all. Ah think she gonna rest sum more." Sister Alma was not a good liar and wanted to keep as close to the truth as she could. "She'll be OK when Ah gets you home. You'll see." Drew turned and ran into the backyard where Sister Alma's two nephews—his two new friends—waited. "Can I be next?" he cried as he ran out the door, wanting another turn on the tire swing.

Drew had found two new friends: Sister Alma's nephews, Leon and Walker, both near his own age. The excitement of the tire swing, the good food, and the way Sister Alma took care of him reminded him of Maude and Reverend Thomas. At least, he'd have some more interesting news for his next letter home, he thought, before remembering his mother had forbidden him to write and had thrown his envelopes and stamps into the trash.

# Chapter 7

## *Letters from Home*

THREE DAYS LATER, Sister Alma sat in the little office at the rear of the Paradise Valley Missionary Baptist Church with the minister. "Brother Joe," she said, "it wuz a pigsty, mebbe worse." Sister Alma shook her head, retelling the story for the third time. Brother Joe Barlow had listened quietly to each telling with a nod here and there. "Dirty clothes an' dirty dishes wuz everwhere. Th' stove wuz caked with grease and dirt, and there wuz things in the icebox so ole you don't wanna even think about. Miz Edith," Sister Alma continued, "Ah thinks she resent the boy. Mostly, she ignores him. What iffen he gets sick, who guine take care of him?"

In each retelling, her chest began to heave with indignation when she related, "An Ah done seen that no-good Ezell, he gone rat in, and ah knows she bedding him down, rat there in front of the boy. He says he's got more uncles. She's, well, Ah'm a Christian and Ah'm not supposed to say, but, she's whoring right in front of that boy. What kin we do?"

Brother Joe now asked a question, "You said the boy talks about a church near Little Rock. What did he call it?"

"Ah thinks Ah got the name right," Sister Alma said. "It's a long name: The Ebenezer Church of God in Jesus Christ."

"Has the boy ever mentioned a preacher? Perhaps a preacher named Aloysius Thomas?"

Sister Alma thought for a minute. "Now tha' y'mention it, he say sompin about a Reverend Thomas several times."

"I may know him. Let's take this a step at a time," Brother Joe said thoughtfully. "Let me write to Aloysius Thomas. I'll do it today and put the letter in the post office tonight. We'll see what he knows about Drew Simmons." He pulled his steel-rimmed glasses off and wiped them with his handkerchief. "In the meantime," he added, "you ask your sister, Imogene, to pass by Drew's house at least once each day. We'll kind of keep an eye out. If the boy seems hungry, we'll arrange for him to get something to eat. If he's been sent into the yard by his mother and it's raining or something, well, maybe we can ask the boy to visit you for a while."

"That pore boy is seeing all kinds of things, and him only five, that he shouldn't be seeing," Alma said gravely.

"Yes," Brother Joe answered, "but I don't need to tell you we're on shaky ground. There's fewer and fewer jobs these days. Times are hard, and the Klan is trying to rile everyone up and blame us colored folks. No telling what would happen if word got out that the colored community was interfering with a white mother's right to rear her child as she sees fit." He saw Sister Alma sit up straighter, draw another deep breath, and he knew a heated response was coming.

He quickly added, holding up his hands to stave off the attack, "Give me some time. You have your sister keep a close eye. We should have an answer in a week or so."

The letter from Aloysius Thomas arrived four days later.

"Dear Brother Joe," it began, "I can't tell you how overjoyed we were to learn some news about Drew. When he left for Union City, we gave the boy some stamped envelopes with our addresses on them and asked him to write. His letters have stopped coming.

"I taught Drew to read and write even though he is only five. During the years when one of our most faithful, Maude Millar, cared for him, we all came to love the boy. He sang in our choir, attended Sunday school, and often Maude would leave him with my wife and me for weeks at a time.

"Members of our congregation took the little boy to heart. He knew all our church songs and also quite a few of our songs that aren't religious but tell of our heritage.

"I will tell you what I can of his background. He was born at Mrs. Lytle's Gentlemen's Club in Little Rock. Maude Millar is a maid in that establishment, and she took over caring for the baby almost as soon as he was born. His mother had no milk, but Sister Beth Bailey from our congregation had more than plenty, having just weaned her youngest, and Maude left the boy with her for the first months of his life.

"Then, earlier this year, a man from your part of Arkansas decided he wanted to buy the boy's mother for himself and move her nearer to his town. I am reliably informed she wanted nothing to do with the boy. The boy's mother said Maude was to keep the boy, which would have delighted all of us. We felt he was simply an orphan, and we knew we could bring him up better than his mother. It was Margaret Lytle who said the boy should go with his mother. Eddie Mackenzie, the piano player at Mrs. Lytle's and a member of this congregation, said that Margaret Lytle, at that particular time, was being assailed from church pulpits across town because of the child who lived in a cabin behind a house of ill repute. She wanted it to be known that the mother and her child had left her establishment.

"All of us have been sick with worry about Drew. Now that it's winter, we worry whether Drew will have warm clothes to wear. And next fall, he will need to start school. I have no doubt that his mother hasn't the slightest idea where to buy school shoes or even care if Drew has shoes.

"Several here in our congregation would be pleased to put together a package of clothes for Drew and send them to him through you, provided you are in a position to give them to him without getting into any difficulty yourself, of course. The clothes we could send won't be new, but they'll be serviceable.

"When you or Sister Alma next see Drew, tell him that all his friends at the Ebenezer Church of God in Jesus Christ miss him, love him, and wish he would write to us.

"And as for you, my friend, may the Good Lord bless and keep you, and you have the thanks of more people than you know for telling us about Drew. If I could impose, I would ask that you write again from time to time. We are all so hungry for news of Drew"

Brother Joe laid the handwritten pages on his desk. Sister Alma had listened to the reading of it, and a tear had rolled down her cheeks from time to time.

"Oh, write 'im back, Brother Joe! Tell 'im to sond the clothes. Tha' little boy has nuthin' he hasn't already outgrown. Mebbe some of us at church can collect sum clothes on our own."

"Let's be careful, Sister Alma," the black pastor said. "The Klan is mighty active around here. You'll need to keep it quiet."

"Yassa, massa, Ah knows," Sister Alma said, rolling her eyes and letting her jaw go slack. She arose from the chair and walked to the door. Turning, her hand on the doorknob, she said in her best English, "We'll keep it quiet, and we'll avoid those idiots in the Klan, but I'm gonna give that boy some help. I'll begin by telling Mist' Henry Deschaes that I'm only gonna charge him for two days a week taking care of Drew but that since my nephews are lonely and want to see Drew, he can come over every day to play with them. I don't think Henry or that boy's mother will even think to look at what the boy might be wearing." She walked out the door.

The clothes arrived a week later.

Brother Joe's old flivver rattled up to Sister Alma's house. He bounded up the steps, carrying a large package. "They are here!" he sang out as he opened the screen door.

They opened the package together, exclaiming at the quality of clothes that had been collected. Neither could have known that Reverend Thomas had shared their letter with Mrs. Lytle and her ladies had chipped in, but their practiced eyes quickly sorted out which clothes were used and which were new. There was a new jacket and sweater, both now sorely needed.

There was an envelope at the bottom of the package, addressed in a bold but clearly feminine hand: To Drew's New Friends in Union City. Inside they found a $10 bill and a note from Margaret Lytle.

"I hope you will put this money," she wrote, "to good use on behalf of Drew. Aloysius Thomas has told me about Drew's circumstances. He says you are to be trusted. Sincerely, Margaret Lytle."

Brother Joe and Sister Alma looked at each other with wide eyes. "Margaret Lytle," Sister Alma breathed, "wasn't it she who insisted Drew come to Union City in the first place?"

"Well," Joe Barlow said, "I understand that when she did so, it was a matter of, ah, business. I would guess that she's a businesswoman before she's a filo—uh—someone who gives away money." He smiled at his attempt to pronounce *philanthropist.*

"When are you going to take these clothes to Drew?" he asked, changing the subject.

"This enin," Sister Alma answered.

"Can I give you a ride?"

"No." She straightened. "You're the one who said we needed to behave as if we were on shaky ground. Let me load it into that old toy wagon that I use to haul groceries and laundry, and I will walk over there as I normally do."

Later, Sister Alma trudged along, pulling her rusty Radio Flyer wagon piled high with Edith's laundry and the new clothes. As she neared the little shotgun house, she noted there were no vehicles around. At least today she would not have to deal with any of Drew's "uncles." Hopefully, she would also find Edith sober, or nearly so.

She knocked at the rear screen door and called out her name while summarily entering.

Edith was stumbling across the room in search of a sliver of ice from the icebox to wrap in a small towel and cool her aching forehead. "Miz Edith, howdy, an' kin Ah ax you sompin'?"

Irritated, Edith turned. "Yes?"

"Well, mah neighbor, she works cleaning house once a week for sum ladies across town, you know, where those rich white folks live. They give her some ole clothes. They're boy's clothes, Ah think they'd fit that boy of yours. You want them?"

"Oh, yeah, swell." Edith waved her hand vaguely as she headed toward her bedroom.

Drew was excited about the clothes when Alma showed them to him. He had no furniture suitable for storing clothes, only an old trunk with broken hinges. Everything he owned had been tossed willy-nilly into the trunk. There was no closet in any part of the house. Alma pulled his old clothes out of the trunk and put those too raggedy or too small in a pile. When she finished, he had only two pair of socks and some underwear left in the trunk and one pair of knee pants. This last was torn in several places, but they fit and would do for play.

She folded his "new" shirts, underwear, and socks and placed them in the trunk. She had brought a hammer and some nails, and she drove several into the walls—Edith screamed in agony from her room as Sister Alma banged on the nails—and placed Drew's new trousers and jacket on wooden hangers and the hangers on the nails.

"Honey," she said to Drew, "ah thinks Ah knows where Ah kin git you sum new shoes. Ah will walk to town with you, mebbe tomorrow, and we'll stop at a shoe store. Yeah, tomorrow, would you like dat? We'll see what we kin do. Now, I gots work to do. You know what I'd like you to do now?"

Drew shook his head.

"Ah would like for you to sit down and write a letter to some folks in Little Rock."

"You mean like Reverend Thomas and Mardie and Max?"

Sister Alma nodded. "Yes."

"I'm not supposed to. Mother found the envelopes they gave me, and she threw them away. She said I wasn't supposed to write to colored folks, except she used another word."

Sister Alma's eyes widened and her chest heaved as she took several quick breaths, trying to keep herself from using several choice words in front of the boy.

"Well, honey," Sister Alma finally said, regaining a measure of control, "tha's OK then. You run outside and play, and I'll talk to your mother in a little while about going to town tomorrow."

As Sister Alma busied herself cleaning Edith's icebox, she mumbled grimly, *If only I wasn't a Christian woman, what I wouldn't tell that . . . that—*

# Chapter 8

## *School Days*
## *1932*

**D**REW WAS SIX years old at the end of summer 1932. And that was when he fell in love for the first time in his life.

Her name was Catherine Ryan, and she taught five grades in one room in the ramshackle schoolhouse at the end of town near the Negro neighborhood where Drew and his mother lived.

She drove an older Ford touring car with the top folded back, and she drove it that way in all sorts of weather. Often it was loaded with both firewood for the school's potbellied stove and full lunch pails for her students, many of whom came to school without breakfast and no prospects for lunch.

Miss Catherine arrived in front of Drew's house one day as August was ending. Drew was sitting on the porch, holding a man's wallet. He was studying it intently as if it could speak.

He had found the wallet one day after his mother threw out what she said was trash. It had been lying on the top of the debris in the garbage can, and Drew had been curious. The wallet was empty, except for a photograph and a card hidden in a pocket inside. The photograph—faded, sepia toned, and mounted on heavy paper—had obviously been cut in two. It showed someone, standing stiffly, staring into the camera. It was a person who looked much like his mother.

On the card was a name, Leslie M. Baker, and listed his profession as attorney. There was no other information other than an address, telephone number, and the name of the city: Oklahoma City. The back of the photograph held a part of a word —*bock*.

Was the photograph his grandmother?

In Drew's imagination, the wallet had belonged to his father. He had been told many times that his father's name was George; but he felt that, somehow, the wallet was a link to his dead father. But why his father would have placed a photograph of Edith's mother into his wallet seemed a mystery. Drew often took the wallet and photograph out from their hiding place and looked at it, wishing it could tell him more about those who were his family.

Who was Leslie Baker? Drew had no idea.

He looked up in surprise as an old topless flivver pulled up in front of the house, dust billowing about. A lady in a gray skirt and white blouse climbed out, slapped dust from her skirt, and brushed back her brown curls, untidy from the wind of her passage.

She walked up to Drew. "Hello," she said. "You must be Master Andrew."

Drew blinked at the intrusion, found his composure, and stood, folding the wallet. "Yes, ma'am. I'm called Drew."

"Well, Master Drew, I'm Catherine Ryan. I'm going to be your schoolteacher. Is your mother home? I need to talk to her." Her green eyes flashed as they met the cobalt blue of his. He smelled lilac perfume.

Drew was a little confused as to why this seemingly impatient stranger was demanding to talk to his mother. He answered, "Ah, she's in the house." Edith was asleep and had forbidden Drew to wake her.

Catherine turned on her heel, her skirts swirled, and to Drew's utter astonishment, she marched past him. He followed her through the front room—his room—and stopped at the door between his room and the kitchen. He saw her knocking on Edith's bedroom door.

There was a whining growl from the other side of the door. "Go away. Don't bother me. I told you to go somewhere and play!" Catherine opened the door, went inside, and shut it behind her. Drew at last closed his mouth, which had remained open and slack-jawed, and put the wallet back in its hiding place, under his mattress. He leaned against the doorway into the kitchen.

Indistinct voices came from his mother's bedroom. He wondered what they could be talking about.

He would never know the details of their conversation. But twenty minutes later, the door opened, and his mother came out followed by this astonishing lady. Edith was dressed, after a fashion, and this in itself was strange. She never got up until it was almost dark and then rarely dressed unless one of his uncles or Henry was coming over. Catherine followed Edith into the kitchen, smiling a tight little smile, as though she knew a secret.

"Drew, honey," Edith called as Drew pulled back from the doorway, "you're a big boy now. You're gonna go to school. First grade. How about that?"

"And new clothes," Catherine whispered, sotto voce, into Edith's ear.

Edith frowned slightly, then, "Yes, yes. We're gonna get you some new overalls. And shoes," she added after a slight prod from Miss Catherine.

Catherine turned her intense green eyes onto Drew and smiled, showing small even teeth. "School starts Monday, Master Andrew. You know where my school is? I'll expect you at eight sharp." Drew nodded.

She laughed, and he heard her lovely tinkling laugh for the first time. Drew felt he would do anything to hear that delighted little laugh again.

"You're going to love school, Master Drew," she said. She laughed again as though hearing a secret joke. She added, "And I'm going to love having you in my school!" She bent down and gave him a quick hug, and he smelled again the lilac perfume that he would associate with her and her delighted laugh for the rest of his life.

As she hugged him, she whispered, "I've been talking to Sister Alma and Imogene about you! That's why I know you're going to love school!"

Then she turned without another word and swept from the room, across the porch, and through the yard. The old car clattered into life and rattled away up the sandy road toward Martinez's store.

Somehow, money had turned up, although Drew knew that his mother never seemed to have any. Early Saturday they walked to town. Edith held his hand, walked rapidly, and, seemingly irritated, jerked him along as he tried to keep up. They shopped first at JC Penny, where Edith snapped at the clerk. At Thom McCann, she seemed in a better mood as a young man helped and was extraordinarily solicitous toward Edith. Drew thought this man might become an uncle. After their final stop at Woolworth's, Drew had new high-top leather shoes, a pair of indigo-and-white striped Oshkosh overalls, and two new shirts along with several Big Chief writing tablets, pencils, and a new yellow-and-green box of crayons. There were only eight in the box, but it was the first time in Drew's life that he could remember having new crayons.

He was never to remember details of those first few weeks of school. It seemed to him in later years when he thought about those days that they had sped by in an incomprehensible blur. He remembered that Miss Catherine wasn't surprised that he could already read but that she was surprised at the words that he knew. He worked hard to hear again and again her delightfully tinkling laughter as he demonstrated more of the things Reverend Thomas had taught him.

There were only six students in the first grade that year. There were three each in the second and third grades, four in the fourth, and four in the fifth. Catherine Ryan taught all twenty children in one of the school's two rooms. The other room was used for storage since the school district had no funds for a second teacher. There were numerous Negro children who lived nearby, but they were required to attend the Harriet Tubman School for Negro Children on the other side of town near the railroad switchyards.

Drew was seated next to a little second-grade girl with large almond-shaped eyes. He learned her name was Kowanda, and she had been born in Hawaii. Her father had been in the navy and after his tour of duty had brought Kowanda and her mother to what she called "the mainland." She told Drew they had lived first in San Diego and only later had come to Union City.

When Drew's Big Chief tablets were used up, Kowanda gave him paper from hers and sometimes gave him shares of her lunch. Drew liked Kowanda, but the other students seemed to avoid her. She and Drew seemed to bond, one with the other, and often walked home together after school.

On one of these walks, he held her hand and discovered that he liked doing so. He asked her about the other kids.

"They don't bother me," Kowanda said. "My mother has always told me, even back when I was little and we lived in Hawaii, that people were often unkind. Most of the time, they don't understand that just because people look different from them, they aren't really different."

Drew nodded thoughtfully as she said this. "I have a lot of friends who are colored. They look different, but they are no different than other people."

"My mother always says just be nice to everyone."

Drew remembered that Reverend Thomas had once said something much like it. Years later, he would wonder at the wisdom he heard from a seven-year-old girl.

One day in mid-October, Catherine pulled Drew aside while the other children were at recess. "Andrew, I'm going to have to talk to your mother again. I think you can skip first grade and go directly into second. Who taught you?"

"Reverend Thomas," Drew answered. "And I learned a lot this summer from the books Miss Imogene brought me from the library."

"And where did you live when Reverend Thomas taught you?"

"Little Rock."

Catherine smiled. "Can I write to him?"

"I know his address. Mother said I'm not supposed to write to him. She threw away the envelopes I had. Reverend Barlow gave me some more and told me it was OK to write when I'm at Sister Alma's house. His address is Ebenezer Church of God in Jesus Christ, Route 4, Little Rock," Drew said a little breathlessly. "Do you know Sister Alma, Miss Ryan?"

A slight frown crossed Catherine's face. "Honey, is Reverend Thomas a colored man?"

Drew nodded.

"And the Ebenezer uh-whatever church, I assume that the people who go there are colored?"

Drew nodded again.

"Then let's keep this between ourselves for now, OK?" Drew would have thrown himself in front of a speeding locomotive if she had asked, but he could only nod dumbly. Any secret she wanted him to keep would go to his grave.

"And," Catherine added, "I'm going to have to spend more time with some of the other children. They didn't have a Reverend Thomas to teach them," she said with a smile. "I'll give you some work that you can do sort of on your own and some books from the library. I'll go see your mother after I hear from the good reverend."

Two weeks later, Catherine again sat at Edith's kitchen table, except this time it was clean. Sister Alma had been there earlier in the day. The whole house was clean, for once, and Edith had made tea. Drew had never known his mother to make tea. They were talking about school and about Reverend Thomas. Drew listened from his room.

"I wrote him," Catherine was saying, "and he answered. It seems that Andrew spent a lot of time at his church, and it seems that the good reverend is himself a well-educated man. Anyway, he seems to have taken a liking to Andrew, and the boy has a smattering of knowledge of not only basic reading, writing, and arithmetic but also a little of the classics."

Edith was at a loss. She had no idea what classics were and was irritated at Drew for making it necessary for her to meet with this person again. "You see," Edith explained, trying to look helpless, "I worked at this place in Little Rock, and there was this old, ah, colored woman, and she took Drew to church when I couldn't. And this Reverend Thomas, well, I guess he was the preacher."

Catherine nodded. "And he was Andrew's teacher too."

"He taught him a little Shakespeare," she added, surmising that Edith was completely unaware of her child's education. Edith had no idea who or what a Shakespeare was.

"He did a good job," Catherine went on. "Andrew's naturally very bright, and Reverend Thomas undoubtedly realized this. Did you know Andrew already knows cursive?"

Edith shook her head, wondering if *cursive* meant she could get money from this woman.

Catherine continued, "I believe he's been taught what we call the Palmer method of forming letters, and that style of handwriting is called cursive."

"Oh, yeah, uh, yes, ma'am, he can write."

"So that's a problem, you see."

Edith didn't see. She was beginning to fidget. Her frustration was becoming evident. Edith lit a cigarette.

"Andrew needs to be with children his own age," Catherine continued, "yet his early schooling along with, well, he's just very bright—ah—he's far above his peers. He needs to be in second grade."

Edith's brow wrinkled as she tried to digest what she was being told and why she needed to know it.

"What Andrew knows is good," Catherine said. "It's just that others may not understand. So if he's promoted in the middle of the school year, he's likely to be the subject of jokes and bullying. Children can be so cruel."

Edith began to weep, not because she cared very much about Drew or whether he was promoted but because she thought this was what a mother should do in this situation. She wished Catherine understood how cruel it was that she had to put up with Drew.

"It's OK. It's all right. There, there." Catherine went to Edith's chair and pulled closely the weeping woman so near her own age. Edith put both arms around Catherine's waist and began wailing.

"No one knows," she cried between sobs. "Since Drew's father died, no one knows what all I've had to put up with."

Drew's ears perked up. His mother never mentioned his father. Maybe now he would learn something more about him. But Edith didn't mention Drew's father again. Instead, she continued weeping as Catherine patted her on the shoulder and continued murmuring, "There, there."

Catherine was under no illusions about how Edith had made her living in Little Rock or who had brought her to this part of Arkansas or why and how she still made her living. But she continued the charade for Drew's sake.

"There, there," she said again. "Don't cry. Everyone knows your life is hard. We'll work together to help Andrew get the education he needs."

Catherine petitioned the school board to allow her to move Drew to the second grade.

It was not usual practice for the school board to become involved in a matter as simple as moving a student ahead in his class ranking. Normally, the teacher and the school principal met with the child's parents, and if they agreed, the child was simply moved.

However, the Paradise Valley School was Catherine's school. She was both teacher and principal, and everyone knew that she had, more than once, asked the school board to allow her to admit Negro children since the Harriett Tubman School was such a great distance from Paradise Valley and her school had two rooms, one of which was unused. Catherine would teach the Negro children in one room, the white children in the other.

The board members, properly horrified at this blasphemy and nervous about public opinion, now carefully watched her every move. Catherine therefore thought it prudent to meet with the school board and obtain their approval before moving Drew to the second grade.

She arrived one night along with Father McClain from Holy Trinity, Reverend Barclay from First Methodist, and Rabbi Berkowitz from the Union City Synagogue. The school board immediately declared executive session but permitted the church leaders present to remain.

Catherine began her presentation. "As shown in the documents I submitted prior to this meeting, there is a first-grade student at Paradise

Valley Elementary whom I believe to be qualified to be moved to second grade. I will ask the church leaders present to each make a statement, if it please the board."

The board president responded, "Are you planning on asking us again to let niggers go to your school?"

"No, sir," Catherine responded. "Perhaps you have not read the documentation I submitted. The boy is white. He has superior intelligence. He needs to be moved ahead one grade."

Rabbi Berkowitz stood up. "I've interviewed the boy. He's been taught by others from the time he was four to read and write. He's already familiar with many of the classics. This is nonsense. I don't need to spend my time with you on this matter. Admit the boy to second grade!" He sat down.

George Matthews, a newly elected board member, shouted, "I've been told he was taught by a nigger!"

While the president banged his gavel, Berkowitz stood and responded with ill-disguised frustration, "Oi vey! Learning is learning even if he was taught by a Hottentot!" He held his hands palm up, shrugged a classic Jewish shrug of goy ignorance, and sat down.

"Sirs!" Catherine said, trying to maintain calm in the room, "Perhaps we could now hear from Father McClain of Holy Trinity."

"Gentlemen," Father McClain said calmly, understanding Catherine's need for everyone to keep calm, "we've all interviewed the boy. Say yes, and we can all go home. He is qualified, and it is in his best interests." He sat down.

Without being asked, Reverend Barclay stood and added, "I agree with both my colleagues. We've all independently interviewed the boy. Admit him."

Catherine's petition was granted, five to four, over George Matthews's objection.

Shortly after the first of January 1933, Andrew George Simmons officially, and quietly, became a second grader in Miss Catherine Ryan's school. And as the New Year rolled onward, Drew's keen mind continued soaking up the education Catherine provided. Imogene, with the assistance of Ursula Schultz, continued to provide books, and he read them voraciously.

The other children quickly realized that Drew's teacher seemed to like him better than she liked them. Catherine loved all her students, but in all honesty, she had to admit—at least to herself—that Drew was special. She treated him differently in recognition of how far advanced he was over the other children, and her task was to keep him challenged. Nonetheless, the other children resented Drew; and despite his obvious poverty, they perceived him as privileged, therefore, a fair subject for taunting and teasing. Drew, for the most part, ignored taunts and teasing when it was directed at him.

But when the teasing included Catherine in its viciousness, Drew rallied. Several times as spring moved toward summer, he arrived home from school with bruises and a torn shirt. Once he came in with a bloodied nose. They could call him names but not his Miss Catherine. He would chase after them, and if they turned around he would fight. He sometimes even fought when they called his mother names. He did not win these fights.

Edith continued to feel frustrated, and she felt Catherine was teaching Drew that he was better than she. So when he came home dirty, disheveled and hurt, and sometimes crying, she utilized her version of discipline, spanking, as a counter for frustration. Edith's discipline verged on revenge. It was revenge based largely on the fact that Drew was even in her life.

One day—it was in May on Drew's seventh birthday—when Edith announced she was again going to spank him, Drew backed away. "No, not this time," the now-seven-year-old boy shouted, his tears forgotten. "I'm not going to let you hit me. I stood up for you when they called you a whore. I stood up for Miss Catherine when they called her names. You can't whip me for standing up for my teacher and my own mother!"

Edith fell into a rage. "How dare you! How dare you back-talk me!" She had a sudden flash memory of her own father saying almost the same thing. She reached for a strap. "I'll teach you respect!"

"No!" Drew turned, heading to the door. He felt the strap whistle past his head, barely missing him. He slammed the door and stood on the front porch, waiting, breathing hard.

He could hear Edith sobbing on the other side of the door.

He waited a long time, it seemed. The sobbing stopped. Drew went to the backyard, to the yard tap beside his shed, and dashed cold water on his face. He went to his shed and found an old dirty towel, went back to the tap, and washed again. He was beginning to feel better and was hungry.

After about a half hour, he went back into the house. His mother was in her room, asleep, an opened whiskey bottle half full on the floor beside the bed. He closed the door to her room and made a cheese sandwich for his supper.

He told himself that he had now learned that after a fight he needed to stop and use the yard tap and wash off before going into the house. Edith was then sure to ignore him if he appeared before her in a somewhat presentable condition.

# Chapter 9

## Summer
## 1935

DREW AND LEON were walking along the railroad tracks north of town, heading to the "swimming hole," a place where the usually narrow creek widened into a deep pool and was suitable for swimming. Someone had placed a rope on a tall elm that overhung the creek, and boys used it to swing out over the water and drop in. Drew and Leon had been there before, and they knew if any white boys were present, Leon could neither enter the water nor remain nearby. However, if the place was deserted, then both boys could enjoy the cool water.

The sun shone down from a brassy blue sky. The boys were dressed alike in faded overalls. They had neither a shirt nor shoes. Drew had experienced a spurt of growth over the past year, and his calves were exposed from the foreshortened legs of his overalls. He was almost as tall as Leon who at ten was a year older. Leon was, by now, Drew's best friend. They had met when Henry had first asked Leon's aunt, Sister Alma, to help with laundry and cleaning at Edith's, and their friendship had grown ever since. Walker, Leon's younger brother, was often included in their games but not today. There was an element of risk in this adventure.

"Reckon we gone git to swim today?" Leon asked nonchalantly.

"Well, this is Saturday," Drew answered. "Since there's a new cowboy movie and a new serial starting at the Rialto today, I'm hoping that's enough for no one to be around. I'm gonna dunk you." Drew grinned as he changed the subject.

"You and who else?" Leon shot back. "Come on, I'll race you to the hole!" Both boys took off running down the embankment and followed the path that led to the creek.

They were in luck. No one was around. The boys, breathless and laughing, stripped off their overalls and jumped into the cool water.

They played and laughed for all they were worth for almost half an hour before Drew noticed a man watching from the shore. He was sitting on a stump in the shade of a large tree at the edge of the sandy creek bank. "Look," Drew said as he pointed out the figure to Leon.

Leon stopped splashing around, and together they stared back at the man, unsure of what was going to happen next. The man on the creek bank arose and waded a few steps into the creek. He was tall but heavy-set, with a salt-and-pepper beard and unkempt graying hair. He smiled. "Don't let me stop you'uns. You was havin' so much fun. I just stopped to watch."

"Who are you?" Drew asked with just a note of uncertainty in his voice.

"I could ask the same to you," the man answered. "But allow me to introduce myself. I'm Honeycutt," he said with a bit of flair and a thumb pointed at his own chest. "That's with two tees. I live over yonder, here in these woods."

"Oh," Drew answered, somewhat embarrassed. "I'm Drew, and this is Leon."

The man waded farther into the water, bent down, grabbed Drew's hand, and shook it. He did the same with Leon.

Their first meeting with Honeycutt ended quickly. He simply told the boys, "Glad to meetcha," turned on his heel, and added over his shoulder that he had to "git on home." He waded to the sandy beach and left. The boys looked at each other, shrugged, and resumed their horseplay. Leon reached down, scooped two handfuls of water, and splashed it toward Drew, who dodged, laughed, and returned the favor. They began to race each other across the creek. Leon won. He always did.

Later, exhausted from roughhousing in the cool waters, the boys lay in the shade of a large elm, waiting for the warm summer air to dry them.

"You gonna go to high school, Leon?" Drew asked.

"Well, I don't know about high school." Leon's brow furrowed in concentration. "That's a long way off. Ma keeps talking about it. Maybe I will. Ma also talks about college. You know she went for two years. But I don't see how there would ever be enough money even if I decided to go. Anyway, maybe I'll just get a job to help out Ma," he continued, looking at the still waters of the broad creek. "She don't make much down at the library, and Aunt Alma makes very little doing laundry. What about you?"

"Well," Drew answered, "I hope I can go to high school. Mr. Scheumack, over at the radio store, talks about high school a lot, and he says great things are going to be happening in radio. Only he calls it electronics."

"You gonna be a radio star? Have your own show?" Leon asked with a bit of sarcasm.

"No," Drew answered, refusing to be baited. "He said anyone that knows how to repair radios or how to work in electronics will have a great future." Drew's enthusiasm slipped into his voice the more he talked. "It'll be a good job. He says someday they are going to have radios that have pictures on them, like at the movies."

"No shit." Leon rose up on his elbows. "Who'd have time to sit and look at a radio all day?"

Drew ignored the question. "Mr. Scheumack said that anyone that wanted to work in radio was going to have to have a high school diploma. So maybe I can go to high school. He said that, in a couple of years, I can work for him in his store."

"Like Ah has said over and over again," Leon observed, "you white asses get all the good jobs." He slipped deeper into his version of Negro dialect. "Well, massa, is you guine to hire me whun you is all rich? Ah does good work. Ah kin sweep up the radio store. Be kind to me, massa!"

"Shut up," Drew said, irritated as he always was when Leon aped others of his race.

The forest sounds, which had been a pleasant background for their lazy chatter, had changed. Both boys were suddenly alert. Someone was coming.

"Hey!" a rough voice from the woods called out to them. Both Drew and Leon sat up and reached for their clothes, pulling them on as quickly as they could. There were other voices too. "Nigger lover!" one of the voices sang out. "Black bastard, what you doin' with that white boy?" Three boys in their early teens emerged from the foliage and walked toward Drew and Leon, who were by now buckling the shoulder straps of their overalls.

"I know these guys," Leon said to Drew in a low voice. "That red-faced guy is called Arnold."

The hooligans were upon them. Arnold grabbed Leon. "Nigger, I said what are you doin' with that white boy?"

Leon resumed his dialect, and his demeanor changed as well. "Nawsuh, nawsuh, suh! Ah ain't doin' nuthin'. Nawsuh, not me!" His jaw was slack, and his eyes rolled. Drool came from one corner of his mouth. In other circumstances, his act could have been considered comical.

Both of Arnold's friends, Leonard and the boy called Smackey, grabbed hold of Drew, who struggled and kicked. Leon continued his loose-jointed portrayal of the Negro every white bigot assumed constituted the entire race.

"Full of fight?" Smackey sneered while holding the struggling Drew. "I know what. Let's beat the shit out of both this little nigger lover and his nigger friend." And so saying, he shoved Drew toward Leonard, turned around, and snapped a vicious right to Leon's jaw. Leon screamed, pulled away from Arnold, and dropped to the ground, covering his head with his arms in an approximation of the fetal position. Drew would have worried if he did not know Leon was a good actor when it was necessary and that he had sustained harder blows. Leon's cries were almost pure sham, but he continued to squall.

"Yeah! Beat the shit out of this little white nigger lover too!" cried Leonard who was still holding a struggling Drew.

None of the three teens expected Leon to do anything but lay on the sand in terror. After all, the teens assumed, it was against the law for a Negro to strike a white person. Leon was hardly terrified. He was angry and simply continued his act until the teen's attention could be diverted. He saw his chance as both his attackers turned toward the still-struggling Drew.

Leon leaped up and smashed his fist into Arnold's jaw. The blow caused blood to spurt from an upper lip and a cut tongue, and the boy sat on the sand in astonishment, spitting red globules. The other two teens turned and dropped their hold on Drew. Leon's fist smashed into another face. Drew swung on Leonard and connected. All three boys were sitting on the sand in surprise and pain.

"Run!" Leon shouted to Drew, who needed no urging, and both boys dashed for the woods.

"That black fucker hit me!" howled Arnold. "That's against the law!" he squalled through his bloody mouth. The other who'd also been hit by Leon rubbed blood and mucus off his nose. Leonard said, "And that little nigger lover hit me!"

"Look," one of the three shouted, "those fuckers are getting away!"

Drew and Leon vanished into the dense woods.

"Shit! Come back here, you little pricks!"

Drew looked back over his shoulder. All three of the boys were charging across the sandy beach, and soon they would be onto the hard clayey soils of the woods. Drew and Leon both realized their lead would vanish quickly.

Leon knew the woods better than Drew and a lot better than their pursuers. All five boys were barefoot. Leon ducked and turned, sure and steady. Drew followed blindly. Once, Leon stopped, picked up a large branch fallen from a nearby tree, and hurled it as far away as he could.

He was rewarded by shouts, "This way! I heard them over here!"

The shouts and curses from the teen boys became more indistinct as Leon led Drew away from the three.

Leon stopped, turned to Drew, and placed his finger over his lips. He pulled a bush aside and shoved Drew into the cavity of a huge hollowed-out log. It was the trunk of a tree that had fallen decades before. Leon followed and pulled the bush back into place.

It was moist and dank, and the dark space was filled with cobwebs and almost too small for the two of them. Leon swept the webs aside with his hand. The surface of the old wood was prickly against their skin, and already Drew could feel a thousand itches blooming that he couldn't scratch. The two boys huddled together. Leon held up his finger, nodding for silence.

Their pursuers came near, and sooner than Drew wanted, they were upon them. "Where'd they go?" the red-faced Arnold sang out as he leaped onto the hollow log where Drew and Leon huddled.

"I think we lost them," Smackey answered. Drew remembered the voice.

"Shit!" Feet stamped in frustration over Drew's head. Debris and loose splinters showered down from the rotted wood.

"I know that white kid," Leonard said. "His ma's that whore Edith, the one that rich guy Henry Deschaes fucks every time he drives over from Newell when he can get away from his old lady." Smackey chimed in, "I know that nigger too. He's Imogene's boy, that nigger that works in the library. I know where he lives."

"Then we'll get them sooner or later." There were more spitting sounds. Drew guessed the lip and tongue were still bleeding.

"You know," Arnold said, "we can take that white boy to his ma, tell her we'll beat the shit out of him unless she puts out for us."

"Yeah! We could do that! Reckon she'd fuck all three of us?"

"I get firsts. No sloppy seconds for me!"

The three sat down on the hollowed log and rolled cigarettes. Drew and Leon waited as they smoked and continued the lewd talk.

Drew cringed at the talk about his mother. He had denied her relationships with the men that she called his uncles for so long it was habit for him. Sometimes for brief periods, he convinced himself that no one else in town knew; but of course they knew, and he always knew that they knew. He was embarrassed that Leon was overhearing this talk. But Leon reached for him in the dank shadows and squeezed his hand. The touch said that he didn't need to worry, that Leon would always be his friend.

It seemed to Drew that Leon waited a long time after the boys left to motion that they should leave their hiding place. Drew was cramped and glad to straighten up, brush away webs and moldy debris, and finally scratch some of the itchy places. They were quiet as they carefully surveyed the surrounding woods. Since dusk was approaching the landscape now seemed dark and forbidding.

Honeycutt suddenly stepped from behind a tree, carrying a long stick.

"Whoo!" Leon shouted. "Man, you scared me."

"I saw it all," Honeycutt said quickly, his eyes wide. "Those boys are mean ones. But you two got the best of them."

"They jumped us," Drew said somewhat defensively.

"Yes, but you bloodied them. They'll be gunnin' for you. My house is right over there." He pointed vaguely over his shoulder. "You two need to come back and see me, mebbe soon. I used to box a long time ago. I could teach you a little," he said with a small note of pride. "Trust me, you're gonna need to know sooner than later."

The boys looked at each other. "It's getting pretty late," Drew said. "We need to be getting home."

"Well, be careful," Honeycutt said with honest concern. "Come over to my place when you can. You're gonna need to know how to fight."

# Chapter 10

## Learning to Fight

"WE SHUDDA COME here that day they jumped us," Leon said. "They wouldn't have caught us like that if we hadn't been foolin' around at the swimin' hole."

It had been a week since Leon had bloodied Arnold Gillis. He and Drew were sitting in front of Honeycutt's cabin, eating a bowl of his unusual stew, which they had learned was generally delicious even if the ingredients were strange or unknown.

"I don't think that matters now," said Honeycutt. "That Arnold— he's had his lip bloodied by a colored boy younger than he and in front of his buddies. And what's almost worse, the whole town thinks that a black boy was the one that done it." Honeycutt shook his head. He was looking at Leon with his eyebrows knitted together. "No, what matters now is that those three are gonna be gunnin' for both of you."

"We'll just have to stay out of their way," Drew said. "Leon can run fast. They won't hurt me if they catch me."

"Well, son," Honeycutt said, turning to Drew, "it'll hurt if they bloody your nose. They might do worse. Remember, they know where each of you live, not to mention you attacked one of them while they were ganging up on Leon. They'll be hidin' and waitin', sneakin' around, and one day soon, I think, they're gonna show up. And you know what, I don't think they're gonna try to catch you two together either. They're gonna try to take you one at a time."

Drew felt a little chill run up and down his spine.

"So, boys," Honeycutt went on, "what are you gonna do about it? Runnin' ain't gonna take care of those three, and you both know it. You're gonna have to think of something else."

Drew and Leon sat quietly for a minute or two.

"What did you have in mind?" Drew asked the old hermit. He had a suspicion that the adult knew perfectly well what they could do in this situation.

"Glad you asked!" Honeycutt answered brightly. He smiled and showed his yellowed and crooked teeth through his dirty beard. "I thought you never would. I told you before that you boys need to learn to fight! And guess what, I am probably the best fighter in this part of Arkansas!" He balled up his fists and held them up for the boys to see.

"You?" asked Leon, grinning and showing his large square white teeth.

"Yep. Me," Honeycutt answered with a grin. "I've done a lot of things in my day, son, and guess what, one of them was boxing. I was twice Golden Gloves runner-up champion of New York City!" He held up two fingers, and Drew noticed his eyes seemed to sparkle with a bit of memory. "'Course, that was when I was younger, just a kid myself. And I didn't have this belly I'm carrying around now." He patted his overhanging belly, a distant look slipping into the edge of his eyes before awareness snapped back in place. "But I ain't forgot nuthin', you can be sure of that.

"And it ain't just boxin'," Honeycutt went on, his experience putting weight behind his words. "I was as good a street fighter in those days as—well, as good as a street fighter gets. If you boys are willing to work at it, show up reg'lar here at my place, well, then, I'm willin' to teach."

The boys began learning the art of boxing and the skills of self-defense from an old hermit in the deep woods east of Union City. On that first day, Honeycutt had begun as soon as they had put their spoons down. "Boys," he said, "the first thing, the very first thing when you get in a street fight, and that's what it'll be when they catch up to you, is you gotta hurt the other guy." He made sure they were paying attention to his words. His voice had lost some of its warmth. It sounded to Drew as if it were hard and stony. "No being nice and tappin' him a little and showin' him you got better footwork or anything like that. Nossir! You got to hurt him, and if you can't hurt him first, you got to hurt him the worst. Worser than he can hurt you! You understand that?" The boys nodded in agreement.

They stayed until it was nearly dark. Honeycutt had furnished both with practice gloves, which appeared to be quite old. The boys had sparred, at first tapping one another lightly, each afraid of hurting the other. Honeycutt had moved around them shouting, "None of that! You each got to know how it feels to hit and to be hit. Protect yourself. Look for an opening in the other guy. Pop 'im one!" Drew saw Leon drop his hands a little. It was an opening, and he found himself hitting hard. Leon fell down.

Tears sprang to Drew's eyes. He had hurt his friend. Leon sprang to his feet as Drew reached down to help him and returned the favor. Drew's vision blurred as Leon's gloved fist slapped into the side of his head. Honeycutt stopped them after a minute or two, laughing and saying that the lesson was at an end. He complimented the boys. Both discovered they were crying—not just from pain but because each had hurt the other. But both nodded agreement when Honeycutt pointed out that this was the way to learn, and soon they were laughing as each proclaimed he had hit the other harder than he'd been hit.

"Pussy!" Leon shouted. "You hit like a girl."

"Look who's talking," Drew responded. "I hardly felt those love taps!"

Both boys had their arms over the other's shoulder as they left Honeycutt's, laughing and teasing.

Leon talked to his aunt that night, sitting on the porch after a late supper. Sister Alma thought for a while and then turned to her nephew. "Leon, I think Honeycutt's right. Those bullies are gonna be layin' for you. I can't teach you, and you don't have a dad around. Is it really true what those boys said, you can't fight back because of your race?" The way her forehead crinkled made Leon's stomach do several flips.

"I don't know," he answered. "Maybe."

"It may mean you miss out on doin' some of the chores around here, but I think it's important. You take off when you can, and you and Drew run on out to that old hermit's cabin. Learn well what he teaches you. But don't hurt Drew or let him hurt you." She grinned as she ended on a pleading note.

The lessons continued all that summer, but Drew found the opportunity to use Honeycutt's first lessons after only three weeks.

It was a Saturday, and Drew was taking a load of his and Edith's laundry to Sister Alma. It was heavy—piled high in a wicker basket— and Drew struggled with the load. He'd taken a shortcut through some brushy vacant lots and had set the basket down at the top of a small hillock. Drew wiped the sweat from his face with one of the dirty towels, put it back into the basket, and reached down to pick up the laundry again.

Something hard hit him in the back. Drew fell, spilling the laundry. He felt the wind knocked out of him. He rolled over and saw the three boys. Arnold had a short but stout tree limb and was brandishing it. "You are one little shithead, and I'm gonna make you sorry you told that lie about that nigger hittin' me."

As Honeycutt had taught him, Drew did not gasp for breath but instead struggled for control and bringing air back into his lungs by taking long and slow breaths. Tears had sprung unbidden to his eyes, but he fought them back. He could hear Honeycutt's voice. "Control the pain!"

Drew rose to a half-kneeling position and looked at his attackers. He kept his fists clenched to hide how much they shook. He felt angry and somehow a little glad that the waiting was over. Instead of tensing too much, his shoulders slacked a little, and he fought to keep his breathing steady. A strange calm came over him. The edges of his vision seemed to have a reddish haze.

Arnold stood by the upturned basket, watching Drew and brandishing the club. Leonard—the shortest of the three, the one with protruding front teeth and unruly black hair—walked to the basket and looked into it. "Hey," he said, "lookie here!" He held up a pair of Edith's underwear, waved it about, and rubbed it on his crotch. "I think I'll keep these," he went on. "I can jack off for a month just smellin' 'em!"

The day, which had been sunny, suddenly seemed to Drew to be blurred. That strange reddish calm feeling continued to roil in his stomach. He was frightened, he was angry, and yet he was overwhelmingly calm. Everything seemed to be happening around him as though he was in the eye of a hurricane.

Arnold and the boy called Smackey turned and looked at Leonard and grinned as Leonard waved the panties about and made lewd motions.

Drew launched himself from his half kneel with his arm outstretched and locked at the elbow. He drove his fist into Arnold's soft belly. The boy gasped, dropped his club, and sat down in the pile of dirty laundry. Smackey stared dumbfounded as Arnold thrashed about, then screamed, and doubled over as Drew turned and put all his weight into a solid kick into his groin. Smackey vomited into the grass before him as he fell onto his side, crying, writhing, and holding his injured privates.

Leonard, still holding Edith's underwear, gawked at his two friends rolling about on the ground, then raised his eyes, and watched in astonishment as Arnold's club smashed into his face. The blow forced his front teeth through his upper lip and rearranged his nose. He fell over backward, blood spurting, and rolled, gagging on his own blood.

Drew turned to see Arnold rising and shouting, "I'm gonna kill you!" He screamed something about *bastard* and launched himself toward Drew. They fell into a heap, Arnold punching wildly and screaming in rage. Drew pulled his knees to his chest and kicked with both feet, dislodging Arnold. He looked around for the stick but wasn't fast enough. Arnold had picked it up and was already swinging it back and forth. Drew backed away, remembering Honeycutt's words. "Watch for an opening. Watch your opponent's eyes. He'll signal the opening. There'll always be one!"

The overwhelming calm Drew felt had another strange feature. It seemed to Drew that everything was happening slowly, almost like the slow-motion effect he had seen at the movies. As Arnold ran at Drew, raising the stick and swinging wildly, Drew could see puffs of dust as the other boy's bare feet hit the sandy clay. Drew felt as if he had all the time in the world as he sidestepped and tripped Arnold as he ran past. As Arnold fell, his club grazed Drew, bloodying his forehead. Drew reached out and grabbed the branch as Arnold put his hands out to stop his fall, Drew pulled it away.

Arnold sprang quickly back to his feet, but Drew was already there with the branch. Drew swung the club and hit him soundly in the side of the head. Arnold's knees buckled, but he did not fall. A scream of rage, the sound somehow strangely distorted, came from Arnold's mouth as he again charged. Drew's next swing missed, and he fell as the larger boy tackled him to the ground using his knees to pin Drew's upper arms. Arnold called to the other boys, "Come on! I got him now. Let's take care of this little bastard!"

Leonard had begun to hope that perhaps his private parts would somehow remain attached to his body, but he was still reluctant to stand. Instead, he shouted between his sobs, "Beat the crap out of him, Arnie!"

Smackey did not answer or get up off the ground but remained there, holding one of the dirty towels over his face in a vain attempt to stem the flow of blood. He too had begun crying.

Arnold looked down at the struggling Drew and punched him solidly in the side of his head. Drew saw the blow coming and turned as it hit, deflecting it a little, but still it hurt. Arnold followed with a second blow with his left and then hit Drew four more times in rapid succession. Drew felt he had only seconds left before he lost consciousness.

Arnold reached for the tree limb, and as he did, his knee rose up off Drew's arms slightly. It was the opening Drew needed, and he pulled his arms free and slid away, climbing quickly to his feet. Both boys sprang for the weapon, but Drew got there first. He immediately turned and hit the overweight boy solidly on his side. Arnold fell to the ground in a heap, holding his ribs.

*Oh, lord,* thought Drew, *I've killed him.* A second later, Arnold groaned and began sobbing. The entire affair had lasted less than two minutes. Drew's mind was still trying to catch up to events when he heard noises behind him.

Brother Joe Barlow stepped from the brush. "Son," he said to Drew, "I saw everything. I tried to get here as quickly as I could. Here." He handed Drew a towel from the pile of laundry. "Take one of these and hold it to your face. You're pretty bloody. How do you feel?"

"I don't know," Drew answered. He wiped his face with the towel and was astonished to see it come away covered with blood. He looked at the black minister. "How did you happen to be here?" he asked.

"Not now, son," Brother Joe said. "How do you feel?"

"It kinda feels like my lip is split. Am I gonna have a black eye?" Brother Barlow nodded yes, his steel-rimmed eyeglasses glinting in the sun.

"Do you feel like you can help me get these three down to Sister Alma's?" he asked.

"Stay away!" Leonard shouted, struggling to his feet. "I don't want some old nigger touchin' me! You leave me alone. I'm gonna go home. I'm gonna tell on you!"

Brother Joe nodded at Drew. "I think he's feeling better."

Leonard stood, wiped at the vomit and mucus with the back of his hand, and turned, moving down the hill. He tried to run, found it painful, and resumed walking with a somewhat awkward gait. He sobbed as he continued to hold his bruised testicles.

Walker had been playing on Sister Alma's front porch and had seen the fray. He came running up and, along with Brother Barlow and Drew, helped Arnold and Smackey down the hill. Walker drew a bucket of water from the well, and Sister Alma brought out clean towels. Arnold and Smackey sat on Sister Alma's porch, sobbing, while Brother Joe wiped their faces with cool wet towels. "Walker," Brother Barlow said, "you run on over to Mr. Martinez's store and ask him to telephone the sheriff. Will you do that please? Oh, and, Walker, before you go, run back up that little hill and bring back that stick they was using."

The sheriff arrived just as the laundry Drew had been carrying was gathered up by neighbors and brought to Sister Alma's house. A small crowd of people stood around.

"Ah don' seen th' whole thing, Sheriff," Brother Barlow said, utilizing his subservient dialect to the sheriff. "Ah wuz comin' across frum th' church, wantn' to talk to Sistah Alma about this Sunday's church supper, and, well, Arnold he'ar, he started it. He snuck up on this youngstah and hit him hard across the back with this he'ar stick. Ah tried to call out, but Ah guess no one heard me. Next thing I knew, Drew, here, he had the club and was knockin' these boys down. But they started it."

"I did not!" Arnold called out. "We was just . . . we was just—" He resumed his sobs.

Felix Martinez had driven his coupe down from his store, and he added, "Sheriff, I didn't see anything, but these two boys and one other were in my store earlier. I heard them talking about Drew and how they were going to 'get him' and how one of them, this boy here"—he pointed to Arnold—"had cut a branch from a tree. They tried to steal a package of cigarettes, but I caught them, and told them to leave. Later, I watched as they whittled stems off the branch."

"No," Smackey sobbed. "We never was in Martinez's store today."

"And that little fucker over there," Arnold added, pointing at Drew as new tears coursed down his cheeks. "He started it all. We were just mindin' our own business."

"Mr. Sheriff," Felix said, pulling himself up to his full height of five feet four inches, "I do not lie."

"I believe you," the sheriff said seriously. He turned to Drew. "Son, walk over here with me a little ways, and let's talk."

They stopped by the side of the sheriff's car, and the sheriff leaned on a fender and removed his hat. "You're Miz Simmons boy, isn't that right?"

"Yes, sir," Drew answered hesitantly, wondering if this man would be an ally or take the side of his attackers.

"Why don't you tell me what happened?"

He listened closely as Drew recounted being struck from behind. Drew worked to keep his voice steady and unemotional as he described the fight and Brother Barlow coming up at the end. The sheriff nodded. It tallied with Barlow's description of events, given privately to him minutes earlier. "Raise your shirt," the sheriff said, "and show me your back." A long diagonal bruise crossed Drew's back.

"You got into a fracas with these three a few weeks ago, didn't you? You and that nigger boy, Leon. I heard about that."

"Yes, sir."

"Was Leon here today?"

"Leon's over at the cotton gin today in Newell. He wants to work there next summer," Drew said.

The sheriff sat silently for a minute, pulling at his mustache. "You know, son, I never did really believe it, back when I heard you bloodied Arnold's nose. I didn't believe that. I thought it was Leon who hit them, just like Arnold said. Tell me the truth now. Was it Leon that first time? Son, don't you lie to me," he said when he noticed Drew's face start to close. "You don't have to protect Leon. I'm never gonna tell another soul, no matter what your answer is."

Drew looked deeply into the sheriff's eyes, searching. After a moment, he said, "Yes, sir, Leon hit Arnold then. But I hit one of the other boys, and then we ran."

"Let's, you and me, make a deal, son," the sheriff said. "You always tell me the truth. And if you think someone needs to be protected, well, that's my job. There'll be times when maybe I won't tell anyone else what you tell me. There'll be times maybe when I have to. But from now on out, if you ever get into any trouble again of any kind, you tell me the truth. Is that a deal?"

"Yes, sir. But I was so afraid for—" The sheriff held up his hand, stopping Drew. "Son, let's reconfirm to each other, man to man. Do we have a deal?"

"Yes, sir. We have a deal." The sheriff stood and held out his hand. Drew shook it.

The sheriff put his hand on Drew's shoulder and walked with the boy back to Sister Alma's porch. "Brother Barlow," the sheriff said, "do you think you all can patch up Drew and get him home? I'm gonna have to take these two home to their mamas."

Sister Alma handed Arnold and Smackey each two fresh wet towels. "You'uns kin keep these towels. They're old, but they're clean."

Arnold turned and looked back as the sheriff was leading him to his car. "I'm gonna tell on you on all you niggers and on you too"—he pointed at Drew—"you little nigger lover!"

The sheriff spun him around and pushed him up against the side of his car. He said loudly, "Son, you ain't gonna do nothin'! You hear me? This business ends now! Right now! Understand!"

Arnold face began to crumble as the sheriff yelled, and soon he was crying again. The sheriff bent down, putting his nose inches away from Arnold's. "I said," he shouted, "Do you understand!"

Arnold sniffled, wiped his nose with the back of his hand, and nodded meekly.

"Lemme tell you something," the sheriff said loudly enough for all the crowd gathered in Sister Alma's yard to hear, "You ever raise a hand to anyone here today, I'm gonna put your little sorry ass in jail!" The sheriff's face was a stone mountain filled with molten rage. "You ever even come to this part of town again, I'm gonna put your little sorry ass in jail! You take on Drew Simmons, ever again, or Leon Arquette, ever again." The sheriff had become a force of nature, and he now shouted at the top of his lungs, "I am going to put your sorry ass in jail!"

Arnold was bawling as he climbed into the backseat of the sheriff's car. The sheriff smiled at the assemblage, tipped his hat, and drove away.

When Drew returned home, he found that Edith and Eugene were having a party, and he was forbidden to enter the house. He spent that night in his shed without supper. He had kept himself from crying all through the fray near Sister Alma's, and during the time the sheriff was conducting his investigation, but now he cried himself to sleep on his blanket in the shed under the chinaberry tree.

# Chapter 11

❖―・❀・―❖

1936

I N LATER YEARS, when Drew looked back on that summer of 1935, he realized that the night after the fight when his mother made him sleep in the shed was the night that he decided to leave home. His mother did not love him, did not care, and had never cared. He did not think she would ever care. But he could not leave right away because at some level he also realized that making up his mind to leave and actually doing so were two different things. He needed to be older, do as well in school as he could until then, and in the meantime find a way to make money and save it.

He already knew that when he left he would go to Little Rock, to his friends, to his real family.

He went to Felix Martinez and asked about employment at the grocery.

Martinez was thoughtful. He knew quite a bit of Drew's circumstances and was concerned and wanted to help. However, as a Mexican selling groceries in a run-down section of Union City, whose principal customers were low-income colored and white families, his margins were slim. He pulled two apple crates to the counter, sat and invited Drew to do likewise.

"What can we do, one for the other?" he asked Drew.

Drew thought about the question. After a few minutes, he said, "I don't know much about the grocery business. I could help in stocking shelves, bringing things from your storeroom to the front, sacking the groceries, and helping carry them out."

Martinez answered, "I already do that myself."

"Well," Drew said as he thought about the issue, "I know you sometimes deliver groceries on Saturdays after you close. Maybe I could make deliveries for you during the day."

Martinez answered after thinking of Drew's response, "That's not bad. Good thinking, Drew, but I use my coupe."

"I've seen a bicycle out in your alleyway shed. Could I use that?"

Martinez arose from the apple crate on which he had been seated and walked around the grocery store, mumbling to himself. Drew remained where he was. There were no customers present.

Felix Martinez came back. He did not sit down. "Drew, you've given me something to think about." He looked away, mumbling again to himself.

He turned, looked at Drew and said, "I need to think some more. Come back tomorrow, after school."

A week later Drew began working for Martinez Grocery, making Saturday deliveries, using the old bicycle from the alleyway shed. Felix explained that years before his son had delivered groceries using the bicycle.

Drew spent his first Saturday cleaning the old bicycle, oiling the chain and other parts, and learning to ride. He discovered that riding a bicycle was not as easy as it looked, but Felix came out into the alley and helped guide Drew as he learned. There was no pay for that first day, but Drew rode with him in his coupe as he made late Saturday deliveries. At each home, he introduced Drew and told his customers that the following Saturday they could receive deliveries all day long.

As time passed, Drew became a familiar sight as he pedaled about Union City on the old bike with the enormous basket fixed to the handlebars. When a delivery was made to a home in the more prosperous part of town, he sometimes got a tip, usually a quarter. Once, he received a whole dollar because the elderly Mrs. Wallace asked him to put the groceries away for her into the refrigerator and pantry. She gave him the dollar tip each time he made her deliveries and put the groceries away. Mr. Martinez paid him a dollar for each Saturday he worked. Drew's tips and his salary went into his tin box, Mrs. Goldstone's Excellent Bath Crystals. He was careful as always to keep the box hidden from his mother.

Drew worried that he might come across Arnold and his friends as he pedaled about the town, and he did. They chased him on their bicycles, but Drew managed to avoid them. Once, several weeks after the deliveries started, they came upon him quickly. Drew pedaled away, but the boys were close behind. As he passed the sheriff's office, Drew skidded to a stop, got off the bike, and stood defiantly. The three young teens turned and left the area quickly.

Drew had hoped that the sheriff's talk after the fight would calm things down, but it seemed that Arnold and his friends continued to harbor a grudge. He never saw the boys in Paradise Valley, so evidently they were taking at least part of the sheriff's threats to heart.

Drew turned ten in May of 1936; and all that summer, he worked full-time for Mr. Martinez, stocking shelves, sacking groceries, taking delivery orders over the telephone, and making weekday deliveries as well as Saturdays. Mr. Martinez noticed the increase in business because of the weekday deliveries and increased his pay to $2 a day. He also allowed Drew to take home canned goods that had lost their labels. Drew thought that sometimes Mr. Martinez removed the labels himself.

While Drew worked at the grocery that summer, Leon turned eleven. He visited the gin in Newell, lied about his age, and was hired to work twelve-hour days for three days a week. Numerous other Negro boys and quite a few white needed summer work, and the gin proprietor limited the number of days each boy could work so that more families could benefit from the cotton harvest.

During long summer evenings and Sundays, when both boys were not working, they continued to visit Honeycutt, who kept up their lessons in self-defense. Both Drew and Leon had begun performing with the choir on Sunday evenings at the Paradise Valley Missionary Baptist Church. It was a good summer for the boys to continue learning and making friends, but both felt their good luck would not last forever.

Two significant events were to occur that year: Catherine's school would be burned to the ground, and Henry Deschaes would at last learn about Ezell.

It was early in August when Henry learned about Ezell's visits to Edith. He had come in earlier than expected one day and discovered Edith and Ezell entwined in her bed.

Henry exploded, "Goddamn it! I can't believe it!"

Ezell calmly and methodically disengaged himself from Edith and walked, naked but with studied nonchalance, toward the crumpled pile of his clothing. He pulled on his pants as Henry, red-faced, continued shouting, "I pay for everything and more, and you fuck anything in pants that comes along! I learned a long time ago about the tricks you turned, and I knew I couldn't expect anything else out of you," he said dismissively. He shook his head in the jerky motion of someone having an itch they can't scratch in the middle of their brain.

"I said to myself," he continued shouting "OK, she's a goddam whore, and doesn't know any better. Now *this*! How long has *this* been going on? How long have you been fucking niggers along with fucking every other Tom, Dick and Harry?"

Edith couldn't think of a reasonable answer, so she started crying while Ezell quietly let himself out the kitchen door. She heard the sound of the engine in his ice truck starting and cried harder.

"And there goes the fucking waterworks," Henry shouted louder as her crying turned to great heaving sobs. "That's what every bitch I ever knew did when the going got a little tough. They fucking cry!" Henry stormed out of the house, slamming the screen door. Then he came back.

"I am through!" he said, his hands shaking, clenching and unclenching. Edith peeked at him through her fingers covering her face as she sobbed and wondered if he was going to try to hit her. He repeated, "I am fucking through!" He paused, panting. He gasped for breath a few times. "I gave you this fucking house!" He continued through gasps of breath, "I paid the fucking bills! You repay me by fucking niggers! Oh god!"

Henry was beginning to calm himself a little. "Well, you can by god keep the house. It's already in your name," he spat. "There will be no more money for you! Lord!" His chest felt tight. He took several long breaths. "I bet everyone in town knew I was fucking a nigger lover! Well, from now on, you pay your own bills. You get your money from your tricks." Henry allowed his rage to build once again. "You go and fuck every nigger in town, see if they'll give you enough money for your booze. By god! I'll never give you another dime or set foot in this house again!" He turned, staggered a little, and crossed to the front room. The screen door slammed behind him.

Edith heard the powerful engine in his new car start, and then the gears ground and the gravel flew from underneath tires as Henry raced away up the hill toward Martinez's Grocery. She knew he meant what he said. There was a cold feeling in her chest that had nothing to do with either her lack of clothes or the ninety-eight-degree August day.

Edith had never been able to put money aside. When she had it, she spent it; when she didn't, she begged Henry for more. Now, she was out of money, liquor, and almost out of cigarettes. Ezell had delivered ice before climbing into her bed, but the twenty-five-pound block would be gone after two days. It seemed doubtful Ezell would keep on bringing ice after Henry's tirade.

None of Edith's tricks—Drew's "uncles"—had really given her much money. Most were refinery workers. Some were truck drivers who had stopped at the BYOB bar out on the highway for a bottle of near beer and a shot of illegal whiskey sold under the counter. Edith frequented the place most afternoons, flirted, and danced with some of the men to jukebox music. Sometimes she only got enough money for a carton of cigarettes. She was a cheap lay, especially since Henry was paying all the bills.

She sat around all afternoon, smoking and letting the enormity of events soak into her consciousness. After a few hours, the cigarettes were gone. She sat on the porch steps and started to cry again, this time as fear slipped past the numbness. She kept trying to come up with some sort of plan.

After a while, she wondered about Drew. She realized she did not know what day of the week it was. It wasn't Saturday because Ezell delivered ice on Tuesdays and Fridays. Since Drew now worked on Saturdays, she had scheduled visits from two of Drew's uncles, truck drivers who had the unusual deviancy of wanting sexual relations to be among three people rather than the standard two. They paid her a little more for this special service. However, they had not come by today as they usually did, so it clearly was not a Saturday.

She decided it was a Tuesday. She remembered Drew worked Saturdays for Mr. Martinez. But today wasn't Saturday, she again reminded herself—it was Tuesday. And school was out. It was summer. She didn't think the little bastard had anywhere else to spend his time.

She found out several hours later. It was nearly dark when Drew rode up on a bicycle with a small sack in the enormous basket attached to the handlebars.

"Where've you been?" she asked accusingly.

"Working," Drew answered flatly. "I told you Mr. Martinez is letting me work full-time at his store this summer."

"What's in the sack?" Edith spat, ignoring his tone for the time being. If he had food, it would buy her some time.

"A pint of milk and the cans are probably soup. Mr. Martinez lets me take cans home when the labels come off. I think these are tomato soup."

Drew noticed his mother's face. She had been crying, evidently quite a lot. Drew knew his mother sometimes cried when trying to increase her price from one or the other of his uncles, but from the look of her face, this was something more.

"What happened?" he asked.

"Oh, nothing you'd understand."

One corner of Drew's mouth turned down slightly. He understood far more about his mother than she knew. "Well," he said, "is Eugene coming over tonight?"

"No."

"Let's have supper then. I'll heat up the soup, and if there's some cornmeal and an egg left, I'll use the milk and make some cornbread, OK?" Drew pulled the bicycle up on the porch. He attached the chain and lock he had bought and went into the kitchen. He could tell that whatever had happened that afternoon, his mother considered it to be disastrous. He expected that he would learn over supper at least his mother's version of events.

She leaned on the kitchen doorway and watched this youngster, seemingly so mature and self-possessed, move about the kitchen, clearing away dirty dishes, mixing bacon grease, cornmeal, flour, egg, milk, and baking soda while heating the oven of the kerosene stove.

"Where'd you learn to cook?" she asked, suddenly curious.

Drew smiled inwardly but did not answer right away. He wondered if she realized that he had done all the cooking for the last year. But, he mused, she was usually too drunk to do more than wolf down a few bites and stagger off to her bed. It occurred to him that his mother was still sober or very nearly so.

"Sister Alma has been teaching me to cook." He opened one of the cans, poured soup into a small pot, placed the pot on a burner, and lit it.

"Cornbread will be ready in a few minutes," Drew said. He moved about the kitchen, ran water into a large pot from the single tap, and placed it on the stove. "I'll wash a couple of plates and bowls," he said. "After supper, I'll clean up the kitchen. Why don't you sit at the table?" Drew noticed his mother's hands were fidgeting. "Ah, you left a pack of smokes in my room the other day, you remember?" he said.

Edith had actually done no such thing. Drew had filched the pack from a full carton, saving it for just such a moment. He'd never tried smoking, although Leon had and had coughed and gagged while Drew snickered.

Drew left the kitchen and returned with the red-and-green pack of Lucky Strike cigarettes. Edith took the pack, opened it, and sat at the table, pulling a cigarette out. Drew held a lighted match.

"You're a lifesaver," Edith said.

"You'll need to make them last. I don't think there's any more in the house. I'll bring some more from the store tomorrow."

Later, as they sat at the table eating, Edith gave Drew a severely edited version of the afternoon. She did not mention Ezell, although Drew had noticed the new block of ice and had no doubts that the iceman visited his mother's bed. She told him Henry had decided to go away and that she and Drew would "be alone now, honey."

Drew smiled. "Just the two of us?"

"Yes," she said slowly. It had just dawned on her that Henry might not be the only one cutting ties. "We'll have to take care of each other."

Drew wrinkled his brow.

"You know what I mean?" Edith said. "Henry paid all the bills. We'll have to pay them now, somehow. How much does Mr. Martinez pay you?" She got right to the point.

"Not much. Not enough to pay the water and electric and buy groceries and cigarettes and other stuff." Drew did some rough math. Then he thought of something else.

"Mother, are we going to have to move?"

"No, the house has been in my name for a long time."

Edith got up and walked around the table. She hugged Drew about the shoulders. "You're my little man, aren't you?"

Drew didn't respond. As he bent his head over his soup, he was thinking about the bills. He always saw them when they arrived, but Henry took the unopened envelopes away in his pocket. How, Drew wondered, does one even pay a bill? He decided he would have to ask Brother Barlow. Both Drew and Edith had a long night of thinking before them.

Edith was basically illiterate but not stupid. She sat around the next day and tried to think about the present situation. She was completely and uncomfortably sober for the first time in a long while, and the withdrawal effects of years of drinking were clouding her thoughts. She was trembling. Her hands shook. She sweated in the August heat, turned on the small electric fan, but turned it off again since she felt cold despite the temperature. She paced about, moving first onto the front porch, then back to her room. Uncharacteristically, she tried to wash dishes, broke two, and stopped. She tried without success to ration the cigarettes Drew had given her the night before. They were completely gone by midday. She continued pacing about.

She realized that she couldn't turn enough tricks in this little town to replace the income Henry had given her. Her basic prices were established. She had never tried to get more than a little extra spending money. She could not raise her price now. There were well-to-do men in town who could afford higher prices; but they would never approach her, especially now, when her activities with Ezell were sure to become common knowledge.

Giving sexual favors to a Negro made her untouchable to white men. This last thought caused her to become even more nervous.

Would her association with Ezell now be blatantly exposed to the KKK? Would they take any action against Ezell? More importantly, she thought with a sudden dart of fright, would they take any action against her?

This last thought frightened Edith more than she could have said. If the KKK got involved, Ezell would surely be hanged. She would, as a minimum, be publicly whipped and beaten. She began to tremble even more, not really caring about Ezell but beginning to foresee significant personal danger. Her fear became palpable, and in combination with the alcohol withdrawal, she was almost overwhelmed. If she could just have a little drink, she thought, she could think clearly. She paced rapidly about.

The thought came to her that she ought to leave town, but she had no money. The list of people who could help her escape was not long.

Eugene was the first name that settled in her head. She knew he had very little money. He often talked about how he wanted to leave Union City and head south to Shreveport. He had told her he knew someone in Shreveport who was making lots of money. This person had asked Eugene to join him. She entertained the thought of going along. She was under no illusion that whatever the activities were in Shreveport they were undoubtedly illegal, but that thought barely bothered Edith.

If they were what she thought they were, perhaps she could work for Eugene's friend. She thought some more. Perhaps she could recruit two or more other women who would work under her directions.

She was sure she could convince Eugene to agree that now was the time to "blow this dirt town," as he'd expressed so often. She had to figure out just what it was she might do when she got there. Were there men in Shreveport who, perhaps, could support her as Henry had? She decided to abandon that thought as part of her plan.

The thought came to her that Eugene was careless about a lot of things, and a new life in another city was certain to have a lot of twists and turns. *Well,* she thought, *I'll just have to see that he keeps his nose clean.*

She thought about Drew. He had never been any help to her and was certainly no help to her now. He wasn't earning anywhere near-enough money to keep her standard of living going. He could just fend for himself, she quickly decided. *Maybe those niggers he thought so highly of would help him. Ha!* she said to herself. *Fat chance!*

Three days later, when Drew bicycled home at dusk, he found Edith and Eugene sitting on the porch steps, apparently waiting for him. He'd seen the evolution in his mother. She had been sober for days. She had washed her hair and cleaned herself up. He could tell she had been putting together thoughts about the future. Now, he thought, she's decided and is finally going to let me know.

It surprised Drew to learn that Eugene was sober too. Both were dressed nicely, his mother was in a summer frock and Eugene in slacks, almost as if they were going to church. Drew found that seeing Eugene cleaned up and sober was somehow more unsettling than dealing with him drunk. He thought about the many times his mother had said, "Just be nice to Eugene." Drew was under no allusions about what she meant, although he was somewhat unclear about the specific details of "being nice." Now here they were on the porch. It filled Drew's stomach with a cold uncertainty that made him keep his distance from the steps.

"Drew, honey," Edith said without preamble, "Eugene here is gonna drive me over to Shreveport tonight." Drew glanced sideways at Eugene's truck. He privately wondered if it would make it out of town before breaking down.

"I'm gonna need to stay in Shreveport for a couple of days," Edith said, "maybe a week, maybe two or three. Eugene knows a fella over there that works in a hotel. Maybe he can put me to work . . . ah . . . maybe has a job for me, you know."

Yes, Drew knew what his mother's skills were. He stayed silent to let her save some face.

"Eugene's gonna stay in Shreveport too. He thinks maybe he can get a job from this hotel guy too."

Doing what? Drew thought. His stomach turned a little, figuring that he had an idea about what sort of work Eugene would do for just "some friend."

"So, honey, you think you can manage here by yourself for a little while?"

Drew did not see much of a choice for him. *Mother is leaving me.* He shrugged to himself. *She never was much a mother anyway.* He answered her flatly, "I'll be fine, Edith. Don't worry about me."

"You're such a good boy," she said, not even noticing that for the first time in his life Drew had not called her mother. Edith stood up from the porch steps and hugged him. Eugene hugged him too, a little too long; but as the man hugged him, Drew noticed something else. For once, Eugene did not smell bad.

Without another word, the two simply walked away and climbed into Eugene's truck. Eugene started the engine, and Edith waved good-bye. The truck rattled up the sandy road and turned the corner at Martinez Grocery.

Drew turned and went into his room. Instantly, he could tell something was amiss. Then he saw his little tin box. It was opened, lying on his bed. It was empty. It had held $40, money he was saving for a bus ticket to Little Rock.

Drew went back out on the porch, fixed the chain and lock on the bicycle, and stood in the gathering twilight, looking up the road his mother and Eugene had taken. He turned and walked into an empty house.

# Chapter 12

❖─•✧•─❖

## *Fall*

## *1936*

D REW STAYED IN the little shotgun house in lower Paradise
Valley throughout the remainder of August and into the fall
after Edith and Eugene left. He talked to Mr. Martinez, who
raised his weekly salary by a dollar. Both Brother Barlow and Honeycutt
offered a loan for expenses, but Drew declined, saying he felt he could
make enough to cover bills.

However, when school started, his hours at the grocery store had
to be shortened; and therefore, his income declined. Someone had
talked to the school administrators (he suspected Miss Catherine and
Miss Schultz), and he was allowed to leave early before the last class
period of the day, so he could continue making grocery deliveries after
school. He, of course, continued working on Saturdays. But there was
never enough money for both savings and bills. Drew decided savings
were more important than electricity and simply allowed the electric
company to turn the power off. Drew brought his old kerosene lamp
into the house from his shed and used that to study by.

About once a week, when he pedaled home, he discovered a
food basket on the porch, filled with homemade biscuits, sometimes
cornbread, along with ham, cheese, butter, and a few eggs. When he
thanked Brother Barlow, the good minister disavowed all knowledge,
though Drew did not fully believe him. There were other of Drew's
friends whom he felt had also decided to help. More than once, he
noticed the package held the residual smell of the lilac perfume that
Catherine Ryan always used, and her basket always included a few
cookies and several times a quart of milk. Other times he was sure the
basket came from Ursula Shultz, the town's librarian, who was a good
friend of Catherine's. As cool weather set in, the lack of ice in the box

became only a minor inconvenience. He always tried to drink the milk quickly before it soured.

The onslaught of cooler weather also brought about a package of winter clothes, which appeared more or less mysteriously on the porch.

Drew felt the time was near when he could leave Union City. He was slowly rebuilding his savings. He worried that Edith might make a surprise visit. To make sure his mother did not again take his money, Drew made sure to hide it in some place other than the tin box, which had so long been his depository. He thought that as soon as he had enough money, he would ask Catherine or Miss Schultz to buy a bus ticket to Little Rock for him.

Edith and Eugene reappeared in Union City several times that fall. They now drove a newer automobile than the old truck they left town in. Both times they returned, they brought a sack of groceries, milk, and a block of ice; but they never left Drew money for bills or for more groceries.

There was never any explanation of why they came back. Nor did they stay longer than a night or two.

One Saturday, as Drew was heading back to the grocery after making a delivery, he stopped at the library for a few minutes and chatted with Imogene. Miss Schultz was away, meeting with the town council. Imogene gave him news; Catherine was seeing someone, a nice man from Fayetteville.

"How did they meet?" Drew asked, interested.

"He is an attorney," Imogene replied, "working with the NAACP and often visits in Little Rock. Miss Catherine," Imogene went on, "is also often in Little Rock, working with the NAACP on her, well, school experiment."

Drew had never heard of the National Association for the Advancement of Colored People and said so. Imogene explained the organization and the goals it set, then went on to talk about the "school experiment."

Catherine had for some time been holding Saturday lessons for Negro children on Sister Alma's front porch, assisted by Imogene. Together, they kept nine children studying at three grade levels. The Negro schools across Arkansas were extraordinarily inadequate teaching facilities, and the Union City Negro school was so far away for the children of Paradise Valley that truancy was rampant.

Through the years, Catherine had approached school board members on numerous occasions, asking if Negro children could be allowed to attend her school, utilizing the extra and unused room and therefore staying within the "separate but equal" standards of the day. Each time, however, the board members had been properly horrified. Catherine had even offered to teach Negro children "after hours" when the white children had left for the day. She was rebuffed at each turn.

The Klan considered the Saturday lessons for Negroes by a white teacher, even if done in a private residence, to be tantamount to heresy. There was already tension in the air over the Klan's activity regarding Ezell. Drew had been busy simply surviving and keeping up with his schoolwork and was surprised as Imogene went on to explain that the Klan had decided to "punish" Ezell. However, the iceman had foreseen that they might target him and had suddenly and quietly left town. There was a rumor, Imogene said, that Ezell was now living in Chicago.

Drew began connecting the dots. This is why, he thought, that Edith had been so anxious to leave Union City.

For some time, there had been threats by the Klan about the children that were being taught at Sister Alma's. The community was nervous. Both Imogene and her sister Alma worried, with some justification that their house would be targeted. Brother Barlow had been to see the sheriff who promised to be on the alert.

When Drew left the library, it was as if he could see storm clouds forming.

As it turned out, the Klan did not burn Sister Alma's house. Instead, they burned Catherine's school—the school that Drew attended. Their plan apparently was to take away the job of that meddling white teacher, and maybe she would then just leave town so that Negroes could "remain in their place" instead of getting all sorts of ideas and becoming uppity.

Drew heard trucks and other vehicles roaring past his house late one night. He got up, stood on the porch, and watched the procession head toward Catherine's school. He ran down the road after them, barefoot and breathless.

A large cross was burning. A number of men in white robes stood around, their hoods off, faces gleaming with sweat. They were throwing burning torches into the school windows. Drew was astonished at how quickly the building burned and at the number of men he recognized. As the fire reached its peak, one of the men saw him standing at the edge of the road. There was a shout. Drew turned and ran, this time through the woods back to his house. He was afraid there would be pursuit; but as he was running away he saw over his shoulder that the sheriff had arrived with two deputies and the fire department, which discouraged the Klan from following him.

After the fire, Drew and the other students at Catherine's school were transferred to Union City's Central Elementary. It was quite a distance from Paradise Valley, but Mr. Martinez allowed Drew to use the delivery bicycle to go to school. The principal at the new school continued to permit Drew to leave early.

On a Saturday, a few weeks after the school burning, Catherine came into the store and asked Mr. Martinez if she could "borrow" Drew for a few minutes. She bought two Cokes, and they sat on apple crates in the storeroom.

"Drew," she said, "I have decided to move. I'm going to Little Rock. I have a job there."

"You couldn't get another job here?" he asked. He tried, without succeeding, to keep the full weight of disappointment from his face.

"Well, I could," Catherine answered, "but after what happened at my school, I've decided I can do more working directly with and for the NAACP." She went on, "Their state headquarters are in Little Rock. There is a lot that needs to be done, and Little Rock is a place where I think I can help more than butting my head against stone walls here in Union City." She grinned as she said this last.

Drew at first felt his heart would break that she would no longer be his teacher but realized he too was planning a change. He told her he was sorry she was leaving, then blurted out, "I'm leaving too! My mother has left for Shreveport. I don't even know if she's still there."

"I've heard about that, Drew."

"I thought maybe you had." He grinned suddenly. "I could smell your perfume on several packages of food left on my front porch. Thank you. I needed the help."

"Drew," Catherine said, "I don't want to intrude on your plans, but I advise you to talk to the sheriff when you make up your mind to leave. He will no doubt want to know where you will be. Everyone knows that you witnessed the school burning. If there's testimony needed someday, you will be asked to give it."

It was as if a cloud had descended into the little grocery storeroom. Drew had known something like this was likely, but hearing it spoken seemed to foreshadow a more immediate event, one that he wished he could avoid.

Catherine stood. "Drew," she said, "I think this is good-bye, at least for a little while. When you get to Little Rock, I want to see you again."

Drew felt a lump begin in his throat. "You were my favorite teacher."

Catherine grinned. "I was your only teacher. Don't you try to sweet-talk me!" She rose and pulled him from the box and hugged him. He felt if he could just continue to remember the lilac perfume, which now almost overwhelmed him, all would be well. He hugged her back.

Drew walked with Catherine to the car. Felix Martinez was standing on the store's wooden porch, holding a camera. "I haven't used this Kodak in a long time," he said, "but it's still got some film in it. Stand here in this sunny spot on my porch, and I'll take your picture."

After the camera had snapped, Catherine shook Mr. Martinez's hand, hugged Drew once again, and climbed into her car. She leaned out the window. "I'll see you in Little Rock, Drew."

A week later, Mr. Martinez handed Drew five $10 bills and a copy of the photograph he had taken. "She asked me to give you these," he said.

"Miss Catherine?"

"Yeah, your teacher. She wanted me to wait until she left town. She was afraid you might not accept it."

It was a huge sum of money. He'd been trying to save for a long time, but his mother's thievery had taken all that he had painstakingly saved. He had been able to replace only a few dollars. The additional money would be very useful.

When Edith and Eugene again reappeared in one of their sporadic visits, Drew made sure his tin box remained empty and that his cash was hidden elsewhere.

During each of these visits, Edith pointedly asked Drew if he had saved any money. Each time, Drew answered quickly and honestly, "I'm barely able to make enough for groceries, kerosene, and the water bill. If Mr. Martinez didn't keep giving me cans with the labels off, I would get pretty hungry. People have left food packages and some winter clothes on the porch. I don't know who did that."

Edith shrugged and lit another cigarette, evidently crossing Drew off her list as someone who could get money for her.

One day, soon after Drew's good-bye meeting with Catherine, as Drew was pedaling up to his house, he found the sheriff waiting for him.

Without preamble, the sheriff said, "I think you're the boy that witnessed the school burning. Are you?"

Drew didn't answer but pulled the bicycle up onto the porch and attached the lock. He went into the yard toward the sheriff.

"I'm not sure what to say."

"You have to tell me the truth, remember? We have a deal, you and me."

Drew thought for a minute. "Could I perhaps just not say anything?"

"I can get a warrant and take you to the courthouse. The judge will compel you to talk to me." It was a statement of fact. He did not want to be cold or mean, but he would be firm.

Drew walked back to the house and sat on the front steps. The sheriff joined him.

"I understand it's a scary thing," the sheriff said as the two sat together. "Here's what I think. I think you heard all those trucks and cars. I think you went over to the school while it was burning. I think you recognized some of the men that were doing the burning."

The two sat together for a while. "Am I right?" the sheriff said.

Drew nodded. It was easier than finding his voice at the moment.

"Son, there's going to have to be an inquest. That's a legal thing, kind of like a trial, but not exactly. It's something we have to do to find out the truth of what happened and punish the people who burned the school. You'll have to testify. And you'll have to tell if you recognized anyone who was there."

"When?" Drew's voice was a trembling echo of how his stomach felt.

"You mean when will the inquest be? I don't know. There are some in town who've hired lawyers, and they're trying to delay everything." Drew knew the sheriff was just trying to help.

"Tell you what, I'll try to keep your name out of it for as long as I can," the sheriff said. "I'll let you know when I finally do have to tell the judge. And I'll keep you safe after the inquest, OK?"

Drew simply nodded.

The next weeks passed by. Edith had now been gone without any word for over two months. Drew spent Christmas Day with Sister Alma and Imogene. They had a great Christmas dinner of ham, gravy, and baked sweet potatoes.

The weather was cold that Christmas, but it was warm inside the little house with the wood-burning stove. There was warmth of family too, and Drew realized how much he loved these people and how much they loved him back.

He had bought two oranges for each person and had carefully wrapped them into separate packages using colored tissue from a crate that had arrived a week earlier at Martinez Grocery. There had been a clothing drive at a church downtown, and the clothes were donated to the Paradise Valley Church. Sister Alma had found flannel shirts for each of the boys, which she wrapped in gay Christmas paper. There was also a sweater for Drew, which had only one small tear on the sleeve.

Drew told them he had met Kowanda at the public library and had given her oranges too. He showed them the warm socks that were Kowanda's gift to him.

Brother Barlow stopped by as presents were being unwrapped and produced three chocolate bars, one for each: Drew, Leon, and Walker. The boys shared, and everyone got a piece of the candy.

At a lull in the festivities, Brother Barlow took Drew aside and asked how things were going. Drew answered truthfully, saying he was trying to save money and keep up with his schoolwork at the same time, but it was hard. Still, he said, he was getting by and his grades were good. He told the kindly minister how much the anonymous food packages had helped, along with the clothing that had also shown up mysteriously.

Drew added quietly, "For whatever influence you had on how those packages came to my front porch this fall, I want you to know how grateful I am."

Afterward, Brother Barlow led them all in a short Christmas prayer service.

# Chapter 13

## Into the Unknown
## 1937

THE NEW YEAR 1937 was a week old when Eugene and Edith returned again. It was a brutally cold day, sleet mixed with freezing rain. When Drew came home, face numb from the biting cold after making his afternoon grocery deliveries, he was surprised to see a car that he had not seen before parked next to the house. Inside, he found Eugene and his mother. Both had been drinking. Drew discovered that the inside was warm; in fact, it was overly warm. The oven in the kerosene stove in the kitchen was going full blast, and the room was stifling. Both Eugene and Edith sat at the table. Neither greeted him. They simply nodded when he came into the house.

Drew opened a window, turned the oven down, and moved about, clearing away the breakfast dishes he had washed and left on the drain board. There was the usual sack of groceries, which had not been put away. He asked the two if they were hungry, saying he would make supper. He noticed that the electric power had been restored. He wondered, what was going on?

He listened as the two carried on their conversation. They seemed angry.

"I told you," Edith said. "You just can't trust that guy."

"Aw," Eugene whined, "he's my friend. What if he does skim a little? We still got paid."

Edith rolled her eyes. "We should have made more," she snapped.

Drew put the groceries away, noting which he could use for tonight's supper. He looked into the icebox. Yes, they'd brought ice, milk, bacon, and eggs. There was a large ham slice. He decided to use that for supper and began mixing cornbread.

Edith and Eugene continued talking to each other, this time whispering, then laughed at some joke only they knew. Then the mood changed again as another point of argument seemed to arise.

"That last kid you brought in," Edith said, disdain coloring her words, "he was too young for this business, and you know it!"

"I didn't get no complaints," Eugene answered.

"Yeah, but a kid like that, he might not be able to keep his mouth shut. You're not being careful enough!"

They lowered their voices again, but after a few minutes, Drew clearly heard more arguing.

"That bitch," Eugene said in his whiny voice, "the new one you brought on board. I don't trust her."

"You don't have to worry," Edith said with sarcasm in her voice, "I knew her from back in Little Rock, and she knows her stuff, unlike that kid."

"Aw, you shudda . . ." Eugene's voice trailed away. The words became indistinct again.

Edith looked up, noticing that Drew was listening. She turned to Drew and told him what a little man he was, making supper for them.

Drew didn't answer but continued with the meal.

He started frying the ham and began slicing potatoes to fry after the ham cooked. He added a little sorghum syrup to the ham slice. As he prepared the meal and listened to his mother and Eugene, he began to perceive what they'd been doing in Shreveport. He learned that the hotel they stayed in was near the train depot. When the late train discharged its passengers, the men who came to the hotel wanted only a few things: supper, a drink, and some of them wanted sexual favors before retiring for the night. Evidently, the room clerk made arrangements for them to visit Edith or Eugene, Drew realized with a disgusted shock. When a man wanted a woman, he got Edith or one of two other women she had recruited. When he wanted sex with another man, he got Eugene or one of several young men Eugene had recruited. Drew hoped his understanding was wrong but knew in his heart that he was not.

Eugene was drinking beer after beer using it to chase slugs of whiskey. He leaned his chair back and watched Drew, who knew what Eugene had on his mind. There were those funny crinkly lines around his mouth, just like there had been so many times before. Drew finished preparing the meal, didn't set the table but instead filled a plate and carried it into his room, and shut the door.

He found he could not eat. While he could not have completely articulated the thought, he now was afraid that Eugene wanted to recruit him to provide sex to deviant men. He heard arguing. It seemed they were now talking about him. Eugene opened the door.

"Come on out," Eugene said. "Let's sit down over at the table. I want you to sit on my lap. You know, like when you were little."

Drew heard a voice that at first he didn't recognize as his own. "No," he said to Eugene and remained sitting on his bed, plate on his lap. There was a ringing in his ears.

"Are you sassing me, boy?" Eugene said. He took a final swallow of beer from his bottle and tossed it, clattering against the wall and floor. Eugene started toward him. Drew remained sitting on the bed. Eugene was across the room at once. It always surprised Drew that the man could move so fast. He jerked Drew off the bed while the plate crashed to the floor. Food scattered. The two of them fell in a heap next to the front door.

"Edith!" Drew cried out as he struggled to move from under Eugene. Then, to his horror, Eugene was pulling at his clothes, unbuckling his belt, ripping his shirt. Damn! It was his only really good flannel shirt. Drew rolled over onto his back, and his arms swung wildly at Eugene, who was now laughing and seemed to be enjoying himself. Soon Eugene had pulled Drew's trousers down to his knees, and he was exposed. Eugene had never done this before. Things had never gone this far!

Eugene laughed. "You ain't got no hair on your balls yet at all, do you, boy?"

Drew was close to blind panic. He renewed his struggles and, somehow, got out from under Eugene. He tried to pull his pants up and run toward the kitchen but was caught before he had gone more than two or three steps, and he was again pulled to the floor. Again, his pants were pulled below his knees. Eugene began laughing with a wild sound, and his long arm pulled back, and he swung his open hand at Drew. The slap echoed through the room.

Drew was shocked at the sudden pain, which somehow tempered his panic. The reddish hazy calm he'd felt before flooded his brain as he remembered Honeycutt's lessons. He stopped struggling for the barest moment. He saw Eugene had unbuckled his own belt and pulled his own clothing down and exposed himself. Drew gagged. Then Eugene tried to flip him over onto his stomach, but Drew pulled his knees to his chest and kicked hard. His feet in hard-soled high- tops connected, and Eugene rolled off him.

"Goddam!" Eugene shouted, holding his privates. "You little shit! I'll kill you for that!" He grabbed for Drew, who had gotten up and was again pulling at his trousers. Drew dodged away, buckling his belt.

Eugene—still on his knees, trousers around his ankles—turned and picked up a large square ashtray from the table next to Drew's bed. It was smoked amber glass—and heavy. He swung the tray at Drew, who dodged the swing. Eugene lost his grip, and the ashtray crashed to the floor. He leaped for Drew, and the two fell. Drew rolled over onto his back. Eugene landed on top of him. The ashtray was next to Drew, and Eugene reached for it and swung at Drew's head. Drew was afraid, and yet that icy red calm continued. He deflected the blow with his forearm and pulled at Eugene. The two rolled across the floor. Eugene dropped the ashtray and slapped Drew again. But as he did, Drew saw his opening and swung his clenched fist into Eugene's nose. Blood spurted. Drew pulled his knees to his chest and kicked with both feet. Eugene rolled away, shouting unintelligible words.

Drew stood. Eugene was still on his knees, his hands holding his bloody nose. Drew kicked hard, and his shoe connected again with Eugene's crotch. Eugene howled and rolled on the floor. Drew thought for a moment that perhaps the fight was over.

But he was wrong. Eugene sprang to his feet, kicked his trousers away, and, half naked, picked up the ashtray and charged again, bellowing and swinging wildly. Drew dodged and tripped Eugene. As he fell, Eugene dropped the ashtray and grabbed onto Drew. The ashtray clattered to the floor as the two fell together. Eugene reached for the tray again as they hit the floor but missed. Drew picked it up with his right hand.

The two rolled across the floor, locked together. Using all his strength, Drew swung the ashtray toward Eugene's head. There was a crunch, the ashtray broke in two, and the man on top of him suddenly became limp and still.

Drew pulled himself out from under Eugene. He was shaking and to his surprise found that he was sobbing. He stood and pulled his clothes into place. Then he looked at Eugene.

The man was still. Vomit along with food from Drew's supper plate was smeared across the floor and matted onto Eugene's body hairs and even into his mustache. The vile taste in Drew's mouth told him he must have been the one to vomit at some time during the fight. Blood oozed from Eugene's high forehead. His thinning hair was awry, and he was still half naked. The part of him that had appeared so vile and menacing lay shrunken and white across the blackness of the vomit-smeared hair where Eugene's legs joined his body.

It was then that Drew saw that Edith was in the room. He wondered how long she had been there. He looked down at Eugene again. Blood continued to flow slowly from Eugene's forehead.

She knelt down and touched Eugene's throat. As she did so, Eugene began to groan and move his legs.

Drew tried to quell his sobs. He felt he had to say something. "I was so scared. I—"

"Shut up!" she shouted.

He was astonished at her anger. Good lord! She had actually wanted him to let Eugene—to let him—he could not finish the thought.

Drew backed away. He drew a deep breath and stopped his reflexive sobbing. He simply stared. *All this time,* he thought, *all this time she has just been someone I made up. Someone I made excuses for. Oh god!* He now fully tasted the vomit in his mouth. He turned and spat.

Edith knelt over Eugene. She touched his throat. "God! What have you done? Now he'll probably go and not come back. What will I do then? How will I get back to Shreveport?"

Drew did not answer. Continuing his deep breaths, regaining some control over his emotions, he went into the kitchen, got a dish towel, ran water from the tap onto it, wiped his face, and rinsed out his mouth. He cleaned vomit and food debris from his clothes, then took the wet towel to his room, and began wiping the blood and vomit off Eugene. He handed the wet towel to Edith, indicating she could clean vomit off Eugene's private parts. Afterward, with another wet towel, he wiped up the floor. All this time, Edith said nothing more but simply continued kneeling next to the moaning man sprawled on the floor.

Eugene began thrashing about. She helped him sit up. "Little fucker tried to kill me," he mumbled.

"It was an accident," Edith said. "He didn't mean it."

*Yes, I did,* thought Drew, although he kept quiet.

"I'm gonna get out of here," Eugene said.

"No," Edith said in a pleading voice, "don't go. We can still have some fun tonight. He'll be nice to you."

*No, I won't,* Drew thought.

"Fuck you," Eugene said. He struggled to his feet and pulled his trousers up and buckled his belt. Somewhat wobbly, Eugene walked to the front door.

"You'll come back?" Edith called as she ran after him.

"You get rid of that little fucker, and we'll see," Eugene shouted back. They heard the slam of the car door and the engine start. Eugene backed away from the house onto the muddy road, and wheels spun as he drove away.

Drew had changed his shirt. He sat on the edge of his small bed. He looked at Edith as she came back from the porch. She did not look at him. Instead, she continued on into the kitchen, where she grabbed the whiskey bottle off the table. He heard the cork squeak as she went into her room and closed the door. Her radio came on.

Drew realized he was finally at the end of this road. He could not continue in this house. She did not want him. She had never wanted him. That she had endured him for all the years of his life was, now, amazing to him. That he had endured her was more amazing.

The boys around town were right. She was a whore—nothing but a drunken whore and a thief. And he was a bastard. He had no father.

He thought back to all the nights, all the uncles, all the times he'd laid under his blankets out in his shed under the chinaberry tree, trying to hide from the truth about Edith. He had always thought that somehow she would stop being a whore and she would be his mother and she would love him.

He knew now with utter clarity that that would never happen.

He moved numbly around the room, gathering his few belongings. Mr. Martinez had given him a knapsack his soldier son had used. Drew stuffed clothes into it. He retrieved the tin box and the old wallet, which still fascinated him, went to his hiding place, and withdrew his cash and the photograph he had been given. He put his money and the picture into the tin box and the box and wallet into the knapsack. He walked into the kitchen and banged on Edith's door. "Go away," she said.

"I'm going," Drew answered the closed door.

He drew a deep breath. He went back into his room and got his jacket and cap off the hanger on the wall. He looked at his schoolbooks and wondered what his teachers would think when he never reappeared in class.

His friends—Sister Alma, Leon—and the others might worry.

The sheriff might assume the worst.

What would Kowanda, the almond-eyed girl who he had sat next to through every grade so far in school, think? He paused, thinking about the girl who had given him gum wrapped in waxed paper and who because of her Japanese ancestry was an outcast like him. Would he never again walk holding her hand on warm spring afternoons? It was almost enough to make him reconsider.

He did not have answers. He picked up his knapsack, put on his jacket, unlocked Mr. Martinez's bicycle from the porch, and rode away into the night.

It was two weeks into the New Year of 1937. He was ten years old.

# Chapter 14

## A Journey

DREW LEFT THE bicycle behind Mr. Martinez's store, locked the chain, and placed the key in Mr. Martinez's mailbox. He was walking away when he heard a car coming. He stepped into the shadows. It was Eugene, which surprised Drew. He thought some more. Maybe it wasn't a surprise.

Drew grinned to himself. *I bet he has a headache,* he murmured. *And I hope his balls are killing him.*

He watched the car as it drove down the hill. It weaved back and forth on the muddy road. Drew nodded to himself. *He's found himself another whiskey bottle.* He continued watching, hoping Eugene would crash into the ditch, but that did not happen.

He returned to the store, climbed the stairs at the rear, and knocked.

"Who is it?" the Spanish-accented voice inside answered.

"It's Drew," he called back.

The door opened. The portly, mustached, and balding proprietor of Martinez's Grocery looked out at Drew. "Come in, come in. What are you doing this late at night?"

"I've left home," Drew said tiredly. "Eugene and I had a fight. I hit him with an ashtray. I was told to leave," the words tumbled out.

Martinez was silent. He nodded to Drew as he motioned the boy into the kitchen of his little apartment. "You hungry?"

Drew nodded. He was suddenly very hungry. He sat down at the table in the warm kitchen, still redolent with spicy odors of the meal Mr. Martinez had eaten earlier. An old radio on the table played softly. A woman was singing something in Spanish. A photograph of a young man in an army uniform hung on the wall over the table.

Martinez noticed Drew looking. "My son," the old man said. "You've been using his bicycle to make deliveries. I've talked to you about him. He was in the army in the war in 1918." There was a pause.

"He died in a forest in Germany. There was poison gas." It was said without emotion as if the old man was reporting an ordinary event that he still could not approach personally.

"Oh," Drew said. Martinez continued toward the electric refrigerator. "I've got some beans, tortillas, and some queso too. I'll heat them up for you."

He took the food from the refrigerator, lit the gas burners on the stove, and put the queso in one skillet, the beans in another, and the tortillas in a third. While they heated, he placed a plate and tableware in front of Drew.

The spices in the beans caused droplets of sweat to appear on Drew's brow. The flour tortillas were tough and so hot from the skillet they burned the roof of his mouth. He barely noticed. While his friend had warmed the meal, words spilled out of Drew. Martinez nodded from time to time but kept silent and let the boy tell his story.

Later, after Drew had finished eating and had gulped two glasses of water to cool the fire in his throat, Felix Martinez said, "What are you going to do now?"

"I don't know. I can't go back. I have the money Miss Ryan gave me, plus a little more, saved from what you paid me plus some of the tips I got delivering groceries, but Edith took the rest of the money I had saved. If I give some money to you, would you use it to buy a bus ticket for me?" Drew wanted to go to Little Rock, to Maude and Eddie and Reverend Thomas.

"I can't buy you a bus ticket," Martinez said. "Drew, if I did that, and if your mother decided to call the law and declare you to be a runaway, she could have me arrested for helping you. Maybe she could have me arrested for even giving you something to eat."

"I wouldn't tell," Drew said, but the old man's body language told the boy that he wasn't going to help. Drew's shoulders slumped, and he kicked his legs aimlessly. No, Edith and Eugene wouldn't come looking for him this night, but they would after they'd sobered up. Drew knew that both would want to punish him. They'd want to make him pay! Yes, they'd come looking. Maybe they'd force him to go with them to Shreveport.

Drew looked up at Mr. Martinez. "If they come here, what will you tell them?"

"I will tell the truth. You came to my door. You were hungry. I gave you something to eat."

"Would you tell them where I was going?"

"Drew, you never told me. And I don't want you to tell me. I can't afford to get in trouble."

Drew nodded.

"I don't want you to have to go out into this night. It's cold. But I'm afraid to let you stay here. You can stay in my alley shed but don't tell me if you do. Drew, I am not a citizen. I could be sent away. I don't know what to do." The elderly Mexican seemed close to tears.

"I can wrap up some food," he continued. "I will put it on the table here. I'm not going to give you food. That would be suspicious. So after I wrap it, I will go into another room for a little while. Do you understand?"

Drew nodded as Mr. Martinez busied himself with waxed paper and a paper sack.

"I've got some old clothes that had belonged to my son so many years ago. I need to throw them out. My goodness, I've just been putting it off so long. I'm going to get a shirt, maybe a sweater, some trousers. I'll put them here on the table to get rid of them in the morning." The tone in his voice told Drew that these too were for him to take.

Martinez left the room, bustled about in his bedroom, then returned and placed a package on the table beside the sack of food. He left again.

Drew knew the clothes would be too big for him and there was little room left in the knapsack. He selected a shirt and sweater and put that and the paper sack of tortillas and beans in the knapsack. Drew found a $10 bill had also been placed on the table beside the sack. He swept the money into his pocket.

When the old man reentered the room, Drew saw him glance quickly at the table, then away. Drew knew he'd done the right thing: the money had been meant for him. Drew knew Mr. Martinez did not have much money. Ten dollars was a sacrifice for him.

The good-byes were quick, and Drew simply walked away. He knew where he wanted to go but had no idea how to get there. Now he was at the paved highway. He had walked maybe two miles from Mr. Martinez's store. He had no watch but knew it was late. A cold misty rain had begun to fall. It had sleeted earlier. Perhaps the rain would turn to sleet again.

He knew that if he turned to the right, the highway would lead into Union City. He didn't know where the highway would lead if he turned left. He simply turned in that direction without thinking further and walked alongside the concrete pavement. There was no paved shoulder or any traffic.

The road curved and ran parallel to a railroad. He came to a crossing. A freight engine sat on a siding several hundred yards from where Drew stood. The engine's light was shining, steam hissing and boiling up around the front of the locomotive. Every so often, the engine would make a clanking sound. There were no signal lights, but it was clear to Drew that the freight was on a siding, waiting for another train to pass on the main line. Almost as the thought came to him, he heard the oncoming train. Drew stepped back into the shadows of a large oleander as a late-night passenger express roared past.

Drew at once realized what he must do.

He jogged back along the highway, next to the waiting freight. The engine whistled loudly and backed suddenly. There was a racketing clatter that moved farther and farther away from the engine and toward Drew as the slack in the car couplings was taken up. Drew saw an opened box car. There was a small embankment. He climbed it, tossed the knapsack inside the car, and jumped, landing hard at the side of the boxcar door. The car had been higher than he'd thought.

The train started to move slowly. His legs dangled toward the ground. Drew kicked. His left elbow hooked onto a handle at the edge of the door. Drew thought he was going to fall under the now-moving train but managed to pull himself up and roll into the car. Soon, the entire train was on the main line, rolling slowly. Drew looked out the boxcar door and saw a man at the end of the train pull a switch, and then he saw the man leap onto the moving caboose as it passed.

As the man disappeared from view, Drew pulled his head back. It had been a mistake to look out. Someone might have seen. The train began to pick up speed. Drew moved away from the open door to the shadows in the front of the car.

It was windy inside and brutally cold. Drew pulled the sweater out of the knapsack, donned it, and put his plaid-patterned jacket back on, pulling it closely around him as he huddled in the corner at the front of the car.

The enormity of the events of this evening began to crowd around him. As he listened to the clatter of the slow freight and the clicking of steel wheels on steel rails, Drew again faced the reality that he might never see any of his friends again. Tears, unbidden, began to roll down his cheeks. Anger too welled up in him. *I'm not gonna cry,* Drew swore under his breath. He was angry at Edith, at Eugene, and at his life.

But despite his resolve, he collapsed into tears. Great sobs of anguish, anger, and frustration racked his body. Tears streaked the dirt on his face. The ten-year-old boy lay huddled in the cold and wind. Reality tore at his soul. Edith had never loved him. She had always considered him a burden.

He knew now that his friends—Mardie, Eddie, Reverend Thomas, Miss Catherine, Sister Alma, Imogene, and Leon—all these people truly loved him. He knew that they loved him still. He continued crying, but the heaving sobs subsided, and hope dawned in his breast. He knew why he was on this train. He would go to those who loved him. He would ride the boxcar all the way to Little Rock. He would go to his family as he had almost blurted out in Mr. Martinez's kitchen.

Finally, his tears were gone, and there were only streaks left in the dirt on his face. Drew raised his head and stood and braced himself against the wall of the car. Holding himself steady, he made his way along the rocking, shaking noisy car until he reached the open door. He looked about the boxcar, filled with cold wind and dust. He looked out at the landscape rushing past. The clouds had moved away, and there was a full moon framed in the open boxcar door.

Drew snapped into full attention, blinking and staring with disbelief at the rising moon. Maybe the moon was setting, and he was looking west. No. He had been right the first time. The moon was rising. He was not on a train heading north toward Little Rock but on one going south. He knew south would take him out of Arkansas, away from Little Rock—away from his friends. Drew slumped down, still clinging to the doorframe. He quickly tried to assess how far he had gone. He couldn't tell if dawn was several minutes or hours away. He might even be in Louisiana already.

He now knew with certainty that his childhood was over. He thought he might again cry, and a sob began in his throat. He sat on the floor next to the opened door and put his head down, his arms folded over. Several minutes went by as he forced the tears back, and as he did, something inside him indefinably hardened. He raised his head and pulled himself up, holding the side of the door. Though he could not know it, his face had somehow changed along with something inside of him.

He stood there, clinging to the doorframe of the wildly swaying noisy car in the cold wind. Drew realized he had taken a step on life's road to maturity and that now he was standing at the threshold of manhood. He held the door frame tightly and was at last unafraid and confident. Whatever life held for him he would meet the challenge head-on. He screamed with defiance into the wind and into the wilderness as it rushed past.

*I will never cry again!*

After perhaps three hours, the lights of a small town shone in the distance, and the lazily moving freight slowed a little more. Houses began to appear, scattered, here and there. A few seemed similar to the house in Union City. Others were larger. As the train moved closer to what must surely be the depot, it slowed some more. Drew thought that it was now going slow enough so that he could jump with relative safety.

He gathered up his knapsack with the package of food Mr. Martinez had given him. The train was beginning to pick up speed again. The locomotive must have already passed the depot. He leaned out the boxcar door, looking toward the front of the train. The depot was in view. He must jump now, if he was going to jump at all. He pushed himself out into space, hit sharp gravel hard, rolled, and pain shot through his shoulder. He had not jumped far enough. He was lying only inches from the rail, and the train wheels roared by. He tried to move closer to the ground, fearing some protuberance from the railroad cars would rake across his back.

Then the train was gone. He turned his head and watched as the caboose rolled away into the darkness, its twin red lanterns growing smaller as it passed the dimly lighted depot and disappeared. He was unprepared for the quiet.

He stood and looked toward the depot. If there had been men around while the freight was rolling through, they had now gone back inside. He was not sure where he was. He looked at the sky. Clouds had returned and now hid the moon. Drew thought it might rain again soon. He realized that it must be close to dawn.

He got up and found his knapsack and cap. He began walking alongside the tracks, away from the depot. A misty rain began to fall.

He came to a highway. There was a closed Skelly Oil gasoline station next to the point the railroad tracks and highway intersected. Drew walked over to the soft drink box. It was open and was one of the newer models. He could insert a nickel, slide a Coke bottle to a gateway, and pull it out.

Drew sat on the curb by the station's front door out of the rain and ate the cheese and bean tortilla Mr. Martinez had given him and drank the Coca-Cola. A car parked at the station, evidently for service the next day, had writing on the door and some sort of symbol. Drew got up and looked at it more closely.

It read, "Claiborne Parish Sheriff's Office, Claiborne, Louisiana."

Drew tossed the waxed paper into a waste container at the Skelly station, drank the last of the Coke, and walked back toward the railroad tracks. A graveled road to his right paralleled the tracks at this point, and Drew followed it for several minutes. There were houses on rather large lots here and garages backed to the roadway he was on. The rain began to come down harder.

Drew stopped at one of the garages and tried a side door. It opened easily. Inside he found the largest most luxurious automobile he had ever seen. He closed the garage door and sat for a minute on the car's running board in his damp clothes, shivering. He wiped his face and hair with one of the shirts Mr. Martinez had given him. Drew stood and tried the rear door of the car. It opened at his touch, swinging outward as if on velvet hinges. An interior light inside the automobile came on as the door opened, and Drew found a lap robe folded over a silver handle built into the back of the front seat. He climbed in and closed the door.

In the darkness, he lay back on luxurious velour seats, pulled the robe over him, and slept.

# Chapter 15

## Reggie and Mama Rose

D REW AWOKE WHEN he heard the garage doors being opened. He remained still in the backseat, covered by the lap robe. A man climbed into the car, started the engine, and backed the car out of the garage. Drew thought the man must surely know that he was in the backseat, but he remained where he was. The man stopped the car, put the gears in neutral, got out, and closed the garage doors. He returned, put the car in gear, and the luxurious machine moved smoothly out into the street. Drew wondered what he should do. *Perhaps,* he thought, *I could quickly jump out and run when the car stops at a traffic signal.* But the car didn't stop; it continued on smoothly.

After a while, the car slowed, turned and left the paved road onto a graveled one, and continued slowly. "You can come out now, if that's what you want," the man said. His voice was smooth, almost like a radio announcer. He spoke slowly with no hint of a regional accent.

"You knew I was here?"

Drew noticed the man was continuously checking his rearview mirrors, not really looking at him, his eyes darting around as he seemed to be looking for something else. The thought occurred to him that maybe the man was looking for someone instead of something.

"Well, sure. I saw you before I even started the engine. I'll bring the car to a full stop if you want to jump out now."

"Why didn't you tell me to get out of your car right away?"

"Because I wanted to make sure I wasn't being followed." The man's eyes continued to dart around. "I needed to get on the road."

"Did you think you would be followed by the sheriff?" It was a wild guess on Drew's part.

"More or less."

"I don't think the sheriff would be looking for me," Drew said. *At least not yet,* he added to himself.

"I didn't say anyone was looking for you, are they?"

"I don't think so. Is someone looking for you?"

The car pulled to the side of the road and stopped. The man turned. "Listen, kid, I'm Reggie. Want to tell me your name?" He was grinning.

"I'm called Drew."

"Are you hungry? I am. You want some breakfast?"

"Sure." Drew wondered if he could trust this Reggie, and he wondered why he was suddenly being solicitous. *But,* he added to himself, *I'm hungry, and he seems to be offering to buy me something to eat.*

Vera's Blue Plate Café was on the main town square. Reggie led Drew to the polished wood counter near the rear. Vera—tall, slender, and probably near middle age, wearing a starched cotton dress—leaned over to Drew, showed her cleavage to the man, smacked her gum, and asked Drew, "What'll it be, sweetheart?" Her eyes danced. It seemed to Drew that she had instantly liked him. Or maybe she just liked Reggie.

Drew was embarrassed since he had never eaten in a restaurant before and was unsure how he should answer this somewhat brash woman. He looked at Reggie, who said, "Get him some breakfast, Vera. I'd like some too. We're hungry." Smells of food almost overwhelmed Drew.

Vera looked at Drew and said, "You're a sweetie, little guy." She turned to Reggie. "Do you fellas want eggs, biscuits, grits, and coffee?" Drew waited for Reggie to respond.

"You got it, Vera," Reggie said. "Bring breakfast for both of us."

Drew suddenly had a vision of the gallons of coffee he'd poured down Edith the numerous times he'd tried to sober her up.

Vera chuckled and said, "Eggs over easy comin' right up, along with hot biscuits, fresh coffee, and grits." She looked at Drew. "And I'm gonna give you some bacon, sweetheart. You need a little meat on your bones!" She bustled off.

Reggie leaned over. "There's a restroom in the rear. Why don't you go and wash up a little?"

When Drew returned, face clean and hair smoothed back, Reggie nodded approval and said, "Can you tell me where you're from, son?"

Drew looked down and then said, "I don't think I'd better. Let's talk about something else."

"OK. While you were washing up, I called a friend of mine. A railroad employee thought he saw someone jump out of a boxcar last night, about a mile from where I keep my car. You know anything about that?"

A huge mug of steaming coffee was placed before Drew. Vera, without asking, poured thick cream into the coffee, added two spoonsful of sugar, and shoved the cup to Drew. As Vera watched, he tasted the coffee and found that he liked it. He smiled at Vera. She trotted away on high heels. Drew looked back at the man.

"That was me," he said tiredly. "I jumped out of the train. I left home. I was told to go. No one wants me back. I climbed into a boxcar. I jumped out. It was raining. I found your car. I went to sleep. You know the rest." After the up-and-down emotions of the past twelve hours, he felt that the shorter version of events was better.

"I've got a feeling that's not the whole story," Reggie said. "You don't need to spill it all right now, but maybe when I feel like a little more would help me, I'll ask. Sound fair to you?"

Drew just nodded as he sipped his coffee.

Vera placed breakfast in front of both Drew and Reggie and asked Drew if he had ever had one of her special biscuits. He had no idea what she meant; but evidently, an answer was not needed because she turned and picked up a pitcher of honey, opened one of the biscuits before Drew, placed it in a fresh saucer, spread butter, and poured honey over the hot bread. Drew found he was more than hungry—he was ravenous. As she left, Vera ruffled Drew's hair, smiling approval as he seemed to enjoy the breakfast she had placed before him.

"Look," Reggie said after Vera had left, "you and I have got to get some things straight between us."

Drew looked up from his plate. He really hadn't looked closely at Reggie before. He had brown hair, small nose, clear green eyes, and was nicely dressed in a brown suit, a blue-and-white striped shirt, and a tie. The tie was impossibly outlandish with swooping designs of yellow and red flowers. He wore old-fashioned spats on his shoes.

"OK," Drew said, "what do we need to get straight between us?

Reggie added, "My last name is Masterson. Reggie Masterson. What's your last name?"

Drew sighed. "I'm Drew Simmons."

"OK," Reggie said, "after breakfast, I'd like for you to ride along with me for a while. Maybe we can talk. I'll drop you off somewhere if you want. How do you feel about the law? You said something about a sheriff looking for you?" This sudden change made Drew nervous.

"I said that I didn't think anyone was looking for me."

Drew went on, "Maybe you could drop me off back on the highway." He was trying to decide if he could ask Reggie to buy him a bus ticket to Little Rock. He wondered if he had enough money. He was still unsure of this man's motives.

"Thank you for the breakfast," Drew added. "I have some people to go to in Little Rock," he blurted out this last nervously, wondering where all this strange conversation was going.

"Well, you're a way from Little Rock." Reggie smiled. "You already told me you ran away." Then Reggie held up his hands in mock protest against the expression on Drew's face. "I know, I know, you said your mama threw you out. But she could still have second thoughts and send someone looking for you. Where's the first place you think she might look?"

Drew had continued eating but now looked up again and into the man's eyes. "She'd look in Little Rock," he admitted grudgingly.

"Exactly," Reggie answered. "It'll be a while before she would consider looking in this direction. Maybe you just want to stay here. Later, I'll check with the law. See if there's a wanted bulletin out on you."

Drew felt a start of alarm deep in his abdomen. "I don't have a place to stay here."

"Well," Reggie said, "maybe I know a place you can stay. Do you want a job?"

Vera laid the check in front of Reggie. "I always pay for breakfasts for my new guys," Reggie said, tossing a $5 bill on the countertop. The check Vera had placed showed a charge of 95¢ for the two breakfasts.

Drew wondered at Reggie's comment about "new guys." He hadn't agreed to work for Reggie.

After Vera walked away, tucking the money in her cleavage, Drew said, "What kind of job do you want me to do?" The suspicion in his voice was thicker than the biscuit and honey he had just eaten.

"We'll figure that out later," Reggie said offhandedly.

As they left the café, Reggie said, "You need a place to stay, and it can't be with me. I'm too busy. I move around a lot. At the same time, you can't be roaming around town while school is still in session."

Reggie went on, "I'm guessing you didn't think about school when you blew town, wherever that was. So if you're in town and not in school, someone is bound to ask questions. I think you're gonna have to come with me out to Mama Rose's."

As they climbed into Reggie's large maroon-and-black car, he patted the dash lovingly. "A 1934 Packard Super 8. They just don't make cars like this anymore." He started the engine. "Listen to that baby purr," he said proudly. He pulled smoothly away from the curb, waving at someone he knew who was passing by.

"That's the sheriff's office over there," Reggie said as they rounded the town square filled with a courthouse and, behind it, several smaller buildings. Reggie waved at a man exiting the sheriff's office. "That's Deputy Griggs. He's a good friend." The deputy waved back. Reggie headed out of town on a rural graveled road. The gravel soon turned to dirt.

Mama Rose's house was twelve miles outside of town on a dusty back road that wound through dense woods. As they pulled into her front yard, Drew saw a tumbledown rambling structure, needing paint, with a well and a hand pump near the front steps. The first floor was high above a ground-floor cellar. The front steps were a once-grand sweeping stairway. Smoke issued from a tin smokestack protruding from one side of the house. There were several outbuildings to the side and rear, and a roofed porch ran the length of the front of the house. The ground in front of the house was barren of grass, simply smoothed dirt with a weed here or there. An enormous old open touring car was parked in front of the steps in what passed for a driveway.

A huge white woman was sitting in a rocker on the porch. She arose as they got out of Reggie's car. She was dressed in a pink woolen sweater with dirty sleeves and a grayish cotton garment that extended to her ankles. It was voluminous and hung from her like a tent. Numerous rings of a gaudy design adorned every finger; some even had two, and each wrist had several cheap-looking bracelets that had once been gold colored but were now tarnished. Several gold and silver chains hung from her neck and were draped into the cavernous cleavage created by two incredibly large and pendant breasts. Her skin appeared blotchy and old, as if it was trying to decide whether to wrinkle. Her hair was frowzily gray and pulled back into a bun.

"Who's this, Reggie?" Mama Rose asked, showing bad and missing teeth. Her small green eyes shifted to Drew as she studied him from under thick lids.

"This is a new friend. I need a place for him to stay for a while, and then I'll get him a place in town. He'll work while he's here. I might have something coming up for him later."

"I already got that little nigger gal Emma and that nigger Maynard to do most of what needs doin' around here," Mama Rose said with a bit of exasperation.

Reggie went on as if Mama Rose had said nothing. "He needs to learn to drive. I figure you or Maynard can teach him in your spare time."

This, Drew thought, was new information. Driving was a whole new world to him.

Mama Rose looked sharply at Drew. "How old are you, boy?" she demanded.

"His name is Drew," Reggie said with just a hint of reproach. "How old are you, Drew?"

Drew looked down, thinking about what he should say. He looked up. "I'm ten. I'll be eleven in May."

"Well," Mama Rose said slowly, "he's a little tall for his age. Maybe he can do it. But he is only ten." She shrugged away her objection. "We'll see."

"Look, Mama," Reggie said. Drew could tell there was a tired note in Reggie's voice. "If he can learn to drive that old junker of yours, he can drive anything. Even if he can't, I can always use another kid for a lookout. Marvin is nearly fifteen now, and that's a little old to be a lookout. If Drew can't learn to drive, Marvin can start being my driver and Drew can take over as lookout."

"I charge for teachin'," Mama Rose said, losing interest at the mention of Reggie's employees.

"I'll pay for his keep," answered Reggie. Turning to Drew, he said, "Do whatever chores she asks. Listen carefully and learn. I'll pay you $10 a week for these first few weeks."

"Yes, sir," Drew replied. Then asked, "You want me to stay just two weeks?"

"No, I want you to stay a few"—he emphasized the word with a hard look at Mama Rose, who rolled her eyes—"weeks. I gotta go now. See you." Reggie turned abruptly and went to his car and started the engine. He leaned out the car window. "Take good care of him, Mama!" The large maroon-and-black Packard purred off in a dusty cloud.

Ten days later, Drew sat on the front steps, a writing pad in his lap. He wanted to write his friends in Union City but was worried about whom to write first. Finally, he decided Imogene would be his best bet and addressed his letter to the Union City Public Library. "Dear Miss Imogene," he wrote. "I am in Louisiana. I had to leave in a hurry and couldn't say good-bye. My address here is Mrs. Rose McCauley, General Delivery, in Claiborne, Louisiana. I am staying here for a while. Don't put my name on the envelope. How are you? Tell Leon and Walker and Sister Alma hello for me."

Drew folded the letter and placed it in an envelope. Maynard picked up mail once each week at the post office in town, and a few days later, Maynard took Drew's letter and mailed it.

A week after that, Mama Rose handed Drew a large envelope with two smaller ones inside. One letter was from Imogene, telling him how worried all his friends had been and asking him to write again.

The other was small and blue and was addressed in an unknown hand. He opened it and found a letter from Kowanda.

"Dear Drew," she wrote, "I miss you. Write back often but send the letters to Imogene or Miss Schultz. I am doing well in school. I don't like the school we have to go to now as well as I did Miss Ryan's school." She signed it simply as "Your friend."

Drew leaned back on the porch steps, where he had sat after being handed the letters. He mused over thoughts of Kowanda. He thought about the almond-eyed girl of Japanese descent, with whom he had often walked home from school, holding her hand. He remembered with distaste the day Kowanda's father had discovered the two and had chased Drew, shouting that he did not want his daughter walking with the bastard son of the town whore.

When Reggie found out about the letters, he cautioned Drew, "Letters can be traced, you know." But Drew decided to take the chance and continued writing, both to Imogene and Kowanda.

Drew learned from his correspondents that Edith had been to the sheriff and that he was now officially classified a runaway. He learned that the sheriff had made contact with people at Mrs. Lytle's Gentlemen's Club (Kowanda's letter admitted she didn't exactly understand what sort of club Mrs. Lytle's was, and Drew did not try to enlighten her) but that they had been unable to provide any information. Drew thanked his lucky stars that he had not yet written to Mrs. Lytle or to Reverend Thomas. He knew that Maude and Eddie would be worried about him but now felt that the less they knew of his whereabouts the better.

Drew did not tell Kowanda that his benefactor was a bootlegger, a fact he had only recently learned by listening to Mama's rambling under-her-breath solo monologues, which seemed to occur at random times.

Drew's life at Mama Rose's was confusing. Reggie had said he was to help Maynard and Emma with chores, and he did, though both seemed reluctant to permit him to do so. Emma, who was the cook, seemed to consider him a threat of some sort. He thought that she might not be all there. Her recipes were monotonous. The day of the week could be told by the oversalted food she prepared. Maynard seemed angry about Drew's presence and was sullen over his instructions to teach Drew to drive. Mama never gave Drew specific directions about which chores he was to perform, so Drew simply pitched in when and where the other two would permit him to do so.

Maynard made weekly trips to town for supplies and mail, driving Mama's old touring car. Drew accompanied him, thinking that these trips could be the "driving lessons" Reggie and Mama had discussed. However, Maynard never explained the controls and permitted Drew behind the wheel only when Mama specifically told him to. Drew felt that with no instruction and only limited opportunities, learning to drive was going to be a slow process.

Much of Drew's time was spent in idleness, which was not in Drew's nature. He searched for books to read but found none. One day, when the noon meal and all chores for that morning had been finished, he found a pack of Mama's playing cards. Years earlier, Margaret Lytle had taken Drew aside and had taught him card tricks.

Drew had practiced what he was taught during long evenings alone in his shed when his mother was entertaining one or the other of his uncles. He had a kerosene lamp and had knelt on his blanket and dealt cards to imaginary players.

On this slow spring afternoon, he sat on the front steps and began his silent "game," dealing cards to unseen players. Mama appeared to be napping in one of the four unpainted Adirondack chairs, but as she observed the boy, her rheumy old eyes widened.

Mama Rose was of an indeterminate age. She had been many things in a long and colorful life, including a teller of fortunes for a traveling circus, who also sponsored poker games when the circus stayed in town more than two days.

Mama now conducted regular poker games practically every Friday night, and she kept these games more or less honest. But now, as she watched Drew, she saw what could be an opportunity for more profit from her games. The boy had the "gift"! He not only dealt from the bottom of the deck, he did it with the Jersey twist. And he was good! He needed to be better, but Mama was sure she could teach him. Her eyes rolled heavenward, and had she been a believer in any sort of divinity or if her enormous weight had been less, she would have dropped to her knees in thanks.

Her only thought was that he lacked guile, but maybe that could serve to her advantage. She would have to think about it.

She told Reggie about Drew's abilities during his next visit. "I hope you don't need him in town just yet," she said with a gleam in her eyes. "I'm studying to teach him a few things. I think he'll be a quick learner."

"And then what?" Reggie said with a bit of an edge to his voice. "You can't put him into a poker game. He's too young, only ten. The other players would smell a rat."

She shot back, "A card game is a sight safer than being a lookout for a bootlegger!" Then she went on, a little calmer, "I'm still thinkin' on the details. They aren't clear yet in my mind. Let me work it out."

"OK," Reggie said, shrugging, his voice carrying dubious tones. "But there's another problem too. That boy is far too straight to be part of any scheme you'd concoct."

"Yeah, I already thought of that. I'll figure it out," Mama said irritably.

Drew had been nearby and overheard parts of the conversation. He was disappointed that once again he was not to return to town for whatever tasks Reggie had in mind. Drew was bored with only the dimwitted Emma, the sullen Maynard, and the old fortune-teller who seemed to sleep a lot. But, he thought, perhaps Mama's plans would give him something to do with his time.

A few days later, as Drew again demonstrated his skills to Mama, she asked how he could remember where all the cards were in a deck. "Well, if the shuffle is facedown, I can't," Drew admitted, "but if the shuffle is faceup, then I know."

"How do you know?" she urgently pressed.

"I don't know how I know. I just know. I can remember. Mostly, it's just the face cards."

*Oh lord,* Mama said to herself. *Please make this fellow a little less straight! Surely there's a way to play this. We could get rich.*

Mama's Friday night poker games had for some time been getting larger. As they did, more and more money changed hands. Mama charged the winners a fee since she was the host, and she also played. From time to time, when she was sure she could get away with it, she dealt herself some particularly good cards. When she won like this, she often won large pots. Drew, along with Maynard and Emma, attended each game. Emma and Maynard's job was to serve the players beer, liquor, and sandwiches. Drew's job was to manage the cash box, maintain a ledger, and hand out chips in return for cash. He'd also been instructed to carefully, and unobtrusively, observe the other players and let Mama know if any cheated. Usually, the only cheater was Mama despite her arthritic hands.

When Mama won large pots, she tipped Drew, generally $10. Once, after a particularly good night, she tipped him $20. All the money Drew got went into his tin box. He wondered about the tips since Reggie had promised $10 a week, but Drew never saw any money except whatever Mama handed him after the poker games.

One of Mama's players, a man named Haskell, seemed to win more often than ordinary luck would permit; and as he watched, Drew saw that the man regularly dealt himself good poker hands. When Drew talked to Mama about this, he explained that Haskell was clumsy. It was a surprise to him that none of the other players noticed.

One Sunday afternoon, with little else to do, Drew was exploring the nearby woods and came upon an oddly shaped tree. Upon inspection, he found a hollow in the tree about six feet above the ground. He cleaned out the hollow and later returned with his knapsack and tin box and placed them in the hollow. Drew had been simply leaving these under his cot. However, as the amount of money in his tin box grew, he remembered Edith's thievery and decided he could not fully trust anyone in Mama Rose's house.

After he placed the knapsack in the hollow, he retrieved it, sat on the ground under the tree, and looked inside. He reread Kowanda's latest letters, then replaced them. He looked once again at the wallet, holding it, wishing that somehow it could tell him of his father. He took out the photograph of the woman who looked so much like Edith but dressed in a style that had been in fashion perhaps forty years earlier. He knew it was not Edith. Could it be his grandmother? He so wanted to know. He placed it all back in the knapsack and put it back in the hollow.

Before he left the tree, he went to a rocky outcropping over a nearby creek. He found several large stones, and these he placed in the opening over the knapsack. He hoped to discourage squirrels and other wildlife from trying to make a nest of his knapsack and the extra clothing in it.

When he returned, he found Mama Rose and Haskell on the front porch, waiting for him.

Mama made the introductions and then said, "Drew, Haskell here is gonna be something like a partner to me, you know, in our Friday night games."

She turned to Haskell. "You wouldn't believe the card tricks this young guy knows."

Haskell nodded, turned to Drew, and said, "I'd like to learn. Would you teach me?"

Drew's first thought was that Mama and Haskell had rehearsed this particular dialogue. The entire setup reminded him strongly of Edith and Eugene.

Mama handed Drew a deck of playing cards and said, "Go ahead, honey. Show Haskell what you can do, you know, with the Jersey twist."

She pulled up a card table and chairs; and Drew sat down with the two, shuffled faceup, and dealt three hands facedown.

"Now," Mama said, "tell us what cards we've got, and then we'll look."

Drew grinned. "Neither of you has anything worthwhile. I've got three kings." He flipped his cards over.

"Do that again," Haskell said with a bit of wonder. Drew again shuffled faceup and handed the deck to Haskell facedown. "Cut," he said.

Haskell cut the cards. Drew picked them up again and dealt three hands facedown.

"What do we have?" Mama said.

"You've got three queens, I've got an ace, and Mr. Haskell has two kings," Drew reported honestly.

"Mama," Haskell said, "why don't we put this boy into your games? We'd get rich!"

"And who'd let us play a ten-year-old boy?"

It was eventually decided that every weekend for the next several weeks Haskell was to return, and Drew would demonstrate and try to teach him his tricks. Drew told Mama later that they had a problem.

"Mr. Haskell's hands are, well, not really very clean, and his nails are broken and dirty. Mrs. Lytle always cleaned my nails and cut them before play. She said always to do that."

"Well," Mama said, "I'll see that he gets a manicure next time he comes."

"His fingers are pretty thick too," Drew added. "He needs to do something—ah, I don't know—like maybe stretch his fingers like this." Drew demonstrated a basic hand exercise, entwining his fingers and pushing his hands away from his body.

"I'll have him start doing that too," Mama said. "Is there anything else?"

"He's gonna need lots of practice."

Weeks went by. Drew could see improvement, but Haskell was never able to locate individual cards as Drew did when he shuffled. His eyes simply were not quick enough. He could occasionally locate one or two, but Drew told Mama he didn't think Haskell would ever get much better. Still, Mama was encouraged at Haskell's progress. *He'll never be as good as Drew,* she said to herself, *but he is more believable at the poker table.*

The poker games got even larger. When Drew had first arrived at Mama's, the Friday night cash flow had been in the hundreds of dollars. As time went on and the games grew in popularity, the cash flow increased along with the number of players. Mama decided to move the games to the parlor, which had been the main room of the original plantation house. When she announced the planned changes one Friday night, she added that a free "grand buffet" would be provided. Several of her regulars offered to invite others.

Mama sang out, "The more the merrier!"

The days before the first grand buffet were busy. Maynard and Drew were set to polishing the old wood floors, cleaning the woodwork, and setting up tables for the players. Early Friday, they went into town and returned with quantities of fried chicken, potato salad, boiled eggs, bread, and pickles from the local café. Drew used the trip to insist that Maynard allow him the opportunity to further his skills driving Mama's car. After the lesson was over, Drew was as pessimistic as the sullen Maynard that he would ever develop into a good driver. Twice, he had almost driven the car into the ditch. The mechanics of operating the clutch and then shifting smoothly continued to plague him.

When the Friday night players arrived, they found food displayed for them, beer iced down in a large washtub, and a quantity of Reggie's potent brew of "white lightning." All during the evening, they visited the loaded table and filled their plates. Emma and Maynard had been sternly instructed to keep the beer and liquor flowing.

As the evening ended, a player named Wendell asked if he could bring "a couple" more players to the next game. One, he told Mama was a well-off realtor; the other was a banker.

When Mama told Drew about this, he nodded and said, "You know, that guy Wendell has been watching Haskell really closely."

"No, I didn't," Mama replied. She sat up a little straighter. "Tell me more."

"I don't know what else to tell. He just watches. When Haskell deals, Wendell usually folds quickly."

"But he never says anything?"

"Not to me," Drew said. "I haven't seen him talking with anyone else other than, you know, just talk. 'Hello, how are you?' things like that."

As more players began arriving each Friday, the cash flow continued to increase. The character of those new attendees changed too. The new people drove expensive automobiles and seemed to be well-off. As Mama's profits grew, the tips she gave Drew increased. After one particularly profitable night, she gave him $50.

It was now late summer, and Drew wondered if Reggie was ever going to follow through with a job offer of some type. School was out, so it would not now be strange for Drew to be seen in town. On the other hand, Drew was beginning once again to think about trying to reach

Little Rock, even if he didn't know if law enforcement was continuing to look for him.

His supply of cash in his tin box had grown over the months. He hadn't counted it lately, but he guessed that he had almost $400. Drew wondered if soon he could get one of the players to give him a ride into town and buy a bus ticket for him.

The last Friday night game that Drew was ever to attend was also the largest to date. Everyone seemed to be in a holiday mood; local harvests promised to be good, and cotton had been a bumper crop. Cash and liquor flowed freely. Drew was kept busy managing the cash box, handing out chips, and managing his ledger.

Drew also was instructed to continue to discreetly observe Wendell and his reactions to Haskell, whose confidence in his own abilities with the Jersey twist had grown far more than Drew felt was warranted. Haskell cheated more often than Mama had instructed and did so clumsily. None of the other players seemed to notice, but Drew was now positive that Wendell knew Haskell was cheating.

The evening went on until after midnight. Haskell won several large pots. Mama Rose, at her table, also had a good evening. And other tables had increased their antes. Drew's cash box was stuffed, and though he was behind in his ledger entries, he thought he must have almost $10,000. He had never expected to see this amount of money in cash.

That kind of money on this Friday night would prove disastrous.

# Chapter 16

## *Friday Night Terror*

ABOUT AN HOUR after midnight there were few people in the room not inebriated—or, at least, they appeared to be inebriated. The final game of the night included only Mama, one of her "regulars," and both Wendell and Haskell.

As the high-stakes game among them began, the other players crowded around, liquor glasses in hand, watching. Drew had converted all the cash to chips, placed the money in the compartmented cash box, and completed his ledger entries. He held the ledger and cash box and watched the game.

It went four hands. Mama let Haskell deal on each hand, and while earlier Haskell had seemed to be very drunk, he now seemed increasingly sober. As the game wore on, Drew noticed Wendell becoming increasingly fidgety. Drew was sure that Wendell was irritated by Haskell's clumsy cheating. He wondered if Wendell was going to call everyone's attention to the cheating, and if so, he wondered what the reason for waiting was. It was then that three of the newer players, men whom Wendell had invited, were edging forward. They had put their glasses down. Their hands were in their pockets.

Then, just after Haskell started the last deal, Wendell stood, reached across the table, and pinned Haskell's hands. He forcibly turned the man's hands, and two palmed cards were clearly shown. Haskell squirmed.

"You've been doing this all night!" Wendell shouted, also suddenly sober. Haskell pulled away. A pistol appeared in his hand. He pointed it at Wendell, who moved back, hands up. The crowd of men standing behind Mama Rose backed away. Haskell pointed his pistol at Drew. "Kid," he said. "Hand me that cash box!" One of the men Drew had been watching pulled a pistol, and a pistol also appeared in Wendell's hand.

Drew did not move, but from the corner of his eye, he saw Reggie Masterson slide into the room. That somehow seemed a little too convenient. He also had a pistol. Haskell's eyes were still on Drew. "Hand me the fucking cash box!" he shouted. Drew moved backward. A pistol shot rang out.

There was pandemonium. Men began running and shouting. Drew backed against the wall. A small silver pistol appeared in Mama Rose's hand. A table was overturned. Several lamps were knocked over. The room was plunged into semi-darkness. There were more loud shots and two popping sounds. "Goddammit!" someone shouted. Drew broke the paralyzing grip of terror that had held him, turned, and ran outside. He was surprised to realize he was still holding the cash box and ledger. "I'm hurt!" a man's voice shouted behind him. There was another shot. A man screamed.

Drew's feeling of terror increased. He was on the verge of blind panic. He ran toward the woods. Maynard dashed past him, shouting incoherently. Emma was screaming somewhere in the house. There was another pistol shot. Her screaming stopped.

Drew continued running, away from that house of horrors.

He had never been as frightened as he was now. Drew ran on, blind and barefoot. Through the summer, his shoes had become too small and he'd simply gone without them. The soles of his feet had become almost as hard as leather. Now, he could think only of escape from the horror of the tragedy behind him. On some level, he called himself a coward, felt that he should have stayed to help Reggie and Mama Rose. But the terror that filled his mind drowned the thought as he ran, sometimes lightly as a deer; other times when the moon was covered by clouds, he stumbled through the brush, colliding with trees, tearing his shirt on brambles, scratching his face and hands. He fell several times.

He could hear shouts in the distance, the sound diminishing as he ran. He could hear Maynard screaming and crashing through the brush ahead and to the right. He changed direction, heading to his left, realizing that pursuit, if anyone was following, would follow the sounds of Maynard's panicked screaming. As he thought about the sounds Maynard was making, he realized that he too was sending signals. He stopped, breathing heavily and leaned over, cradling the cash box; and vomited.

He spat the taste from his mouth and moved more deliberately and quietly away from Maynard and away from the sounds his own retching had made. Calm rationale was beginning to return.

*No matter what had taken place back at Mama's house*, his mind said, coldly and with unassailable logic, *the law can't ignore it. There'll be questions, maybe charges of murder. You can't become involved. You're already wanted back in Union City. Others know you've lived at Mama Rose's since winter and through the summer. They've seen you driving that old car of Mama's. Maybe the sheriff here will decide to put you in jail. You've already run now. Maybe others will blame you for what has happened. Both Reggie and Mama might be dead.*

He could still hear shouts in the woods. More distantly, he could hear sounds toward Mama's house. Once, he heard two more pistol shots. He could not tell where they came from.

It was clear to Drew now that Wendell had for some time been planning the attack and had recruited others. As panic subsided into calmer thought, Drew kept running but at a more deliberate and sustainable pace. His mind continued sorting out the awful events of the past few minutes.

With a stunning shock, Drew realized that he was at his hollow tree.

Drew immediately put the cash box and ledger down and clambered up for his knapsack. He jumped back to the ground, reached inside the money box, and withdrew handfuls of bills. He folded the ledger.

After a minute or so, he looked up. A man stood in front of him no more than ten feet away. His face was in shadow. Moonlight glinted on the pistol in his hand.

"Hand me that money box," the man said. It didn't sound like either Haskell or Wendell.

Drew bent down and picked up the box. Another voice, Reggie's, said, "Hold it right there!" Drew froze. Reggie was behind the man. His shirt glistened blackly. Was it blood?

Drew threw the cash box at the man, turned, and in one quick motion slung the knapsack over his shoulder and ran.

There were two shots. Someone screamed. It didn't sound like Reggie. Drew continued running.

He ran for perhaps another mile through the woods. A rivulet of water coursed down the middle of a small creek. Drew, breathing heavily, fell to his stomach and drank deeply. Afterward, he rested for several minutes, listening for pursuit. He resumed a sustainable jog.

Drew looked up to the sky through the trees. The moon had moved past its zenith toward the western horizon. Using it as his guide, he continued his deliberate pace through the woods.

Was Mama dead? Drew thought that she might be and grieved for her. Despite all her faults, cunningness, and deceit, she had taken Drew in, given him food and shelter, and Drew had liked her though he'd never trusted her. Maynard and Emma were almost certainly gone.

Was Reggie dead? There was no way to know.

As the eastern sky began to lighten, gray dawn clouds could be seen scuttling before the wind. Drew found himself at a graveled highway. He was drenched with sweat but felt chilled. As he pulled his jacket and cap from the knapsack, he realized it was mid-September.

He walked along the deserted highway, alone in the dawn grayness. His bare feet were now sore and bleeding from numerous thorns and deadfall.

He was eleven years old.

# Chapter 17

## *Traveling Again*

I T WAS NEAR the end of the next day. A tired, dirty, and hungry Drew rested beside the road. He figured he had gone perhaps twenty miles, maybe more. During the daylight, he stepped aside into the brush alongside the graveled highway as vehicles approached, fearing police patrols or worse, so his progress was slow. He had not dared to try hitchhiking.

Several times he came upon a small community and thought about trying to buy food and shoes but was sure that he would be noticed and remembered. He was thirsty but had found several springs alongside the roadway during the day, so his thirst wasn't as severe as his hunger. He had thought about skirting around the towns, crossing through fields and some woods, but realized it was a Saturday. There would be more people in town than on a weekday. He hoped no one would notice him among the Saturday crowds if he simply passed through.

That night he found another spring several yards from the highway, sheltered beneath a large rocky outcropping. He slept there beside the spring, huddled in his jacket and hungrier than he could remember. While he had gone barefoot most of the summer, and the soles of his feet were tough, they were still sore from his panicked run through the woods. They were now blistered from his walk along the graveled highway. He soaked his feet in the cool spring waters and afterward dried them with one of his shirts.

Dawn came. He continued on his way, wincing as the blisters continuously announced their presence. He would have to find food and shoes today.

That Sunday afternoon he passed through another small community. The sign on the roadway called it Bloomsdale. On the other side of town he saw a Magnolia Petroleum gasoline station with a small shack next door. A sign said Hamburgers, 10 Cents.

Drew pulled his cap down tightly about his ears, hoping to hide his reddish-hair; and bought three hamburgers, along with a Coca-Cola; and fished coins out of his knapsack. He took his hamburgers in a sack, drinking the Coke as he walked away. He was pretty sure no one other than the man in the hamburger shack had noticed him. Even so, he moved rapidly; and as soon as he could, he stepped into the woods. He wolfed one of the sandwiches down. It was only meat and bread, but it seemed nothing had ever tasted so good.

As he was eating the last of the second burger, he looked up. A young boy—about six or seven, ragged and unkempt—was standing nearby, looking at him.

"Mister, those hamburgers shore looked good to me," the boy said in a broad drawl.

"Ah, well, hello," Drew answered. "How long have you been standing there?"

"I watched you eat them burgers. I shore am hungry. You gonna eat that other burger?" Drew handed the sandwich to the boy.

"I've got some Coke left," Drew said. He handed it to the boy, who gulped the last two swallows greedily. "That was the first Coke I ever drank," the boy said, wiping his mouth with the back of his hand.

Drew looked closely at him. Dirty overalls, no shirt, blond unkempt hair, blue eyes of a sort of washed-out blue, not quite the cornflower blue of Edith's, but more faded, almost gray. "Where do you live?" Drew asked.

"I live over yonder," the boy answered, his voice somehow sounding thick. "My ma and pa are there. We've camped out. They're hungry too."

Drew handed the boy the last sandwich, and he wolfed it down without speaking, almost without chewing.

Drew pulled a dollar out of his knapsack. "Here," he said. "Take this to that gas station over there, hand it to the man in that shack, and tell him two hamburgers and two Cokes."

The boy stared at the bill. "I ain't never done nuthin' like that," he said.

"OK," Drew said. "I'll go with you."

As they walked back to the hamburger shack, the boy said, "Could you buy one more, maybe? My ma and my pa are powerful hungry."

Drew bought four more hamburgers and three Coca-Colas and walked with the boy back to the woods. "This here's our camp," the boy said.

The camp was nothing more than an old Ford parked well off the road at the side of a small clearing. Quilts had been hung onto the tops of the car's open doors and made into shade with sticks guyed upright with line. Two cots and a pallet of old blankets were apparently the family's sleeping arrangements while cooking was evidently over an open fire. Several suitcases were scattered about, and others tied to the top of the car. A man and a woman, almost as unkempt as the boy, were sitting on one of the cots.

The man was balding, his remaining hair greasy and stringy. He was extraordinarily thin. His overalls hung loosely on his frame. The woman was more heavy-set. Like her husband, she was dirty, wearing a print dress that might have been made from flour sacks. Her hair had evidently not seen a brush or comb for days. Both had eyes of the same washed-out blue as the boy.

No one spoke, but the smell of the hot sandwiches had preceded Drew and the boy. Their eyes focused almost exclusively on the sack of food Drew carried. He handed the sack to the man, who opened it without a word, and eagerly pulled the food out, handed one to his wife, and both began eating. The boy grabbed a sandwich, too. Drew handed them the other sack of Cokes but realized he had no way to open them. The man took the sodas out, held the bottle cap on part of the car's bumper, and snapped it off. All three gulped the drinks. There was one sandwich left.

"Ain't you gonna eat?" the man said in the same broad drawl the boy had used. Drew shook his head.

"I'll save it for later." The man put the burger back in the sack.

They introduced themselves: Arvin Nettles; his wife, Anne; and their son, Tad.

As they shook hands, Drew said, "I don't want to tell you my name. I . . . I've got some troubles."

Nettles said in that same almost annoying drawl the boy had used, "You don't need to worry about us none, mister. We ain't close to the law. It was the law what threw us off our land back in Alabama. You look like you been travelin', maybe walkin' a lot?" He looked down at Drew's blistered feet.

Drew nodded. "My name's Drew. You shouldn't call me mister. I'm only eleven."

The woman said, "Drew, we proud to know you. You tall for your age. We sure appreciate the food. We're travelin' too, out of gas and money, now. Arvin here he trapped a rabbit the other day. I made rabbit stew. I found some poke. It's all gone now. It gave all of us the runs."

Arvin added, "we've done run out of flour and meal, got a little salt left, no bacon or nuthin'."

Drew said, "Does the car run?"

"Why, sure, mister," Arvin said. "It's nearly out of gas, though. There's no money for gas neither. We're just stuck. I wuz tryin' to find work, but this here town's too small. Nobody's building nuthin'. I'm a good carpenter."

"Tell you what," Drew said, "I'm tryin' to get to Arkansas, to Little Rock. Could you drive me? I've got a little money. I could buy gas."

"Mister, if you got some money, I can get us wherever you want to go. Maybe I can get a job in Little Rock."

They talked a while longer, and Drew reached into his knapsack and handed Arvin a $20 bill. "Go into town and buy some gas and maybe some more hamburgers and Cokes for the road."

Arvin and Anne disconnected the quilts from the car; and Arvin left for gas; while Anne, Tad, and Drew folded up the cots and gathered up the family's things. Arvin came back twenty minutes later.

"Boy, howdy!" he shouted. "You shudda seen that gas jockey's eyes pop out when a guy like me handed him a $20. Ah . . . here's your change." Anne looked at her husband sharply. He continued, "I bought a carton of Cokes and some oil for this old car." Drew nodded and took the money. It was a mistake, he thought, to use large bills. The gas guy will surely remember.

The Ford was soon packed with the family's belongings. The hamburgers Arvin had bought were packed into one of the suitcases that evidently served as the family's pantry.

They pulled out of the clearing, down the path to the highway, and turned away from the town. Drew asked Arvin, "Do you have any road maps?"

"I did have, but we used them for fire starter."

"We need to get some, maybe at the first large filling station we come to."

The old Ford ran but not well. Moreover, its top speed was no more than forty; and when it exceeded that, coasting downhill, the front wheels shimmied terribly. Several times, Drew doubted whether the car would be able to make it up a particularly steep grade as the straining engine rattled and shook and steam issued from the radiator cap. Twice, Arvin stopped and added water to the overheated radiator.

The worn tires gave out quickly. Arvin had two spare tires and a package of tube patches and glue. They lost almost an hour for each puncture, replacing the punctured tire with one of the spares and extracting the tube and applying the patch.

During one such stop, Anne looked closely at Drew's feet. "Honey," she said, "we got an old pair of shoes in one of our suitcases. Let me see if I can find them. Maybe they'll fit."

Darkness was falling earlier than Drew wanted.

"Mister," Arvin said, turning to Drew, "we ain't gonna git much farther today. I don't think we should keep on drivin' much after dark. We're gonna have to camp for the night."

Arvin pulled off the road into a clearing next to a small group of trees. They stopped, and Drew helped set up camp. Anne built a fire. Everyone ate another hamburger. Arvin and Anne both said that Drew must sleep on one of the cots, but Drew refused. He and Tad slept in the car.

The next morning they arose early and loaded the car. The engine started reluctantly, and they pulled away from the camp.

They were headed east, and while Drew was confused about their exact location, he was fairly sure the road they were on paralleled the Louisiana-Arkansas line. He was right. By the time they found a road heading north, they were nearly to the Mississippi River. It was late afternoon when the decrepit Ford crossed into Arkansas.

They found no large towns, but at one small community, they found a road map at a Sinclair station, where they were told Okies weren't welcome. "You people need to get outta here!" the gas station proprietor said to them. Drew said nothing; paid for the maps, gas, cigarettes for Arvin and another box of tube patches; and they left the station.

The shoes Anne had found for him were canvas high-tops with rubber soles. She had found some salve, and Drew rubbed it into his badly blistered feet. He pulled his only pair of socks from the knapsack and thanked Anne for the shoes. As he did, thinking of their slow progress, Drew said,

"Folks, I think we're going to have to buy some supplies." No one had eaten since the evening before.

"We ain't got no money," Anne answered.

"I've got a little," Drew said in what he hoped was an innocent tone of voice. "Let's use some of it in the next town, restock what you need. Get some cornmeal, coffee, flour, bacon, things like that. Maybe some eggs for both supper tonight and breakfast tomorrow morning."

"That's mighty generous, Drew," Anne answered, though Drew noticed she avoided his eyes as she said this.

"You giving me a ride is mighty generous too," Drew answered.

Just then, another tire went flat.

They bought supplies in the next town. Drew remained in the car. He had handed Anne another $20. He noticed she had watched closely as he'd extracted the money from his knapsack. When she returned, she did not give him any change from the $20.

They camped again that night next to the road. Coffee, bacon, eggs, and cornmeal fritters fried in bacon grease the next morning were a welcome "wakeup."

They continued north, looking for a highway heading west or northwest. Progress was slow as one and then another of the worn tires gave way, and they stopped to work on the punctures. That afternoon, Drew dozed and finally fell asleep next to Tad in the back seat. When he awoke, it was late afternoon, almost sunset. They were parked on a graveled road. The engine was idling in its clattering way. Drew could see Anne and Arvin standing a short distance away from the car, talking. Anne was gesturing, pointing back at the car. Tad was nowhere to be seen. Drew did not move but listened carefully.

Twice he heard the word *money*, and several times he heard his name. With sudden clarity, he realized they were talking about robbing him. Drew slid down in the seat and pulled his jacket and cap on. The rubber-soled high-tops were on the floor of the car. He slid his feet into them and tied the laces. He gathered his knapsack to him, leaned across the front seat to the door handle, and quickly opened the car door and ran.

"He's gittin' away!" he heard Anne scream. "Go after him!" Drew ran down the graveled roadway. Arvin followed for a short while, then turned around. Drew heard the sound of the car door slamming and the car's engine spluttering as the revolutions increased. He turned to his right, crossed a wire fence, and ran across an open field, up a slight rise. As he topped the rise, he was quickly out of sight.

He turned sharply to his left toward a small grove of trees. Once in their midst, he stopped to catch his breath and turned back to look. Arvin evidently had cut the fence, or maybe simply driven through it, because Drew could hear the old car straining as it topped the rise. He could see the headlights as it started down the slope toward a small creek. It would be a good time now, Drew thought, for another puncture. Evidently, the tires held, for the car continued on to the creek.

Drew turned and ran through the trees and out the other side. He was pretty sure the Nettleses had not seen him and likely had no idea which direction to look, but he kept jogging along the creek and into another small grove. He went farther into the grove as he followed the creek. The stream meandered, and Drew crossed it, jumping as far as he could, but nevertheless landing in shallow water on the other side. He jogged on as full darkness fell, and his path became illuminated by starlight. He kept the creek between him and the Nettleses. He could still hear gears grinding and engine noises. He looked back over his shoulder several times and could see the dim headlights of the old car as it zigzagged through the fields, searching. He came to another roadway that crossed the creek with a small bridge. Drew crossed under the bridge and continued jogging. He soon turned away from the creek and across open, but rolling, countryside. He could see no houses. The pain from his blistered feet in the now soaked high-tops was intense. Drew slowed to a walk. The soles of the high-tops began to come loose.

He had no idea where he was. He stopped at another small creek, fell onto his stomach, and once again drank deeply. He pulled his shoes and socks off and soaked his blistered feet. The high-tops were disintegrating rapidly. Drew was convinced that, at first light, Arvin and Anne would be patrolling the roads, hoping to cross his path. Drew put his socks and the deteriorating shoes back on and sat with his back to a large tree. He pulled his sweater out of the knapsack and put it on, pulling the jacket on afterward. He leaned against the tree and slept.

Drew awoke. It was not yet dawn, though he had no idea of the time. He listened for the Nettleses' car. He neither heard nor saw anything. There was the dim light of a quarter moon.

He exited the grove and walked across open country, heading, he thought, generally northwest.

After an hour or so, he limped up another slight rise and found a dirt road. He decided to walk along it, thinking that the Nettleses would still be camped for the night. A farmhouse was displayed down the hill, a barn, windmill, and other outhouses nearby. Drew was tired, and his feet hurt. He had trouble organizing his thoughts. A light shone in a window of the farmhouse. He was tempted to go to the farmhouse and, perhaps, beg for food. But he did not.

He kept on walking. The dirt road turned, and this part was graveled. Drew limped onward, needing to put as much distance as possible between him and the Nettleses before full daylight. He felt that when daylight came, he would need to find shelter, somewhere that he could be concealed, perhaps a haystack or another grove of trees.

The road crossed yet another creek, and Drew turned and walked along it for several hundred yards. There, he found what he needed: shelter under the tall creek bank. He slid down, pulled himself into an overhanging part of the bank, and fell instantly asleep.

# Chapter 18

## St. Timothy's

I
T WAS LATE afternoon, and soon darkness would fall. The clear day had changed, and there were clouds low in the northern sky. An occasional lightning flash could be seen. Drew left his shelter under the high creek bank after sleeping only a few hours. He had thought he would stay through the daylight hours and continue walking after dark, but hunger had awakened him and was too severe to ignore.

He walked along the now-graveled road, alert for the sounds of approaching vehicles, but heard none. The dark clouds continued their approach, highlighted with red and gold from the setting sun. Drew could smell rain in the air. He was very hungry. Even if he found nothing to eat, he was going to need more substantial shelter tonight than a creek bank. Perhaps, he thought, he could find a farm tool shed or some other outbuilding. As he looked around, he saw a sign next to a drive that led up a slight rise.

It announced, in peeling paint, that St. Timothy's Missionary Catholic Church held Vespers every Sunday and Wednesday evening and mass twice on Sundays. He saw the church building set back quite a distance from the road, at the summit of a grassy rise.

It was small, apparently of whitewashed clapboard. A rude steeple, sheathed awkwardly in this same clapboard, extended upward from one side of the church. He could see no bell. The steeple had a tiny pointed roof and was adorned with a simple wooden cross that, upon closer inspection, leaned somewhat from the vertical.

The church was overwhelmingly plain. Neither contrasting trim nor stained glass could be seen, and no shrubbery of any kind graced the church or grounds. A huge maple overhung the rear, its leaves showing the dusky dark green of late September. The graveled drive before him wound up the slight rise and circled back toward the road.

There was a cemetery to one side of the old church, which extended almost to the road. There were modest-sized markers and what was evidently a low iron fence surrounding the graveyard.

Drew looked again at the sunset, which now had spectacular rays and colors from the changing cloud shapes of the approaching storm. He looked back at the church and saw it suddenly framed in the red and gold of the sunset, and for just a moment, its plainness was transformed. It somehow spoke to Drew of peace. Though he did not think the word, the old church also spoke to him of sanctuary such as had been offered in the great cathedrals of Europe in ancient times.

Reverend Thomas had once, long ago, shown Drew pictures of many of Europe's magnificent cathedrals. St. Timothy's was not among them. Its only adornment was the spectacular sunset colors now cascading over its whitewashed walls.

Drew quietly approached the building and was a little fearful at what he might find inside. Perhaps, he thought, the doors would be locked, but the heavy door was only warped. It swung outward awkwardly, noisily, on its hinges. He pulled it open.

The floor plan of the church was that of a cross, and Drew entered through the left arm of the cross, directly into the sanctuary. It was dark and cooler inside. Drew walked slowly to the center of the building; the altar was on his right. It was as simple and plain as the rest of the building and overhung with a wooden cross. There was no carpet, only several statues, evidently of saints, but no other images of any kind. The wooden pews were old and scarred. An upright piano stood to the left of the altar. A few votive candles on the right side of the altar flickered in the gloom.

With a start, Drew realized for the first time that he was not alone in the building. A black-robed man stood quietly in the gloom at the altar with his back to Drew.

Without turning, a voice came from the robed figure. "Welcome."

The voice had a strange lilt to it. "I was just about to say Vespers," the priest said. "Will you join me in evening prayers?"

Drew nodded, though he realized the man could not have seen the nod since he did not turn around. He sat down awkwardly in a pew, which squeaked in protest.

"I'm so glad to have company," the priest said. "Having someone here makes Vespers much more meaningful."

Drew wondered at this without speaking. Would the priest have held his service anyway even if the building had remained completely empty? He decided that he would have.

The man at the altar had not yet turned. He was smoothing a piece of cloth. A match flared, the man lit two tall candles and began Vespers, sung a cappella. As he sang, the final rays of the setting sun were thrown onto the plain crucifix above the altar. Drew's mouth opened slightly as he stared and for the briefest of moments felt this was the light of God. Drew blinked, the light changed, and the instant of otherworldliness vanished.

Drew was pervaded with a feeling of being safe and calm. In some unique way, he was profoundly moved by the changing patterns of light and by the rhythms of the Roman Catholic evening service as the priest sang the liturgy. Drew pulled his jacket about his shoulders and relaxed, pulling his cap off as he did so. He became drowsy, and while he heard the man's voice, he could not have told what it was about. Vespers were over quickly. The white-haired priest snuffed out the candles, stepped down from the altar, made obeisance, and walked to Drew, who started awake. The man sat beside him. "Thank you for attending evening services with me. You are not Catholic." It was more a statement than a question.

"No. I went to a church a long time ago. The preacher called it evangelical. At another church, it was called Baptist, so I don't know what I am."

"Almost everyone in this part of Arkansas is Protestant, son," the priest chuckled. "This church, St. Timothy's, is Catholic, but it's small. Ah, we can get into all that some other time. I think now we need to be acquainted, you and I. I'm Father Tom Byrne. Many people call me Father Tom. Some call me Father Byrne. And quite a few just call me Tom. You can have your choice."

Drew nodded, thinking again of that strangely entertaining lilt in the man's voice. He saw that the priest was quite elderly, but as he looked at Drew from underneath a shock of startlingly white hair, Drew also thought that he radiated friendliness and concern.

Drew answered, "I'm called Drew."

"Is that short for Andrew?"

Drew nodded.

"You're running away?" The priest's eyebrows rose.

"I guess so." Drew was very tired. He had no use for debate.

"You think your folks are worried about you?" There was perseverance in the priest's voice.

"My father is dead. My mother told me to leave." Drew's voice was flat.

"Well, then, you're not really running away, are you? Hungry?"

Drew nodded again, this time with more interest. He was almost faint with hunger. He had not eaten since his breakfast with the Nettleses the morning before.

"Mrs. Calumet is my housekeeper. She goes home before Vespers, but she usually leaves more food for supper than I can eat. Come, let's see what we have."

Drew had not noticed earlier the small residence behind the church or the closed sedan that sat between the church building and the house. He followed Father Tom as he exited the church and walked past the car and onto the screened porch at the rear of the little house.

Drew followed into the kitchen, which had been made inordinately hot from the dying embers in the wood cook stove. The walls were whitewashed. A small table, covered with a red-and-white checkered tablecloth with two chairs, sat next to an open window. Curtains of the same material as the tablecloth framed the window. A single place had been set.

There was a sudden clap of thunder. Rain finally began, pouring down in torrents. The curtains stirred, and Father Tom pulled the sash halfway down. He motioned for Drew to sit. Rain continued to collect on the windowsill, but the slight breeze helped cool the stifling kitchen.

Another plate and bowl along with tableware and a large tin cup were placed in front of Drew. There was a large bowl, and what was evidently an iron skillet of cornbread on the sideboard of the stove, covered with dishtowels. The kitchen was filled with the smells of cooking, and Drew's stomach growled alarmingly while his mouth watered.

"There's a wash-up sink back there, Drew, with soap," the priest said. "We've no hot water, just the one tap." Drew went to the back porch and washed. He found a comb and, after wetting his hair, combed it back from his eyes. When he returned to the table, the priest nodded his approval.

Father Tom set the skillet of hot cornbread in front of Drew. He took a piece, broke it into several smaller pieces, and placed it in a bowl, which sat in the middle of Drew's plate. He then ladled a beef stew—meat, onions, potatoes, and carrots swimming in rich brown gravy—over the cornbread.

There was a small electric refrigerator by the wall opposite the table; and from it, Father Tom withdrew a pitcher of milk, after stirring to mix in the cream, filled the large cup at Drew's place, and then filled his own. He looked at Drew. "I didn't think before I poured the milk, but there's also a pitcher of buttermilk. Would you rather have buttermilk instead of sweet milk?" Drew shook his head as the priest pulled a butter dish from the refrigerator and placed it on the table. Drew waited expectantly.

"May we thank the Lord for what he has provided?" the priest said. Drew bowed his head, hoping that the Catholic blessing was not nearly as long as Reverend Thomas's had been.

He was not disappointed. Evidently, Catholics got their blessings over quickly and moved on with the business of satisfying their appetites.

Father Tom crumbled a piece of cornbread into his milk and began eating it with a spoon. Drew began eating his stew. The flavor of fresh meat, combined with that of fresh vegetables, was new to Drew. He found it was delicious and hoped he could keep himself from wolfing the food down.

As they ate, Father Tom asked, "Where are you from, Drew?"

"I'd rather not say the name of the town," Drew answered between bites.

"When did you leave?"

"Last January."

"May I ask where you've been these last nine, no, almost ten months?"

Drew sighed and reluctantly put down his spoon. He drank some of the milk and then looked at the priest for a long time. Here again was another person to weigh his trust against past experience. Drew's recent feelings from inside the church, however, stirred up words from his lungs and out of his mouth.

Drew said, "I'm not sure how much I should tell. A man took me in—he took me to live with—ah, someone. I don't know. I think she was some sort of relative of his. He called her Mama, but she wasn't his mother."

"She was?" the priest queried. "She's not alive anymore?"

"Oh. I don't know. I hope she's alive." Drew also hoped that no one had been injured on that terrible night four days ago but was sure his hope was in vain.

"He's a bootlegger, the guy who took me in," Drew continued. "He wanted me to work for him."

Lightning flashed. There was a clap of thunder. The single electric light hanging from a cord in the center of the room flickered. A breeze entered the room and stirred the checkerboard curtains.

The priest's pale-blue eyes had widened as his bushy eyebrows rose. "Work for a bootlegger? Doing what?"

"I'm not sure. He said something once about me being a lookout, but I was never asked to do anything like that." Drew was jumping around in telling the story. He wanted to tell everything, but his recollections were as jumbled as his words. Images from the months of boredom conflicted with those of the horror of robbery and murder, and they flooded his mind in a confused montage. "They were nice to me most of the time. I had chores to do around the house. They were teaching me to drive a car. I don't think I was very good. Then Mama R—" Drew stopped before completing the name. "I mean, then this woman he had me living with, well, she found out I knew how to do the Jersey twist, and she wanted me to teach another man, one of her players, how to do it when she had some poker games. She made a lot of money playing cards. She had poker games every Friday night."

"What's a Jersey twist?" Father Tom said, shaking his head and wondering at the events this boy was trying to tell, trying to organize the sequence of events in his mind.

"It's something I can do with cards. Not everyone can do it. It's cheating, but Mama—ah, this woman—said that it was OK if I taught someone else to do it. That way, it wouldn't be like me that was cheating. That sounds mixed up. She had me working the cash box. Anyway, last Friday night I was at one of her games, and one of the men had a pistol, waved it, and someone said he was going to rob everyone, and then things got pretty confused. The pistol went off, and it was really loud, and some lamps got knocked over, and two other men had pistols and, well, I just ran and ran. I don't really know what happened. Maybe the sheriff is looking for me. I didn't do anything, but he might be looking for me as a witness or something.

"I don't want to be found by anyone," Drew finished.

The priest nodded. It would all come out in time, he was sure. For the present, he needed to be silent and helpful.

Rain began hitting the windowpane. There were more lightning flashes, followed by thunder. The storm was fully upon them. Heavy rain rattled on the tin roof of the little house. The electric light flickered and went out.

"Well," the elderly priest said, match flaring as he lit a kerosene lamp, "we'll see that they don't find you. If you'd like, maybe I can ask around and find out if anyone wants to talk to you. Where did all this happen?"

"Down in Louisiana. It was near a little town not far from Shreveport."

"That's quite a ways from here," the priest observed. "How did you get here?"

Drew shrugged. "Some people gave me a ride. I walked."

"When you first left home, was there someplace in particular you were trying to go, I mean other than to Mama's?"

Drew buttered a piece of cornbread before answering and looked longingly at the stew. Father Tom indicated he should help himself to another serving, and he did. He chewed a piece of meat, swallowed, and drank a little more milk. The priest waited patiently.

"I wasn't trying to get to Mama's when I left home. I just sort of wound up there. I didn't know where I was going to go. I have friends in Little Rock. I thought I might go to them, but when I left home, I jumped into a boxcar, and the train was heading south, not north. So I wound up in Louisiana."

"Tell me about your friends in Little Rock."

Drew realized that he had an overwhelming need to talk about his life to an understanding and sympathetic adult whom he could trust. Now, though nothing had changed, it seemed that somehow everything had changed. Drew looked deep into the old man's blue eyes, not the cornflower blue of Edith's or the washed-out blue of the Nettleses, but still very different from the cobalt blue of his own. He felt as if the elderly priest was, in some way, a kindred spirit and that he could trust this man.

Though Drew did not know it, his own eyes radiated an intensity that fascinated the thin and wrinkled old Irish priest. Tom Byrne silently vowed that whatever this boy's troubles were, he was going to help. As he made this silent vow, his nephew Charly came to mind.

Drew found himself telling everything. He had torrents of words dammed in his throat, and he was now desperate to say them. But the words did not come easy to Drew, and he struggled, searching for the right word, the correct phrase that would result in clear understanding. This, and Drew's hesitant speech as he jumped around in the chronology, but nonetheless with a voice choked with emotion, somehow made the words more powerful than Drew could have known. Father Tom found himself moved by the rawness of this boy's life and hoped that he could formulate the proper response when Drew had finished.

Drew held almost nothing back. He told about Mrs. Lytle's in Little Rock where his mother had worked and called it what it was. He told about the Ebenezer Church of God in Jesus Christ, about Reverend Thomas; about Maude, whom he called Mardie; about Eddie Mackenzie, whom he had called Max; and about the rest. He told about Margaret Lytle and how she had taught him the Jersey twist; and he told about his best friend Leon, the fights. He even told about Catherine Ryan and the Klan attack and the school burning. Finally, his speech, now even more halting and with embarrassment clouding his features, he told about Eugene and his disgusting interest in young boys.

Drew, finally coming full circle in his talk with Father Tom, even told the name of the small southern Arkansas town where Uncle Henry had taken him and his mother, though he now called her Edith. The only thing he did not mention was the cash stuffed inside his little tin box in his knapsack.

The priest had been transfixed throughout the story as Drew had continued in the yellow lamplight.

When he had finished, the old priest was quiet for long moments. Finally, he said, "Drew, I'll never tell another soul all this unless you tell me to. This is just between the two of us and God. Tomorrow, we will talk about what you want to do next. It may not be wise for me to ask around. We will decide later what to do."

Changing his tone, the old priest added, "How old are you, Drew?"

"I'm eleven. I'll be twelve next May."

"Well, Drew, tonight we need to get you some fresh clothes, a hot bath, and I'll make up the divan for you to sleep."

"I have three spare shirts and some socks. I don't have any other clothes," Drew said, adding, "These high-tops are just about gone. They are coming apart."

"Fortunately, I have extra clothes and some shoes too," Tom Byrne answered. "We're able to collect clothing from time to time, and I just happen to have a quantity on hand. They're for the unfortunate, and candidly, you seem to qualify."

Then the priest added, "We don't have a modern water heater. You'll have to make do with a couple of kettles from the stove's tank and the galvanized washtub out on the porch. Move the tub into the kitchen. There's a garden hose connected. After you bathe, turn the little handle you'll see at the base of the tub, and it'll drain outside. Mrs. Calumet will move it back onto the porch in the morning.

"I'll keep the door closed, so you'll have your privacy."

As Drew washed, he luxuriated in the feeling of at last removing dirt and odors that seemed to have collected on his body ever since leaving Union City. He had of course bathed during his time at Mama Rose's, but this bath, somehow, seemed to cleanse not only his body but his soul.

As Drew drifted to sleep on the old sofa in the cabin's front room, his last thought was that finally he was with someone he could trust. Rain pelted the metal roof of the little house, but now the storm did not seem threatening. Drew felt safe. As he slept the storm slackened and then stopped entirely.

The next morning the sky was crystal clear. The air of an early October Arkansas morning was cool and somehow seemed full of promise and hope.

# Chapter 19

## Father Tom

A S DREW TALKED at the supper table, Tom Byrne wondered if in his own life he could have faced what Drew had already faced. His life had few direct parallels, but even so, he found that he could relate to the story Drew had told.

Tom had been sent as a young priest to a parish in Philadelphia, later to one in Ohio, and, still later, Indiana. He served well but without any special distinction. When a country church in southeastern Arkansas whose parishioners were Negroes became his, he found his calling at last. The desperate poverty and tragedies his parishioners experienced in the years following the Great War and, later, the dreadful years of America's Depression touched him profoundly. The Irish immigrant priest loved the people in his small and poor parish, and they in turn loved him back. It was only incidental that the skin of the elderly Irish priest was white in contrast to that of his parishioners.

St. Timothy's had not begun its life as an all-black church. In the beginning, its parishioners were exclusively white families. Father Tom, in his ignorance of white Southern America and Arkansas's Jim Crow laws, had welcomed Negro families who lived nearby. They were the children, grandchildren, and great-grandchildren of former slaves. The owners of those slaves had followed the Roman Catholic faith.

When the Negro families began attending mass, white families refused to support the tiny parish and instead made the trip into town for their worship services. In a very short time, St. Timothy's became exclusively black. Father Tom had, of course, noticed the change, but he did not have the heart to refuse his Negro neighbors.

Tom Byrne was alone but not lonely. He became a familiar sight on the roads in that part of Arkansas, dust billowing behind his Graham-Paige sedan as he toured the farms in the rolling countryside surrounding St. Timothy's. He taught first through third grades at the church, Catechism on Saturdays, and encouraged his parishioners to send their children to town to continue their education, there being no rural public schools for Negro children.

He often visited St. Michael's Cathedral in Little Rock as he sought both financial and other types of help from His Eminence Monsignor Father Richards. St. Michael's often had clothing drives, and Father Tom gladly transported many of the things thus collected to St. Timothy's for later distribution to needy children. One day a few years before Drew's first appearance at an evening's service, Tom was visiting the monsignor.

The office door was suddenly flung open, startling both men.

A woman stood at the entrance, dressed in a gown that had been stylish some fifteen years earlier. A large lavender hat with a heavy veil hid her face. A light-colored Negro man in a chauffeur's uniform held the door for her. Both men knew without being told that they were in the presence of the town's notorious madam: Mrs. Margaret Lytle.

"I've seen every preacher in this damn town, and now it's your turn, Father Richards," she announced without preamble while the two priests forgot their manners and, in their astonishment, remained seated. Tom Byrne had heard of Margaret Lytle but had never expected to meet her.

His Eminence coughed. "Come in, Mrs. Lytle. What can I do for you?" He began to rise but sat back down quickly as she motioned him to do so. She moved into the room with an imperial air and sat in a chair next to Father Tom, raising her veil. Both she and Tom Byrne sat facing His Eminence across his desk.

And so began one of the strangest chapters of Father Tom Byrne's life. In return for Father Richards' agreement to consult and counsel with his fellow ministers regarding recent pronouncements concerning a certain gentlemen's club, which had come from a variety of pulpits though not from St. Michael's, Margaret Lytle agreed to sponsor ten of the Negro children from St. Timothy's. Her sponsorship extended not only to their boarding costs in town but also $12 for each child each semester for clothing and school supplies.

Tom Byrne was not quite sure how it had come about but accepted his and the children's good fortune and offered to provide Mrs. Lytle with an annual accounting.

She shook her head. "I can tell an honest and good man from a mile away, Tom Byrne," she said in her imperial manner. Tom understood he was in the presence of a strong-willed and independent businesswoman. Margaret Lytle concluded briskly, "I'll need no accounting from you."

Nevertheless, he had given her one with samples of the children's schoolwork and grainy photographs taken with his Kodak Rainbow folding camera. He was to follow this routine throughout the years.

Tom had therefore discovered himself to be more than astonished when Drew confided his early life at Mrs. Lytle's. He had fought to keep his expression bland as the boy had talked and had said nothing.

Drew assumed that a priest would be innocent about things of a sexual nature, but of course, he was wrong. Tom had experienced all the passions and lusts of any young man, even to the point where he and Sister Novice Mary Margaret had fallen in love. Tom knew that their transgression—which resulted in her pregnancy, removal from the sisterhood for her, and a disciplinary transfer for him—was doubly a tragedy. Later, when the baby was stillborn, both Tom and Mary Margaret wept that God had so summarily terminated a life that they, in their sin, had so thoughtlessly started.

As Tom grew older, the lusts of the flesh diminished and finally disappeared altogether. Mary Margaret eventually became a teacher in the church school of the Archdiocese of Galveston and died in a great September storm at the threshold of the twentieth century.

The clothing Tom provided Drew had not, of course, come from local families. The trousers, shirts, and shoes Tom Byrne now gave Drew had come from his "benefactor" in Little Rock. It made no difference to Drew, who had been delighted with the new clothing.

"I can take you to Little Rock if you still want to go," Father Tom said at breakfast the morning after the storm, "but not until next week. You are welcome to stay here until then."

Drew cast his eyes down when Father Tom made his offer. "Ah, sure thing, Father," he said. Tom's eyes narrowed for the briefest of instants. "Or you could stay here for a while," he said, his voice becoming brighter. "We have loads of chores that need to be done. My nephew, Charly, is coming soon. He's a policeman in Dallas. Maybe I could ask him to look into your, ah, special situation, you know, better to know the facts, right?"

Drew had experienced a start of anxiety when the word *policeman* was used. But he'd already decided to trust Father Tom. *OK,* he thought, *let's take this one step further.*

"Yes sir," Drew answered. "I'd like to stay here. I'll work for my room and board."

# Chapter 20

## A New Life

TOM BYRNE ASKED Drew after breakfast the next day, "Would you be interested in attending church services here?"

"I don't know much about Catholics," Drew answered honestly, "but I want to go to church, so the answer is yes, I'd like to attend."

"I promise that we Catholics are nice people," Father Tom said.

Mrs. Calumet poured each of them another cup of coffee and then busied herself drawing water from the single tap on the back porch.

"I don't want you to have to sleep on that old divan," Tom said. "The church used to have a live-in handyman who stayed in the shed out back, and when they strung the electricity to this house, they put a line out to the shed too. Maybe we can fix it up, clean it out and all, and it'll be private-like, and you can live there for a while." He added a thought, reflecting on Drew's telling about his life the night before, "This shed has flooring and is likely a little more comfortable than the shed in Union City that you told me about."

Furniture—of a sort—had been found, dusted, and cleaned. The window screens had been repaired. When they'd finished, the shed/room had been made as comfortable as limited resources could have made it. Drew thought it was a good place for him to call home. Father Tom placed a tiny crucifix on one of the walls; and he, Drew, and Mrs. Calumet had a short blessing ceremony.

"You need to know," Father Tom said at lunch one day soon after Drew had moved into the little shed/room, "that our parishioners here at St. Timothy's are Negroes."

"That doesn't bother me," Drew said immediately. "But, Father, aren't there white Catholics in this neighborhood?"

"To be sure, but they mostly go to mass in town. Those who can't travel, for one reason or another, sometimes call me to come to their house, and I say mass for them. It seems white people in the neighborhood around here won't go into a, well, they call it a nigger church."

In addition to Father Tom and Drew, there were seven other white faces that attended Sunday services at St. Timothy's.

The convent, eight miles from St. Timothy's, was on 150 acres of land left to the church by a wealthy widowed parishioner. The Sisters of the Holy Sepulcher had been granted ownership; and now a population of seven nuns ran the place and bred, raised, and showed Norwegian Shetlands. The bloodlines of their horses were prized and becoming known nationally.

The convent's mother superior was a crusty lady of indeterminate age. She reminded Drew of the librarian in Union City, Ursula Schultz. The good sister tried mightily to appear intimidating, but Drew sensed that she had a wide streak of kindness, which she tried to hide within her stern appearance. He instinctively liked and trusted her.

That first Sunday, Drew asked Father Tom about the nuns. He had noticed them walking.

"Yes, they walk every Sunday," Tom answered. "They have a tractor at their convent and a truck that they use to pull horse trailers around to the shows and all, but Mother Superior feels it is unseemly for all of them to ride in the truck. So they walk. I used to pick them up in my car—it's not quite large enough for them all—but now that the parish has grown, I'm too busy on Sunday mornings. Sometimes one of the parish families will give them a ride but not often. Most of our families don't own automobiles. A few have farm trucks, but most have only mule-drawn wagons."

"I could give the sisters a ride," Drew said.

Tom Byrne's eyebrows went up.

"Well, you'd have to loan me your car," Drew said, smiling. "You remember I told you I was learning to drive when I stayed at Mama Rose's?" He added somewhat tenuously, "I'm not very good. I'll need lessons, but I'd like to try it."

"Well, I don't know why not," Tom answered with a sound of hearty agreement in his voice. "If four of them could crowd in, one in the front with you and three in the backseat, then the remaining three could come in their farm truck. They could be at church earlier, and goodness knows I need help getting things ready for the service. As soon as I get some time, let's have some driving lessons."

The next afternoon, Drew was replacing the hinges on one of the doors inside the main church building when Father Tom interrupted, "Let's go start our driving lessons now. You can finish those hinges later."

Drew had never had the controls of an automobile explained. What he knew he had learned by observing Maynard. His principal problems had been coordinating the shifting and clutch while still keeping his eyes on the road. He tended to focus on his feet and hands as he depressed the pedal and moved the shifting lever while the car roamed about the roadway on its own. Maynard had, more than once, screamed as Drew steered the car toward a ditch or tree.

Father Tom patiently explained the controls and, behind the wheel, showed how the clutch, accelerator, and shifting should be coordinated. There was an added complication for this automobile: it had four forward gears instead of the more standard three. Reverse was in a somewhat awkward position.

Drew understood quickly and, with a little relief, understood what he had been doing wrong in Mama's car. They practiced on the drive, going up and down, each laughing as mistakes were made. Several times, Father Tom clapped and cheered when Drew mastered some particularly complicated maneuver.

The lesson ended after about a half hour, both laughing at Drew's clumsiness and inability to maintain the car onto the graveled driveway. Drew promised Father Tom that he would get better, and Tom gave him permission to practice alone in the car when chores had been completed. He was not to exit onto the county road without someone in the car with him.

The following Sunday afternoon, Drew asked Sister Arabella if she could help with his driving lessons and work with him. When it was time for her and Mother Superior to return to the convent, she asked Drew to drive them.

Drew did fairly well. Mother Superior only screamed twice, and he returned to St. Timothy's by himself, driving slowly and carefully.

Several days later, Tom interrupted one of Drew's chores and directed him to the car. They exited the drive onto the county road. Drew's shifting had improved. Tom opened the windshield and asked Drew to try a little speed. Drew pressed on the accelerator pedal, and the car surged ahead. Wind whistled through the car. When the speedometer showed forty miles per hour, Drew took his foot off the pedal and coasted to a stop at the side of the road.

Both Drew and the old priest had been exhilarated at the speed and laughed as though experiencing a rare thrill. Father Tom clapped his hands.

"More! More!" the priest sang out. "Do it some more!"

Drew smiled. "I think I'll need a little more practice in your car before I try more speed. That was fun! Father, your car has a lot of power! And it's so smooth! Mama Rose's car was rough. You could feel every bump in the road, and it wouldn't go more than thirty-five, and that was when it was rolling downhill," Drew ended on a joking note.

"You know, Drew," Father Tom said, "I'm really getting too old to drive. I've nearly run into the ditch several times these last few months. When I have to drive after dark, these old eyes have trouble seeing the road. I need a driver."

"I'd love to drive you," Drew answered.

"Well, you'd still have chores to do. We haven't had a handyman at St. Timothy's for a long time now, and things are falling apart," Father Tom assured him.

"I'll be your driver. And I'll try to do whatever chores need to be done. I don't have handyman experience, but maybe some of the men of the church can give me instructions on Sundays, after the service."

So the white face of Drew began blending into the fabric of the tiny rural black parish. He met several white farm families, but as Father Tom had warned, they did not come to church.

In addition to driving Tom around in his visits to parishioners and giving the sisters rides to church, Drew, along with Sister Arabella, began assembling a church choir. After church services, when families were visiting, Drew and Sister Arabella gathered the children together and taught songs from the hymnal as well as spirituals. They planned to use these as entertainment for church socials and similar gatherings.

Drew recalled some of his early lesson in tap dancing at Mrs. Lytle's and began teaching several of the children a few elementary steps.

One day, Father Tom went into town and talked to the local school officials and was given lesson plans and was loaned a few school books. Sister Arabella began using these to bring Drew to grade level, making up for the school he had missed during the past year. Both Tom and the Sister were astonished at how quickly Drew absorbed the lessons.

Harvests that fall had been good, and when Drew proposed a church social as a celebration, the congregation eagerly participated. The children provided entertainment, with Drew leading the children's singing and tap dancing, while Sister Arabella played the piano.

It seemed to Tom that Drew's presence at St. Timothy's had somehow brought the congregation closer together. He felt they were becoming a true church family. Other Negro families who had not regularly attended mass began doing so. The men of St. Timothy's had begun talking of adding another room to the school for a fourth-grade class. Sister Arabella had volunteered to teach.

Somehow, Drew had made this all come about, not because he'd planned it but because of his trust in his mentors and the people of the congregation. They brought out Drew's natural friendliness and easy manner, and that encouraged others to enjoy one another's company.

# Chapter 21

◆◇━━●◆◇◆●━━◆◇

## *Meetings in Little Rock*

O N THE SAME fall day Tom was giving Drew his driving lesson, Catherine Ryan Browning was meeting in her husband's Little Rock office with a private investigator she had hired, a man named J. William McWilliams.

"I'm at a dead end," the prematurely gray J. William confessed. "I've had people throughout central and northern Louisiana, as well as southern Arkansas, looking for the boy, and nothing has turned up. I've sent people back to Union City, and they have talked to everyone we could find that had any sort of relationship with the boy. We even talked to an old ex-vaudeville player, now a hermit of sorts living in the woods around Union City. My people have found nothing. It is plain and simple. We have lost track of him. Barring some unforeseen and possibly lucky circumstance, we aren't going to find him."

"What did the, ah, old hermit have to do with Drew?" Catherine asked.

"Oh, that's an interesting thing," J. William answered. "It seems that Drew and a colored boy named Leon frequented the hermit's home. He said he taught the boys self-defense. He also said he taught the boys what he remembered of his own tap-dancing days onstage in New York. One summer the boys had a shoe-shine stand at the railroad depot, and they sang and danced, trying to encourage men getting off the train to get their shoes shined."

"I never knew about that," Catherine said, grinning at this unknown facet of Drew's life and picturing the boys at the depot. "I was in Union City at the time, so I maybe should have known."

She became serious once again and changed the subject, "What's happening on the inquest issue in Union City?"

"There's been an election. Judge McCoy has been replaced. The new judge is busily going about cleaning up old business that he says

McCoy simply ignored for whatever reason. Also, there is a lot of talk around Union City about the Klan. They know Drew witnessed the school burning and that he could testify and identify many of them."

"So you think the Klan is still looking for Drew?" Catherine asked.

"I would expect that they are," J. William said. Then he continued, "McCoy issued a summons for Drew to appear, but it seems the Klan squelched it. The new judge says he's going to tell the sheriff to follow up on that summons and find Drew and then reopen proceedings. We can hope that the Klan does not find him first."

McWilliams glanced at a notebook. "Also, the warrant that was issued when the boy's mother declared him a runaway is still operational."

Catherine looked dismayed. Since receiving Ursula Schultz's letter earlier in the year, telling of Drew's disappearance, Catherine's concerns about his safety had increased. After several months of making calls and trying to work on her own, Catherine talked to her husband and hired J. William.

"Also," the investigator continued, "there was a shooting down in Louisiana at some old fortune-teller's place, way out in the country. She was involved in illegal gambling and is an associate of some sort with a bootlegger. Anyway, one of the men shot down at whatever happened that night died. Apparently, one of the servants of that old fortune-teller also died, and another was badly injured. Mama Rose herself, well, she's still in the hospital and not expected to live. The sheriff is calling it murder. Everyone who knows anything has clammed up."

Catherine was close to tears. She shook her head, wondering what this had to do with Drew.

The investigator continued, "There is quite a bit of evidence that a boy answering Drew's description lived at the gambling place for a number of months, but he is nowhere to be found now. The sheriff down there asked a judge to issue two warrants, one for the boy whose name they do not know and the other for a man named Haskell. Right now, they're looking for the boy as a witness."

"The bootlegger, a man named Reggie Masterson, is also looking for Drew. I haven't been able to find any details on why yet. I've been told that a great deal of money was missing after the shooting, but there's no hard evidence that I can find."

"And we still have no idea where Drew is," Catherine said, feeling a little hopeless.

"No. However, if we don't know where he is, it's probable that no one in law enforcement knows either. You know, there is a line of thought you could pursue that would lead one to the conclusion that it might be better, for Drew, if he simply disappeared—took another name, went to another state maybe," the investigator explained. Catherine considered this for a moment while he continued, "If the law can't find him, and if Reggie Masterson can't find him, and if those Klan hotheads from Union City can't find him, well, I think he'd be the better for it to simply disappear."

"Miss Catherine," J. William went on, "all this has cost a lot of money. I know you and the senator are concerned about the boy, but shouldn't we call off my search, for the time being, at least?"

"So Reggie Masterson is also looking for Drew?" Catherine asked, seemingly ignoring the question.

"Apparently so," the investigator replied. Her sidestep did not escape his notice, but she was the customer, after all.

"I told you about the allegedly missing money. It seems Reggie may believe that Drew has it."

"I talked with Theodore again yesterday," Catherine said once more, changing the subject. She was finding it hard to keep her thoughts organized.

"Senator Browning?"

"Yes. He's in Washington this week, but we talked long distance. He said he's talked to the Justice Department, and they've assigned a case number." Catherine folded her hands on top of the desk. She looked J. William in the eye, resolution settling there.

"What does that mean?"

"It means that the case will be given to the next available agent, but nothing will happen soon. When the Justice Department agent gets the case, he'll begin by reviewing the files. That will take several months. But the Justice Department is interested primarily because of the school burning. The issue of a runaway boy is only peripheral."

"So no matter who finds the boy, he's still likely to be in danger. Would the Justice Department protect him?" J. William asked. This case was already full of more knots than he would have thought possible for simply a runaway kid.

"I just don't know," Catherine answered. "You know, the senator is a distant cousin of the First Lady. He told me he'd talked to her, and she agreed to let the Justice Department know that she has a personal interest in the case. Maybe that will help."

In the end, Catherine and J. William McWilliams agreed. The search for Drew was to be called off, at least until there was more information. As he was leaving the senator's office, J. William stopped at the door and turned. "Oh, one more thing. It probably doesn't mean anything. However, the name of Father Richards of St. Michaels here in Little Rock keeps coming up but not in any way that indicates he knows anything. I haven't interviewed him. I just thought it was interesting that I keep running across the name of a Little Rock churchman while I'm rattling around in southern Arkansas and northern Louisiana."

J. William paused. He had no hard information but only a suspicion. He considered what he should say.

"Maybe he's just good at helping wayward souls," he concluded, somewhat lamely.

Several hours later, the investigator boarded a train for St. Louis.

The wife of Arkansas senator Theodore Browning thought about J. William's final comment for several days. She made up her mind. She would visit St. Michaels. Maybe it was fruitless, but she had no other plan.

Catherine parked the senator's car and walked to the rear entrance, looking for the monsignor's office. As she approached the door, an elderly white-haired priest, extraordinarily thin, opened it. He was wearing a black suit, a clerical collar, and was putting on his hat. Something about his face, kind and caring, made her want to know more about him.

She asked about the monsignor's office.

"It is right this way," the priest said, speaking in a somewhat entertaining lilt. He added, "I'm just leaving after my own meeting. I'll walk with you back to his office. Do you have an appointment?"

"No," Catherine replied. "I called, but no one answered. My name is Catherine Browning."

Had she been looking directly at the elderly priest when she said her name, she would have seen a change in his expression. He knew he was talking not only to the wife of a US senator but someone from Drew's past. As it was, he had already turned and was motioning her down the hallway. He knocked once at an ornate walnut-carved door and then opened it. "Mrs. Catherine Browning is here," the priest said, ushering Catherine into the room and starting to close the door.

"Yes, Mrs. Browning," Father Richards said, rising. Tom closed the door.

He did not leave. He sat in a straight chair in the hallway outside the monsignor's office. He felt that something unusual was about to happen, something that would impact Drew's life. He did not have long to wait.

The door opened. Monsignor Richards did not seem surprised that Tom was waiting. "Father Byrne," he said, "I think you will want to meet this young lady."

"Surely," Tom said as he entered and closed the door.

Catherine was sitting in one of the two chairs in front of the monsignor's desk. As he returned to his chair, Father Richards said, "Father Byrne, I would like for you to meet the wife of our senator, Mrs. Browning. She was once a teacher in Union City. Her name then was Catherine Ryan."

He turned to Catherine. "Mrs. Browning, this is Father Tom Byrne who has a parish in southern Arkansas, the region called the Arkansas Delta." Tom extended his hand in a courtly manner, and she took it.

As Father Tom sat down, Catherine turned to Father Richards, her eyes flashing. There was the beginning of a thought. Why would he mention Union City? She made the connection quickly and blurted breathlessly, "I've figured it out! You two know where Drew is, don't you?"

"Mrs. Browning," Monsignor Richards said, nodding and smiling, "we have a lot to discuss, we three. But at this point, I will admit only that we know of an eleven-year-old Caucasian boy who has told us his name is Drew." Tears began to trickle down Catherine's cheeks.

She fumbled in her purse, withdrew a handkerchief, and dabbed at her eyes. "Oh, I've been searching everywhere for so long! Here, look!" She fumbled with her purse again and this time pulled a small envelope from its recesses. It held a photograph of her and a young boy, standing on the wooden porch of a run-down grocery store, with the photographer's shadow extending across the foreground. Drew had shown Father Tom his copy of that same photograph.

"We've been told a lot," the monsignor continued, "or rather Father Tom has been told a lot. The boy is safe. He has been in danger, and we have tried to protect him," Father Richards said, trying to reassure the well-dressed woman in front of him.

"Much of what we know was told," Father Richards said, "in the form of a confessional disclosure. Therefore, what was said must be treated by us as sacred and confidential. We believe it is likely the boy, Drew, will want us to disclose to you what we've been told, but we will have to talk to him first."

Catherine burst into tears.

The two priests nodded and smiled sympathetically. Tom Byrne patted Catherine's hand.

"Let's set up a time when you can travel to Father Byrne's church," Monsignor Richards said, reassuringly. "I suspect you and Drew will have a lot to talk about. But we must first talk to the boy."

"I am sure he will want us to tell you everything," Tom Byrne repeated some of the monsignor's words, "and that he will want you to come visit at St. Timothy's."

Then he added. "And I too want you to come to St. Timothy's. Let's plan on you coming to visit very soon."

# Chapter 22

## Visitors to St. Timothy's

FROM THE TIME Drew had entered St. Timothy's on that first night, as Tom Byrne heard the boy's story over supper, he had thought that here might be an answer to prayers he had offered to God.

Tom cared very much for his nephew Charly, his only living relative. Charly had been devastated by the death of his wife, now more than ten years in the past. At the time of her death, Charly had begun drifting, his life purposeless. He was still drifting. It seemed to Tom that Charly was searching for something. Perhaps it was not for another woman, but certainly he was searching for love, for some way to put meaning and purpose back into his life.

Perhaps Drew could in some way help this lonely man. In turn, it would seem that perhaps Drew could find safety with Charly. Tom's initial ideas had been hazy but were becoming clearer in his mind. He needed time to think the issues through and seek guidance from God.

This led to two broad currents of concern converging. Tom thought that his prayers might soon be answered, and he praised God and wondered at His mysterious ways. First, though, he would have to see how each, Drew and Charly, would feel about the other.

On a Saturday shortly after Drew's arrival at St. Timothy's, Charly's blue Ford turned into the drive.

Men in the congregation had instructed Drew, and he was engaged in systematically removing the old pews, one at a time, into the building in the rear churchyard used for maintenance. He set about sanding them down to bare wood preparatory to staining and varnishing. He looked up from his sanding as the car had turned off the road. His coppery hair was matted and wet; drops of perspiration ran down his nose that pleasantly cool autumn afternoon.

Drew had been told about the visit, but he also knew Charly was a policeman. He experienced a start of concern, deep in his abdomen.

He stopped his work for a while when Charly came up and was introduced by Tom.

Charly quickly pitched in and helped Drew with sanding the church pew. As they worked, drops of perspiration appeared on Charly's brow, and sweat began soaking through his shirt. Charly showed Drew some techniques with the sanding blocks that actually made the job easier. Later, both now dripping with perspiration, Charly and Drew carried the pew into the church for staining and varnishing at a later time.

As they put the pew into place, Charly said, "That's enough work for today. You need a break. I need a break. How about playing some ball?" He went to his car and retrieved a football.

Drew was astonished by his actions. He had never held a football in his hands. He had certainly never seen a game. He had no idea what to do with the ball.

Charly patiently showed him how the ball was handled, and the two began tossing it back and forth. The closest Drew had ever come to playing a game with a ball was kickball at Catherine Ryan's school, but the older boys had tended to play among themselves at recess and only included the younger children when their teacher demanded that they do so. Throwing an oddly shaped ball back and forth, with a grown man, was an entirely new experience.

Drew watched Charly carefully and tried to mimic his handling of the ball. He learned quickly that he needed a lot of practice. That first afternoon Drew found it was fun to toss a ball back and forth. Charly ran from Drew, turned sideways, and caught Drew's toss, explaining to Drew that the maneuver was called passing. Drew found it hard to accept that simply tossing a ball back and forth could be fun, but it was.

Supper that night was a happy affair. Charly talked about his home and his life in Dallas. He had missed the radio broadcast that afternoon of a college football game, but Charly declared that teaching Drew a little football was better than any game he could have listened to.

Drew had enjoyed tossing the football back and forth. He also enjoyed the supper talk. While he carried his end of the conversation, he also studied Father Tom's nephew.

Charly was a big man, tall, with the only evidence of his approaching middle age being a slight thickening of the waist. His face was round, like his uncle's, with a hint of rosy glow in his cheeks. His eyes matched his uncle's eyes perfectly; they were bluer than a summer sky. Unlike Tom, who had a thick mass of hair though he was in his seventies, Charly's light-brown hair was thin on top and he'd cut it short all around so that his incipient baldness was clearly evident.

Drew's impression of Charly was that he cared not a lick what others might think of him. He was what he was with no overtones of bluster or braggadocio, completely unselfconscious. He liked to laugh, showing his white teeth, and he genuinely cared about the feelings and opinions of others.

After supper, while the winter sun was setting, Father Tom went to his office in the church to finish preparations for the coming Sunday services. Drew and Charly walked around the church grounds and stopped at the iron fence that surrounded the graveyard. Drew showed Charly the grave markers he had carefully cleaned and righted. He had replaced several of the old rotted and illegible wood markers with new ones from treated wood one of the men in the church had supplied. Using church records, he had carved the proper information about the souls interred there.

That evening the sky was full of color as the sun began its journey to the other side of the planet. The facade of the church was washed in gold, much as it had been the first time Drew had seen it. As they leaned on the iron fence and watched the sunset, Charly pulled a Chesterfield from a package in his shirt pocket, lit it, and said, "Drew, I want to know about your life. How did you come to St. Timothy's?"

Drew was silent for a few minutes. He was unsure how much he should tell him and how much he could trust this man. Just then, something clicked inside of Drew. He realized that he and Charly were somehow developing an easy camaraderie. He decided he liked Charly. He also realized that, in much the same way as he knew he could trust Father Tom, he knew he could also trust this man.

He told Charly about his life.

Charly did not say anything while Drew talked. He simply smoked and listened, lighting one cigarette from the stub of the previous. He noted that despite the emotion evident in Drew's body language and face, he nonetheless kept his voice steady. There was a noticeable lack of tears. Several times, however, Charly felt tears of his own starting. He held them back.

Drew left nothing out, but neither did he embellish. Unlike his telling of the story to Father Tom, this time Drew kept the narrative organized as he related the facts of his life that had brought him to this southern part of the Arkansas Delta. He discovered that he could tell Charly even the more sordid facts without embarrassment or resorting to euphemisms. He was unsure why he felt as easy as he did when he related these parts of his story.

When Drew finished, Charly said, "I guess that was a little strange, one guy asking another about things, but I wanted to know. Thanks for telling me."

Drew nodded. "How about you?"

"You mean my life? OK, I guess that's fair enough."

Charly was a widower and had been so for ten years. He and his beloved Rebecca had married with the full blessings of the church and had waited confidently for children that were sure to follow.

Charly chuckled grimly, mostly to himself. "I guess the good Lord knew things we didn't because we never had the children we wanted."

Drew kept silent.

"It was a cancer," Charly said. "She was very sick for a long time. Then she died."

"How long were you married?" Drew asked.

"Five years. The first three were wonderful. When she was sick, though—"his voice trailed away. Drew noticed that Charly's eyes were full of tears.

She had died in agony as her body deteriorated and the pain that drugs could not assuage increased. "I was almost glad," Charly said, "you know, when she died. I knew she was free of pain."

Charly was not free of pain, though. He grieved and was devastated. He was grieving still. Charly had not looked at a woman since Rebecca left him, though this last fact was left unsaid.

Drew waited as Charly's emotions seemed to subside. "Tell me about being a policeman," Drew asked. He thought, *If Charly is going to arrest me, take me back to Union City or Claiborne, now will be the time.* He felt a tightening in his midsection.

Charly did not arrest Drew. Instead, he simply continued talking.

Charly told Drew about his job as a Dallas policeman and how he had one of the few patrol cars in Dallas that was equipped with a two-way radio, although, he said, other cars would soon be so equipped. He liked his job, he said, but that now he was approaching the twenty-year mark, maybe it was time to think about retirement.

"I don't know," Charly said. "I'm still a young guy. Maybe I'll stay on a few years after retirement. On the other hand, maybe there's a better job I could get. I'll have to think about it."

Charly went on, segueing into his boyhood in New Jersey and his life in the house that he and his wife had built in Dallas's Oak Cliff. He told about his roses.

"I take her a bouquet, you know, almost every Sunday."

"Rebecca?" Drew questioned.

"Yes, yes," Charly answered, smiling. "She always enjoyed them so much. I just know she can see them now. I take a lot of care, putting them together just right. I leave them there, so she can see them until I come back."

Charly, Drew learned, was more than enthusiastic about sports. He followed professional sports teams, especially baseball in season, and played in a softball league in Dallas's White Rock Park. He also followed American college football. Games were broadcast over the radio, and Charly listened to each broadcast.

The Milky Way soared across the indigo blue of the Arkansas sky when Charly finished telling of his life. Drew and Charly stood together, neither talking. Both thinking about the other.

Father Tom exited the church, waved, and headed to his little house.

Charly left the following morning. He would return several times.

Monday, December 20, in the Arkansas Delta that year, 1937, was clear, cold, and windy. Fields were brown, for there had been a light freeze. The leaves of the huge maple behind St. Timothy's had not yet fallen; and the bright fall colors, against the blue of the Arkansas winter sky, provided a backdrop for the white clapboard building that distracted from its plainness.

After a Friday night supper, Father Tom asked Drew to come into his office. "I need to tell you a few things," the elderly priest said.

"In Little Rock, some weeks ago, Father Richards and I met with an interesting lady. Her name is Catherine Browning."

Drew looked up. His eyes brightened. "You did? How is she? Has she seen Mardie? Max? Reverend Thomas?" The words spilled out of him. The need to touch even a tiny piece of his old life surged through him like a mighty wave, threatening to overwhelm all else.

"Hold on, hold on," the priest said, smiling and holding his hands up. "Let me tell you about her and your friends, and then we need to get back on the subject. Your Miss Catherine is well. She is now, as you may have heard, the wife of Senator Browning." Drew nodded, listening carefully, barely keeping his enthusiasm in check. "She works with several organizations," Tom went on, "but primarily with the National Association for the Advancement of Colored People, the NAACP. It seems that both she and the senator are quite passionate about Negro rights. She's happy in her work and deeply in love with Senator Browning."

Drew realized Father Tom was working toward some point and wanted to be careful how he presented it. "I didn't see your Mardie," Tom continued with what was evidently a speech that had required a lot of planning, "or Max—isn't his name Eddie?—or Reverend Thomas, but Mrs. Browning has seen them. They did not know that you were safe, but of course, now they do. They do not yet know where you are."

It was a long speech for Tom. "Your friends are well," he concluded.

Drew remained sitting. A feeling of unease came over him, but he held his head up and looked Father Tom in the eye, waiting for whatever was to come.

"The three of us—Mrs. Browning, Charly, and I—may have a plan for you. One that we hope will keep you safe so that you can go to school and live a normal life," he began. He studied Drew's face for a reaction.

Drew continued to remain quiet, waiting for Tom to continue.

"You know you need your schooling. It's already nearly Christmas. You've missed half of the current school year, not to mention the past spring semester."

"Are you telling me I have to leave St. Timothy's?" Drew had come to the conclusion before Tom could say it. Tom waited for a moment, knowing what he had to say.

"Yes. All of us want you to think about living with Charly, in Dallas."

Drew did not know what to say. "He might not want me," he blurted.

Father Tom chuckled. "I don't think so. I think he wants very badly for you to come and live with him. I believe you two will get along splendidly. I want you to think about it. Mrs. Browning wants you to think about it."

Drew nodded, silent, sitting with his hands clasped between his knees.

Father Tom continued, "None of the three of us know how your, ah, legal situation can be resolved. Mrs. Browning has been talking to an attorney, and Charly has talked to a friend of his, a Judge McGowan, in Dallas."

Drew still said nothing, waiting for the priest to continue.

"You see," Father Tom went on, "while all of us work to clear your name, it seems best for you to live in another state, not Arkansas or Louisiana. You are not safe here."

He continued, "Mrs. Browning has information that the Klan from Union City is looking for you. She has also learned that the bootlegger, Reggie Masterson, is looking for you, and the sheriff in Claiborne Parish is looking. We believe that if you were in Texas, under another name, then you'd be fairly safe while everything got worked out."

Drew interrupted, "I want to keep my name: Drew."

"Only your last name would need to be changed," the priest assured him.

Father Tom moved his hands in a gesture of impatience. He did not want to be more specific until more information was available. He changed the subject.

"Oh, I almost forgot," Father Tom retreated. "Mrs. Browning is going to be visiting us first thing tomorrow morning. I told her that I would have to ask you if you wanted to see her," he said as casually as a greeting. He looked at Drew with an expression between innocent curiosity and sincere amusement.

Drew nodded, thinking that he would move mountains in order to see his Miss Catherine.

After breakfast the next morning, when Catherine turned the senator's car into the drive, Drew ran down the slight hill. Catherine stopped, opened the door, and tried to stand as Drew hugged her.

# Chapter 23

❖ ⸎ ❖

## *1938*

T WO DAYS AFTER the New Year, Drew and Father Tom set out for Texarkana. "You drive, Drew," Father Tom said. "After last night, I'm very tired." Drew obligingly slid under the wheel. He was now much more confident about his driving abilities. It was a sunny, clear winter day; and while they'd planned to start early, Mrs. Calumet's niece's baby had decided to arrive even earlier. Father Tom and the convent's mother superior had stayed up most of the night.

Before they left, the radio had foretold of an approaching cold front. After Father Tom entered the car, he pulled a lap robe over himself and fell asleep quickly as Drew drove through the country lanes to the paved highway.

Texarkana, Tom had explained to Drew, was an interesting place. The state line between Texas and Arkansas ran down the middle of the city's main street so that by crossing from one side of the street to the other, one could go from Arkansas to Texas. At around ten that night, Charly would be waiting in his car, parked on a side street on the Texas side. Tom would park on the Arkansas side, and Drew would simply walk across the street. Neither man would therefore have transported anyone, especially not an under-aged young man, across state lines.

After about an hour, Father Tom awoke. Drew asked if he wanted to stop for coffee or anything, but Tom shook his head, asked if Drew was tired of driving, and then relaxed again as the miles passed.

"How about singing a little tune, Father?" Drew asked.

"You sing something, Drew. If I like it I might join in."

"Swell," he replied happily.

Drew began with a favorite, one he had heard frequently over the radio during the last several months and over the loudspeakers at the record store in town in one of his rare visits. He wondered if Father Tom would know the words. He knew from church services that the good

Father had an excellent singing voice. He wanted to see how he would do on popular music. Drew launched into the song.

But he changed the lyrics. His rhyming was awkward but clearly a tribute to his passenger. Both Father Tom and Drew laughed at the butchering of the popular lyrics and at the times Drew's voice had cracked. Then the priest added his own voice as they cruised down the road, and he too changed the lyrics around, making Drew laugh.

They continued on in this manner, each laughing at the other's jokes and changing the lyrics of first one popular song, then another. Sometimes, they sang together in harmony. Other times they serenaded each other. The miles passed quickly as they rolled through town after town. Several long stretches of highway were paved, but others were graveled. The singing and the laughter reminded Drew strongly of his times with Reverend Thomas, and suddenly he missed him more than he could have said. He let Father Byrne continue his song for an instant as he sat quietly and steered.

There was a maroon-and-black Packard in the rearview mirror.

Drew frowned. Father Tom continued singing while Drew tried to figure out how long the Packard had been behind them. The priest finished his song, laughing and clapping, and turned to Drew. It was then that he noticed something was amiss.

"What's wrong, Drew?" Father Tom asked.

"Don't turn around and look, but there's a big car behind us. I think it's been there for a long time," Drew said, his voice tight, but determined to be calm. "It looks like Reggie's car."

The Packard suddenly pulled from behind them and roared around the priest's car, leaving a trail of dust as it sped away.

"It's Reggie," Drew whispered.

"Are you sure?" Father Tom asked.

"I saw him. His hat was pulled down over his eyes, but I saw him. I'm sure. Besides, how many cars are there like that in this part of the world?"

Several hours earlier, Mrs. Calumet answered the ringing telephone mounted on the wall in the office parlor. "Hello?" she answered, somewhat loudly, for she distrusted a device that purported to transmit a human voice over vast distances. Surely, one could not speak in a normal tone of voice and expect the person on the other end of miles of wire to hear clearly.

She could hear an operator's voice telling the caller to deposit 35¢ for the first three minutes from El Dorado, and then she heard coins being dropped into a pay telephone.

A male voice said that he wanted to speak with Father Tom Byrne.

"He is not here," she shouted. She thought she could hear a very soft curse word under someone's breath.

"How can I reach him? It is quite urgent," the caller said.

"He is traveling. Who is this?"

"I'm Father Richards of St. Michael's. I am calling from Little Rock. Is he coming here?" Mrs. Calumet knew Father Richard's voice. This was not Father Richards. Moreover, she had heard the telephone operator use the words El Dorado.

"No. I heard him say he was going to Texarkana."

"Oh. Perhaps I can reach him in Texarkana. When do you expect him to arrive?"

She was now very suspicious but did not know what to do other than speak the truth.

"Not until late tonight," she again shouted. "And he is supposed to be back here tomorrow afternoon. You will have to call back then. Give me your name again. I will tell him you called."

The connection was abruptly terminated.

Drew and Father Tom had elected to drive through El Dorado and bypass Union City, even though they were sure no one would recognize Drew in a moving automobile. Still, there was no use in taking chances. The more southerly route to Texarkana also took them over highways that were generally in better condition.

They had not reckoned with highway construction operations. These had slowed them down considerably, and in one instance, they'd been forced into a long detour on a graveled county road. It was here that Drew first saw the maroon Packard.

As Reggie's car disappeared into the dust ahead of them, Father Tom said to Drew, "Keep driving. He may know where we are, but we also know where he is. So we both have an advantage." The priest began rummaging in the seat pockets behind him and withdrew several highway maps. Detour signs announced they were approaching the end of construction. Soon they would be on concrete pavement.

"Turn left at the next crossroad," Father Tom said, "before we come to the end of this detour." There was a momentary opening in oncoming traffic, and Drew turned left.

"Now go on up to that wide space up there, and let's turn the car around."

Drew pulled over and swung the car in a wide arc, stopping just short of the roadside ditch, grinding the gears as he found reverse, backed the car, shifted into first, and completed the turn.

"At the detour turn right."

"That will take us back the way we were coming," Drew said.

"According to my map, if we return to El Dorado and go north and then west, we can bypass this construction. It may take Reggie an hour or more to figure out what we've done. By then, we can be forty or more miles from here."

"Won't that take us through Union City?"

"Yes, but we'll have to risk it if we're to outrun Reggie. You can hide in the backseat when we're close to Union City. I'll drive then. We'd planned that we might rest a little during the afternoon. My suggestion now is to keep driving."

"We're gonna need gas before too long," Drew said, eyeing the fuel gauge.

"Let's keep going as long as we can."

The bright and happy day now seemed dark and grim, although the sun still shone as brightly as before. Drew continued driving, watching as the indicator on the fuel gauge moved inexorably toward the *E*. Finally, he turned to Father Tom. "At the very next town, we've got to get gas."

Tom had him turn off the main highway. Three blocks over, they found a small grocery store with a hand-operated gasoline pump out front. "Keep on going," Father Tom said, "past the little store. Stop two blocks farther down and get out. I'll take the car back and fill it with gasoline. No one needs to see you." Drew nodded and exited the car when Tom told him to do so.

Later, Tom relinquished the wheel to Drew again. "Go two blocks farther down and turn right," Tom told him.

They zigzagged across country all that afternoon. Drew wondered if they were, in fact, drawing closer to Texarkana or if they were driving in circles. Shortly after sunset, Drew saw a sign in the car's headlights that announced an upcoming small town and that Texarkana was forty miles away. He told Tom, "I'm really tired of all this. Let's just make a run for it into Texarkana. We'll park on the busiest street around and dare Reggie to try anything."

Tom just shook his head and motioned to Drew to head south, past the city.

It was after dark when Tom turned the car into another gasoline station, telling the attendant to "fill'er up." Drew remained in the backseat, cap pulled low over his eyes. Father Tom exited the car to pay. "Where," Tom asked the attendant, "can I get something to eat around here?"

"The Dew Drop Inn," the attendant said as he cleaned the windshield. "It's just down the road. Best steaks in the county! Do you want your oil checked?"

The Dew Drop Inn was brightly lit, and the parking area around the little café was filled. Tom pulled the car to the rear and parked it in the shadows. He had long since removed his clerical collar, and he now removed his white collarless shirt and pulled from his luggage the most outlandish print shirt Drew had ever seen. He grinned self-consciously to Drew. "I don't want them to remember a priest. Is this colorful enough?" He chuckled. "You stay here. I'm going to buy us some sandwiches and Cokes. We'll eat them in the car."

It was nearly eleven when they pulled onto State Line Avenue in downtown Texarkana. The street appeared deserted as they rounded the new post office, constructed so as to straddle the boundary between Texas and Arkansas. Tom parked three blocks from the post office.

"This is it," he said, turning to Drew. "Charly should be parked across the street in that alleyway over there." As he spoke, the headlights of a parked automobile came on then were extinguished. "That's him," Tom said.

"Father," Drew began, "I don't know how—"

"Sh!" the priest stopped him. "Thanks go to God."

"You've been mighty good to me," Drew said.

"Drew," Tom Byrne said, "you've given more to St. Timothy's than you've taken. Many of us are beholden to you. Now, let's thank the Lord for our safe passage." He bowed his head, and Drew followed suit. The priest said a short prayer, asking God to grant Drew safe passage and a good life. Just as he was about to say amen, Drew interrupted.

"And, Lord," Drew prayed, "please grant Father Tom safe passage back to St. Timothy's."

"In the name of the Father, Son, and Holy Ghost," Father Tom concluded.

Drew pulled his luggage from the backseat of the car—the old knapsack and a small suitcase that had been in a closet of Father Tom's parsonage. "I'll never forget you," he whispered.

"Go with God," the priest whispered. Drew turned and ran across the deserted street. Halfway across, two items dropped from the knapsack. Drew turned and stopped and picked up the rusty tin box that had once been gaily colored and the wallet, whose importance he did not know. He stuffed both back into the knapsack and ran on to the dark car in the darker alleyway.

At about five thirty the next morning, Father Tom stopped his Graham-Paige at the side of the Dew Drop Inn and went in. He was still wearing his outlandish shirt. He sat in a booth at the rear of the diner.

As he was eating his pie, a man slid into the booth across from him and ordered coffee. He said, "Father Tom Byrne, I believe."

"So, Reggie Masterson, we meet at last," the priest said without looking up.

"Yes. I suppose you're not about to tell me the whereabouts of Drew Simmons."

"Not in the slightest."

"I checked the car. He's not there. My guess he's halfway to Dallas or Fort Worth or Houston by now."

Father Tom said nothing.

"Look," Reggie said, "I just wanna get back something he's got, something that's mine."

Again, Father Tom said nothing but continued nibbling at his pie, his head down.

"Look, he stole upward of $10,000 from me that night. He told you about that night, right?"

Tom couldn't help himself. He flinched at the amount.

"Yeah, I didn't think you knew about the money. So we know he didn't donate it to the church. What did he do with it?

"What I don't get is," Reggie continued, "him always so nicety-nice, so honest-like, those big blue eyes looking so innocent and all. Why'd he steal the money? It isn't like Mama didn't pay him well. She told me she'd given him upward of $300 as his cut when he helped with those games."

Finally, Tom put his fork down, took a sip of coffee, and looked at Reggie. "You'll never make me believe that boy stole money. I know he had some money. He kept it in a tin box, but that box wasn't anywhere near large enough to hold something like $10,000."

"And yet, I don't have the money. I'm sure the fellow I shot didn't have it, even though Drew threw the cash box at him. That box was empty. Remember, Padre, I was there."

A memory stirred. Tom was silent for a few moments, thinking of Drew's telling of that night of mayhem and terror. "Look, Reggie, I'm going to tell you something. Before I do, I need you to contact me if I'm right, and if so, I want you to tell me that Drew's safe from you or Mama Rose from now on."

"Mama Rose is dead. What if you're wrong?" The bootlegger did not sound as if he was prepared to make deals.

"Well, I need you to tell me that too. And if I'm wrong, I promise to help you find out what happened to your money."

"You can't trust me. I'm a bootlegger. I make my living by lying."

"Oddly, I think I can trust you. Your last statement tells me that."

"You're a sneaky old bastard, Padre. OK, you've got a deal." Reggie was grinning in spite of himself.

Tom put out his hand to Reggie. "Shake my hand and tell me that." Then, when the bootlegger and the priest had shaken hands, Father Tom said, "OK, Reggie. Here it is. That night, Drew had the cash box, all right, and a ledger. He ran through the woods. Did you ever think he wasn't running randomly but rather to a specific place?"

Reggie shook his head, wondering where the priest was going.

"Drew ran to one particular tree with a hollow in it about five or six feet above the ground. He'd hidden his knapsack and that little tin box we've both seen in that hollow. And he put your money in the hollow. I wouldn't be surprised if you don't also find that he folded the ledger and crammed it into the hollow. I know he'd used stones to keep squirrels or other varmints from nesting there, and I suspect he put the stones back over the entrance to keep them from your money. I think he was planning on throwing the cash box away in some other place in the woods. But the man you killed caught up to Drew before he could run away."

"I didn't kill the guy. I just shot him. He'd already shot me. It was turnabout fair play."

"Never mind. Drew threw the cash box at him, right?" The priest was quickly trying to ignore the blatant admissions to violence.

"Yeah, then I shot him. But the cash box was empty," Reggie repeated. He shrugged.

"Then where do you think Drew put the money?"

Reggie chewed on his lower lip. "Did Drew tell you this?"

"I never asked Drew many questions about that night," Tom said. "I'm making a lot of deductions from what he did tell, plus I know Drew. He would never steal."

Reggie leaned back and chuckled. "Yeah, he's an honest little prick. Mama always said he was too honest for his own good.

"OK, Padre. We have a deal, you and me. I'm gonna go back and check that tree out. If I find the money, I'll let you know. If I don't, I'll let you know," he said this last with a bit of finality. Father Tom did not want to know how he "would know" if the money wasn't there.

"I want you to do it in person. Don't telephone me. Don't send a telegram. Don't write. You come and see me," Father Tom said sternly.

Three weeks later, Reggie pulled into the drive at St. Timothy's one afternoon as Father Tom was pulling out. Reggie leaned out of the Packard and held his hand out, thumb up. He then reversed onto the county road, slipped the car into gear, and roared away, leaving a trail of dust behind him.

# Chapter 24

# Dallas

ON THE SAME dawn that Father Tom and Reggie Masterson were shaking hands in the Dew Drop Inn, Charly's blue Ford topped a slight rise and the Dallas skyline could be seen. Drew had been sleeping fitfully in the passenger seat while Charly had driven through the night.

"Wake up," Charly said. "Get your first look at Dallas."

Drew opened his eyes to a blue-and-gold dawn and saw the largest city he had ever seen. The rising sun behind the car highlighted the skyscrapers and gave the buildings a warm glow against the blue of the western sky. Drew was stunned at the sight of the magnificent skyline. Unbidden, words from "America the Beautiful" filled his mind.

Drew felt he was looking at one of the "alabaster cities" that made for a beautiful America. One building stood out from the others. It was taller and had a giant red sign on top. "Wow," Drew said, rubbing sleep out of his eyes. "What's that red sign? How tall is that building, anyway?"

"That's the Flying Red Horse, the emblem of the Magnolia Petroleum Company," Charly answered, smiling. "That's their home office. It's twenty-nine stories tall, the tallest in Dallas."

The car slowed. Charly pulled off the highway and into a small grove of trees, currently with bare limbs. There was a view of the skyline. "Drew, you and I need to talk, one more time," he said, grinning and switching off the motor. "Let's let the old bus rest for a minute. There'll be plenty of time later for you to tour Dallas."

Charly got out of the car and sat on a front fender. He lit a cigarette. Drew followed and sat on the opposite fender. Both looked at the city's skyline on the horizon before them.

"Drew," Charly said, not looking at him, "you need to know I'll never lie to you. You can always trust me." Drew somehow knew that he needed to remain absolutely silent and listen carefully.

Charly inhaled deeply on his cigarette and exhaled a large cloud of blue smoke. "Drew, I wanted you to come and live with me the first time we met and maybe even before we met when I began learning about you from my uncle. I'm still sure. I hope you believe this move to Texas, and to my house, is a good move for you. I want you to be happy and be able to go to school.

"I don't make much money," he went on, "but I guess you figured that. A policeman in a radio car earns about twenty-two hundred a year. That's not bad. Not good but not bad either. It's more than a lot of people make. I get by. I make the payments on the house, and I get all the bills paid. There's not a lot left over. Still, there's enough for me. There's enough for the two of us, for that matter. We can get by. You won't have to work or anything. I want you to concentrate on school."

"I've almost always had a job," Drew said.

"I didn't say you couldn't have a job," Charly said, grinning, "just that you didn't have to. You missed a lot of school last year. You might need some, ah, time off to do some 'catching up,' so to speak."

Drew nodded and grinned. "You may be right."

"And there's something else I gotta say," Charly said.

Drew smiled at this warm and caring man sitting on the fender of his car across from him, both of them feeling the heat of the cooling engine through the metal, which was beginning to become uncomfortable.

"What is it, Charly?"

"I want you to know that you're going to be safe with me. Safe from anything—anything at all, like what went on in Union City. Do you know what I mean?"

"I think so," Drew answered.

"Let me be plain," Charly said, his voice choked with emotion. "You are safe with me from anything like that Eugene fellow had in mind, OK?"

Drew turned and looked at Charly. "I was never worried about that."

"I hope not, but I felt it had to be said," Charly answered. "And," he went on, "you're going to be safe with me from anything that happened in Louisiana too, OK?"

Drew nodded his head.

"But to make that happen, we're going to have to change your last name," Charly said. "Father Tom talked to you about this, I hope. Tomorrow, I'm gonna take you downtown to meet with a judge I know. He's a friend of mine.

"He's gonna help get you into school. So that's why your name—just your last name—is gonna have to be changed, at least temporarily. So you be thinkin' about it, OK?"

Drew nodded again. "I don't want to be called Andrew. Can it be just Drew?"

"We'll still need a last name."

Charly continued, "Judge McGowan told me he has talked with the investigator Catherine Browning hired, and he has provided an affidavit that your mother cannot be found. So you will need someone appointed temporary guardian at least until you're eighteen. I told him I'd ask you if I could be that man. Drew, would that be all right with you?"

Drew looked again at Charly, still sitting on the fender, now lighting a new cigarette from the butt of the previous one, staring straight ahead, as if afraid to look at him. Neither Drew nor Charly realized that this moment was the beginning of love, one for the other. The love of a father and the love of a son for his father.

The eleven-year old Drew, mature beyond his years, rose off the fender, stood in front of Charly, and reached up and pulled the cigarette from his lips. He dropped it onto the ground in front of the car and stepped on it, then grabbed both of Charly's hands. "Charly, you smoke too much, but would you be my guardian, please?"

Charly grinned. "I only smoke these coffin nails too much when I'm nervous," he said, stepping off the fender and hugging Drew, who at first squirmed in embarrassment but shortly returned the hug.

"I'll try to cut down. Now, let's go and see Dallas!"

They both climbed into the car and turned back onto the highway. The day, though cold, was bright and sunny and would be warm later. Winter would be at bay for a short while in north central Texas.

Charly turned off the highway onto Main. "That's the courthouse. We call it Old Red for rather obvious reasons." The building with late-nineteenth-century architecture seemed imposing and stately. "That's where we'll go to meet Judge McGowan. Over there is the Adolphus Hotel, Dallas's finest." The twelve-story skyscraper towered over the street. "Over here is Dallas's famous department store," Charly went on, "where all the rich people across Texas come to shop." He pointed out a modern-appearing art-deco building with an understated sign Neiman Marcus. Drew studied the sign for long moments until the car turned a corner and the department store was hidden from sight.

"Here's the police station."

"Is that where you work?"

"Yes. Now let me show you your new home."

Charly's house was not large. It was a white bungalow with blue shutters and a porch that extended across much of the front of the house. Carefully trimmed cedars framed the porch, whose roof was supported by enormous brick pillars crowned about two-thirds of the way with a decorative molding. Wood framing extended past to the porch ceiling. There was a porch swing and a carefully manicured lawn, now brown and sere, but with summer would be a lush green. Two small trees stood on each side of the concrete walk leading to the front porch. "Those are pecan trees," Charly said. "My wife and I planted them the year she died."

The street in front was paved and curbed, and both sides had concrete sidewalks. Charly turned into his driveway, two concrete strips placed just far enough apart for the car's wheels. The garage was at the rear of his property.

There was a screened back porch with a washing machine covered with an oilcloth tablecloth, a tiny kitchen, a small dining room, and a small living room. The house had two bedrooms and one bathroom. The bathroom floor was white-and-black checkered tile. There was linoleum in the kitchen, and the other floors were shining hardwood. There were rag rugs scattered about and comfortable furniture.

"This is your bedroom," Charly said, leading Drew to the smaller bedroom located at the rear of the house. "Mine's up there," he said, nodding toward the front.

Drew thought Charly's house was the most luxurious place he had ever seen. With a start, he realized that for the first time in his life, he would be living in a place that had indoor hot water—more than a cold-water tap and a sink.

"I gotta go to work today at three," Charly said. "And after drivin' all night, I'm pooped. I'm gonna take a little nap. You make yourself at home. There's bread in the kitchen, sandwich meat, eggs, and milk in the fridge. You get hungry, you fix yourself anything you want. This place is now your home as well as mine."

While Charly napped, Drew sat in the living room, thinking about all the possibilities. He was now in the safest place he had ever been. After a few minutes, Drew leaned his head back and relaxed. He felt he had not completely relaxed for a long time. Drew slept.

Charly woke at two, shaved, and put on his policeman uniform. He and Drew ate a sandwich together before he left for work. "If I don't see you tonight, I'll see you first thing in the morning," Charly said as he was leaving. "Tomorrow's gonna be a busy day. We've got to buy you some clothes for school next week. I may even get to show you some more of the sights of your new hometown. Make yourself at home."

Drew stood in the driveway watching as Charly backed out, turned his car onto Cliff Heights Drive, and drove away down the street.

Drew remained motionless in the driveway long after Charly had driven away, looking both up and down the street. The few times he had gone to movies in Union City, he had seen places depicted like this. Never, he thought, would he have believed he would actually live in such a safe, secure place. Yet something was odd about this place. He couldn't quite put his finger on it.

Drew went back inside and explored the house. He examined the console radio-phonograph, which appeared to be new, and looked at Charly's record collection, being careful not to disturb anything. Almost all were classical music and unfamiliar to Drew. An upright piano was in one corner of the dining room, and Drew decided he would try a few chords. He opened the fallboard and struck the keys. The piano was not in tune. He closed the cover.

He walked around outside, looking at Charly's woodworking tools, stored neatly in a lean-to workshop at the rear of the garage. A low fence of an open wire design, a type of fencing Drew would later learn was called chain link, marked the boundaries of the small lot. Across the fence in both directions were the backyards of other houses—some with laundry hanging on clotheslines, others with children's swings and toys scattered about. Charly's backyard was festooned with rose bushes, most now in a state of dormancy.

He unpacked his few things, folded his clothes, and put them in drawers of the chest next to the closet door. He hung his trousers and shirts in the tiny closet. He thought about his clothes. He had grown a lot this past year. His shoes no longer fit. Neither did the trousers and shirts that Father Tom had given him.

During the year 1937, Drew had grown to almost his full adult height. He would grow another two inches by the time he was seventeen and one more after that; but already, five months before turning twelve, he had grown to five feet ten inches. His body was now consolidating its rapid growth spurt; bones, muscles, and sinews were becoming stronger as they adapted.

Drew suddenly realized that his voice had changed along with everything else.

He would no longer, or would he ever again, sing as an alto. The voice he would later add to the choir at the Methodist Church nearby was becoming a rich tenor—mellow and pleasing. His hair was also changing as it evolved from its light sandy-reddish color. Now, it was already a coppery auburn, and while it would darken, it would retain its auburn shade for the rest of Drew's life.

Across from Drew's bed was a small desk. A lamp was mounted over it on the wall. Its drawers were empty. He sat at the desk and took his tin box from his knapsack. He counted the money inside. He had $326.49, the residual from the money of his various adventures. The total was what remained after all that he had spent while with the Nettleses, the money saved after Edith's thievery, the money he had earned from Mr. Martinez, gifts from both Catherine and Mr. Martinez, and the money that Mama Rose had given him. He put the cash back in the box and the box in the middle drawer of the desk. He also took the wallet and two photographs out of the old knapsack. One of the photos was mounted on heavy paper, showing a woman in an old-fashioned dress. She looked a great deal like Edith. The other photo showed a younger Drew and Catherine Ryan, squinting into the sun. He placed both in the drawer beside the tin box and stored his knapsack on the closet shelf.

Drew sat in the porch swing. The winter day had warmed and was cool but not cold. At other houses, up and down the block and across the street, children played in their yards or ran along the sidewalk or rode their tricycles. Dogs barked and chased after children. He could hear radios playing. Someone down the block was practicing scales on a piano. Drew winced as the piano player hit several wrong notes in succession.

Women visited with one another on the sidewalks or pushed babies in carriages. Some houses were identical to Charly's, others only slightly different. A mailman walked along the sidewalk. As he delivered mail, he greeted children, women in their yards, and those walking along the sidewalk. He walked up to Charly's front porch and gave Drew a cheery smile as he handed him a small folded bundle of mail. Two boys about Drew's age on bicycles rode past, waving and calling out to him.

Drew had a hard time gathering his thoughts. Just yesterday, he and Father Tom were making a desperate run across Arkansas. Possible danger had lurked at every side road and over the brow of every hill. Today, he felt safer than he'd ever dared dream. And yet, he continued to puzzle, what was it about this place that felt so different, so subtly discordant from every other place he had lived?

It came to him. He could see no black faces. In every other place he had lived, there were Negroes, his friends, people whom he knew instinctively that he could trust. All the people he could see, up and down the street, were white.

He thought about this for a few minutes. Then, he remembered that just this morning Charly said to trust him. *I trusted Father Tom,* Drew mused. *I told Charly I would trust him. OK*—Drew nodded—*this place is my home. I trust Charly. I will learn to trust these white people.*

As he stood from the porch swing, the folded bundle of mail dropped off his lap and onto the floor. *Life* and *Time* magazines parted from the bundle and lay face up. He bent to the scattered mail. There was a photograph of a Swedish ice skater on *Life*. *Time*'s cover had a stylized drawing of a man seated at some sort of huge pipe organ and a caption that said, "From the unholy organist, a hymn of hate." He picked up the scattered mail and placed it on the coffee table in the living room. Someone came to the front screened door.

"Whatcha doin'?" a nasally voice said. A red-faced boy about Drew's age with an outstanding case of acne was standing on the porch, looking into the living room.

"Oh," Drew stammered. "Hello."

"You the guy that's gonna be livin' with Charly?" the boy asked. He brushed greasy blond hair out of his eyes as he talked.

"Yes. My name is, uh—" Drew paused. What should he tell this boy? What had Charly said about changing his name? "My name is Drew," he finished, somewhat lamely.

"Charly sometimes shoots hoops with me. He said a guy named Drew was gonna be livin' here with him."

"Oh. Well, I, uh, I guess that's me."

"Okay. You're Drew," the boy said. "I'm Richard. People call me Richie. I live three houses down. What grade you in?"

"Seventh," Drew answered. At least, he hoped that the school people would let him be in the seventh grade.

"I am too. You wanna play ball?" Richie asked. He clearly was done with introductions.

"Sure. But I don't have a glove. Charly bought one for me, but I think it's in his car."

"I'm not talking about baseball," Richie said with some scorn in his voice. "I'm talking about this!" He held up a basketball.

Drew had seen boys playing basketball, but he'd never held one in his hands. "I don't know how," Drew said, nodding at the ball. "Then I'll teach you," Richie said, grinning and showing yellowed and uneven teeth. "C'mon out."

# Chapter 25

## Eddie Mackenzie's Song

I T WAS EARLY April. Drew was sitting at the dining room table working on a Texas History paper when he heard the radio announcer say, "Here's that latest hit 'Tears in My Eyes' written and sung by that newest musical sensation Eddie Mackenzie!" Drew turned his head sharply to the radio in the living room. There was a soft piano introduction, unmistakably Eddie's sure and soft touch on the keys; and then, backed by a full orchestra, Drew heard Eddie's clear mellow voice singing to an unusual beat. Drew ran to the living room, dropped to his knees in front of the radio, and turned up the volume.

The song was a ballad; but it had a unique rhythm that was upbeat, somewhat bright, a little quirky, but sad at the same time. As the voice he knew so well came into the living room, Drew could visualize the dreamy expression, the dangling cigarette, smoke curling as he leaned away from the piano and became absorbed in his music. Eddie's soft mellow voice filled the room.

"It's Eddie!" Drew shouted, laughing. Charly walked into the living room from the back porch, drying his hands on an old towel. "Who?"

Drew held his finger to his lips as he listened. The song ended, and the announcer began a commercial.

"It was Eddie Makenzie, you remember? He was the piano player at Mrs. Lytle's in Little Rock. I called him Max when I was little. I'd heard that he had written a song that had been published in Nashville, and now I guess he's written another. Wow! Wasn't it swell? The next time I'm in the record store, I'm going to buy his record. Could I write him?"

This brought on another thought that followed just as quickly. "In fact, I'd like to write to a bunch of people that I know. Charly, I want to write my friends. I know Miss Catherine has written them, but now I want to write them."

Charly sat in the overstuffed chair, still holding the damp towel. He was wearing an old sweatshirt and dungarees, his sleeves damp from feeding clothes through the wringer and into one of the rinsing sinks. "I don't know, Drew. Let me talk to Judge McGowan. I'm concerned that if you send a letter, well, maybe someone else might see it and see the Dallas postmark. I guess all I'm saying is we need to be careful."

The late spring day was bright and clear, but it now seemed to Drew as if the brightness was somehow changed. It was fifteen months since he had jumped into a windy, noisy, and cold railroad car. It had been three months since he raced across State Line Avenue in Texarkana and hopped into Charly's car.

Much of those months were a blur to Drew. Some things stood out. He could remember clearly the day when he and Charly met with Judge James McGowan.

The venerable jurist was in his late fifties, somewhat stout, with a gray fringe of hair around his ears and gray eyes resting in a kind face. They had met in the judge's office, a large paneled room in Old Red, the courthouse in downtown Dallas. Photographs of the judge with various dignitaries hung on two walls along with diplomas and testimonials. One wall contained no adornment other than a large photograph of President Roosevelt.

After greetings and introductions were completed, the judge said, "I have talked with the superintendent of the Dallas Independent School District." He looked over the tops of his glasses at both Drew and Charly. "He told me that he will accept a confidential letter, and he will keep that letter under lock and key."

He again looked at the two sitting before him, ensuring himself that they were not only listening but understanding his remarks.

"He will then instruct the principal at the Oak Cliff Junior High School," the judge went on, "to admit Drew." His eyes shifted and focused on Drew. "They'll test you in about two weeks and see where you best fit academically. Texas History is taught in the seventh grade and is mandatory for all students."

He paused again for a moment, letting it all soak in. "You'll have to attend Saturday catch-up classes on Texas History. They're taught at Central High. They last the entire semester, but if you catch up, you can take the Texas History classes at junior high."

The judge now focused over his glasses at both. "Drew will need to have a guardian until he is eighteen. I will appoint Charly Byrne as your guardian unless either you or he objects." He shifted his eyes to some paperwork before him.

The judge raised his eyes and continued, "Hearing no objection"— he smiled—"I am now going to call Mrs. Ellsworth in. She is going to transcribe notes of this meeting."

Drew had thought since the day before what he would say when asked about his new name. "I'm Drew Allen Neiman," he said when asked. "Not Andrew. My name is Drew."

The judge dictated a memorandum, and Mrs. Ellsworth left. Papers concerning Charly's guardianship of Drew were prepared and signed by the judge and by Charly. Drew looked at his copy of both documents. Mrs. Ellsworth had consistently misspelled what would become his last name.

"So," Drew asked as he studied the document, "from now on, I am Drew Allen Neilan?"

The judge and Charly both smiled. "Unless you want it to be something else," the judge smiled, not catching the difference between Neiman and Neilan. Charly simply sat in his chair, grinning, his obvious emotions showing with a tear glistening in his eyes. He did not catch the typographical error either.

Soon, there were handshakes all around. Judge McGowan asked for "regular reports, oh, say every three months, on how you're doing."

"I can send them, Judge," Charly volunteered.

The judge shook his head. "No. I want Drew to send them. Will you do that, son?"

"Yes, I will, sir!" Drew answered, a huge smile on his face. He had the strange feeling of being completely at home.

"So, Drew Neiman," Charly said after they left the judge's office and as they were climbing into the car, "you want to stop at the Pig Stand?"

Drew remembered laughing at the secret only he knew. "Charly, Mrs. Ellsworth got my last name wrong. She typed it up as Neilan, not Neiman."

"Why didn't you say anything?"

"I thought about it, but you know, I never knew my father's last name. So, really, almost any name would do. I only picked Neiman because it was the name of that ritzy department store you showed me, and it was the only name I could think of. So I'm Drew Neilan. I like it. I like the way it sounds.

"Now," Drew asked with a change of expression and mock seriousness, a suppressed grin playing across his features, "what the heck is the Pig Stand?

The Pig Stand, Drew learned, was the name of a drive-in restaurant. Charly informed him that drive-in restaurants were invented in Oak Cliff, and the one on Chalk Hill Road had been the very first such establishment in the world. Pig sandwiches were barbequed pork on a bun, dripping with sauce. Charly had bought them each two, with battered and fried onion rings, plus a chocolate malted milk for each. Drew told Charly that not only was it the first time in his life he'd had a pig sandwich it was also the first time he'd had a malted milk. "And it's the first time I've ever been to a drive-in restaurant too." Drew grinned as he wiped sauce from his chin.

The weeks that followed were a montage of "firsts." Among them were a trip to a dentist, immunization shots at a doctor's office, his first ride on a street railway car, and his first Technicolor movie, *A Star is Born*.

Drew caught up quickly with the other seventh-grade students at Oak Cliff Junior High and worked on his Texas History Saturdays. He soon caught up with Texas History and entered the history class in junior high. He found Texas History to be rich in lore, pageantry, suffering and triumph, heroes and villains. Drew also thought privately that much of the history he was taught was likely more myth than fact. But even so, he thought, it was no wonder Texans seemed such a proud lot; their history read like an adventure novel.

As baseball season began that year Drew learned, through Charly's enthusiasm, to love the game. Whenever possible, he and Charly listened to game radio broadcasts, and their cheers could be heard up and down Cliff Heights Drive.

Both Drew and Charly had hoped that they would like each other. During these past months, as they learned more about each other, they developed an easy compatibility and a strong friendship. On weekends, after chores were done, they would often play catch in the front yard. Richie would sometimes ask them to his house to join in a game of horse basketball. Occasionally, one of the other men on the street would join the three. The grown-ups played against the boys, and always, the boys won.

Charly's favorite place was White Rock Lake Park, across town from Oak Cliff. On weekend afternoons, there was almost always a softball game in progress. Charly was well-known and liked; usually both teams competed for him to play on their side. Drew was beginning to learn the game and quickly found baseball to be a game of strategy, grace, planning, and execution. He was less interested in basketball, much to Richie's disappointment.

Charly's strong Catholic upbringing led him to attend mass regularly. Drew often went with him. Sometimes Drew attended the Oak Cliff Methodist Church down the street from the junior high school. And sometimes, both he and Charly stayed home, slept late, and read the Sunday papers over strong black coffee, Charly's special omelets and Drew's hot biscuits, which he called Sister Alma's biscuits, dripping with butter and, often, honey.

Spring and the summer of 1938 passed pleasantly. Drew turned twelve. He knew there was another world—war clouds in Europe and war in China. But war and the turbulence of the rest of the world seemed far away from this quiet corner of north central Texas.

Drew and Charly often sat before his radio and listened to President Roosevelt's "fireside chats." Drew's mind was at peace, and listening to the president only enhanced that feeling. There were times that a line from a Negro spiritual haunted him: "A band of angels, comin' after me." He wondered if it really had been angels that directed him to this place and this time.

Drew had been thinking of angels one Saturday when his reverie was interrupted. His mind snapped back to the present. Charly was speaking.

"I've talked to Judge McGowan about your interest in writing your friends, and he has talked with Mrs. Browning. The answer is, yes, you can write your friends."

However, after sealing and addressing the letters, they were to be placed in a larger envelope and addressed to Catherine Browning. She would see that they were distributed. And so through his friend Catherine, Drew was able to keep up with the lives of other of his friends.

Ursula Schultz's letter was as straightforward as she herself was. She offered to facilitate a correspondence between Drew and Kowanda along with astonishing news. Ursula wrote, "Your mother has married Eugene McElroy after his wife divorced him. I heard that they were working in a hotel in Shreveport, but I've also heard that they left Shreveport for Galveston."

Drew put the librarian's letter down. Edith. Married! His mouth turned down, and there was an acrid taste in the back of his throat as he thought of Eugene. *I didn't kick his balls hard enough that night,* Drew thought. *I knew when I saw him going back to the house after I left that I should have kicked harder, done permanent damage.* He gritted his teeth, thinking about the smelly and awful man, then realized, with mounting disgust, that, technically, Eugene was now his stepfather. Drew buried his face in his hands. "God!" he heard himself say in an anguished voice.

One day in late August, a letter from Eddie arrived, postmarked from Tennessee.

"Dear Drew," he wrote, "Mrs. Browning was good enough to give me your address. I promised her I would not share it with anyone. I want to tell you that the third Saturday of this September, I will be in Dallas. My band has a date at the Ebony Club. I want to see you. At three o'clock that Saturday afternoon, I will be waiting for you at the train station. Look for me in the colored waiting room. Don't worry if you can't be there. I'll wait for an hour, and if you can't make it, I will leave at four. All my love, Eddie."

Drew felt that it would take some sort of major calamity for him *not* to be there. Charly drove him to town that day, and both of them met Eddie. Drew had hardly slept the night before and was up early that Saturday, even though the meeting with Eddie was hours away. After Charly parked the car, Drew ran across the street and burst into the waiting room, filled with Negroes waiting their turn to board a train after white people claimed their seats. Eddie was sitting on a hard bench, his cigarette drooping and his eyes half shut as he listened inside his head to music yet to be heard by the rest of the world.

Eddie stood as Drew dashed across the room, and the crowd stared as the white youth hugged the Negro man. Eddie's eyes filled with tears as he returned Drew's hug. Drew would not let himself cry but felt the emotion and to cover the moment began laughing as they hugged each other and clapped each other on the back. Soon, both were laughing at nothing and at each other.

Charly drove Drew and Eddie to 1247 Cliff Heights Drive. Eddie sat in the rear seat as befitted a Negro in a white man's car. Neighbors up and down the street noted the black man exiting from Charly's car and hoped the policeman wasn't bringing a black roommate to live in his little house. They nodded to one another; surely, this was a servant or a handyman. But why, they wondered, would Charly Byrne bring him to his house so late in the day and why permit this person to enter his house by the front door? That boy living with Charly had even held the screen door open for the Negro! Gossip buzzed.

Drew had talked almost nonstop from the train station to Oak Cliff. Eddie had smiled and answered when he could get a word in, but generally, he let the excited youngster simply chatter on. Once in the house, they sat in the living room, and Eddie handed Drew a package he had been carrying. It contained six records, everything that he'd recorded thus far, and sheet music with lyrics for all the songs he had published. There were sixteen.

"Play your music for me, Eddie," Drew said. "I'll listen to the phonograph later. We had the piano tuned just last week. I've been taking lessons this summer. I want to hear you play."

Eddie smiled his lazy trademark smile as he settled down at the piano and ran his fingers across the keys, testing their touch, looking unobtrusively for flaws or idiosyncrasies. He lit a cigarette and placed it dangling in his lips. He didn't need sheets of music: it was in his soul and flowed through his fingers and onto the keyboard seemingly without effort. Charly thought he'd never heard the old pedestrian upright produce the concert-hall quality sound that he heard with Eddie at the keyboard.

His touch was as Drew had remembered, and as Eddie leaned back in his easy and relaxed manner and closed his eyes, the neighbors heard his magnificent music through the opened door and windows. They stopped talking and listened. A soft and mellow voice was singing a ballad—it seemed as if they had heard that music somewhere before. It had an odd and quirky beat, which, somehow, sounded familiar. Several teenagers walking by stopped, looked at one another, and snapped their fingers to the unique music.

Eddie played for the better part of half an hour. Then he asked Drew to play. Drew had been taking lessons during the summer from the school's band director and was glad to have the chance to show Eddie what he knew. He arranged the sheets of Eddie's music, studied them for a few moments, and began to play. Eddie watched and showed him ways to better blend his chords with the melody. Drew played "Tears in My Eyes," trying to match Eddie's beat. As he played, Eddie told him about his life.

"Yes, Drew. I married that little gal in Dardanelle that I was sweet on forever, you remember? We got us five fine black boys now, and they are a real handful. Here are their pictures." Drew smiled and leaned over as he continued playing and looked appreciatively at the photographs of the smiling boys and their mother. "Maybelle is beautiful, Eddie," he said, his fingers finding their way across the keyboard, "and your boys, Eddie, I hope I have boys just like them some day."

Eddie laughed. "Well, not exactly like them. Your babies will be white!" Drew grinned and ducked his head to the keyboard, opening another sheet of music and segueing with a series of piano riffs into the newest of Eddie's songs.

The visit was over sooner than anyone wanted. They were surprised at the crowd of young teens standing on the front porch and in the yard. Someone had learned that Eddie Mackenzie—the Eddie Mackenzie!—was in their neighborhood. Eddie signed autographs for almost fifteen minutes. And the neighbors all breathed a sigh of relief when Charly, Drew, and Eddie finally climbed into the car and drove away.

After they dropped Eddie off at the Ebony Club, Charly said to Drew, "I talked to my chief today, and it's OK if I check out a police car. I talked to Eddie about it, and he's going to see that the doors of the Ebony Club are opened for twenty minutes at eleven thirty tonight. An ordinary car with two white guys in it in that part of town that late, well, someone might think it strange. But a police car wouldn't be considered unusual. We patrol that part of town regularly when there's a big party at the Ebony Club. You can sit in the backseat where no one will notice you. We can listen to Eddie's music."

That night, while Drew and Charly were sitting in a Dallas Police patrol car across from the Ebony Club, an automobile pulled up down the street from Charly's. The man inside switched off the motor and lit a cigarette. Another man came from inside the house and sat in the car.

He too lit a cigarette, and the two smoked quietly for a while. A third person was sitting in the backseat.

"Is that where he lives, over there?" the driver said, pointing by nodding his head in the direction of Charly's house. "That's where you saw that nigger go in by the front door, and then you heard all that nigger music?"

"Yes," the second man said, "there may not be anything to it. Maybe that nigger was some old family nigger or something." He shook his head. "You know, things have been strange in that house for a long time."

"Strange in what way?" the driver asked.

The second man rushed to explain. "I mean, that Charly Byrne guy ain't married. His wife died a long time back. Now, he's got this kid living with him. Then yesterday he brings a nigger in through his front door, and they play nigger music."

He stopped to light another cigarette, then went on, "A couple of years after his wife died, my wife and I introduced him to my cousin Mabel. They went to the movies a time or two, but Mabel said he just didn't seem interested.

"That Charly guy didn't go after Mabel, and that's a fact. Even if she is my cousin, I can tell you she'll sleep with anything that wears pants. She told me he turned her down flat."

The driver lit another cigarette. "He's got a kid living with him?"

"I'm just worried about what's going on in that house," the second man continued using a somewhat sanctimonious tone. "You know, that Charly guy, well, he's Catholic, and I admit I don't like Catholics. But he and his wife, the one that died, well, they were married for over five years and they never had children. Now, explain that to me, will you? You know Catholics can't use nuthin'. That's one reason they always have so many kids. And now he's got that kid livin' with him. He ain't kin, I asked. Charly said he'd been appointed guardian. What's that mean? Where'd the kid come from?

"And the kid plays the piano," he went on, "and sings and can tap dance, my boy told me. Also, my boy told me that that kid couldn't even throw a football. If that kid ain't a sissy, then that Charly Byrne is tryin' to make him into one."

"You may be right," the driver said, flicking his cigarette butt into the street and lighting another. "It sounds like you think that Charly guy is a sissy homo as well as a nigger lover."

The driver turned to the backseat passenger, a young person, about Drew's age. "You know that kid, Lonny?"

"Yeah, Dad, he's in my homeroom."

"Is he in your gym class?"

"No."

"Good. No telling what might happen in the showers. You watch out for him. He might be queer. Anyway, we know he's a nigger lover. I'm gonna see that you go back to that private school. I don't want you hanging around queers and nigger lovers. That Byrne cop is Catholic, and that's almost like a Jew, and you can't ever tell about Jews."

# Chapter 26

## *1941*

DREW TURNED FIFTEEN in May of 1941.

Later that summer, Drew opened a letter from Kowanda. The two had written each other through the years and now that Drew's so-called legal issues were finally cleared up, he had visited Union City several times where, under the chaperonage of Charly and Ursula Schultz, he and Kowanda had sat and talked in the library basement.

He smiled as he read Kowanda's latest letter. She described a day that had been particularly pleasant for her: an outing with several of her friends. Drew knew that her life in general was increasingly unpleasant. Her father was growing more verbally abusive. There were a number of people in Union City who worried about the girl and her mother, fearing that the verbal abuse could turn physical.

It had been a year since Judge McGowan reported that there was no longer any interest in Drew by the authorities. There were still worries that the Klan might retain interest, but because of the passage of time since the school burning, they hoped the Klan would also have lost interest. The fact that Edith had left Union City and was herself in some undisclosed location, likely pursuing less-than-legal activities, had also been pointed out to the local authorities. Drew felt he could return to Union City anytime he wished.

There had been several visits. Charly and Drew had shared a meal with Leon's family, at Imogene's insistence. Drew had renewed his friendship with Leon while Charly chatted with Brother Barlow, Imogene, and Sister Alma. But to Drew, the focus of each of the trips was the hours he and Kowanda spent together.

Their most recent trip had been a very special occasion. Charly had stopped at the town square, handed Drew the keys, and sauntered off to the soda fountain at Wilkinson's Drugstore. Drew had driven away and met Kowanda at a tiny park on the other side of town from where she lived, and the two had a small picnic. They walked along a shaded glen beside the creek, held hands, and talked of things that meant nothing and everything. Their first kiss was on that walk.

They had stopped talking and stood facing each other, holding hands. The afternoon sun streaming through the late summer-green trees seemed to infuse the little clearing in which they stood with a golden haze. It highlighted her silky jet-black hair and seemed to make her large almond-shaped eyes appear luminous and glowing. Drew could not know that, to her, his auburn hair sparkled in the dappled sunlight with highlights of red and his cobalt-blue eyes held her attention in such a way that she dared not breathe. The sharp tinkle of the rushing creek waters, the rustle of the leaves in the light breeze, and the calls of birds were forgotten by the two. They stood together enveloped in a silence broken only by the beating of their hearts.

Neither would ever know which had first moved toward the other, but without thought, they found themselves in each other's arms and her lips were warm and full on his as her young slender body pressed into him. Her sweet breath filled his senses as the world stopped turning on its axis.

It was Drew who broke away. An embarrassing, inevitable, and entirely normal physiological reaction had begun to occur and he broke the embrace, embarrassed. He pushed her away from him, turned her, and with his arms about her shoulders laid his cheek against the side of her head and said huskily, "I hope you're never sorry we did that."

She turned her head and looked up at him. "Are you?" she said.

"No, and I never will be."

"And neither will I," she said and meant it.

The world in which Drew lived perceived him to be sixteen now, although chronologically, he was fifteen. Charly had taken him to Judge McGowan, who had issued a "hardship" affidavit, and Drew had then been permitted to take (and pass) the Texas State driving test. He now had his license and hoped that, one day soon, Charly would agree that he could make the trip to Union City by himself.

In contrast to the turmoil and her father's threats of violence that permeated Kowanda's life, Drew's life continued to have a dreamlike quality. He was well liked at school, enjoyed baseball, and had discovered that he had an aptitude for it. Coach Aubrey Baker and Charly had spent much of the summer of 1940 coaching Drew. Charly attended almost every game of Drew's first season in high school the following spring.

Drew had been in several junior high school productions, and the first high school production he was in, the *Musical Review of 1940*, had been a big hit. Drew had renewed his tap dancing, taking lessons at a dance studio near Highland Park. It was quite a trip via street railway and electric bus, but Drew enjoyed the dancing and considered it fun.

Drew's early lessons from Eddie Mackenzie and, later, Honeycutt had been simply taught by demonstration of various rudimentary steps. Now, he learned, choreography could be written or sketched and each symbol indicated a different movement. It was a whole new world that, to him, was not only fun but as exciting and interesting as learning to read music.

The manager of the Oak Cliff radio station, KDOC, approached Charly after the school production and, after receiving approval to do so, offered Drew a half-hour guest spot on a Saturday morning radio show.

Drew and Charly had agreed to four shows, for which he would be paid nothing. However, Drew's easy speaking manner quickly assured every teen listening that here was one of their own, and he had convinced the show's host to play the music they all liked, leaning heavily on Eddie Mackenzie's latest records. The show's popularity swelled. After three weeks, Drew was asked to make a thirty-minute appearance on the show every Saturday. He was to be paid $10 for each.

The soft drink company Dr Pepper had a large bottling and distribution center in the Dallas area. Drew began the second show by saying, "Good morning, everyone, this is Drew Neilan. It's ten o'clock, and Dr Pepper says you should drink one of his refreshing sodas every day at ten, two, and four." He popped his thumb in an empty bottle, simulating the opening of a soft drink, and said, "So let's sit back, have a cool drink, and here's some of the latest hot music!" Eddie's mellow voice and quirky rhythm issued from radio sets across Oak Cliff.

On Monday morning the station's switchboard was jammed. Advertisers whose products targeted the teen market were clamoring for Drew to hawk their wares. On Wednesday, one of Dr Pepper's advertising personnel visited the station to talk about Drew's free and impromptu "plug" of their product. He noted to the station manager that sales of Dr Pepper in and around Oak Cliff had risen since the previous Saturday. The thirty-minute show quickly evolved into an hour-long show and became "Dr Pepper's Drew Neilan Teen Radio Show," and Drew's salary was upped to $15 for each show.

Drew had written Kowanda about his radio show. "You might be able to hear it," he had written, "if you go and talk to Mr. Scheumack at the radio repair store. I used to hang out at his store sometimes, and he has these huge aerials out back that he says can pick up any radio station in the country. I'd be so thrilled if I knew you were listening!"

Scheumack closed his radio store that first Saturday after Kowanda talked to him. A small crowd gathered at the store, consisting not only of Kowanda and Scheumack but also Ursula Schultz, Sister Alma, Brother Barlow, Leon, Walker, and Imogene. Felix Martinez, the proprietor of Martinez's Grocery, also came to hear Drew's show. Leon had made a special trip to the woods east of Union City and invited Honeycutt. To everyone's relief, the smelly old hermit had evidently bathed and trimmed his beard before arriving at Scheumack's.

The crowd cheered and clapped as Drew's voice came over Scheumack's twin speakers. "Good morning, everyone. This is Drew Neilan bringing you the latest and hottest music for Dr Pepper's Drew Neilan Teen Radio Show! So sit back, relax, its ten o'clock on a fine Saturday morning! Let's follow Dr Pepper's advice. Pop open a cool Dr Pepper (pop!) and let's listen to some hot music!" There were a few more cheers as Eddie's latest record began playing.

Ursula Schultz excused herself and quietly moved to the back of the room. No one must see the tears that had sprung, unbidden, to her eyes. Kowanda, Imogene, and Sister Alma wept unabashedly; and Honeycutt pulled a rag from his back pocket and honked noisily. Leon executed an impromptu soft-shoe, dancing to Eddie's music.

Charly's little house had become a haven not only for Drew but for scores of teens who quickly learned that 1247 Cliff Heights Drive was a place to grow, learn, and have fun.

Drew realized with clarity, one day, that no male figure in his life before had filled the role of a father, a role that he now understood he yearned for. Not Reverend Thomas or Eddie or anyone in Union City had been the strong male figure for which the young Drew yearned, although he often felt that possibly the hermit, Honeycutt, might have at least partially filled the role.

Charly was Drew's friend. Father Tom had been Drew's friend too but in a grandfatherly sort of way. When Drew's thoughts focused on Charly, he realized that the burly policeman was not only his friend; he was his father. Drew respected Charly's authority, subordinated himself to his directions, and was careful to observe Charly's rules—both spoken and unspoken. Charly, in turn, respected Drew's privacy and was careful to set limits and boundaries. The initial steps Drew and Charly had taken toward love, one for the other, that winter morning as they gazed on the Dallas skyline were becoming complete.

Charly's chest swelled with pride every time his eyes fell on Drew bounding up the front steps eager to share his day with him or running onto the baseball field, splendid and handsome in his team uniform, or tap dancing across the stage in a school musical production. Charly never missed a single performance of any school production or any baseball game in which Drew's team played. Charly had changed his work hours from the three-to-eleven shift to the eleven to seven so that he could be at every function, regardless if they were school or extracurricular related. He missed sleep but was determined not to miss out on Drew's exuberance of life. A father's love had blossomed, and Drew loved him back. It was this that brought out the natural friendliness that Drew had always possessed but kept hidden as he walked through difficult times.

The rusty once-gilded tin box Mrs. Goldstone's Excellent Bath Crystals was still in the middle drawer of the small desk in Drew's bedroom, but it no longer served as repository for cash. Charly had introduced Drew to the concept of savings and the wonders of compound interest. The $326 it had contained when he arrived in Oak Cliff was now invested in US postal bonds, drawing interest at the princely rate of 2.5 percent per year.

Drew originally offered the money to Charly, who refused and who had, in fact, added to the principal the quarterly mysterious and anonymous cashier's check that came from Memphis. Drew's cache of postal bonds now amounted to over $800, and Charly's safe-deposit box allowed Mrs. Goldstone to receive her well-deserved retirement. Rather than cash, she, in her retirement, now contained only the torn photograph that Drew continued to study in rare moments of introspection. The mysterious wallet always lay next to Mrs. Goldstone.

Drew often accompanied Charly to mass. The youngster had become comfortable with the ritualism of the Holy Roman Catholic Church and could see meanings and power where others might see empty repetitions of religious words and phrases. Charly never pressured Drew to study the catechism, and Drew never offered to do so but was comfortable merely being with Charly as he communed with God.

Any woman, on first meeting Charly Byrne, could have told Drew or anyone else who cared to listen that when it came to women this man was a hollow shell. It was true. The death of his wife, Rebecca, had profoundly affected Charly. Her photographs filled his bedroom. Every other Sunday afternoon, he visited her grave, where he sat for hours, talking. He had long ago told her of Drew's coming to share the house. He now told her, with pride, of Drew's every achievement and victory, as well as occasional disappointments. He took Drew's team photos with him and proudly pointed out to her the tall smiling, good-looking youngster in the middle. Charly dug his Kodak Brownie Hawkeye out of a bottom drawer and took candid photographs of Drew and his friends. He showed these to her on his Sunday visits.

Charly once took Drew to the grave early in the boy's stay in Oak Cliff, but both were embarrassed by Charly's obvious emotions. The visit did not last long. Drew perceived, correctly, that the visits were something Charly wanted to do in private. Sundays after church, Charly drove Drew home and then went alone to the cemetery, usually taking a huge bouquet of roses from his own yard, carefully arranged in a large vase.

Neither Drew nor Charly fully realized the impact each was having on the other's life. Drew had sought safety and found it. Charly had found meaning for his life. Both had sought love, and both found it.

But while life was peaceful in this quiet corner of Dallas, Texas, it was far from peaceful throughout the world. In September, 1939 Germany invaded Poland. In the summer of 1940, Drew and Charly listened intently to the Battle of Britain fought in the skies over London but heard through the magic of radio around the world. Now, they listened nightly to radio news broadcasts of the war in Europe and the terrible toll German submarines were having on the convoys transporting lend-lease war materiel to Britain. They watched newsreels of the war at the Texas Theater on Jefferson Avenue and continued to be avid listeners to President Roosevelt's fireside chats.

Drew and Charly, in concert with almost all Americans, were focused totally on the war in Europe. Little attention had been paid to the Japanese invasion of China in 1937. Unseen war clouds gathered in Asia, and in September 1941, the world was moving rapidly toward what would become a turning point of history.

Drew had added additional height to his frame by the time school started that September of 1941. He was now one-half inch shy of being exactly six feet tall. His thick wavy hair had completed its change to a rich-dark auburn, which showed highlights of red in sunlight. His intense blue eyes, straight teeth and nose, strong jawline, and ready smile topped a trim and athletic build. It would have surprised and embarrassed Drew to know that more than one girl daydreamed of him while doodling in the rear pages of her notebook: Mrs. Drew Neilan, Mrs. D. A. Neilan, Mrs. Drew Allen Neilan.

The soft down on Drew's upper lip and cheeks had changed too. Charly accompanied him to the drugstore on Jefferson to buy his first safety razor. Drew was initially embarrassed when Charly wanted to go along but quickly lost that feeling as he realized, blinking in surprise at himself, that, of course, this was something a father would want to do with his son.

Sunday, December 7, 1941, caught Drew and Charly by surprise as it did most of the rest of the world. It was a warm, clear late-fall day in Dallas. Charly and Drew had returned from early mass that Sunday and Drew had changed, preparing to do some needed yard work. After a quick cup of coffee, Charly left for the cemetery, carrying a large bouquet of roses. Drew watched Charly drive away and went into the garage for the gardening tools. A wind and rainstorm two nights earlier had blown leaves and other debris into the yard. He finished raking and decided to trim the walks.

He was on his knees with a pair of hand clippers, shearing off the tough tendrils of grass that had initiated a trial run across the walk, when he looked up in surprise. Charly's blue Ford was racing down Cliff Heights Drive, and tires squealed as a white-faced Charly wheeled the car into the driveway. "Drew!" he shouted, "Quick! Go inside! The radio! Japanese planes are bombing Pearl Harbor!" Charly left the door of the car open in his rush to the house. Drew dropped the shears and followed. The Sunday *Dallas Morning News* lay open and ignored on the coffee table. The headline said, "Japanese Ambassador to Meet with Cordell Hull."

Together, they heard the bombs falling and the Hawaiian radio announcer say over and again, "This is the real McCoy, folks!" There could be no doubt. War had intruded its ugly visage onto the quiet streets of quiet neighborhoods in cities and towns across America. Charly and Drew stared at each other in disbelief and horror as the radio news continued. Up and down Cliff Heights Drive, other radios could be heard in other homes with the same horror flowing from their radio speakers.

One of Drew's first thoughts was of Kowanda. She had relatives in Hawaii. Would any of them be harmed? He would learn only later that the beginning of the war also foreshadowed the end of Mitsui's marriage to Kowanda's father and the subsequent internment of Kowanda and her mother in a remote camp in Kansas.

Drew made a fresh pot of coffee during one of the lulls in the battle in the Pacific, and during another, he and Charly noticed neighbors gathering on the street. They joined them, coffee cups in hand. People looked at one another with wide worried eyes and spoke in hushed tones. "I thought the peace envoys were meeting in Washington today," one person was heard to say. "Will the Japs invade Hawaii?" "What about California?"

Drew brought the coffeepot and more cups out onto the porch. When that coffee was gone, he went inside and made another pot. Sometime later Charly and another man carried the console radio out onto the porch and turned the volume up. A neighbor lady brought her coffeepot and plugged it in to the dual-outlet extension cord Charly had used to power up the radio. Someone brought a tray of sandwiches, but few were hungry. Other neighbors, from up and down Cliff Heights Drive, arriving from a late Sunday lunch after church or a Sunday outing, stopped their cars and joined the small crowd standing in Charly's front yard and listening to his radio.

People's expressions could not hide that they were frightened. A father put his arm around his eighteen-year-old son's shoulders, knowing that the young man would surely be called very soon to war. Many women in the crowd wept, for they knew that it was their sons and husbands who would go to this war and might not return.

Men talked about enlisting. "Tomorrow, by god!" one man shouted.

Finally, it seemed the attacks were over. Reports coming through the radio were incomplete; but it was clear that significant damage had been done to US naval, air, and land forces in the Pacific. More than one battleship had been destroyed and sunk. Dead and wounded were only just now beginning to arrive at hospitals throughout Oahu. Many airplanes had been destroyed, and only a relatively small number of the hundreds of Japanese planes had been shot down. Brave sailors, soldiers, and airmen had fought back valiantly. The surprise had been complete. Fires were burning not only at Pearl Harbor and other Hawaiian military bases but also in the city of Honolulu.

The radio reported rumors that a Japanese invasion of Hawaii was imminent. There was no confirmation.

The golden orb of the afternoon sun in the clear blue Texas sky seemed indifferent to the turmoil. What would have otherwise been a quiet Sunday afternoon in a quiet neighborhood in Dallas, Texas, was now transformed. War had intruded directly and viciously not only into remote Hawaii but into their very lives, and they were frightened. When someone in the crowd in Charly Byrne's front yard started singing "God Bless America," everyone joined in and sang as one voice, many holding hands with their wife, husband, children, or neighbor.

Charly and Drew had just come out onto the porch with more coffee and a pitcher of iced tea. They put the refreshments down, their arms over one another's shoulders, and sang along. Charly wept unabashedly as he sang, as did many in the crowd; but Drew simply squared his shoulders, put his arm around Charly, and sang dry-eyed, though his emotions, like everyone else's, were in turmoil.

As the last note sung by the crowd ended, Drew turned up the radio. Kate Smith was singing the same song, and her clear sweet voice rang out over Cliff Heights Drive. The men in the crowd and their older teenaged sons—their heads up, shoulders squared, tears coursing down many of their cheeks—gathered their weeping women and wailing siblings about them and drifted toward their homes.

Charly and Drew moved the radio back inside and retrieved the cups scattered about the porch and yard. They continued listening, but the broadcasts were now becoming repetitious and were interspersed with patriotic music. Drew washed dishes. This ordinary task had a calming effect. Charly dried and put them back into the cupboards.

Drew walked out onto the back porch, put his wet dish towel into the Maytag, and stood, looking westward. The sun was low in the clear blue of the Texas winter sky. Drew thought about the Japanese flag, the rising sun, and how this sunset represented a new and different world in which the United States, and all the world, was in danger. Charly came out onto the porch and stood for a moment, looking at the tall young man who had so changed his life, silhouetted against the sunset. He put his arm across Drew's shoulders. Drew leaned against the man he had come to love. Charly said simply, "My son." Drew turned to Charly and buried his face in the older man's shoulder. Drew said, "Dad."

The two stayed like this as the sun dipped below the horizon and the day faded to an early December twilight.


The next day, President Roosevelt asked the Congress of the United States to declare that since December 7, 1941, a state of war existed between the United States and the empire of Japan. Three days after that, Germany and Italy declared war on the United States.

## Chapter 27

# March 1942

DREW WAS SITTING in the high school gym locker room, pulling on his shoes. It was late into sixth period. Spring baseball practice was due to start. However, the March day was cold, drizzly, and rainy. Coach directed a half hour of calisthenics and then dismissed the team. Drew had showered and finished dressing and was cramming his sweaty gym clothes into a mesh bag.

"Hey, asshole!" a sharp voice said, "You're sitting in my place!"

Drew looked up in surprise. It was Lonny Skaggs, a boy who had previously been in a private school and only recently transferred to Oak Cliff High. Drew looked up and down the bench. Other boys in various stages of dress were scattered about the locker room. A few heads turned toward Drew and Lonny.

"There's plenty of room," Drew said. "But if it's important to you—" He shrugged and moved a couple of paces down from his locker.

"That's my place too!" the disagreeable boy said loudly. More heads across the locker room turned.

Drew felt a flash of embarrassment and anger and then said, "Well, you can suit yourself. I'm leaving anyway. You can have the whole place." He picked up his books and slung his gym bag over his shoulder. He turned his back on Lonny and began walking toward the door, calling out to his best friend on the team that he was leaving. Carlton Matthews sang out, "I'll be along in a minute. Wait up."

"I hear you're a fag!" Lonny shouted at Drew.

Drew stopped and turned, astonished and angry, but said nothing.

The boy advanced two steps toward Drew and shouted again, "That's right, nothing but a fairy sissy queer!" Drew looked hard at Lonny. The boy was about his height but was a little pudgy. He outweighed Drew by at least fifteen pounds. Even so, Drew thought he could take him if it came to blows.

Carlton moved up behind Lonny. "You shut the fuck up. Drew ain't queer!"

"Are you protectin' him?" Lonny shouted. "He can't take up for himself?"

"Watch it, Carlton," Drew said in a quiet voice. "Lonny, I can take up for myself, and you can just go to hell." He again picked up his gym bag and books.

"I hear you're a Jap lover too!" the ugly voice shouted.

Drew's upper lip curled in disgust.

"You're a Jap lover and a nigger lover! I hear all that nigger music you play over the radio!" It was clear Lonny had no qualms about his prejudices. The acid of his tone stung Drew's pride but little more.

Drew shrugged and said, "I'll say it again, Lonny. You go to hell." He turned his back on the boy, again slung his gym bag over his shoulder and opened the door that led into the courtyard at the rear of the gymnasium. As he moved through the doorway, Lonny pushed him hard, and Drew stumbled into the schoolyard. Books scattered as he tried to keep his balance.

Drew turned. Lonny was coming through the door. Carlton and other boys were following him, their faces showing excitement. A fight!

The courtyard behind the boys' locker room was between the gym and behind the football bleachers and could not be seen from any of the school windows. If a fight was to be held away from a teacher's prying eyes, this was the place to have it.

"Nobody tells me to go to hell," Lonny said, "especially not a fairy-queer, nigger-lovin' cocksucker like you!"

Drew frowned. A red calm flooded his mind as an icy coolness came over him. "Lonny, exactly what is your problem?"

"I hate queers!" the boy answered. "I hate niggers!" he continued. "And I hate Japs!"

That wasn't it, Drew's mind said. He thought hard. He considered what sort of circumstances could lead to this reaction. He'd done nothing to this boy. Now he obviously wanted to fight.

Drew remembered he'd seen Lonny hanging around Mary Alice Johnson. Drew had walked home with her last week. He had no idea Lonny had any interest in the girl, but Drew certainly didn't. Talking his way out of this wasn't going to be easy, but blind prejudice and anger rarely are easy things.

"Look, Lonny," Drew said calmly. He held up his hands casually and extended one in an offer to shake. "I don't want to fight you. If this is about Mary Alice"—he smiled—"why, she's just a friend. I've got a girlfriend."

Lonny pushed Drew in the chest—hard —and Drew stumbled backward. "Yeah," Lonny shouted, "and I hear she's a Jap! I hate queers, and I hate Japs!"

Drew shook his head. There was no logic at all in what Lonny was saying. The boy just wanted to fight someone. Drew braced himself and dropped his gym bag. His feet moved slightly farther apart, and he bent his knees slightly as he prepared to enter the stance that Honeycutt had taught him so long ago. This was so unnecessary!

Unknown to Drew and to the other boys, Lonny had sat in the backseat of his father's car as Charly's down-the-street neighbor had complained several times to the local leader of the KKK. Both men had been unreasonably concerned over Eddie Mackenzie's visit, Charly's Catholic religion, and Charly's lack of a female companion. Lonny's father was obsessed with hatred for Negroes, Jews, and Catholics, along with homosexuals, and had indoctrinated his son with frequent beatings. He had told his son to "show that bastard livin' with that cop that we don't cotton to nigger lovers and queers."

The other boys crowded around, excitement showing in their faces. Drew heard fragments of shouts: "C'mon, Drew, bust him one!" "Which one's the sissy?" "Show him what you've got!" Carlton suddenly stepped between Drew and Lonny. "Cut it out, Lonny. You guys are gonna be on the same team, for chrissakes! You don't need to be fightin'." Carlton crumpled and spat blood, holding his hands over his face. Lonny had sucker-punched him even before he finished talking. "Goddamn!" Carlton shouted, "That hurt, you sonofabitch!"

Carlton stood and aimed a quick blow at Lonny who deflected it and smashed his right fist into Carlton's nose. Blood splattered as Carlton fell backward and sat heavily on the ground.

Lonny turned back. Drew was standing quietly in a slight crouch, his arms raised, his fists not yet balled. "You want to fight me, Lonny?" Drew said quietly. "OK, come on. I'm ready for you." The reddish hazy calm feeling Honeycutt had taught him took over his senses.

Lonny laughed and threw a strong right that Drew deflected with his left forearm, ducked, and came up with a quick series of strong right jabs to Lonny's face, splitting his upper lip. Drew danced back. Honeycutt's lessons came back to him in a series of flashes. He could hear the old hermit saying, "You gotta hurt the other guy first and worst. Always! Protect yourself!"

Lonny came at Drew, swinging wildly. Drew dodged and danced away, looking for an opening. Lonny swung more blows, Drew blocked two, but Lonny scored with a right to Drew's cheek. His teeth cut the inside of his cheek, and Drew tasted the metallic salty taste of his own blood. Seconds later, Lonny dropped his guard. It seemed to Drew that he had all the time in the world to lean in and smash his right into the side of Lonny's head near his left eye. Lonny did not raise his guard again, and Drew dropped low and drove his right fist deep into Lonny's stomach while his left jabbed a split second later into Lonny's mouth. The boy's teeth cut Drew's knuckles.

Lonny dropped to his knees and vomited, gasping for the breath Drew had knocked out of him. The fight had lasted less than forty seconds.

"Jesus, Neilan!" someone said. "He never even touched you!"

Drew leaned over and spat blood, giving lie to the inaccurate observation.

"Where'd you learn to fight like that?" someone else said.

Drew leaned over to Carlton, helping him up. "You OK, Carlton?" he said. "C'mon, let's find a clean towel and put some cold water on your face and nose." He led Carlton back into the locker room. As they entered the door, he turned to the group of boys. "Someone help Lonny back in here and get a wet towel for him. He's gonna need to get cleaned up too. I'm afraid that eye is going to swell up."

As Lonny entered the locker room helped by two boys, Drew held out his hand again. "C'mon, Lonny, let's shake. No hard feelings! I'm sorry I hurt you." Drew grabbed Lonny's hand as he spoke and shook the limp hand as though its owner had genuinely proffered it.

The next morning every student at Oak Cliff High School knew about the fight. Senior boys who normally deigned it beneath their dignity to even speak with lower classmen went out of their way to call out to Drew as he made his way to class. Teachers that knew kept quiet. Someone had telephoned Coach the night before, but no one was sure what action he would take, if any.

Drew met Lonny in the hallway and put out his hand. "C'mon, Lonny, let's shake again. C'mon, there's no reason to have hard feelings." Lonny ducked his head, turned, and walked away without responding to Drew's overture. Carlton was standing next to Drew, a bandage across his nose. "Jesus, Drew. You gave Lonny the most beautiful shiner I've ever seen!" He clapped Drew on the back as they headed to their classroom.

That evening there was a knock on Charly's front door. "Come in, Coach," Drew said, opening the door. "Can I get you some coffee? We've just finished supper." Charly walked into the living room as Coach said, "Charly, can we speak in private?"

"If it has to do with Drew, no sir, we can't. I think it's only fair that he hear firsthand whatever you've got on your mind."

"OK, may I sit down?"

"Of course you may," Charly said, dropping into his easy chair as Drew entered carrying a small tray with three cups of fresh hot coffee.

Lonny's father, Coach explained, had made a considerable nuisance of himself throughout the day. "He made all sorts of allegations," Coach was saying, "all of which I knew to be false, and I said so. I had already interviewed everyone who'd witnessed the fight, including Carlton, and feel I know exactly what happened. Drew," he said, turning, "I didn't talk to you because I didn't feel I needed to. I was confident the other boys were telling me the truth. Now, however, you need to tell me your version."

"Sure." Drew gave as accurate an account as he could, after which Coach confirmed matched the accounts of everyone except Lonny.

"Well, what does he say?" Charly asked. Drew could hear the tone in his voice that said Charly had a feeling he knew where this was going already.

"He says, of course, that Drew started it. Started hitting him for no reason at all. He says it's proof that he didn't even fight back because Drew wasn't hurt at all."

"Well," Drew said, "he did hit me. I bled on the inside of my cheek."

Charly chuckled. "Drew outfought him, that's all."

"You'll have no argument from me there"—Coach smiled—"but that's not the end of it," he added, his expression changing. "It seems that Lonny's father is a big-time local architect who does a lot of business with the school board. He's a big political supporter of the school board president, and he's going directly to a school board meeting to ask that Drew be suspended from school!"

Charly and Drew were dumfounded. "For God's sake," Charly said. "It was just a simple little squabble between two boys and will be forgotten in a week. No one was seriously hurt!"

"That's not the way he sees it. I advise you to make plans to be at the school board meeting and defend your boy."

"What are you going to do, Coach?" Drew asked.

"Me? I'm going to do nothing. But if the board directs me to suspend one or the other of you or both, then I'll have to do it. I wanted you to hear that from me."

After Coach left, Drew looked at Charly. "What are we going to do?"

"Well," Charly said, "I guess I need to go see Judge McGowan tomorrow morning."

Drew never knew how, but the issue seemed to simply disappear. It was not brought up at the school board meeting, and Coach never mentioned it again. As time passed, Drew realized it was easier for his life if he joined everyone else in putting the incident out of mind. He made sure to treat Lonny just like anyone else even if he did remember what happened that afternoon.

# Chapter 28

◆╴──╴•╶∅♪╶•╶──╴◆

## *Two Weeks Later*

I
T WAS SATURDAY morning. Carlton had just come over. He had for some time been taking guitar lessons, and he and Drew were practicing a piano-guitar duet they planned to play live over the air on Drew's radio show. Carlton's voice blended well with Drew's, and they were debating whether or not to sing during the duet.

The doorbell rang. "Package for Mr. Drew Allen Neilan," the deliveryman said when Drew opened the door.

"I'm Drew Neilan," Drew said, taking the large box the man handed him. It was marked stylishly with the elegant but understated Neiman Marcus logo. Drew stared as the man returned to his truck and drove away. Several neighborhood women had stopped what they were doing and stared as the delivery had taken place.

"Who was that?" asked Charly, walking in from the kitchen and wiping his hands on a dishtowel.

"A delivery man from Neiman Marcus. Look!" Drew held out the box.

Carlton pointed to a small card attached to the box with a tiny square of cellophane tape. "Who's it from?"

The card was blank. Drew opened the box.

Inside, he found an extraordinarily well-tailored dark-blue single-breasted man's business suit, white shirt, and a silk handcrafted tie in muted but tasteful colors, and a pair of black men's dress shoes. Drew lifted the suit out on its hanger. Charly whistled. "Where are you going to go and preach in that?" he asked teasingly while Carlton laughed. Charly added in a more serious tone, "Go and try it on, Drew. Let's see how you look."

Drew came out of his bedroom a few minutes later, wearing the suit and shoes, holding the tie. "Charly, everything fits perfectly." He grinned. "I don't know how to tie a tie." Charly whistled appreciatively.

"You handsome dog," he said, smiling.

Carlton said, "I can tie a tie, buddy. Let me know when you need it done."

All turned at another tap at the front door. "Telegram," a young man in a Western Union uniform said, looking at them through the screen door. Charly signed for it.

"Drew, it's for you," he said, handing him the yellow envelope. Drew tore it open.

"BE AT LOBBY ADOLPHUS HOTEL TWO PM TODAY STOP WEAR SUIT." The telegram was signed Catherine Browning.

Carlton whistled. "You're gonna be in tall company today, man. I'll come back later and tie your tie. You need to start getting cleaned up."

Traffic was heavy around the Adolphus when Charly and Carlton dropped Drew off. The front door was almost hidden by a large crowd of stylishly dressed women. "I'll park the car," Charly said, "and Carlton and I will wait for you in the lobby." Both Charly and Carlton, along with Drew, were mystified as to the purpose of Catherine's message and whom Drew was to meet.

The lobby was crowded with women, all chattering and smiling one to another. Drew tried not to gawk at the spectacular lobby with its elaborate paneling, thick Oriental carpeting, and stunning artwork as he made his way through the crowd, unconscious of admiring glances from several of the younger women. Drew went to a large overstuffed chair and sat.

Almost immediately, it seemed to Drew, a uniformed bellhop carrying a silver tray stood in front of him. Drew looked up. "Mr. Drew Neilan?" the Philip Morris advertising logo lookalike asked. Drew nodded, and the bellhop handed him the silver tray. He frowned when Drew removed the piece of paper he was carrying and did not leave a tip in its place. The bellhop turned on his heel and walked swiftly away. Drew opened the note. It was in Catherine's strong flowing hand.

"Drew," she wrote, "I will meet you in the twelfth floor elevator lobby. Please come right away."

The elevator operator pulled the door handle; and the ornate doors opened onto a hallway filled with overly dressed women, many wearing furs, all seemingly talking at the same time. Drew worked his way through the swarm of women as they converged on the open elevator, which filled quickly. Drew stood to one side of the hallway as the crowd surged toward the next set of elevator doors and wondered what he should do. He saw Catherine working her way to him through the crowded hallway.

"I am so glad you made it," she said, "and right on time too. That's good. We haven't much time. Sorry to be so mysterious, but as they say, there's a war on. One can't be too careful, and besides that, I just really haven't had enough time. Step in here for a minute, and I'll tell you what this is all about." She ushered Drew into a small anteroom that evidently led into a much larger meeting room and quickly explained.

She next led an amazed Drew into the meeting room, filled with tables containing the remains of uneaten luncheon salads, water glasses, and plates with uneaten portions of food. A long table covered in white cloth spanned one end of the room and contained a huge bouquet of fresh flowers along with a speaker's dais behind a phalanx of microphones. Catherine led him toward the speaker's dais. A slightly stout woman in an olive drab women's army uniform had her back to them and was speaking softly to two women and a man, all of whom were taking notes.

The First Lady of the United States turned as they approached. "Mrs. Roosevelt," Catherine said, "I'd like you to meet—"

"Drew Neilan!" Eleanor Roosevelt said, interrupting Catherine and smiling, showing rather crooked teeth. There was no mistaking the obvious warmth behind the flawed smile as she went on, "I am so pleased to meet you!"

Drew was afraid he would stammer, but he did not. He tentatively offered his hand, and she took it in her gloved one as he smiled and said, "I am happy to meet you, Mrs. Roosevelt." Butterflies swooped and dove inside his stomach, colliding at times with his stomach walls.

Still holding Drew's hand, Mrs. Roosevelt turned to Catherine. "You did not tell me what a charmer this young man is," she said. "But we must hurry," the First Lady added with a tone of urgency. "I understand there is a weather system moving toward Dallas from the west, and my people tell me we must take off very soon if we are to return to Washington by later tonight." She turned back to Drew. "Will you accompany Mrs. Browning and me to Love Field? I want to talk with you. She has told me so much about you!"

While she had talked, a woman had fussed about behind the First Lady, adjusting and finally pinning a billed army cap upon her head.

She whispered to Mrs. Roosevelt, who said, "Come! We must depart at once."

Drew's mind perceived a kaleidoscope of images. A man in a business suit led the way to the elevator and the walk through the lobby to the waiting limousine, with dozens of women and men clapping and cheering and photographers aiming their cameras. There were flashbulbs popping and people staring at the entourage. They were followed by a second man in a business suit. Nothing stood still, nothing was permanent, and though Drew hoped he could retain all the impressions in his mind for later review after this astonishing day was over, he somehow knew that he would never hold on to all of it. It seemed that before the walk through the lobby had begun, he was seated in what Mrs. Roosevelt had called a jump seat, and the limousine was speeding toward Harry Hines Boulevard. He heard only vaguely the sirens from the motorcycle policemen who preceded and followed the motorcade.

"Catherine has told me," Mrs. Roosevelt was saying to him, "that you were one of her first students in that little country school in Arkansas.

"You have many friends who are Negroes, I understand," she added, changing the subject.

"Yes." Drew wondered where this was going.

"I also understand," the nation's First Lady continued, "that you were brought up until age five by a Negro congregation. Later, you lived for a while with a white priest whose parish consisted entirely of Negroes. So you see, you have a unique perspective on the plight of the American Negro, especially those in the South.

"Son," Mrs. Roosevelt went on, "Catherine has told me you witnessed her school burning."

This was news. Drew was stunned to learn that the First Lady of the United States knew of his presence that night. Mrs. Roosevelt continued speaking,

"Things need to change, son," Eleanor Roosevelt said with emotion. "Segregation throughout the South must come to an end. Hate and prejudice in all corners of our nation has to come to an end too, but an end to segregation must come first. We cannot dictate an end to hate, but we can legislate to bring an end to segregation. We can end hate only by setting an example for others to follow and then let the bigots swelter in their own juices. Eventually, we will win. Do you see that, Drew?"

Drew nodded a bit uncertainly.

"I see," Mrs. Roosevelt said. "Well, you will, I'm sure. It will be like a war, son, though not one fought with airplanes and tanks and battleships. And it will take decades, but I believe in the goodness of the American people, and I believe that in time they will all see. This country will truly become one nation, and it will be a nation where all men are created equal! I believe that. Will you join me in this war?" Drew could positively hear capital letters in the way she spoke.

"Of course, I will, but, Mrs. Roosevelt, we've got a pretty hot war going on right now."

She chuckled grimly. "Well said, Master Drew! Yes indeed. We do have a pretty hot war going on. And this present war does require battleships and airplanes and tanks and the lives of so many beautiful young men and women!" Tears had sprung to her eyes as she said this last. Her obvious emotions choked the words. The motorcade turned onto Mockingbird Lane from Lemmon. Drew realized for the first time that there were people standing along the roadway, waving flags and cheering as the four-car entourage sped toward Love Field. He looked back at Mrs. Roosevelt.

"We will win this present war, Drew!" she said with emphasis. "And after we do, I want you to join me in the next one. I need men of your sort—the nation needs men of your sort—men without prejudice, with love for their fellows, and men who are color blind when it comes to pigmentation. I ask you to join me."

The car stopped. Someone opened the door for the First Lady. As she began climbing out, there was a turn to Drew. She had a questioning look in her eyes. "Mrs. Roosevelt, you have my promise," Drew said.

Out of the corner of his eye, he saw Catherine nodding and smiling, almost proudly, as though she had wanted Drew to respond in this way.

"Good!" was all the First Lady said as she exited the car, turned, and waved to the crowd. Catherine gave Drew a quick hug as she and others in the car climbed out. "That was wonderful!" she whispered as she followed the First Lady. "I'll write you next week."

The car pulled ahead several car lengths and stopped. The driver motioned to Drew, and he got out. Other cars were discharging passengers behind him, and a number of people were moving toward the giant olive-drab-painted airplane. Its right engine was already idling with a throaty clatter. Photographers were shouting, and flashbulbs popped. As Drew watched, he saw the uniform of the First Lady as she climbed the three steps to the oval-shaped door of the plane, flanked by the two men in business suits. She waved and entered. Catherine followed. Other people climbed in, the two men followed, and a steward leaned out and folded the stairway into the plane and closed the door. The propeller on the left engine turned, and the exhaust spat black smoke and orange flames as the engine caught. The crowd around the plane began moving hastily toward a low fence that separated the terminal area from the tarmac. Drew followed.

The twin engines of the Douglas C-47 Army Skytrain roared, and the plane turned. A sharp wind tore at the crowd, and men's hats blew away while ladies tried to hold down their skirts. The plane moved slowly away, the clattering roar diminishing as the distance between the plane and the crowd increased. It reached the end of the runway and turned around. The engines roared again; and the plane began rolling, slowly at first, and then, gaining speed, lifted from the earth. It banked over the crowd as it folded its wheels into the fuselage and climbed into the sky, turning northeastward. Soon, it was a dot in the sky, and then it was gone.

"What was that all about?" Charly said as he touched Drew's elbow. Carlton stood nearby, his eyes round in amazement.

Drew turned. "I'm not sure. I'll tell you about it later at home." Charly realized that it was the first time Drew had referred to 1247 Cliff Heights Drive not as *your house* or *Charly's house* but as *home*.

He put his arm across Drew's shoulders. "Yeah, I kind of thought you'd be needing a ride. Carlton and I followed the motorcade all the way from town. C'mon, Carlton, Drew and I will drop you off, and then we need to go home."

"Miss Catherine," Drew told Charly later over coffee, "summarized it all for me right after I got off the elevator and before I ever met Mrs. Roosevelt. She said that when the Klan attacked the school in Union City, a newspaper reporter from Little Rock had written about it, and the Associated Press picked up the story. Mrs. Roosevelt had been interested in the school for some time—behind the scenes, of course—and that interest is what had kept the school open as long as it had since Miss Catherine had been proposing limited integration to the school board. After the attack, she asked the Justice Department to open a file. This is what protected me when the sheriff wanted me to come to an inquest. I never had to testify."

Charly whistled appreciatively. Drew continued, "There was concern that if I testified and identified the Klansmen—which, of course, I could—there might have been Klan retribution of some sort or another. There was nothing law enforcement could do, anyway, short of jailing a number of the town's leaders and creating even more unrest. So the best course was to make everything quietly go away."

Drew stared into his coffee cup. He was still organizing all the information himself.

"Later, Miss Catherine said, the Justice Department's involvement also protected me from several Klan retributions that I never even knew about. In fact, I never knew any of this. Besides, this was when Edith threw me out, so I ran off to Louisiana and eventually wound up at St. Timothy's.

"I guess that if Mrs. Roosevelt knew about me and whatever role I played at that little school, then she must have known about the teacher who made it all come about. That would, of course, have been Catherine Ryan, now Catherine Browning, the wife of Senator Theodore Browning, who is Mrs. Roosevelt's cousin."

"So," Charly said, "I've been living with a famous person."

"Hardly," Drew answered, smiling a little self-consciously, "besides, I don't want to be famous. I just want to live here with you, Charly." Drew's voice broke a little, "I really like having a home here with you."

Charly stood and put his cup into the sink. He punched Drew lightly in the shoulder as he passed. "And I like it too, buddy," he said.

Photographs of the First Lady's visit to Dallas were on the front page of the *Dallas Morning News*, the *Dallas Times-Herald* and the *Fort Worth Star-Telegram* the next morning. Drew's face was easily recognizable as part of the background of faces behind the First Lady as she swept through the lobby of the Adolphus into her waiting limousine. He was not identified in the captions or mentioned in any news story. But he had been noticed.

Sunday night, the darkened car was again parked down the block from 1247 Cliff Heights Drive. Two men with Lonny in the backseat were talking. They had talked before, and the topic was familiar to them.

The driver said as he smoked, "I told you. I checked out Charly Byrne the first time you called me. That was more than a year ago.

Byrne is a straight arrow. I told you then, and I'm telling you now. There's nothing goin' on between him and that kid."

"Lemme tell it to you again, then," the man in the passenger seat said as he lit his third cigarette from the stub of the second. "That kid plays nigger music all the time on his radio show. He's got every kid in Oak Cliff listening and dancing to that nigger music.

"Finally, and I've seen this more than once, that Charly Byrne and this kid are getting all brazen. They're always hugging and touching each other right out in public. In addition to that, now that kid goes off to the Adolphus and rides, brazen as you please, with Mrs. Roosevelt. You know she likes niggers. What did she and that kid cook up?

"You know," the speaker continued, "I have a cousin from Union City. He told me about a kid several years ago that saw one of our crusades up close when a school up there got what it deserved, and then the kid disappeared. Now there's this kid that shows up here living with Charly Byrne, answering to that kid's description. Could he be the same kid?"

"Look," the driver said while lighting another cigarette of his own, "I told you. Byrne's a straight arrow. Now, the nigger business, that's different. I agree Mrs. Roosevelt likes niggers an awful lot. I agree that kid needs to stop pushin' niggers into our face with his nigger music and havin' that nigger Eddie whatever-his-name-is over to his house.

"You may be onto something about the school thing in Arkansas, though. I'll have some guys check it out."

The driver turned to his son, Lonny, in the backseat. Lonny said, "I bet he is the guy from Arkansas. I know he's got a girlfriend who lives in Arkansas, a Jap girlfriend."

The two men in the front seat nodded. Yes, that would fit the facts as they saw them.

"We need to make one more check," the driver said. "You talk again to your cousin. Check out what Lonny said." He turned back to Lonny, grinning. "You may get to even your score with that kid."

He turned back to his front-seat passenger. "Let's have the boys give them a little teaser, maybe next week."

A week later, Charly pulled his police radio car onto Cliff Heights Drive, the red light on its roof flashing. It was three thirty in the morning. Fire trucks and a small crowd were in front of his house. He stopped in the street next to the fire truck and walked to his front porch past the still-smoking, rag-wrapped cross in his front yard. Drew was sitting tiredly on the steps.

"I heard about it on my police radio," Charly said, "and got here as fast as I could. I was answering a call of my own at the time. Are you OK?"

Drew looked up at his guardian; there were soot smudges on his face. "I'm all right, Charly. I was asleep, and something woke me up. The cross was already burning."

"Did you see who might have put it here?"

"I didn't see anyone. My first reaction was to get the garden hose and try to put the fire out. Mrs. Baker across the street called the fire department. I'm glad she did."

A fire department captain said, "He's OK, Charly."

Mrs. Baker came up. "He's so brave, Charly. He was out here trying to put that fire out all by himself."

"Thank you so much for calling it in," Charly said sincerely. "Did you see anyone?"

"No, it was burning, and Drew was out here with the hose when I woke up."

"Do you want us to pull it down and haul it away, Charly?" the fire captain asked, nodding his head toward the cross.

Charly looked at the smoldering obscene relic from the days of reconstruction. "No, I want you to pull it down and haul it to the police station. Put it in the side parking lot. I'm going to ask a couple of Dallas detectives to go over it tomorrow with a fine-toothed comb. If we can find any evidence—anything at all—I'm going to file a complaint."

Another man was standing in the small crowd in the street. He turned and went to his car. Later, he stopped at a telephone booth and made a call. "Byrne's going to have some people go over that cross. You need to get yourself over to the police station when it gets there and see to it that nothing is found."

# Chapter 29

## *April 1942*

NOTHING WAS FOUND in the remains of the cross that would point to any one individual or group of individuals. At the Dallas Justice Department field office, a note was made in a file, and the file was placed in a cabinet marked Secret.

As time went by, and the incident moved further away in people's minds, it seemed nothing more happened. Drew and Charly began locking the doors at night and both the doors and windows when they were to be away. Charly bought a large padlock for his tool shed, and they put the car away at night, locking the garage doors. But even these precautions soon seemed pointless.

Spring arrived in Dallas. Charly's roses seemed to compete at producing the most gorgeous or elegant among all the blooms that crowded the back yard of the little house on Cliff Heights Drive.

Spring had also come to the Arkansas Delta. The grassy field between St. Timothy's and the county road seemed, to Father Tom, to be filled with boundless color from the wildflowers. He felt that were he younger, he would have run down the slope, jumping as he ran, for the sheer joy of being in the midst of such beauty strewn about carelessly by Mother Nature.

But at seventy-seven years of age, he did not run laughing down the slope. He felt the fullness of his years in this springtime, but he felt it from the cautious standpoint of a man on whom the years rested heavily. He often felt tired, more so than usual, and sometimes fell asleep while working in his little office. Mrs. Calumet had chided him, urging that he see a doctor or at least take a dose of a tonic she'd concocted and given to her own family two days earlier. He laughed and told her it was nothing more than a severe case of spring fever.

He was to drive to the Millet's farm. Margaret Millet's baby was due soon, and he wanted to discuss the baby's baptism and name. As he climbed down the back steps of the tiny parsonage, Mrs. Calumet called out to ask him where he was going and when he would return. He told her, but somehow, her voice and his seemed loud enough to hurt his ears. He climbed into his Graham-Paige, switched on the ignition, and depressed the starter pedal. The engine ground for a second before it caught, and while it was well tuned and ran smoothly, it too seemed loud to him. Everything since before breakfast had seemed so vivid. He felt he could feel every nerve, muscle, and sinew of his body. All sounds were quite loud. When Mrs. Calumet moved the skillet onto the kitchen stove, the clang was loud enough to startle him.

The day seemed bright, which was odd. When he'd risen from his bed, the morning had been dark and overcast, threatening rain. In fact, it was still overcast; but to him, it seemed extraordinarily bright.

He shoved the gearshift lever into the reverse position and backed slowly, turning the car so that he could drive forward down the rise to the road. He felt he could hear every blade of grass as it crumpled underneath the tires. He waved to Mrs. Calumet, let in the clutch, and moved down the driveway.

After several miles, he turned off the main road onto a long straight lane that eventually would lead him to the Millet's farm. He settled back into the scarred and cracked leather seat cushions and increased the car's speed slightly, remembering the day when Drew had first driven the car and, when they'd come to a straightaway, how he'd told the boy to open the throttle and enjoy the speed. That day had been warm, and they'd opened the windshield. The wind had blown through the car as they'd laughed at their own audacity. This April day was cool, but nonetheless, he wished he'd opened the windshield before starting out.

At that moment, he felt significant pain in his chest.

Father Tom was no stranger to pain—his and the pain of others. He'd spent countless nights praying over someone who was sick or hurt or in childbirth, writhing in pain. He'd felt pain in his chest before, but it had been mild and easy to ignore. It had always gone away. This pain was new and dramatic. It took his breath away. He took his foot off the car's accelerator pedal, and the vehicle coasted to a stop at the side of the road.

Tom Byrne took a deep breath. *This will pass,* he thought as he switched off the engine. *I'll just sit here and wait for a few minutes. It will pass,* he repeated to himself. An old brown mule was grazing in the pasture across the fence from the car. Tom watched it as he continued taking one deep breath after another. The day remained very bright. At one point, he shaded his eyes from the gray brightness.

The pain did not pass. Instead, it increased in intensity and spread across his chest, radiating out into his left arm. Tom now knew what it was. He faced his adversary with the equanimity of his years. Everything dies, he thought, and if this was now his time, he was ready for it.

Except—except—there were a few things that needed to be finished. There was the coming of the Millet's baby, for example. There were so many other things. He wondered what would eventually become of those for whom he cared so much: the people in his parish, the boy, Drew, who'd somehow become more important to him than he'd thought when the youngster first ventured into his church that evening five summers ago. He wished he could see the boy once more. Photographs Charly had sent showed clearly the boy had grown and was becoming a fine-looking young man. *I would like to see that,* Father Tom said to himself.

A refrain from a Negro spiritual "Swing low, sweet chariot" played itself in his mind. He could hear Drew's strong voice, always on key, singing the majestic and moving old song. He scolded himself, saying that it was hardly a proper song for a dying Irish Catholic priest. He thought it should be something more Catholic but was hard-pressed to think of an appropriate hymn at that moment. *Comin' for to carry me home.* There was a soothing character to the song and to the voice in his head that sang it.

To whom would he say his final confession? He looked over at the mule across the fence and smiled to himself. Not the mule, certainly. A mule couldn't hear final confession. Could he hear his own final confession? *Hail Mary, full of grace!* His mind began the prayer, but then he remembered the times Drew had sung the Negro spiritual that rang in his head, and it filled his spirit. He could see Drew with Sister Arabella at the piano, the Negro children crowded around, singing along with Drew and the good sister. It had seemed to him then, and it did now, that when the Negro children sang this old spiritual with Drew leading, his soul had soared to new heights. *Comin' for to carry me home. Hail Mary, full of grace! Swing low, sweet chariot.*

He looked over at the old mule and silently asked the mule if he heard the singing too; but evidently the mule did not, for he simply stood quietly on the other side of the fence and ignored the old dying priest.

There was another upward surge in the level of pain. Tom gasped and cried out. His mother's face, careworn and tired, swam in a blurry outline before his eyes. She had been gone for almost five decades, having died well before the new century had begun. He was surprised that he was now seeing her face and thinking of her. Then he saw the sweet face of a twenty-year-old Mary Margaret, his Mary Margaret. Her face was blurred too, and the image shifted through the haze of pain that enveloped him.

But all at once, he saw her clearly. She was running across the meadow that day they'd picnicked on Long Island, running to show him the wildflowers she'd picked, both of them laughing at nothing, at foolishness, and at being young and in love. Somehow, as the flower-filled meadow from that day sprang to his mind, he saw it merged into his memory of the sloping field in front of St. Timothy's, also filled with vibrant color.

He pushed words into his head:

*Hail Mary, full of grace! The Lord is with thee. Blessed art thou among women and blessed is the fruit of thy womb, Jesus. Holy Mary, Mother of God, pray for us sinners, now and at the hour of our death. Amen.*

But through his prayer, Drew's voice in his head was still singing. It continued through the refrain, *Comin' for to carry me home.* He wondered for the briefest of moments if the boy had somehow miraculously appeared nearby.

Quite suddenly, the pain was gone. He breathed in the sweet air of relief, but he felt incredibly weak. He leaned back on the seat cushions. Oh, Blessed Virgin!

*I looked over Jordan, and what did I see? Comin' for to carry me home, a band of angels, comin' after me, comin' for to carry me home.*

Drew's voice rang through Tom's head, singing the Negro spiritual. He relaxed. He looked over at the pasture. The old mule was lying down, possibly to roll and scratch his back. The incredible brightness of the day increased. The brightness overwhelmed him.

Was a band of angels coming for him? It seemed that perhaps they might be, but it was hard to see anything at all over the brightness that was all around. He wondered if he would recognize any of the angels. Would the Blessed Virgin Mother accompany them? But surely, the Blessed Virgin had more important things to do than attend to the death of one old priest in a small, unimportant parish in the delta of Southern Arkansas.

Tom Byrne died.

It was Saturday, the twelfth of April, in the year of our Lord nineteen hundred and forty-two. He had been born in Dublin the year the United States was still locked into a conflict that was then called the War Between the States. He immigrated with his parents to New York when he was seven and had lived to see the end of one century and four decades of the next. He was seventy-seven years old.

They found him several hours later, sitting upright behind the wheel of his old sedan, his head slumped forward onto his chest.

In Oak Cliff, later that same day, Charly answered the doorbell and signed for the telegram. He opened it and sank into his easy chair. After a few minutes, he called Drew who put down his pencil and math book. Drew came into the living room.

"Father Tom is dead," Charly said simply, handing Drew the telegram. Drew sat down on the couch. He didn't know how he felt at that moment.

"I'll have to go," Charly said. "There's no one left of our family. The people in the parish and the church will want someone from the family to concur in funeral arrangements. I'll call in to headquarters. I've got vacation coming."

"Charly," Drew said, "I want to go too. He was important to me." Charly nodded. It was Father Tom who had brought Charly and Drew together. Drew often wondered what his life would have been like if the good priest had not intervened. "I'll call the radio station," Drew said. "They'll get someone to fill in for me if we're not back by Saturday."

They buried Father Tom Wednesday afternoon in the cemetery next to the old white clapboard church that was St. Timothy's. Charly had visited with the undertaker in town and ordered a small stone. It would be placed over the grave within several weeks.

Monsignor Father Richards from St. Michael's Cathedral in Little Rock had come for the funeral and conducted the services. The small church was overflowing with quite a few standing outside in the warm April afternoon. The field of wildflowers that sloped from St. Timothy's to the county road was filled with automobiles, farm trucks, and wagons. The colorful flowers, crushed beneath rubber and iron tires, filled the air with fragrance. The simple coffin was carried on the shoulders of six strong Arkansas Negro farmers to the little graveyard and gently set onto two sawhorses beside the open grave. Although Father Richards had instructed that this was not a day for weeping but of jubilation in the certainty that Father Tom was with Christ, most of those present wept anyway.

Drew's eyes were dry in contrast to the tears coursing down Charly's cheeks. Drew walked alongside the burly balding policeman, his arm across the older man's shoulders. As he walked, he remembered his vow in a windy, cold boxcar rattling into Louisiana. Father Tom had been his benefactor, his friend, had led him to Charly and to his present life in Oak Cliff; and Drew was incredibly sad that he would not again in this lifetime see the frail white-haired priest. But he would not, and did not, cry. He walked beside Charly with his head held high and his shoulders squared. The day of Father Tom's funeral was a day that Drew took another step toward being the man he was destined to become.

A young black priest, Father Vincent, who would be Father Tom's replacement, conducted prayers at the gravesite. When he finished, Father Richards nodded to the pallbearers and, straining, they began lowering the earthly remains of Tom Byrne into the Arkansas Delta soil. As they did, a rich baritone voice began singing in a slow majestic cadence. It came from somewhere near the outskirts of the crowd surrounding the open grave.

*"Mine eyes have seen the Glory of the Coming of the Lord!"*

Beryl Lancaster, whose eleven children Father Tom had baptized, and who had thought he would die of heartbreak when four of those did not survive their first year and Father Tom buried them, was singing his own tribute for Father Tom.

*"He is trampling out the vineyards where the grapes of wrath are stored!"*

Beryl's seven surviving children had all graduated from high school at a time when funds for such were not available. Somehow, Father Tom had found the money. Beryl continued the old anthem, picking up the cadence a little as others began joining in, tenuously at first and then with more confidence.

*"He has loosed the fateful lightning of His terrible swift sword!"*

One of Beryl's surviving children was an intern at a Chicago hospital, another an attorney in Indianapolis, and two were teachers at Negro schools in Mississippi. Father Tom had somehow made all this happen, and Beryl continued through the old verses as he wept for a man he knew to be holy.

*"As He died to make men holy, let us live to make men free, while God is marching on!"*

As more Negroes and now even whites scattered among the mourners joined in the singing, the cadence gained even more of a triumphant beat. In the final victorious chorus, all those in the cemetery were singing. There was no black or white, no farmer or businessman, no rich or poor in this simple final farewell to a man who had walked in their midst and whom all believed to have been truly good.

*"Glory! Glory! Hallelujah! Our God is marching on!"*

Unnoticed by everyone, a large town car of indeterminate age, driven by an elderly liveried light-skinned Negro chauffeur, sat at the side of the county road with its engine idling as Father Tom's coffin was lowered into the waiting grave and Beryl began singing his final tribute for the old priest. Heavy curtains shielded the rear of the town car from prying eyes. Had anyone been nearby, they would have seen the curtains pulled back slightly by a wrinkled hand, heavy with jeweled rings and bracelets.

The gloom inside the automobile was such that, even if there had been an observer, he would not have seen the tears that flowed down the powdered cheeks of an old and retired bawdyhouse madam as Beryl Lancaster led the final ringing tribute to Father Tom Byrne. As the song ended, the hand closed the curtains, a cane tapped the chauffeur's shoulder, and the ancient town car drove away from St. Timothy's down the dusty road that led to the new paved highway.


Drew and Charly stayed for three days in the little parsonage behind St. Timothy's, going through Tom Byrne's things and settling the few affairs left unattended. Tom's car and most of his material things were donated to the parish. He had left no insurance, but neither had he left any unpaid debts. Monsignor Father Richards had asked for a large file folder they found, filled with photographs and copies of letters. They forwarded it to him at St. Michael's. Neither Drew nor Charly had looked closely at the file, for if they had, they would have seen among the dozens of old letters and photographs a few of a young Drew. Drew would have known the intended recipient of the originals of these letters, but had they asked Father Richards, he would not have told them.

That Saturday, as they were driving away from St. Timothy's, Drew asked, "Charly, do you think we could stop in Union City for a couple of hours on the way back to Dallas?"

"You bet we can." Charly grinned. "Wouldn't happen to be a certain someone you'd want to see, would there?"

Drew looked with a serious face at this man he loved. "Yeah, maybe."

Drew met Kowanda in the basement of the town's library while Charly and Ursula Schultz had a cup of tea in her office. It was nearly dark by the time Charly and Drew left Union City heading toward Dallas.

On the other side of the world the Pacific Ocean was seeing the dawn of Sunday, April 18, the day that General Jimmy Doolittle launched his fleet of B25-B Mitchells from the deck of the carrier *Hornet*. The bombers were bound for Tokyo and Yokohama.

# Chapter 30

-◇-•-◯-•-◇-

# *April 1945*

THE LUMBERING TROOP train inched across the Texas Hill Country west of San Antonio on an early spring day in 1945. Eighteen-year-old Drew Neilan looked out the open window at the semi-arid scenery. There were tall columns of "dust devils," rather flat-topped limestone mountains, a blue cloudless sky, and the strange shapes of cacti lining the right-of-way. The trip across Texas seemed endless. At stops along the way, none of those on board had been allowed to disembark.

Their destination was unknown, a military secret. Several with whom Drew had talked had assured him they had inside information that the West Coast was their final disembarkation point; they were all to be part of the invasion of Japan.

The US Red Cross met the train at each stop. Women walked along the cars distributing cold drinks and sandwiches. Drew accepted a sandwich and Coke gratefully. At one stop—Drew thought it was San Antonio because of the depot's Mission and Spanish colonial revival architecture—the train stayed motionless for six hours. At another stop in a small town in Central Texas, they stayed four hours. At none of the stops had anyone been allowed to leave the train.

Six or seven soldiers, one with a guitar, were singing in the front of the car: "Deep in the Heart of Texas." Periodically, they would all clap four times: "The rabbits rush, around the brush (*Clap! Clap! Clap! Clap!*) Deep in the heart of Texas!" Drew smiled and turned again to the opened window, wind whistling, thinking of the last three years.

Drew was not in the army. He was a member of a USO entertainment troupe traveling with the soldiers to their undisclosed termination point. There, they were to give shows every evening for a week. Drew was in a car at the front of the train. Other white USO performers were scattered throughout. However, the remainder of the troupe—Eddie Mackenzie's orchestra—were in rough seats installed in boxcars at the rear of the train. There were a number of boxcars filled with Negro troops, along with Eddie's people, and they rattled along behind the passenger carriages reserved for white soldiers and white USO performers.

Drew had protested loudly when he'd learned of the traveling accommodations and had gone to a nearby telephone to call Catherine Browning to see if she could have any influence on the United States Army. Before Catherine could be connected, a master sergeant had opened the booth door and pulled the earpiece hook down, terminating the call. "You can't make any calls!" he'd shouted. "This train and everyone on it is subject to secrecy—a military secret!" Drew had boarded his assigned car while the master sergeant mumbled, not quite under his breath, "Nigger lover!"

As Drew sat in his seat on that hot, dusty trip, he felt as if the last three years might have been something of a dream—most of it a very good dream—but some of it a nightmare. He thought about the tragedy of a father, so consumed with racial hatred that he would send his own son, Lonny, on a mission of murder.

Drew remembered vividly the sight of Lonny's knife as it withdrew from his body, the blade covered in thick red blood. He had watched in disbelief while he pushed Kowanda out of the way, Lonny shouting something about Japs, niggers, queers, and how he hated them and then something about Union City. Lonny continued on, knife pointing, this time at Drew. Before Drew could dodge or try to deflect the blade, it had, seemingly in slow motion, entered his body. He remembered the surprise he'd felt at the time; there was no pain. But then the blackness enveloped him, and later pain was his constant companion for a very long time.

Drew had driven to Union City, picked up Kowanda at the public library, and brought her back to Dallas for the 1944 senior prom. She slept in his room. He slept on the couch. Charly had promised Kowanda's mother that he would strictly chaperone the youngsters.

Drew had worn his Neiman Marcus suit that Saturday morning before the prom and had taken Kowanda downtown to the prestigious department store. The clerks recognized the suit, and Drew invoked Catherine Browning's name, causing the department manager to be called. Everyone scurried about. In the end, Kowanda had a beautiful pink prom dress in the very latest of fashion, one that accented her dark almond eyes and hair. It had been costly. Drew had cashed quite a few postal bonds to pay for it but thought it all worthwhile. Charly had been impressed when Kowanda modeled the dress before they left for the prom. He unlimbered his Kodak and took flash pictures.

They made a beautiful couple, easily the most attractive at the prom. Boys envied Drew. Girls envied Kowanda's dress. Drew had made prior arrangements with the band leader, and he and Carlton practiced together before the prom with their dates. Drew, as class president, and Carlton, as class vice president, had the job of welcoming the seniors, the faculty chaperones, and the band. At the proper time, Drew, Kowanda, Carlton, and Mary Alice Johnson walked out on the stage before the closed curtains. Drew announced his part of the obligatory welcome speech, holding Kowanda's hand; and Carlton, holding Mary Alice's hand, completed the remainder of the welcoming speech. They introduced the band. The curtains opened, music started, and both couples performed what appeared to be an impromptu but graceful soft-shoe. They danced off the stage as the band segued into Glenn Miller's "In the Mood."

It was late. The band was taking its final break. It would return for two or three more songs, and the evening would be over. Kowanda and Drew, along with a number of other students, had moved outside into the cooler night air. The gymnasium was stifling. Both boys and girls crowded around Drew and Kowanda, and everyone seemed to be talking at once. Carlton was the first to see Lonny.

He looked disheveled, shirt tail partly out; he weaved as he walked. He carried an opened pint bottle of liquor.

"Hey, Skaggs," Carlton called out, "are you OK, man?"

Lonny focused on Kowanda, standing next to Drew and chatting excitedly with Mary Alice. "I hate Japs!" he shouted. He continued shouting; it was mostly unintelligible. He moved into the crowd. It parted. People moved aside.

Carlton stepped between Lonny and Kowanda and then doubled over, holding his middle. There was a knife. The blade was bloody. A girl screamed. Lonny dropped the liquor bottle and rushed toward Kowanda who stood transfixed, feet rooted to the ground. Drew moved quickly. He pushed Kowanda, who fell; and as she did, Lonny's knife entered Drew's body.

Drew was sick for a long time. Charly had been waiting in his car to drive Drew and Kowanda back to 1247 Cliff Heights Drive after the prom. He was chatting with a friend, a motorcycle patrolman, when he saw the disturbance. The kids moving about, girls screaming, set off his internal alarms, and he rushed over along with several teachers. Carlton was dead. Lonny was pinned to the ground by several boys, screaming obscenities. Drew was unconscious and bleeding. Kowanda was on the ground, holding him, crying and screaming, his blood staining the beautiful pink prom dress.

It never occurred to Charly to wait for an ambulance. He picked up Drew and raced to his car. Kowanda followed. Someone handed Charly a towel. Kowanda took it and held it tightly to the gushing wound. The towel quickly turned red. The motorcycle patrolman led the way to Parkland Hospital, his siren blaring, his red lights flashing.

There was surgery and days of unrelenting pain, relieved only by morphine-induced blackness. Soon, though, it began to appear that all the skills of Parkland Hospital's physicians would be unable to suppress the rampant infection. Drew did not know, could not know, but he was visited by many, including Judge McGowan and Catherine Browning. Flowers crowded his hospital room. A number of telegrams from the nation's First Lady were strewn about. Doctors told a weeping Charly to prepare himself, for Drew was not likely to survive.

Penicillin was a new drug and in short supply, but Catherine had appealed to doctors she knew at Bethesda. Somehow a supply had appeared at Parkland.

One day in early June, Drew woke and looked around the flower-filled room. A nurse was standing beside his bed. "Well," she said brightly, "you've decided to rejoin the living?"

Drew's small intestine had been damaged. He would regain his strength, but the draft board would nevertheless classify him as 4-F. He would never be a member of the armed forces of the United States.

Drew resumed his radio show that August. Then, two months later, the USO began tryouts for a stage production as part of a Dallas War Bonds Drive. Drew had seen James Cagney in *Yankee Doodle* at least six times. His dance instructor in Highland Park had transcribed the choreography, and Drew practiced the outstanding dance steps Mr. Cagney performed. The USO show was to include production numbers based on several movies and Broadway productions, including the Cagney movie. The producers needed a lead dancer who could mimic Cagney. Drew tried out and was selected.

Weeks of rehearsal followed. Eddie Mackenzie agreed to perform. The idea of an all-Negro orchestra rankled some of Dallas's elite, but they were somewhat mollified when it was pointed out that the lead performer would be a white boy from Oak Cliff. Drew was well-known through his radio show.

The performance opened in McFarland Auditorium one cool fall day. There was a dinner in the adjacent hall, speeches, pleas for more money for war bonds, then the tuxedoed and beribboned crowd moved into the auditorium. Eddie and his players were in the orchestra pit, tuning up. The lights dimmed, the crowd hushed, and the curtains opened to the full cast singing and Drew dancing Cagney's timeless *Yankee Doodle Dandy*. The crowd roared.

There were other production numbers, all with a patriotic theme. Then at the end, the entire cast began singing *"God Bless America."* Drew motioned and shouted to the crowd, "Sing along with us!" The crowd stood and sang. Women wept. Men pulled out their checkbooks. Ushers went along the aisle, collecting checks and pledges.

Drew and the cast had what seemed dozens of curtain calls. In one, a perspiring Drew motioned to Eddie who joined the cast on stage and bowed along with the entire crew. Eddie motioned to members of his orchestra to stand and bow.

The audience began chanting, *"Yankee Doodle Dandy!"* Drew held up his hands and walked to stage front and center. In the hush that followed, Drew shouted, "OK, folks, but only if you sing along too!"

Eddie's orchestra crashed into the opening bars, and Drew began his performance. The audience sang along, and *Yankee Doodle Dandy* soared into Dallas history.

The show was a success. There were clamors for another performance. Three more were held. Drew had clearly been the star of the show. Charly was so proud of Drew his friends laughed, saying that he was going to burst the buttons on his chest.

A few days later, the USO approached Eddie. The Dallas show had been such a hit the USO had decided to continue the show and planned to schedule performances at a number of military bases. Funds had been found to meet Eddie's fees. Not all the cast of the original Dallas production would be available, so some of the numbers would have to be changed and the overall show abbreviated. This suited the USO well since several of the new shows were to be part of coast-to-coast radio broadcasts with Hollywood stars and radio personalities. Thus, the radio portions would fill the deleted portions of the original show. Eddie asked the USO to ask Drew to join. Drew thought he'd like to do it and planned to talk with Charly the next morning.

But that was the morning Charly died.


Charly's early morning habit, after ending his eleven-to-seven shift, was to stop at a local bakery a block down from the Texas Theatre. The elderly, palsied Jewish proprietor and Charly were good friends. Abe always expected him and had fresh cinnamon buns and a steaming cup of coffee waiting.

On this morning, just before Charly was expected, a Negro boy, about twelve, entered the front door of the bakery. It was decided later that the boy—whose name was never known—meant no harm. He was simply hungry; and the smell of the freshly baked breads, buns, and doughnuts were more than he could stand. He had entered to beg.

But Abe did not interpret it that way.

A black boy had entered through the front door, which in itself would be a threatening thing to some. Abe was frightened. With shaking hands, he pulled a double-barreled shotgun from under the counter. "You get outta here!" Abe screamed, brandishing the gun.

Charly walked in at just that moment and quickly factored the situation. "Hold it, Abe!" Charly shouted. "He's just a boy!" Charly walked up behind the Negro, preparing to hold him and escort him out of the store. Abe's shaking fingers pulled both triggers.

Number six buckshot tore through both bodies.


Drew was making breakfast, eggs frying in the skillet. At a knock on the door, he turned the gas off and went into the front room. Two Dallas policemen were standing on the porch.


Drew would never remember details of the funeral. Catherine attended as did Judge McGowan. Mrs. Roosevelt sent a handwritten note. The mayor spoke; there was an honor guard of Dallas policemen, and as the cortege moved through Dallas, men stood at the curb with hats removed. While the mayor had given the eulogy, everyone expected that Drew would also speak, but he did not. Charly was laid to rest beside his beloved Rebecca.

The day after the funeral, a taciturn Drew cancelled his radio show.

Two weeks later, Judge McGowan rang the bell at the front door of 1247 Cliff Heights Drive. "May I come in?" he asked.

Without preamble, the judge seated himself at the dining room table. "Would you offer me a cup of coffee?"

The judge withdrew several files and other papers from his briefcase, setting them on the tabletop.

As Drew delivered the hot coffee, the judge said, "Get one for yourself. Please sit down. We have a great deal to discuss."

Charly had left a will and two insurance policies. One policy paid off the mortgage in the event of his death. The other was a $10,000 whole-life policy. Drew was the sole-named beneficiary. The city of Dallas held a $5,000 policy for policemen killed in the line of duty, and Drew would also receive this. In addition, there was a $5,000 savings account; most now invested in war bonds.

The judge next reminded Drew that for several years, an anonymous check, drawn on a bank in Memphis, had appeared in his office at quarterly intervals. It had been marked For the Benefit of Drew Allen Neilan. Charly had, at first, used the checks to buy postal bonds for Drew but later converted the postal bonds to war bonds. The current total of the bond account was $3,700.

The house, bank, and savings accounts and all the bonds were now Drew's, as was the car, all the furniture, Charly's woodworking tools, and his roses. Charly's will appointed Judge McGowan executor until Drew turned twenty-one.

"And since Charly was with the city of Dallas for more than twenty years," the judge said, "as his sole heir, you will receive his pension. It won't be much, probably $100 a month, maybe a little less. You'll receive it until you reach the age of twenty-five."

As Drew was digesting all this, he said, "Those quarterly checks. I've known about them for quite some time and often wondered. Do you know who they came from?"

"No, I don't know. They came from a Memphis bank. The letter accompanying each said they were from someone who wished to remain anonymous. Both Charly and I respected that person's wishes. You should too."

The judge changed to a different subject. "Your reports to me over the years have kept me well informed about your life. Now, I need to talk about that girl, Kowanda, from Union City. After the prom, she returned home. All the time you were sick, Charly wrote regularly, giving her updates on your condition. At one time, Charly planned to go to Union City and bring her to Dallas to visit you, but right about then, you took a turn for the worse.

"Later, when you started to get better, Charly wrote her again, planning again to bring her to Dallas. However, that was about the time we learned that when Kowanda's father found out about, her 'sneaking away' to go to the prom with you. He became enraged."

Drew shook his head. "He never did like me. He called me the bastard son of the town whore."

"Well," the elderly jurist continued, "as I understand it, things began getting really bad about that time. Kowanda's father threw both she and her mother out of the house. I don't know all his reasons, but evidently, he had become obsessed about his wife's Japanese heritage. Kowanda and her mother moved in temporarily with Ursula Schultz."

"I knew about that," Drew said. "Kowanda and I wrote back and forth during the time I was recovering, after I got out of the hospital. Things were pretty rough for her. We decided to stop writing for a while so that, perhaps, Kowanda's mother and father could work things out."

"But," Judge McGowan said, "that didn't happen."

"No. Miss Schultz wrote me several times. Maybe she wrote you too. She said Kowanda's father was trying to rile up the Klan over Mitsui's Japanese ancestry."

"Mitsui?" Judge McGowan interrupted.

"Yes, Kowanda's mother. Anyway, things were getting nasty. Miss Schultz said that even she was going to stop writing me to be sure the Klan didn't connect me with their hate campaign."

"When all that was happening, I got involved in the USO show, and things were awfully busy. Then, Charly—" Drew paused, unable to continue.

"Kowanda's father," Judge McGowan said in a flat voice, "initiated divorce proceedings and reported his wife and daughter to the War Relocation Authority, the people who've taken those of Japanese descent in the West, and placed them in detainment camps.

"Kowanda and her mother are in a camp in Kansas."

The slow uncomfortable train crawled across the west Texas landscape. Despite the calendar proclaiming that spring had arrived, the inside of Drew's railway carriage was as stifling as if it were already summer. Windows were open. A hot, dusty west Texas wind blew through the car. Drew drowsed uncomfortably, leaning against the windowsill. He sensed another presence nearby and looked up. A man in a United States Army uniform was standing in the aisle next to Drew's seat. It was Eugene.

The surprise was complete. Drew could only stare.

"Gotcha!" came from the whiny, nasally voice Drew remembered well as Eugene sat down in the seat next to him. "Didn't expect to see me, did ya?" Eugene's hand rested on the seat near Drew's thigh. "You gotta remember," the nasty man went on, "I'm your step-pappy now. How about a hug for your step-pappy?"

"Touch me, and I will do my very best to kill you," Drew said. This was not said in a growl or a whisper but instead calmly and as a statement of fact.

"Aww. Is that any way to treat me? I'm an old friend." Eugene's hand moved closer.

"I was never friends with you," Drew said. "I'm not likely to be."

"Ain't you even interested in how I happened to be here?"

"Why don't you go to hell?" Drew pulled his cap down and moved closer to the window.

"You need to be nice to me. Your momma and me, we're gonna be rich. We're on our way. We'll cut you in if you're nice to me."

"You keep your hand to yourself!" Drew felt the gorge rise in his throat.

Eugene pulled his hand back and smiled. Drew noticed the US Army had evidently paid for dental work. The missing front tooth had been replaced, and the smell of rotten teeth was gone.

"Oh, I'll back off for now," Eugene said, still smiling. "But you'll learn to be nice to me. I told you, your momma and me are gonna be rich. You'll come begging."

Drew answered, "I already said touch me and I'll do my best to kill you."

"You can't do that. You're a civilian traveling on a US Army troop train. It's against army regs for a civilian to strike a noncommissioned officer."

Drew's head spun around. Good lord! The disgusting man was wearing master sergeant stripes.

"I suspect," Drew said, "that homosexuals are also against army regs."

"Hey, hey, hey. I ain't no homo."

"You could have fooled me."

The wayward hand again rested on the seat beside Drew. "And I don't think you're likely to fool that lieutenant watching us from over there," Drew said, nodding in the lieutenant's direction. The hand was withdrawn.

"I even got somebody working for me that I just know you'll know," Eugene chuckled. "He's a nigger. I use him to sweep up and deliver stuff to the nigger companies. You know a guy named Leon?"

Drew felt he would vomit at any moment.

"Yeah," Eugene went on, "I had to have my guys hold him down while I slapped him around a little but, you know niggers." The casual way the word rolled off his tongue made Drew's teeth grind. "Hit them a time or two, and then they're all 'yassa, masta,' stuff like that. He folded easy."

Eugene laughed, and his mouth got the funny crinkly lines Drew remembered so well. "I may even try out some of that nigger stuff, you know? It's all pink inside, they say."

Drew gagged and got up. "I'm going to the restroom, up there," Drew said, nodding toward the front of the car. "I assure you I will lock the door. If you are here when I come back, I will complain to the lieutenant."

By the time he was finished, had washed his face, and opened the restroom door, Eugene was exiting the car at the rear.

As he sat at the dining room table with Judge McGowan, he tried to calm his feelings. Drew said, "I'll call Catherine Browning. Surely, she can get Kowanda out of there."

"I already did," the judge said, "right after I learned about the internment. She and I, along with Ursula Schultz, have been working together for some time. Mrs. Browning has pulled quite a few strings, I understand. She has even talked with the First Lady. But even so, the administrative details to have someone released from one of those camps are extraordinarily tedious. You were involved in *Yankee Doodle* at the time. Charly asked that we avoid mentioning anything to you until we could report progress."

"And?" Drew questioned.

"We've made progress. Mrs. Browning and Ursula Schultz and several others are preparing affidavits about them being loyal Americans and so on. I need to prepare an affidavit that they have a place to live."

Drew sat still in his chair for a long time, coffee cooling. The judge waited patiently, expectant, for Drew's answer to the unspoken question.

Drew got up and walked to the hall from the dining room and toward the door to Charly's room. He had not entered since he and someone from the police department picked out the uniform for Charly's body. Drew looked at Charly's toiletries and electric razor clustered on the bureau, along with an opened Chesterfield carton. He stood in the middle of the room and looked at Charly's dozens of photographs of Rebecca. He looked for a long time. He opened the closet door. It seemed to Drew that he could smell Charly. He felt his heart breaking all over again.

Drew turned, shut the door to Charly's bedroom, and went down the hall to his bedroom. There were two photographs on his desk: a small, silver-framed, creased, and dirty photograph of a young boy and his teacher, standing on the porch of a run-down grocery store, squinting into the afternoon sun; the shadow of Felix Martinez sprawled across the foreground. The other was a framed photograph of Charly, taken by Drew, showing Charly in one of his softball team jerseys, holding a bat as though waiting for a pitch. Drew remembered asking Charly to look aggressive, stare hard as though facing a real pitcher instead of the camera. Charly had burst out laughing instead, and Drew snapped the picture. Drew stood, looking at the picture of Charly. As he did, something inside Drew changed. The metamorphosis crystalized. Drew straightened up. He was now a man. His father was dead.

Drew walked back into the dining room. "Charly was my dad, and I loved him. I'll always love him." Judge McGowan remained sitting. He waited, his expression neutral.

"But Charly's gone," Drew said, seemingly standing a little taller. "I've got a life to live. I've got a place for Kowanda and her mother." He paused. His eyes shifted away from the judge, searching, looking into the distance. Then Drew looked back. It was as if he had returned to the present. "Didn't you just say I own this house? They can live here with me. We'll put twin beds in Charly's room. Kowanda can have one, her mother the other. I'll keep my room. We'll be fine."

The judge relaxed. He had achieved his objective. He chuckled. "Don't you think the neighbors might think it's improper? Kowanda's mother can't chaperone you and Kowanda all the time."

"Then I'll marry Kowanda," Drew said firmly. "That'll shut them up."


The train rattled into a town. Drew looked around. *This must be El Paso,* he thought.

Someone was running alongside the slowly moving train as it pulled into the depot. It was a young Mexican boy, about twelve, holding up newspapers and shouting.

President Franklin Delano Roosevelt was dead.

# Chapter 31

<h2 style="text-align:center">El Paso</h2>

THERE WAS NATIONAL grief over the president's death. Some of the soldiers on the train wept, and Drew himself was saddened. His thoughts were centered on Mrs. Roosevelt as he exited the train and asked permission to go to the Western Union Office.

"Son," a captain told him, "you're a civilian, but while on this train with these troops, you're under military supervision. You can go, but someone has to accompany you and review your telegram before it's sent. No phone calls, though."

He assigned a lieutenant, not much older than Drew; and as the two walked across the station, Drew asked about the secrecy. "There's not much I can tell you," the lieutenant said. "I know army trucks are on the way to transport everyone that was on the train to Fort Bliss and two buses are on the way for the USO troupe on board. You're part of that, aren't you?"

"Are the troops to stay at Fort Bliss? I'd heard they were headed to the West Coast."

"I don't know anything about that. I can say that I understand the troops will be in Bliss only temporarily. Two or three weeks, maybe a month. Then after that, no one knows."

After Drew had written the text of the telegram, an expression of sympathy for Mrs. Roosevelt, the young lieutenant leaned over. "I can't let you send that."

"But the president just died," Drew said.

"I know, but Mrs. Roosevelt is under military guard. We don't know if the president's death was a natural thing or some sort of enemy plot."

Drew shrugged. He addressed a new telegram to Judge McGowan and asked him to convey his regards and sympathy to Mrs. Roosevelt. This met with the lieutenant's approval.

As they were leaving the telegraph office, Eddie Mackenzie walked out of the colored waiting room. "Drew, we're leaving on a couple of buses the USO has provided. Our shows are going to be at Bliss."

Just then, Leon also walked out. Drew shouted. Leon turned. "Eddie," Drew said, "you and your guys go on ahead. I'll take a taxi later. Leave my name at the front gate. I'll catch up." He and Leon ran to each other.

The lieutenant had followed. Drew grasped both Leon's hands, and each boy began talking at the same time. The lieutenant stood by with a bemused expression on his face.

Drew turned. "Lieutenant, you know I've gotten permission to travel to Bliss in a taxi. Could Leon ride with me?"

"Maybe. I don't know. Let's go talk to the major. He's right over there."

"Look," the major said after listening to both Drew and the lieutenant, "you need to talk to that captain. He's part of the MP squad accompanying us to the base."

The captain listened and then nodded. "I'd heard you Southerners are funny about your niggers. Is this guy one of your house niggers?" Drew kept his mouth shut. Leon looked angry.

"Yeah, sure. Go ahead. What the fuck do I care?"

Eugene saw both as they were heading out of the depot. "What are you shits gonna do?" he said. "You gonna go suck each other's dick?" Eugene laughed the nasty laugh that Drew wished to never hear again.

Drew and Leon kept moving out to the taxi stand.

The Mexican taxi driver at first refused to let Leon ride in his cab, but a $5 bill from Drew served to change his mind.

They talked nonstop for several minutes as the cab negotiated El Paso traffic. The front gate of Fort Bliss came into view before Drew wanted. He asked the driver to pull over for a minute.

"You hungry?" he asked Leon.

"You knows me, massa," Leon said. "Ah is always hongry." He rolled his eyes.

"Not funny," Drew said. He turned to the Mexican driver. "Is there someplace we can get something to eat?"

"Not both of you," the driver answered. Then, after another $5 bill was produced, he said, "Well, I know this little place down by the river.

It's really small. I think if I talk to the guy what runs it probably he'll let you both in." All this in highly accented, somewhat tortured English.

"I'll buy lunch for all three of us," Drew said.

"I gotta warn you, white guy," the driver said, "the food—it's hot."

A memory of tortillas and beans in a small kitchen late at night, over a small grocery store, flashed into Drew's mind for just an instant.

"We'll handle it," Drew said.

For $20, the proprietor closed the little three-table restaurant. Drew and Leon were seated at a table away from the front windows. The café's proprietor and the driver sat at a back counter, talking in Spanish.

The food was delicious. It was spicy beyond all belief but delicious. Other than Mr. Martinez's beans and tortillas, Drew had never before eaten Mexican food. Disregarding Texas's liquor laws, the proprietor brought both of the under-twenty-one-year-olds frosty mugs of beer to help control the flames.

They talked, laughed, and Leon even cried a little. The lunch lasted over two hours. They had three mugs of beer each and ate more than either had thought they could hold. As the lunch ended, the proprietor brought three saucers over to the table. On each was a small glass with a slightly amber liquid and a quarter lime. The boys looked up in puzzlement. The proprietor picked up his lime and bit into it. He next picked up the small glass and in a practiced movement tossed the liquid into his throat. He smiled. Both Leon and Drew looked at each other, shrugged, and did as the proprietor had done. Each coughed after downing the tequila.

As they walked back to the parked taxi, Drew realized that for the first time in his life he was a little tipsy. Perhaps he was more than a little tipsy. Leon was unsteady too.

While the taxi made its way to Fort Bliss, Leon said, a little thickly, "Drew, I gotta tell you sompin."

As he talked, both he and Drew began to become sober.

Drew had the driver stop twice so he could hear it all before they got to the base.

Eugene was running a huge black-market operation as part of his job as battalion supply sergeant. When orders for new goods came to him, he increased the amounts and sold the excess when the military supplies arrived. There were enormous profits. Each of the noncommissioned officers in the supply unit, as well as the captain in charge, was part of the scheme. Eugene had also offered money to the major, and he'd accepted. There was no one Leon could talk to.

"What's your job in a white supply unit?" Drew asked.

"Oh, massa," Leon answered, "ah rolls mah eyes, ah mops floors, ah carries stuff, and ah keeps mah mouth shut." Then in much better English, he told Drew that there were other white service units that had a few blacks assigned for menial chores, so the whites wouldn't "dirty their hands."

Leon talked about the approaches Eugene had made. "I might have to kill him one of these days," Leon said hopelessly. Drew could see the signs the stress was having on him, now that he could take the time to look.

"Maybe we could put him in jail instead," Drew said with a bit of steel in his voice.

Leon snorted and smiled grimly. "He'd probably like that. Think of all the men he could feel up."

"Your testimony would at least start an investigation," Drew said, with what he hoped was a positive tone. "I could contact Judge McGowan. He'd tell us how best to get someone's attention."

Leon grew serious. "There's no way I can go to anyone without Eugene finding out. I can't even go around that major Eugene's paying off. If military police come in, Eugene will suspect me, deny everything, and the major would assure them that it was just some nigger blowing smoke. Then Eugene would take it out on me."

Both were silent for a while.

Drew looked up when Leon said in a whisper, "But there is a ledger."

The driver let them off at the front gate of Fort Bliss. Drew showed their passes. They were admitted.

"We can't walk together," Leon said. "You go on. I'll turn here and find out where I'm supposed to go."

Later, in a large base theater usually reserved for weekend movies, rehearsals were under way. Sound and lighting technicians from the USO were busily installing lights, microphones, and supplemental speakers. Their first show would be within four nights.

Drew was taking a break at the side of the stage, perspiring heavily. Spring was warm in El Paso, and the hall had only a few electric fans scattered near the ceiling. Doors were opened on both sides of the stage.

Hot, dry desert air blew in, quickly drying Drew's sweat-soaked T-shirt, but uncomfortable nonetheless. He was talking to Eddie.

"I know we don't *need*," he accented the word, "another dancer but I need to get him away from Eugene." Drew had recounted his entire taxicab conversation to Eddie. "If he doesn't have to work for Eugene anymore, maybe then he could blow the whistle."

"He likely hasn't danced in years," Eddie said doubtfully.

"He was good when we were kids. I think he may be a natural, so to speak. I'm confident I can whip him into shape before the show. Honeycutt taught us both to fight, and he also taught us a little about tap dancing. He always said Leon was better than me."

"Yes, but you kept up your lessons. I'd be surprised if he kept up with his." Eddie continued his objections, even though he knew he would eventually give in to Drew. "You've only got four days. That's a tall order even if Leon is Fred Astaire in blackface."

Eddie went on, "Drew, if you guys pull off what you've told me, try and steal that ledger from that Eugene guy, well, he's likely to kill both of you."

"No," Drew said. "I think stealing the ledger is a pipe dream, but if we can get to the inspector general and he moves quickly to find the ledger, then Eugene will be sunk."

"You boys have seen too many movies," Eddie sighed with resignation. "But I'll see what I can do to get Leon assigned to us."

Eddie's USO contacts worked their magic, presented the need for another dancer to the base commander, and pointed out the morale benefits to the soldiers when one of their own was introduced as a cast member.

"But he's a Negro," the general had said, frowning.

"And you know how those niggers love to sing and dance," his adjutant had responded.

Eugene protested, complained to "his" major, kicked up quite a fuss, but in the end told Leon, "Good riddance!"

Leon was billeted temporarily with members of Eddie's orchestra. He and Drew started to work.

Eddie was right. Leon had forgotten a lot and hadn't danced in several years. He had never seen a sheet of choreography. Drew would have to demonstrate every movement. Moreover, Leon's army boots were completely unsuited for the current task at hand.

However, somehow, suitable shoes were found, taps were added, and Drew and Leon worked throughout that afternoon.

The next day they worked from early in the morning until dusk, not even stopping for lunch. At the end of that second day, Drew handed an exhausted Leon a tube of mentholated salve. "Rub this into your leg muscles tonight. Tomorrow, they're gonna hurt like the dickens."

Leon complained loudly the next morning and told Drew he'd never learn quickly enough to fool anyone. Drew handed him two aspirins and a full cup of water, led him out onto the stage, and turned on the portable phonograph.

The next day there was a full run-through and that night a complete dress rehearsal. Afterward, as Leon limped away to fall exhausted into his cot, Eddie approached Drew, saying, "I think he's gonna make it." Eddie then launched into a discussion with Drew on a "few" things Leon still needed to work on.

The first three shows, beginning on a Thursday through Saturday, were more or less dress rehearsals except with an audience of soldiers. But Sunday night was to be the grand finale. A coast-to-coast radio show would begin after the intermission. A Hollywood star would sing in two of the numbers. Radio technicians from Los Angeles had already arrived, and both checked and changed much of the sound equipment the USO technicians had installed earlier. Big-time radio personalities weren't available, but a lesser-known comedian had accepted, hoping that his appearance on the show would be his big break.

The first shows were smash hits as far as the soldiers were concerned. They roared when Drew stopped the show, invited "one of their own" from the audience onto the stage, and then Leon and Drew launched into their well-rehearsed duet, dancing soft-shoe to Eddie's inimitable quirky beat. The soldiers went crazy, their applause and shouts stopped the show. Leon and Drew repeated the duet and soft-shoe.

On the final *Yankee Doodle Dandy* number, Drew performed mostly solo but in a well-rehearsed part brought Leon out from the wings, and both tapped in unison as the orchestra blasted the hall. In an impromptu moment, soldiers stood and sang along with the cast on stage. After the show ended, Drew lost count of the curtain calls. The soldiers cheered even more loudly when Drew shouted, "A tribute to Franklin Delano Roosevelt! Sing along with us! The 'Star-Spangled Banner'!" Leon and Drew led the cast and the audience.

The radio broadcast part of the show the following day required an abbreviated "onstage" cast performance after the intermission. When the radio performance was starting, Leon had told Drew the two of them could dash over to Eugene's supply room and simply steal the ledger.

"He keeps it in his foot locker," Leon said. "It's a small padlock and easy to pick. I've even done it while Eugene looked on when he had locked the key inside."

"And no one is going to be around when we dash over there during intermission?"

"I'll bluff my way," Leon answered.

"No," Drew said. "Eddie's right. We've seen too many movies."

By Sunday morning the radio producer had changed his mind again. He'd met with Eddie and the script was changed. When the intermission ended, the announcer would begin the show by introducing the Hollywood and radio personalities. The coast-to-coast audiences would then be told about the show in progress. Drew and Leon would step forward, announce that the show was to be a tribute to the late president, and lead the cast and audience in singing "Star-Spangled Banner."

Drew was surprised when Eddie told him, "The change was Mrs. Roosevelt's idea. I have no idea how she knew about the show and your part, but she said that a Negro and a white boy performing the National Anthem together as a tribute to her husband would in some way lead to a better relationship between blacks and whites.

"There won't be another show for a while," Eddie continued. "There have been far too many delays. I've got some club dates coming up in New Orleans. I've asked the USO about Leon, and they're going to move him temporarily to a USO troupe in Los Angeles. We're supposed to do another show in July at some base in New Mexico. Leon can come back to us then."

"What base in New Mexico?"

"Some place in New Mexico called Alamogordo. I never heard of it. They've got an army air force base there named Holloman. There's some kind of secret operation going on. We're to perform several shows."

# Chapter 32

## *Dallas*

DREW WAS NOT unhappy to be back in Dallas. Both Mitsui and Kowanda were comfortable at 1247 Cliff Heights Drive and had started secretarial school. Judge McGowan had arranged for their bills to be paid out of Drew's accounts. Spending money had been provided along with secretarial school tuition.

Kowanda met Drew as the train pulled into Union Station. He was first off the train and ran to Kowanda. He had her in his arms and said, "I need to ask you something."

She looked up into his eyes, her large almond-shaped dark ones meeting the impossibly intense blue eyes of the man she'd loved since childhood.

"Will you marry me?"

"You don't even have to ask."

They kissed on the station platform, their bodies blending together almost as one. Passersby smiled and grinned. The two lovers paid no attention.

Mitsui stood beside the two. "Don't I even get a hug?"

They piled into Charly's blue Ford. After crossing the viaduct into Oak Cliff, they turned into 1247 Cliff Heights Drive. A man was running along the street, leaping occasionally, waving his arms, and shouting.

Drew got out of the car. "Don't you know?" the man shouted. "It's VE Day! Victory in Europe! The war in Europe is over!"

All ran into the house. Drew snapped the console radio on.

Pandemonium erupted across Dallas that day, the eighth of May 1945. Indeed, it erupted across the United States.

Times Square was mobbed. Thousands thronged the National Mall in Washington. Thousands crowded Main Street in Dallas and into Dealey Plaza. Across America, automobile horns blared, people shouted, sang, kissed one another, wept, and prayed. Yes, there was still a war in the Pacific. An invasion of Japan would cost tens of thousands of lives, but at least the killing in Europe was over. Americans prayed that in some way the war in the Pacific could be over soon too.

Drew was reminded of words he'd read once spoken by a British prime minister a long time ago. "Peace in our time," he had said. It suddenly seemed like it could be a possibility.

Drew and Kowanda walked along the street after lunch the next day. The May weather in Dallas was balmy; new leaves graced the trees and shaded the sidewalk. "Ko," Drew said, "when we're married, I'm not sure I want my wife to work."

Kowanda looked up at this tall young man whom she loved more than she could have said. She shook her head. "Nonsense. Drew, I want to work. Earn my own way, at least until babies start coming."

Drew stopped, turned her, and they kissed for a long time. He said, his voice a little hoarse sounding, "We could make that happen pretty quickly, you know."

Kowanda shook off the trembling warmth she always felt when Drew kissed her and replied, "That might be a mistake. I've thought about this a lot. You've talked about college. I want you to go. I know you've got Charly's money, but things could still get tough while you're in school. If babies come, well, they come. I know we'll love them, but before that, I want to work."

Drew's telephone rang that evening. It was long distance: Eddie Mackenzie calling from Dardanelle, Arkansas. "The USO called. They want another show in Dallas using as much of the same crew as possible that we used in El Paso. This time the theme is to be both a VE Day celebration plus a resolve to get the Japs and end the war. We've got two weeks before our first show."

"We'll have to change some of the numbers," Drew said. "It's going to be hard to get everyone we had in El Paso. Some are simply not going to be available."

"Can you find Leon?" Eddie asked. "I've given him leave from Los Angeles to visit in Union City. I can't locate him. Some phone lines are down or jammed or something. Ursula Schultz isn't answering. Leon's folks don't seem to have a telephone.

"You know everyone there," Eddie said, "so find Leon for me. The USO wants a black performer onstage. We'll make do if we can't find many of the others."

"Will the president be there?"

"No. As I understand it, President Truman is preparing for a trip to the South Pacific to meet personally with General MacArthur."

Drew telephoned Mr. Scheumack at his radio store. He was in luck; the genial proprietor was working late. Yes, of course, he'd do what he could to help find Leon.

Leon called back the next morning, complaining of the amount of the long-distance charges. Drew told the operator to reverse the charges, then asked Leon how soon he could be in Dallas. "You can stay here with the three of us," he said after explaining about Eddie's call and the resumption of the USO shows.

Drew slept on the couch, Leon moved into Drew's old room, while Kowanda and her mother bunked together in the twin beds Drew had bought for Charly's room. The first day Leon was there, Drew and Kowanda visited the ladies in homes on either side and across the street from 1247. At each, Drew discussed that he and Kowanda would be married soon; but before that, Drew said, there were to be several additional USO shows. One of the shows, he explained, was to be in Dallas and would be a celebration of VE Day but otherwise would be much like the USO show at McFarland had been some months earlier. Drew promised the ladies he'd arrange complimentary tickets. Then he said, "There's another USO performer who'll be staying with us for a while. You know, what with the war and all, hotel rooms simply can't be found."

Each of the ladies had complimented Drew on his engagement and gushed over how pretty and attractive Kowanda was. Drew added when these comments were made, "You know Kowanda is Japanese American. She was born in Hawaii and is an American citizen."

He chuckled in a self-depreciating way and said, "Mrs. Roosevelt has said almost the exact same thing about Kowanda that you ladies have said. It's nice to know I have your approval as well as Mrs. Roosevelt's. Charly was proud to know Kowanda. I wish he could be here for the wedding."

The ladies clucked sympathetically.

"Oh, one other thing," Drew said over his iced tea. "The USO performer who'll be staying with us, well, he's a Negro." Eyebrows went up. "His name is Leon Arquette."

Drew nodded at the elevated eyebrows. "I could hardly say no to a direct request from the USO." It wasn't strictly true. He had been asked to "find" Leon by Eddie Mackenzie. When Drew and Kowanda had discussed this bit of diplomacy prior to the visits, they figured such a request from Eddie was "close enough" to the actual truth.

"Besides," he added, "you know show-business folks. They're just about color-blind. Leon is one of the lead performers. I can get you his autograph if you like."

Later, the three women talked and agreed, "We need to be nice to that young Negro. After all, there is still a war in the Pacific, and we need to support the war effort." As things turned out, most of their neighbors agreed, especially when the ladies said they were almost sure that "Charly's boy" could get additional complimentary tickets.

On the night of the show, the streets leading to Fair Park were jammed, and the performance was a sell-out. A twelve-seat section near the front of the auditorium had been set aside for Drew's neighbors, all dressed in their finest. Several of the men had rented tuxedos and grumbled under their breath about the money their wives had spent on new clothing, makeup, and permanent waves. The cream of Dallas society attended, and several newsreel cameras had been set up in the rear of the auditorium. The radio broadcast of the performance was to be live throughout North Texas. Kowanda stood in the wings and watched her husband-to-be and Leon as they led the show to the crashing sounds of *Yankee Doodle Dandy*.

Kowanda lost count of the number of curtain calls. At what Drew expected to be the last, he held up his hands. Relative quiet swept across the hall. "Folks," Drew shouted, "I want you to meet the woman that I'm going to spend the rest of my life with!"

He led an astonished and embarrassed Kowanda from the wings out onto stage center. She recovered her composure and bowed and smiled along with Drew as the crowd cheered. Then Drew shouted, "And Eddie Mackenzie and Leon Arquette are going to stand with me when we're married! I'll have two best men!" Leon stepped forward and bowed. Eddie turned in the orchestra pit and bowed. The audience could hardly stop applauding.

The next day the Dallas newspapers devoted much of their front pages to the show, which, even though truncated from the original war-bond show, received glowing reports along with prominent photographs of parts of the performance. On page three, there were a number of photographs of Drew, Kowanda, Eddie, and Leon as the mayor stepped forward to congratulate the happy couple and then displayed a telegram from Mrs. Roosevelt.

The day after that, the ladies of Cliff Heights Drive stumbled over themselves to visit Drew, Kowanda, and Mitsui and to meet Leon. The men of the neighborhood weren't quite as ready to accept even this limited racial integration, but their wives had been won over, and Kowanda said that was 90 percent of the battle.

And more progress was made when Drew and Leon accepted invitations from the Oak Cliff Rotary and the Oak Cliff Lion's Club to speak and perform an impromptu soft-shoe.

Three days after the performance, Eddie called again and announced they were all to be "on the road" by the first of the following week. This time, Eddie said, there would be no train rides in cattle cars. "No, the USO is providing several air-conditioned buses. We'll be crossing Texas in style."

He listed their itinerary: Fort Sam Houston in San Antonio, Fort Bliss in El Paso, and the army air field at Alamogordo, New Mexico. The shows in San Antonio and El Paso were to be repeats of previous shows and include radio broadcasts, though not coast to coast. The show in Alamogordo was not going to have a radio hookup, and the USO had been encouraged to limit publicity over the location of the final show. It seemed that Alamogordo and Holloman Army Air Force Base was simply some place that the United States Army did not want discussed.


The war in the Pacific and the dying continued on both sides of the conflict. American and Japanese soldiers died in island battles. Thousands upon thousands of Japanese civilians died horrible fiery deaths as Tokyo and other Japanese cities were carpeted with incendiary bombs.

An invasion of Japan was imminent. Thousands of men, women, and children—soldiers on both sides as well as civilians—would die.

# Chapter 33

❧ ⟶ • ✶ • ⟵ ❧

## *Alamogordo, New Mexico*

I T WAS A little cooler than El Paso, but July in Alamogordo nonetheless is summer. While early mornings in the high desert can be pleasant, crisp, and dry, as the day progressed, so did the heat.

Barracks on the base were rows upon rows of what appeared to be fifteen-man tents, all with wood floors raised an inch or two above the ground. Latrines and showers were in small concrete block buildings and were used by several companies. A few new-appearing unpainted two-story wood barracks were assigned to officers and to battalion supply.

Drew learned that many of the soldiers now at Holloman had also been on the troop train that had transported him and the USO troupe to El Paso. These soldiers, whom everyone had assumed were heading for disembarkation for the invasion of Japan, had now been issued desert camouflage uniforms and equipment. They trained on maneuvers in the desert. It all seemed strange, unlikely to be suitable for war in the Pacific.

Quite a few of those from the Negro companies had been assigned duties in camp. They cleaned latrines and performed yard cleanup around the rows of tents and KP duty in the numerous concrete block mess halls.

The assignment of Leon to the USO had somehow become permanent. Leon told Drew, shortly after their arrival at Holloman, that Eugene had acquired another Negro to provide services for him and his men. Ironically, the boy was from the Union City area.

"I know him," Leon said. "His name is Elton Martin, from Newell. He worked at the same gin where I worked a couple of summers."

For Eugene, life was good. Edith had followed the troop train to El Paso driving a newly acquired but several years-old two-tone DeSoto.

Later, she'd come to New Mexico and had rented a small apartment near downtown Alamogordo. Eugene obtained permission to leave the base every afternoon. Edith met him in the DeSoto at the base entrance at five.

Eugene's operation was complex, and much later, Drew was to wonder how the illiterate Eugene could have put it all together.

In Lubbock County, early in Edith's life, her schooling had included only four grades. Later, in her teens at Margaret Lytle's, Edith had simply done nothing more than she'd been asked. Still later, in Union City, she'd been so well taken care of by Henry she'd seen no reason to do more than stay close to the friendly alcohol as she turned a trick or two on the side for extra spending money above what Henry gave her.

But Edith was not stupid. Upon losing Henry's support and leaving Union City, she quickly realized that life with Eugene and his many schemes would need organization and planning to stay at least one step ahead of law enforcement. Eugene's competence was exhausted after he'd concocted his illegal schemes. Someone needed to organize his activities, or both she and Eugene were likely to land in jail. Edith discovered an organizational ability she did not know she had. She dramatically reduced her intake of alcohol and taught herself additional reading skills by frequent trips to the public library, first in Galveston, later Houston, and still later the massive Central Library on West Market Street in San Antonio. As Edith learned to read, she also learned that she had an instinctive understanding of basic mathematics. Eugene had needed organizational structure and a bookkeeper. He got organizational leadership and an accountant.

Sex with Eugene had always been an inadequate affair from Edith's perspective, and at any rate, she had progressed to the point where it was nothing she cared about, with Eugene or anyone else. She accommodated Eugene when he made advances, but it had long ago become a simple duty and she was glad when he looked elsewhere.

For Eugene, looking elsewhere for sexual pleasures had begun in Union City and had continued as something of an obsession during the time he and Edith had spent in Shreveport and Galveston. During the early years of World War II, Galveston had ample supplies of both women and men eager to provide services of various types for a few dollars. And there were several of both sexes who worked for Eugene.

There were organizations in Galveston in those years who felt that they should have complete rights of employment of sex-for-hire individuals. Eugene and Edith had been encouraged to leave.

Houston, however, was just up the road, and they discovered that they could organize a similar business venture near the Houston Ship Channel Turning Basin. It was successful and profitable, for the most part, although Houston Police had an annoying habit of arresting both their male and female employees.

They decided to try San Antonio, which proved very profitable until the nation's draft caught up with their customers and employees alike. Eugene too joined many of his customers as he reluctantly became a soldier at the request of President Franklin D. Roosevelt.

Had he been asked, and had he had an inclination to do so, it is possible that Eugene could have explained how the use of sexual favors and outright bribery had produced an extraordinary and stellar rise to the rank of master sergeant of supply. Edith did not care how he had accomplished this miracle but gave guidance as he bribed his way. The profit potential of a supply unit was enormous. Edith coached Eugene on ways to have loyal men assigned to his supply unit, men who had an understanding both of the profit potential and also the opportunity to further their own deviate sexual adventures.

Both Eugene and Edith had been dismayed when they learned that the battalion to which his unit had been assigned was to be sent westward, presumably to be shipped overseas to take part in the invasion of Japan. However, when supplies of desert camouflage uniforms and other equipment began arriving, both were sure that Eugene was not headed for Japan. And then when Eugene learned their destination likely would be the desert in New Mexico, he began to search a little deeper.

It was Edith who learned more about what was going on in that remote desert. Eugene had urged her to turn at least one more trick, a colonel he was sure had additional knowledge. Edith had done her best; and in that relaxed period following sexual climax, the alcohol she'd provided, together with a valium tablet, had loosened the colonel's tongue to a remarkable degree. No, he did not know precisely what was going on; but he did know it was huge, important, urgent, and could win the war in the Pacific in one blow.

In such an atmosphere of urgency, Eugene and Edith both realized that their business could become even more profitable. There would be little, if any, oversight. She left for El Paso in the DeSoto as Eugene's unit boarded the troop train that had come from Dallas and was delayed for six hours in San Antonio so that additional cars could be added to the already overly long train.

"I want to talk to Elton," Leon said. "I want to clue him in on what we know Eugene's doing. Maybe he can help if we ever get the MPs or the FBI interested."

Both young men had talked with Judge McGowan who, in turn, had talked with men he knew with the FBI's Dallas office. They had no idea if anything had happened since then.

Elton was sure he could pick the lock on the trunk that held the ledger and volunteered to do so when Eugene's back was turned.

"No," Drew said. "We've agreed for some time that this business needs to be left in the hands of professionals. You're already involved more than I think is safe."

"He's right," Leon said. "Watch your back, brother."

The show had been scheduled for 8:00 p.m. the night of July 15. However, that morning they learned the show had been moved to 5:30 p.m. and was to be abbreviated to not more than an hour, less if possible. A large contingent of the base population was going on desert maneuvers, so the audience would likely be small. There would be no second show, not tonight or ever. After the five thirty show, the entertainment troupe could leave. In fact, they were urged to leave as early as possible the next morning.

The stage was open-air and faced west. Five thirty in the afternoon would be quite warm and uncomfortable for both the audience and performers. And when the makeshift stage curtains opened, there were less than fifty soldiers in the audience.

Nevertheless, the performance went on. At the final number, about forty-five minutes after the show had begun, the small audience rose and clapped and sang along with the heavily perspiring cast. A few curtain calls later, the show was over. Drew, Leon, and Eddie, along with all the other cast members, could go home or to other assignments. The USO buses would be waiting for them at seven the next morning. Eddie would return to Dardanelle and spend some time with his family. Leon was scheduled to return to the Los Angeles USO troupe but could take a few weeks off to go to Union City. He had confided to Drew that he'd found someone there, and they were serious; Drew planned that he and Kowanda would at last schedule a wedding.

Drew and Leon caught a ride into Alamogordo. There was a small club where Eddie's orchestra members planned to "jam." Drew and Leon decided to join the session. It looked to be fun.

They were walking along a side street not far from the center of downtown Alamogordo, heading to the club, when Elton came running up to them. "They raided supply," he said, somewhat breathlessly.

"OK," Drew said. "They've finally caught that bastard."

"No," Elton said. "That's what I came to tell you. I think Eugene got word somehow. I saw him about four or so. He got the ledger and left. Someone drove him to the gate in a jeep, and someone in a two-toned car met him."

Two jeeps loaded with MPs stopped beside them. A man in tan civilian slacks and a white shirt with the sleeves rolled up exited one of the jeeps. He contrasted so starkly with the olive-drab uniforms of the military police accompanying him, Drew was at first unsure if he was in charge of the soldiers.

His demeanor and first questions made it clear that he was in charge, whoever he was. "Are you Drew Neilan?" he asked briskly. Drew nodded. The man turned to Leon. "And are you Leon Arquette?" Leon also nodded. "How about you?" the questioner said, turning to Elton.

Drew found his voice. "This is Elton Martin. He works in the supply unit."

"I need you boys to come to my office right now." His tone implied that if they did not come along, the soldiers with him would encourage them to do so. "I need to know as much about Eugene McElroy as you can tell me. He's on the run. We're searching high and low."

The boys climbed into already-overcrowded jeeps and were driven rapidly toward a two-story building: Alamogordo Police.

They were ushered into a rather sterile office on the second floor. The room was bare except for a filing cabinet with an electric fan on top, a small metal green-colored desk and four straight-back metal chairs. The man in civilian clothes followed them in and turned on the fan, which began oscillating and stirring the hot air.

He introduced himself, "I'm Agent McCuskey, Josh McCuskey. I'm with the FBI." He motioned for the boys to sit as he leaned on the edge of the desk. He turned to Drew. "Were you once called Drew Simmons?"

Drew nodded. "I feel as if I've known you for years," McCuskey said, smiling at Drew. "I was the original Justice Department agent assigned to your case years ago when Mrs. Browning asked us to look into threats made against you by the Klan in Union City. I've been tracking you ever since, though I lost you for a while when you were holed up at that old carney woman's place down in Louisiana. I was pretty sure who you were when you climbed into my jeep.

"So," McCuskey said, holding out his hand to Drew, "I'm glad to finally meet you, Drew Neilan.

"We've been working this case along with the military police. We've been on Eugene's trail for quite some time, but while we know what he's been up to, he's a slippery soul. I've been told what you've told Judge McGowan about a ledger, but now I want it repeated to me."

Leon told how he'd been assigned to the supply unit and how he'd seen the ledger firsthand, but the web of payoffs was so large that he'd had no one to go to. He said he'd thought of stealing the ledger but admitted he could not figure out how to get it to an authority who could call the police. Elton confirmed that he too had seen the ledger. Drew added that Leon had told him the same.

McCuskey looked at Drew and said, "You and Eugene McElroy go back quite a ways, don't you?"

"Yes. I've known Eugene since I was six," Drew said and paused. "When I was seven, he molested me."

McCuskey's eyebrows went up. "How old did you say you were?"

"The first time I remember, I was seven. He might have done something before because he always talked about how 'nice' it was when I sat on his lap. But I only remember the time when I was seven."

"Good lord!"

"Well, he didn't stop. There were other times, and then when I was ten, I hit him with a glass ashtray and Edith threw me out."

McCuskey turned to Leon.

"He felt me up a number of times there in the supply unit. Once, he had his guys hold me down. They pulled my pants off, but I kicked and carried on, and Eugene couldn't get it up. So he just had his guys kick me around a little."

"Did you go to a hospital?"

"No. One of the guys in my barracks patched me up with iodine and bandages and such. They didn't break any ribs, but it felt like it."

Elton added, "They did worse to me. But Eugene didn't—ah, actually—ah,"

"Penetrate?" McCuskey said, softly as though acknowledging Elton's embarrassment.

"Yeah," Elton said, his head cast down. "He rubbed it around on me and then—ah,"

"Ejaculated?" It sounded dull and imposing at the same time, the way McCuskey said the word.

"Yes," Elton whispered. It was loud enough to hear, but even as Drew gagged, he knew that Elton was cringing on the inside.

Leon went to a wastebasket and threw up.

"We have an all-points bulletin out for him. We know it's a two-tone car."

"Two-tone green," Elton said, regaining his voice, "A DeSoto."

The telephone rang. McCuskey picked up the receiver and listened for several minutes. Then he looked up.

"Sounds like we got him cornered about twenty miles from here. It's a two-tone green DeSoto all right. A woman was driving. We think Eugene may be hiding in the brush nearby."

McCuskey added, "I've got to go. I want to be in on the arrest. You guys are free to leave here. Stay where I can find you." Then he added to Drew and Leon, "I know you're supposed to leave on the USO buses tomorrow. I don't want you to do that. Tomorrow morning, when you get your things together, I want the three of you to come here to the station. I'll put you up somewhere for a week or two. I'll square it with whomever I need to square it with. I need depositions from each of you."

He turned to Elton and Leon. "I'm going to see that you each get honorable discharges from the army. I need you as witnesses. I don't want you getting your asses blown off in any invasion of Japan or anything," McCuskey spoke quickly, barely giving himself time to think, much less leave any room for the three other men to interrupt.

"Oh, and one other thing. I'll arrange transportation for each of you when all this is over, back to your homes or wherever you want to go."

Once out on the street in downtown Alamogordo, feeling relieved but still wanting to excise some of the tension of the past half hour, Leon said, "You know what, I bet that jam session is still going on. What say? Want to join them?"

"No," Elton said, "I'm going back to base. There's a bus stop right over there. See you guys in the morning." He was still feeling embarrassed over the discussion of deviant sex.

"Wait," Drew said. "Eugene's guys—they might be looking for you."

"Nah," Elton said. "Those assholes are running around now like trapped rats trying to find a hole to hide in. I'll be OK. I know a couple of guys in the MP at the base. They'll put me up." He walked toward the bus stop, waving as he walked away.

Drew thought the jam session was great, and apparently, so did Leon. The orchestra members invited Drew to sit in at the piano and handed Leon a guitar. "I didn't know you knew the guitar," Drew said.

"I'm a man of many talents." Leon smiled as he strummed an introductory chord.

Leon, it turned out, was very good with a guitar. The session was splendid. Both men were relaxed and felt better than they had in quite a while. Life was good. Drew had a happy thought. He was soon to go home to Kowanda.

He and Leon launched into a piano/guitar duet, and the orchestra members accompanied them. They sang "I Wanna Go Home."

# Chapter 34

## *Trinity*

IT WAS AFTER midnight when Drew and Leon left the small club. The orchestra members had borrowed several jeeps, which were parked a few blocks away. Drew and Leon stood in front of the club, waiting for the others to retrieve the jeeps and pick them up. They were chatting and enjoying the warm afterglow of a pleasant evening. The lights inside the club went out as club employees continued shutting the establishment down for the night.

A nondescript Chevrolet sedan pulled up to Drew and Leon.

Eugene got out of the passenger side of the car and walked up to the two. Drew was so astonished he could only stare in open-mouthed disbelief. "I need you two to get in the car," Eugene said in that whiny, nasally voice that always turned Drew's stomach a little.

"No," Drew said.

"I think you will." Eugene giggled. He had a pistol in his hand.

Just then, the neon lights on the front of the club went out as the club employees completed their nightly close-down. "Run!" Drew shouted to Leon as he charged Eugene. There was an awful pain in his head. The world swirled. Drew dropped to his knees.

He was having trouble figuring things out. There was a confusion of voices. Someone was pulling at him. He was in a moving vehicle. He opened his eyes.

He was in the rear seat of a two-door sedan. Leon was beside him and was supporting Drew with his left arm around Drew's shoulders. Drew sat up.

"I'm sorry, brother," Leon said. He had never called Drew brother before. Drew realized they were in bad trouble.

Leon had run only two or three steps when he was stopped. A blonde curly-haired woman had stood in front of him. She was holding a small silver pistol.

The car they were in seemed to be moving at a high rate of speed. Drew looked at the driver. "Edith," he said.

"You shut the fuck up, you little shit," Eugene said. He was looking over the seat back at them, holding his pistol. His eyes were filled with the wild intensity of an animal that realizes there is nothing but a wall behind it.

Drew rubbed his temples, trying to clear the cobwebby feelings and the sharp ache at the side of his head. His hand came away bloody. "What's going on?" he asked.

"I just paid you back for that ashtray. You remember?" Eugene whined then giggled, apparently pleased with his own wit.

"They're gonna catch you," Drew said. "There are cops all over looking for you."

"Nah, they're looking for a green DeSoto. And that's twenty or more miles from here. They ain't looking for a beat-up Chevy."

"The FBI is looking too. You're going to spend a long time in prison."

"We're taking you boys to a place where you'll have a hard time finding your way back. And when you do, we'll be long gone." Eugene started giggling again. There was not a lot of amusement in his giggle. It was more like the edges of a violence barely contained.

The car slowed. Edith turned into what appeared to be a secondary road and then several miles later turned into a graveled lane across the desert. Dust boiled through the opened windows and into the car. After three or four stricken minutes, the car turned onto a dirt track. A gate was just ahead. Headlights shone on the words Restricted Area! The Chevrolet increased speed and crashed through the gate.

No one spoke.

After about a mile, the Chevrolet stopped. Drew's head had cleared. And he was frightened.

Both Eugene and Edith got out of the car. "Come on, get out!" Eugene said. "This side of the car."

Edith had slammed the driver-side door and walked around through the headlight beams. This was Drew's first clear view of the woman he had called mother for so long. She was dressed attractively in a light-blue women's business suit, her blonde hair cut in the latest fashion, and unsuitable for the desert, she wore high-heeled shoes.

As the boys began to climb out, distant sirens could be heard. Drew looked to the south. There were headlights and flashing red lights. They were a long way off.

"Back! Back!" Edith screamed. "Get back in the fucking car!"

Leon had been exiting the car ahead of Drew. When Edith started shouting, Eugene turned and pushed hard. Leon fell against Drew, and both fell back onto the car seat.

Edith leaped behind the wheel and put the car in gear. It accelerated forward. Eugene hung onto the open passenger door and nearly fell. He shouted. Edith slammed on the brakes. Eugene pulled himself into the car and shut the door. Edith floored the accelerator, and the car leaped forward.

The following jeeps, police cars, and ambulances careened through the broken gate and continued on into the desert, following the distant taillights ahead.

After several miles, a young lieutenant ordered a stop to the caravan. "What the fuck!" McCuskey shouted, clambering out of his jeep. A nearby cactus snagged his slacks, tearing them.

The Chevy continued speeding along the dirt track. Eugene sat in the front seat with his pistol held in his left hand across the seat back and pointed at the boys.

"You're not gonna let us walk back, are you?" Drew said, realizing the full extent of the danger he and his brother were in. "You're gonna kill both of us," he added calmly.

"Shut the fuck up!" Edith screamed. Drew knew that desperate tone, knew he had hit too close to the bone.

"All my life, all you've ever done is fuck things up. I hate you! I've had to put up with you all these years! You fuck everything up for me! You never helped me out! Henry left me because he couldn't stand you!" Her voice was shrill.

"Really?" Drew said calmly and, now, sarcastically. "I thought he left because of Ezell."

This seemed to increase Edith's shrillness. "It's all your fault! Everything is your fault!" She was screaming now. "I hate you! I thought I was free of you! You aren't going to fuck things up for me anymore! We're gonna fix that! I'll finally be rid of you!"

Drew looked into Leon's eyes. There was fright. Drew was feeling the reddish calm Honeycutt had taught him slipping into his head. The car was still speeding across the desert, but to Drew, it seemed to be moving slowly. He hoped Leon could hear his thoughts, *we've got to fight, and we've got to fight now.* He could see Leon's eyes get hard around the edges as though he knew what Drew was thinking.

They focused on finding the opening that Honeycutt said would always be.

Eugene shifted his eyes toward the speedometer. The car was going almost fifty. It was weaving from side to side. Edith was close to losing control on the dirt track. The pistol in Eugene's left hand draped over the back of the front seat was pointed down. Simultaneously, Drew and Leon seized the moment.

Leon grabbed Eugene's hand to twist the pistol out. Drew grabbed Edith about the shoulders and began wrestling her away from the steering wheel. Her pistol was nowhere to be seen. The car veered off the dirt track and careened across the desert, colliding with bushes, becoming airborne as it crashed over hillocks. The car lost headway.

McCuskey was screaming obscenities at the lieutenant who was shouting back and pointing at his wristwatch. "I said," the lieutenant was shouting, "everybody out! We're too far into the restricted zone! Go to that ditch over there! Get down! Cover your head. No matter what happens, don't look up!" He was pointing to a low depression in the desert floor.

McCuskey grabbed him by the shoulders. The lieutenant turned and said, "Sir! In about a minute, the army is going to test a weapon! We're way too close! I was supposed to keep you from coming this close! The weapon is a huge bomb. No one is sure how big this is going to be, but it's supposed to end the war! And it's gonna go off right up there!" He pointed to the north, where the taillights of the speeding Chevrolet could still be seen.

To the east, the ridges of the desert were outlined in an orange glow. Dawn was breaking.

Edith was screaming. Drew had both arms around her, pulling her toward the backseat. She bit him, bringing blood. Leon pulled Eugene from the front into the back, punching wildly with one hand as he pulled with the other. Eugene screamed and kicked as Leon bit his ear off and spat it out. Eugene's foot struck Edith. The car began to skid sideways. Eugene's door came open.

McCuskey and the lieutenant were running around the cluster of vehicles. Confused policemen and ambulance drivers were climbing out. Orders were being screamed, "Go, over there! Quickly! Lie down. Don't look up no matter what happens!" Men were beginning to move. The lieutenant shouted, "Time is running out!"

The Chevrolet rolled. Drew felt himself tossed against sides of the car. Eugene screamed as he was propelled through the opened door.

The car bounced upright, began another roll, and fell into space. It was a deep ravine. Drew lost his grip on Edith as he felt himself being flung from the car. He thought about Leon. There was a sensation of falling.

McCuskey and the lieutenant had everyone in the ditch. "Do not look up!" the lieutenant shouted. "No matter what happens, keep your nose in the sand, hands over your heads!"

He and McCuskey fell to the floor of the shallow ditch, joining the others. McCuskey covered his head. "Stay down!" the lieutenant shouted one more time. Then he too covered his head.

The world turned white. Intense and powerful, it blotted out all sight and sound. Drew fell heavily onto solid but sloping ground and rolled; his breath knocked out of him. He put his hands over his head.

The light faded. A powerful wind rocked the desert. Brush and sand cascaded down upon Drew. The wind stopped and then returned from the opposite direction. He saw the wrecked car nearby.

There was sound now—incredible, roaring, otherwise indescribable, and awful sound. The ground shook. Drew raised his head. The entire northern sky was filled with a huge ball of orange, red, black, and purple. It was a cloud of some sort, boiling, rolling, and moving upward in the sky. It was magnificent, awful, terrifying, and terrible. Drew thought it looked as if the gates of hell had opened and the devil himself was rising to the heavens to do battle with God. Drew lay on the ravine floor as he stared at the boiling cloud.

He turned his head and looked at the car. It was upside down. Both doors were gone. He could hear Edith screaming. As he tried to rise, there was sharp pain in his chest and shoulder. Pain shot through his foot. His forehead was bloody. He limped to the car.

The dash was now above his head, and Edith was crammed into the space around the steering column. She was undoubtedly badly injured. A wheel was still spinning aimlessly. There was a powerful smell of gasoline.

She looked at him. "I hate you," she said in a croaking voice. "See what you did to me! Get away from me!"

Flames licked at the engine compartment. "Edith!" Drew shouted. "I've got to get you out!"

"Get away from me! I'll get myself out!"

There was a whump! The engine compartment was on fire. Drew shied away from the heat, holding his hands over his face, and stumbled away for a few feet. He fell to his knees, looking back at the burning car. "Mother!" he screamed as the car exploded. Drew fell back onto the desert floor and lost consciousness.


Drew Allen Neilan, of Dallas, Texas, formerly from a small town in southern Arkansas named Union City, had witnessed, without knowing it, the detonation of the world's first nuclear device at 5:29 a.m., July 16, 1945, in the New Mexican desert north of Alamogordo. The government scientists who had triggered the explosion called it Trinity.

# Chapter 35

## *El Paso to Dallas*

DREW AND LEON had been airlifted to a military hospital in El Paso. Drew had insisted that the two remain in the same room no matter where they were being taken. He said over and again, "He's my brother! We need to be in the same room!"

At Alamogordo, the hospital nurses and others had looked first at Drew and then Leon. They had shaken their heads and clicked their tongues, but they capitulated when Leon, rising from the web of pain that enveloped him, said, "Mama always said we wuz the spittin' image of one another."

Both of Leon's legs had been broken along with two ribs as he was thrown from the tumbling automobile. Fortunately, his leg injuries were not compound fractures. There were dozens of bruises but no apparent internal injuries. The doctors assured Leon that within six to eight weeks he would be "as good as new." He was placed in plaster casts and had to remain in bed with his legs elevated by a series of pulleys and lines. Within two weeks, the doctors said, the casts could be converted to walking casts and he could get about on crutches instead of wheelchairs.

Drew had also escaped without internal injuries other than a cracked rib and numerous cuts and bruises. His foot had several broken bones. It was possible that he would walk with a limp for the rest of his life. It was also possible that he would not, but one thing was more than probable: his tap-dancing days were over.

Drew did not care. He told Leon one day, "A career as a dancer or entertainer was never in my plans. I thought it was fun, but it was not what I promised Mrs. Roosevelt that I'd do with my life. I'm going to try to go to Southern Methodist in Dallas and then law school."

At Leon's raised eyebrows, Drew further explained, "There are all kinds of law. I'm not yet sure which field of law I'll choose to practice in."

It seemed that there was something called radiation sickness that concerned the doctors, but apparently, both Leon and Drew had somehow been protected enough from the blast that they received minimal dosage. The doctors had shaken their heads, perplexed. Even though both young men had been thrown to the bottom of the ravine, doctors felt that their radiation dosage should have been higher.

After the show had closed in Alamogordo, Eddie McKenzie had told both Drew and Leon that he'd been asked to take his orchestra to Los Angeles. There was to be a movie and Eddie had been asked to bring both along.

"I'm going to try for the Hollywood thing," Leon said. "I like California. 'Course, I gotta get out of these casts and the army. Maybe McCuskey really can get me out like he said. And with this bomb we saw back there in the desert, maybe the war will be over any day now."

McCuskey visited them almost every day. First at Alamogordo when they'd arrived at the hospital and now at the Fort Bliss military hospital. Often, he brought a stenographer.

Eugene had been badly injured. He was arrested at the wreck site. Eugene would be sick from radiation. McCuskey said he had been told that Eugene would probably die of cancers after a few years.

A small suitcase had been found containing both the ledger and almost $20,000 in cash. The FBI located three bank accounts in Mexico. All together, they contained over $150,000.

The woman driving the green DeSoto had been a decoy and was innocent of involvement in the black-market operation. She would be charged with aiding and abetting a criminal activity and would likely receive probation in return for testimony.

Elton Martin was temporarily in protective custody in a hotel in Alamogordo.

"How did you find us?" Drew asked one day.

McCuskey chuckled. "It wasn't easy. Some of the people at the club saw you two getting into that Chevy, but we were at a loss as to which direction to look. We had patrols in every direction.

"A police car checked on a car parked in the desert. Two people were 'making out,' to put it mildly. They were told they were near a restricted zone, and they said another car had gone by. It was our only lead, and we took it."

"What about your mother's body?" McCuskey asked Drew shortly after they'd arrived in El Paso. "She was burned beyond recognition, but of course, we know who she was."

"I don't care," Drew answered. But after a few minutes of silence, Drew said, "Well, maybe I do. Edith will always be the grandmother of my children, and someday they may want to know about her and where she is buried."

He was quiet for a few more minutes. McCuskey simply remained on Drew's bedside chair and waited. "Here's what I want," Drew said at length. "Lubbock, Texas.

"No tombstone. I want just a small marker, one of those flat-on-the-ground things, maybe brass, just listing her name and dates of birth and death. That's all. How much will that cost?"

"Nah," McCuskey said. "Uncle Sugar will take care of it. We'll let you know where she is after we make the arrangements."

"I will never go there unless my children want me to take them."

Shortly afterward, Colonel Brownson sat with Drew. "We've performed dozens of tests, as you know," the colonel said, "and as we've told you, it doesn't seem that the radiation dosage you received is severe. However, there is one area of concern. We don't think it was caused by radiation. Perhaps it was caused by some prior illness or maybe just genetics. Maybe your mother drank when she was pregnant."

Drew chuckled grimly. "I can promise you she drank when she was pregnant."

"Well, in any case, these things happen. You might be sterile."

"I can't have babies?"

"It's all a matter of statistics. There's a lot we don't know. Your count is slightly low. However, the motility ratios are high. The reason we tested you was we were concerned about radiation, and if that had been what caused the low count, then likely, motility would have been affected too. That doesn't seem to be the case.

"You know, all it takes is one sperm cell. You may have a dozen babies. We just don't know."

"Is it probable or simply possible that I can impregnate a woman?"

"We don't know," Brownson said. "I want to say it is likely and probable and that you will have children." He shrugged. "That could be wishful thinking on my part. I just want to be completely honest with you."

"Is Leon OK?" Drew asked.

"That's supposed to be private, between me and Leon. You'll have to ask him."

"Well, if I read you right, then Leon's OK," Drew said. "I guess I'll have to look him up if I want to bounce babies on my knees. Maybe they'll like their uncle coming to visit."

Brownson changed the subject. "You know, your low sperm-cell count doesn't make you less of a man. If you want, I could arrange some counseling."

"No, I'm OK. I know a man's reproductive system doesn't define him." Drew tapped his chest. "This is what does."

"I guess I can agree with you, Drew." Brownson smiled. "You don't need a shrink."

Then he chuckled. "I'm pretty sure I know the answer to this next question, but are you and Leon truly related?"

"In our hearts," Drew said, "in our hearts."


On August 15, 1945, the empire of Japan surrendered. The United States had dropped atomic bombs on two cities in Japan. Thousands of Japanese citizens had been killed or maimed, or would die of radiation sickness or cancers years later. There had not been an invasion of Japan.

On September 2, 1945, formal surrender documents were signed in Tokyo Bay aboard the battleship *USS Missouri*. World War II was over.

And on Monday, September 3, 1945, a C-47 Army Skytrain landed at Love Field, Dallas, Texas. Drew Neilan got off and limped into Kowanda's waiting arms as Mitsui and Judge McGowan stood proudly nearby. The plane took off again after a few minutes and carried Elton Martin and Leon Arquette, with honorable discharge papers in large manila envelopes on the seats beside them, to an air field in El Dorado, Arkansas. They were met by two small motorcades: one from Newell and the other from Union City.

Drew and Kowanda were married on September 15, 1945. Reverend Aloysius Thomas, now eighty and his hair a white fringe, performed the ceremony in the Oak Cliff Methodist Church alongside the church's pastor, John Frederichs. Some of the church members had wrinkled their brows over a black minister in a white church; but the attendance of the mayor of Dallas, a guest of Judge McGowan, calmed their feelings.

Catherine could not attend, but she had arranged for Maude to travel with Reverend Thomas. The bowed and arthritic old Negro woman had never felt more proud as she did when Drew introduced her to the assembled guests as his mother.

Eddie McKenzie and Maybelle had, of course, come. Eddie was to be one of Drew's two "best" men. They'd brought their five boys. The two eldest, now in their teens, served as ushers.

Imogene, Sister Alma, and Ursula Schultz had made the trip from Union City to Dallas, all three crowded together in the single seat of Ursula's coupe.

Leon was out of crutches. He and Eddie McKenzie stood with Drew; and a new member of Leon's family—a lovely girl from Union City named Genevieve, Leon's bride of only two days—stood beside Kowanda as matron of honor. Mitsui, now secretary to Judge McGowan following the retirement of Mrs. Ellsworth, stood with Maude.

When Reverend Thomas asked, "Who gives this man and this woman?" Maude and Mitsui together stepped into the church aisle. Maude said as loudly as she could muster, "I give this man to be married." Mitsui then said, "And I give this woman." Drew and Kowanda turned and stepped down to the church aisle, and Kowanda hugged and kissed her mother as Drew hugged and kissed Maude.

Following the ceremony, as the newly married walked down the aisle to applause, Drew stopped. A portly man—clean shaven, wearing a stylish double-breasted business suit—was part of the applauding assemblage.

Drew looked at the man closely. "Honeycutt?"

Honeycutt moved into the aisle, and Drew hugged him. "Thanks for being here," Drew said, a catch in his throat. "Wouldn't have missed it for the world," Honeycutt answered.

At the reception in the fellowship hall following the ceremony, Eddie sat at the church's upright and played a waltz as Drew and Kowanda danced. As the waltz neared its end, Leon took Kowanda from Drew and danced with the bride while Drew danced with Genevieve. Then, by prior arrangement with Eddie, though unknown to Drew, Leon and Kowanda did a short soft-shoe routine. As they did, Drew stepped over to Maude and led her gently to the dance floor for a few minutes.

Later, at a faster beat, Eddie played his newest music, which was to be part of the movie filmed in California. His quirky beat had been updated and expanded. While the young people present had no trouble dancing to the beat, older folks sat the song out while laughing and saying, "Too fast for me!"

Judge McGowan and Honeycutt were the exceptions. The judge led Mitsui onto the floor, and both kept up with the beat along with the younger people. Honeycutt joined, dancing with Genevieve, and performed an impromptu tap dance.

The honeymoon was a car trip in a blue Ford to Little Rock, Union City, and St. Timothy's. At St. Timothy's, Drew knelt at the gravesite of Father Tom Byrne and silently thanked God for leading him to Father Tom, who had given him Charly and therefore given him his life.

### *The End*

# Epilogue

❖ᴥ❖

# *Washington DC*

**T**HE MANAGING PARTNER of a prominent Washington law firm walked into the office of one of his young attorneys. It was a sunny seventeenth of May in 1954. Washington was already beginning to feel the warmth that foreshadowed the sultry heat of a Washington summer.

"Good work, Neilan," he said, "assisting the NAACP on their lawsuit. The decision just came down: the Supreme Court has sided with the plaintiff in *Brown v the Board of Education*. Thurgood Marshall called and asked me to congratulate you."

"I didn't do much other than legwork. Mr. Marshall is the one deserving congratulations," Drew answered in the humble way he was known for.

"Nevertheless," the managing partner said, "I think this day is historic."

Drew smiled. "Maybe so. But you know what, this day is my twenty-eighth birthday." He grinned. "That's pretty historic for me."

That night, Drew and Kowanda, now a legal secretary, had an intimate birthday dinner at a small Georgetown bistro. Drew proudly showed his wife the congratulatory telegram Mrs. Roosevelt had sent. As they were enjoying dessert, Kowanda announced she was going to have to stop work in a few months.

"Why?" Drew asked, suddenly worried about her health.

"Because, my love, I'm three months pregnant."

Three years later, a White House attorney stood in an anteroom off the Oval Office and watched, through a slightly opened door, as President Dwight David Eisenhower signed the Civil Rights Act of 1957. Following the signing that September day, as the president was preparing to leave for his golf game, he passed by Drew Allen Neilan's office in the West Wing.

He stuck his head in the door. "Good work, Drew."

"Thank you, Mr. President. But you know, the fight is not yet over."

Eisenhower turned, eyebrows raised.

"There's a fellow down in Atlanta, a Dr. King, who's frankly saying, 'It ain't over,' sir."

"Well," the president said, "we've made a start, haven't we?"

"Yes, sir."

The senior White House legislative liaison attorney decided to take the rest of the afternoon off and go home to his wife and son. He did not know it at the time, but eventually, there would be two more children. None of the three children suffered in any way from any possible radiation their father may have received that July morning in 1945. They were strong, beautiful, intelligent, and wonderful.

In the delivery room, as each was born and the baby handed to his father, Drew broke a vow he had made to a lonely and frightened boy in a cold, windy railroad boxcar so many years earlier.

Drew wept.

# About the Author

J IM COLE IS a retired civil/structural engineer. While traveling around the world on various engineering projects, he always dreamed of becoming a writer. When he retired after 42 years as a consulting engineer, he saw his chance to fulfill that dream. He attended Rice University's Glasscock School of Continuing Studies in Houston, taking classes in creative writing. Later, he joined the Houston Writer's Guild and was fortunate to be under contract for several years to the Houston Chronicle for stories for their Sunday supplement magazine, Texas.

Today, Jim and his wife Marian live quietly in their hometown, Victoria, Texas, where Jim continues his interests in writing and studies Victoria's rich history and heritage.

Jim currently authors a monthly newspaper column for Victoria Preservation, Inc., where he is a member of the Board of Directors. His well-received column, 'Vanished from Victoria', published in The Victoria Advocate, documents Victoria's vanishing nineteenth and early twentieth-century architectural heritage.

Never Cry Again is 80-year old Jim's debut novel. The action and events of his historical fiction saga take place during a time-frame in which he is personally familiar, the 1930s and 40s. The sweep of his narrative covers locations and events throughout the five-state region of Arkansas, Oklahoma, Louisiana, Texas and New Mexico, set against the backdrop of racial prejudice, depression-era southern America, the turbulence of World War II, and its aftermath.